Nothing To See Here

This is a work of fiction. The characters, incidents and dialogue are creations of the author's imagination and are not to be construed as real. Any resemblance to actual events or persons living or dead is entirely coincidental.

Published in the United States by
Beckham Publications Group, Inc.

ISBN: 0-931761-29-8
10 9 8 7 6 5 4 3 2 1

Library of Congress Cataloging-in-publication data: 2006939764

Nothing To See Here

A Novel

David L. Post

THE Beckham
PUBLICATIONS GROUP, INC.
Silver Spring

Before you embark on a journey of revenge,
dig two graves.
   —Confucius

The cranium is a space-traveler's helmet.
Stay inside or you perish!
   —Nabokov

Chapter 1

A BAD MARRIAGE can last forever, but a marriage brushed by insanity will crash and burn in no time at all.

Alan Sarnower—psychiatrist, father, and devoted practitioner of the up-early, home-late middle class work ethic—swung his legs off the stale, rumpled bed on to the already hot summer floor and reviewed his situation. Things were tanking. Fast.

Three weeks ago, after returning home from a family outing at a local crafts fair, his wife Cassie had locked herself in their bedroom, slamming the door. Sarnower and Mitch, their ten year old son, heard banging drawers, and things being thrown. Something smashed. A crazed, raving monologue with screamed obscenities and sharp bursts of laughter accompanied the tornado.

They stood outside the door, frozen in disbelief at what was happening on the other side. Time to take charge Sarnower finally decided, shaking off the paralysis of shock. He knocked loudly on the door several times. "Cassie! Cassie! Open up. Open the door. Now!" But the manic destruction continued. Sarnower leaned into the door with all his weight and pushed, but the new locks he'd installed resisted him.

Gradually the noise abated. Cassie was apparently focusing on something specific and purposeful. Sarnower banged again and this time the door was opened. A packed suitcase sat on the middle of the large double bed. The room was a complete disaster. Dresser drawers were pulled out, clothes strewn and piled on the floor, pictures ripped from the wall. Sarnower's night table lay on its side, the phone off the hook bleating like an injured lamb. The antique leather change and jewelry caddy, a treasured gift from his late father, was on the floor in several pieces. Its contents—coins, cuff

1

links and his beloved gold Vacheron dress watch were flung everywhere. Books had been pulled from the small bookcase and lay opened and splayed out in painful cheerleader splits. A copy of his own book, *Ice Fishing in the Unconscious: Trusting Your Midlife Self*, a self-help paperback written quickly years ago, was torn in half at the spine. His own publicity photo, with early-eighties loud wide tie and over-the-ear haircut stared up at him idiotically from the floor. The absurdity of seeing his twenty-year younger self dampened a growing rage.

"Cassie," he said quietly.

"Don't give me that fucking shrink voice of yours," she screamed. "Save it for your patients. You should be getting some serious psychological help yourself."

She was trying to close the suitcase, which bulged with a random assortment of clothes.

"Where are you going?" he asked.

She smirked. "You'd really like to know, wouldn't you?"

"Yes, I would."

"I would too," Mitch said. In the melee, both had forgotten the boy was standing right there. He'd seen and heard everything. What kind of bleeding hole was this scene going to leave in his psyche? Sarnower had spent much of his practice working with divorcing parents, and now all their detritus was washing up on his own beach.

"Let's calm down and figure this out, shall we?"

"Shall we? *Shall we?*" she mocked. "You're truly pathetic Alan. It's already figured," she said as she finally closed the suitcase.

"Would you mind telling me what this is all about?" he asked. The pointlessness of the question almost made him laugh. She ignored it and took their son by the shoulders.

"Mitch, I'm going to be gone for a while, ok?" He started to cry. Quickly, Cassie wiped his tears with a corner of her dress.

"Where, Mom?" There was a jagged, torn element in his voice. Something primitive was rising in the boy.

"Oh, that's really not important, honey."

"Yes it is. I want to know. Can I call you?"

In the past, Cassie would have shown at least a semblance of support, a gesture of tenderness. Now Mitch's anguish was just an annoyance. She ignored his question, picked up the suitcase and headed downstairs through the hall to the front door.

Sarnower had to act. But do what? Barricade the door? Take the suitcase from her? Given things as they were, any intervention would make matters worse. He tried to comfort himself with the thought that she would cool down and call later, but out of the fog of wishful thinking, it seemed an unlikely possibility. Better just to let her go. Whatever this was, it might wear itself out.

At the front door Cassie turned to him, straining with the bulging suitcase.

"I don't suppose you'd help me carry this out to my car?"

He played the request over in his mind. Help his wife leave their safe, predictable house to start off on some haphazard, possibly dangerous adventure in this condition? Her fury had temporarily pried him away from his own moorings like an out-of-body experience. No, this was crazy.

"You won't help me? Fine. I'll do it myself." One hundred and twelve pound Cassie heaved the case, which must have weighed at least half of that, opened the door and started down the front steps. Enraged people temporarily acquire super-human strength he remembered reading somewhere. Here was a textbook in psychopathology brought vividly to life. She popped open the trunk to her car and hurled the bag in with the fluid arc of a professional shot-putter.

"You were never there to help me. *Ever!* You dumb *fuck!*" she screamed.

Over the din of his lawn mower, Fred Cerillo, the neighbor across the street stopped mowing and looked up. He cut the power and crossed the street.

"Alan, everything all right?" he asked. At that moment, they saw Cassie peal her Celica out of the driveway and on to the road. Although Sarnower was numb with anger and confusion, he chuckled in spite of himself. *Peeeooon!* The Road Runner taking off in a cloud of dust. He must have seen those cartoons hundreds of times as a child on his parent's old black and white TV. "Beep beep," he said softly to himself. Then, turning to Fred he said "yeah, everything's under control."

About a year ago, he'd begun to notice Cassie acting strangely, or more accurately, stranger than usual. Always something of an oddball, Cassandra Kelly had an infectious, funny, irreverent take on things that Sarnower had found refreshing while they were dating. She was the sixth of seven children from an old-fashioned Irish Catholic family and was full of outrageous anecdotes of drunken parties, older brothers getting into slapstick scrapes with the law, comical priests and nuns from parochial school, all of whom could easily have stepped out of an old Mack Sennett comedy. She would deliver stories with wonderful timing and wicked accents and hold an entire table of beer drinkers at Chances R, the local watering hole, in the palm of her hand.

Sarnower had been smitten immediately. The long strawberry blond hair, the fresh scrubbed looks, a seductive, mischievous smile all promised naughty fun; a welcome balance to his tendency to be buttoned-down and overly studious.

They had married after college before medical school, but had gotten off to a rocky start. Cassie resented his long hours. She felt his dedication to becoming a doctor was "self-indulgent." Away from Chicago, living in Cambridge where Sarnower was busting his hump at Harvard, there were no ready-made audiences to entertain. The world had gradually spun into a new appreciation of sobriety, twelve-step programs, aerobics, healthy eating and natural highs. The drunken madcap antics had lost their humor. Things had moved on, but Cassie hadn't.

Last year, on a trip to Disney World with Mitch over spring vacation, Cassie had started giggling out of the blue, at odd times, and at things that weren't funny—at the weather report, at a sappy song on the radio, while cooking dinner, it could be anything at all. At first, Sarnower didn't know what to make of it, sensing perhaps she was finally relaxing after a long and difficult winter during which her mother had died suddenly of a massive stroke. He was tempted to write it off as a delayed grief reaction. But when he asked her about it, she had turned on him with an unexpected, frightening rage: "Can't a person laugh a little in this goddamn house?" she shouted.

"Sure...of course."

"Does everything have to be so fucking serious with you? Do you have to control everyone all the time?"

Sarnower backed off, as much from the surprise of her attack as from not knowing how to respond, particularly since Mitch had come into the room and had stared wide-eyed and disbelieving at his mother. He'd let it slide.

Gradually the giggling was accompanied by strange facial movements, almost grimaces, as if she were responding to some private, internal drama. He'd become concerned. As a first year resident in psychiatry, he had seen the same kinds of contortions in

4

the faces of patients on locked wards. Of course they were heavily medicated with anti-psychotic drugs and frequently over time, began to show the unmistakable signs of tardive dyskinesia, the involuntary spasmodic movement of facial muscles that would forever place them in the ranks of the profoundly ill. Even after the meds were withdrawn, the side effects would set like an indelible stain.

Then Cassie's thoughts and speech began to race. At times, Sarnower couldn't understand what she was talking about. She would drift from subject to subject, misusing common words, even inventing new ones, talking as if the whole word salad made sense. "Back up, slow down," he would ask. She'd look at him with contempt.

"Why is Mom mad at us?" his son had asked him one Sunday afternoon while they were clearing dead winter leaves from the yard.

"I don't think she's mad at us, Mitch," he answered slowly. "She's had a hard time, you know, with Grandma dying. Sometimes when people are sad like that, they get angry about things they've lost."

Mitch had stopped raking and looked Sarnower right in the eyes, something he almost never did. The urgency in his gaze was alarming and flashed something a ten year old shouldn't be expected to handle.

"She's not sad, Dad, she's different. Really different." Nothing had been lost on him. What else had he picked up that he wasn't letting on?

"I know what you mean," Sarnower admitted, giving up any pretense at invention. Sometimes his son reminded him of an ancient Buddha connected to an ageless stream of wisdom. At times, Sarnower had come upon him reading quietly, deeply engrossed in a book, and was struck by a resemblance to an old sepia photograph of his own father as a young boy. His father, with deep brown eyes and a Buster Brown haircut had been caught reading a book by a clever photographer, in a rare (for those days) spontaneous shot at roughly the same age Mitch was right now. He wore the fleeting incandescence of the fictional world he was immersed in, yet showed the beginning of surprise at being yanked by an old sulfur flashbulb into the present moment.

"What's wrong with Mom?" Mitch pressed. How to explain, or even try to explain at all? What could he handle? He was smart enough to see through any attempt at evasion; that would just put distance between them at a time when they needed to trust each other. Mitch would tolerate a gauzy version of the truth, but was too old for fairy tales.

What *was* wrong exactly? Sarnower wasn't completely sure himself. Everyone's screwed up somehow to one degree or another, but when do the little character twists, the annoying idiosyncrasies begin to pile up and become something else?

Never particularly warm, Cassie had basic decency and a need to see that everyone was having fun, though under that demeanor lay a dark, guarded shyness. She'd been an observer, not a player in her family, adept at hiding from her father's unexpected wrath or embarrassing behavior from her mother. Her siblings dominated the stage—Cassie managed the props and scenery. It was easy for her to get lost in the constant movement and buzzing blur of family life. Her mother, either out playing bridge all afternoon or getting smashed on gin in front of the daytime soaps. Cassie learned to get her own after-school snacks, always walking softly to the kitchen. Her father was often tied up for over an hour each way in commuter traffic. His series of dead-end sales jobs ate away at him from the inside out so he'd come home roaring, a purple vein in his forehead ready to burst. An advantage to growing up in a large family, she learned; the swells could wash over you as you hid at the bottom of the ocean floor.

Sarnower himself was an only child, introspective and precocious, envied and resented by his parents. His birth had been an accident he overheard his mother whisper one day when he was eight, to a distant cousin out in Ohio.

He read voraciously: history, philosophy, biographies of scientists: Marie Curie, Albert Einstein, Louis Pasteur. Paul deKreuf's *Microbe Hunters*, Hans Zinsser's *Rats, Lice and History*, anything related to science or disease. Why wasn't he out playing baseball, getting some fresh air his father would ask. Leave him alone, his mother would fire back, can't you see he's reading? He identified himself early on as the source of their constant bickering. Was that the way all parents were? He would go over to friends' houses and stay for dinner. There was civil conversation, interest in the other person's life, a warm, low-keyed atmosphere of give and take, often some light music in the background. Why wasn't his life at home like that?

And his own marriage. Could he honestly say he'd done his best? There'd been so many demands on him, his time and his resources. There was medical school, internship and residency. Weeks and months would go by, sometimes without even so much as a day off. On the occasional free weekend, he'd be preoccupied thinking about cases or an impending presentation. Cassie would want to go out to dinner and a movie, sometimes making plans with other couples. Sarnower would drag himself along, to an inexpensive Indian or Mexican restaurant in Cambridge and a movie at the old Orson Wells Theater afterwards, often so tired he'd sleep through it.

Inevitably, his fatigue and disengagement would lead to an argument. Cassie was right to be angry, he could have looked interested in dinner conversation, made more of an effort to be genial. The few friends they managed to make were puzzled. More than once each had been asked what they saw in the other. He'd always found the question surprising. Weren't they compatible? Didn't all couples get on each other's nerves? Certainly his parents did, and from what he'd seen of Cassie's family, well, they were easily as dysfunctional as his.

Did that mean they weren't supposed to be together? When his mother had asked him before they got married if he loved Cassie, the question caught him off-guard. He supposed he did. It was a question he pondered late at night when he'd look over and see Cassie sleeping on her side, snoring quietly. No one had a great marriage, did they? You got married as a ticket into adult society. You could have children and all the routine, boring sex you wanted. There'd be someone to rock with on the porch later on in life.

But now things had changed. As Cassie's illness progressed, so did his awareness of all that had slipped by, the years he could have spent challenging himself, asking the tough questions, struggling for answers rather than settling in passively for the long ride. Her craziness had moved in like a fog, imperceptible at first, then overtaking everything until all the familiar landmarks in her personality had vanished.

Sarnower sucked in his gut and began. "Mom is ill." He looked into his son's eyes and they held each other's gaze with the intensity of trapeze artists. "Not ill like when you have a cold or the flu. Sometimes, people's thoughts and feelings get very mixed up. Did you ever get really confused about something, like you didn't know what was right or wrong? Or you didn't know whether something was real or out of a dream?"

He stopped. Mitch was getting scared, wanting to know more, but not liking the direction in which this was going. Crazy people were creepy, something ten year olds joked about. Like a haunted house, you didn't want to get too close.

7

He retreated, his gaze shifting to the ground. "Yeah, kind of."

Sarnower continued. "Well, Mom's a little mixed up right now. She's trying to figure out a lot of things."

"Can I help her?" Mitch asked. "I'll really try to keep my room cleaner and put my stuff away." Sarnower looked at him, the words bringing an unexpected flush of tears to his eyes. This was Mitch's all, his maximum effort, the best he could do. He was hurting and had to be reassured.

"She's going to be ok, buddy. I promise."

He could tell Mitch wasn't satisfied but had enough grace to let his father off the hook. They finished raking in silence.

Cassie's condition continued to spiral downward. There were joint visits to a series of psychiatrists and psycho-pharmacologists, the new high priests of brain chemistry management. There were temporary respites where the three of them could enjoy a Sunday afternoon at the Arboretum or a day trip to a North Shore beach, but things quickly reverted. Soon there were pressured late night calls to doctors, all of them difficult to reach, despite Sarnower's professional connections. Medications were prescribed and changed, side effects analyzed and debated, courses of treatment considered, including short-term hospitalization. Nothing seemed to be effective, and Cassie's anger at the process was mounting.

Two days after her unhinged, surreal departure, Sarnower received a call from the Boston Police Department. Her car had been found parked in front of a fire hydrant in the North End near Logan airport. It had been towed to a city lot near the wharfs. They were calling to let him know they had the car and that fines were accruing at the rate of $300 per day. A note in her handwriting had been found taped to the inside of the windshield. "Split for the coast," was all it said. One of the windows had been smashed and the car had been looted.

Sarnower canceled a day's worth of appointments and made the unfamiliar trip out to the city's municipal lot. To get a taxi to take him there from sleepy Newton was not easy, but he finally persuaded a dispatcher to entice one of his hacks with an added fifty-dollar bonus to make the trip. They rode through decrepit neighborhoods, past abandoned lots and rotting factories; places he'd never seen before despite his decades in the Boston area. But the driver, a swarthy Middle Eastern, surely in this country for only a fraction of that time, got him there quickly in his shock-less, strut-less cab.

The lot was huge. As far as he could see there were rows and rows of cars radiated curling waves of heat in the baking sun, all enclosed in a high chicken-wire fence with a razor-wire coil running along the top. A small office looking more like a worn beachside seafood restaurant displayed a weathered sign assuring him he was in the right place. Sarnower entered and was immediately assaulted by the odor of sweating bodies and stale junk food. A bored cop in shirtsleeves was reading the *Boston Herald* in a chair propped up against the wall, a toothpick playing in his mouth. Inside an old wire cage, a fat, sweating clerk, bursting through his soaked uniform, stamped multi-copied forms with a crisp rhythmic beat. Cash or credit card only, a sign announced. The sergeant who had contacted him about the car had reiterated that message several times. No checks under any circumstances.

Sarnower fished out his wallet and began hunting for his Visa card. Subsidizing insanity does not come cheap. The original ticket and towing were $225. Two days of storage, another $600. The cab ride with promised bonus, ninety dollars. Your wife in a loony bin? Priceless at this point. He was out almost a grand. And let's not forget her fantasy trip to the coast. The ticket, impulsively bought, and God knows what kind of accommodations in LA or San Francisco, or wherever she was. She would burn through his money in a hell-bent fury. He wondered what it would take to put a stop on her credit card.

He gave the clerk Cassie's name and the plate number of the car. While the man thumbed through a stack of forms, Sarnower heard him sing the unmistakable strains of *E lucevan le stelle* from *Tosca*.

"An opera buff, eh?" Sarnower asked, glad for the novelty and distraction.

He nodded as he pushed a set of forms and a cheap plastic pen through the cage window. "Here, here and here," he said, pointing with a huge finger to lines that required signatures. The voice was full and melodious, not at all the expected deep cigarette growl. He smiled at Sarnower, who ordinarily would have given a compliment or made small talk. But today he was too far-gone, fried from his heated thoughts.

After signing the papers and the credit card receipt, the clerk opened the cage window and leaned his enormous bulk out.

"Lot on your left. Row M," he said with a lilt, gently tipping his head. Sarnower nodded in thanks, and in that moment, from nowhere, in his own craggy bathroom baritone, he started singing:

"Oh Danny boy, the pipes, the pipes are callin'"

On the second phrase, the clerk himself joined in. At the door, Sarnower stopped at the door and turned while the clerk took over and brought the ballad to a heroic conclusion. As he hung on the last note, as clean and shimmering as Pavarotti, Sarnower could hear fellow co-workers in the back offices applaud wildly. Even the sleepy cop against the wall was roused to attention, and Sarnower who was always affected by the easy sentimentality of "Danny Boy" felt a lump rise in his throat and struggled to keep from tearing up. Singing Irish ballads with John McCormick: priceless. He was well out of the door and heading for Cassie's car before he broke down sobbing.

All that was three weeks ago. Today was going to be tough; seven patients in a row without so much as a lunch break. Mitch was now in day camp, so logistically things should have been easier, but Sarnower's new role as a single parent was proving difficult. Even simple decisions had become hard to make. It was Thursday, late June and hot. What to wear? His patients would expect the crisp laundry-pressed cotton shirt with a tasteful tie. Sharply creased khakis and polished cordovan loafers completed the modified prepped-out look that Sarnower had cultivated since starting practice. While many of his colleagues wore business suits even in the summer, he had felt them too rigid. His patients weren't applying for a bank loan after all. A neat but casual appearance more easily equalized power, invited trust and encouraged openness.

But today would have to be different. He was running out of clean clothes. A crumpled polo shirt lay across the back of a chair and Sarnower put it on in a quick motion. Since Cassie's departure, basic housekeeping had eluded the sporadic, halfhearted attempts he and Mitch had made to bring order to things. Several days worth of dirty clothes overflowed the hamper. A pile of shirts needed to go to the laundry. The kitchen floor was getting sticky, and the increasing heat and humidity only accelerated the process. Half-eaten salads and cartons of take-out Chinese food liquefied in the refrigerator in various shades of brown and gray. This weekend we're really going to get organized. Set aside a whole day. Top-to-bottom clean up. A handsome cash incentive offered to Mitch would increase the chances of things happening. Probably. Maybe. Maybe not.

Kids today didn't have the same zest for earning money that he'd had as a boy. In his son's room, he constantly found change under the bed and strewn all over the floor as if the coins were worthless as old gum wrappers. At Mitch's age, he'd eagerly saved the quarters and dimes he earned at simple household chores, for a movie, or a paperback book. But Mitch and all his peers had grown used to transacting their business in bills and had no use for the nuisance of metal currency. At the mall, some of the more audacious stores had even starting asking their young customers if they wanted their change at all.

"Mitch!" he called. "Get ready. Tracey's going to be here in a minute."

Tracey Bowen, a seventeen-year old living down the block had been engaged to help Sarnower navigate Mitch through the day after Cassie had left. She was spindly and gawky as a colt, an honors student at Newton South High School, already aiming for pre-med in college. She would drive Mitch to and from camp, play-dates, do light shopping and run errands. Always prompt, always reliable. Despite several pleas to drop formality and call him Alan, she persisted in calling him Dr. Sarnower, and to his relief, she had no boyfriends, tattoos or body piercings. That was as close as you could get these days to the wholesome American girl. But as eager as she was not to flaunt any shred of sexuality, Sarnower felt himself oddly stirred in her presence.

In fact, since Cassie's departure, he was stirred in the presence of nearly every woman he came in contact with. Was he just horny after several weeks, months really, without sex? No, something else was going on, something deeper, some kind of liberation. He was looking at women with a reawakened teen-age eye. "Middlessence" was how he had heard it described by a colleague, common in men beginning a midlife crisis. It gave him a fresh view, with a full-color spectrum of possibilities.

Mitch bounded down the stairs as Tracey, reliable as a Greenwich clock, appeared at the screen door.

"Good morning, Dr. Sarnower," she smiled, beaming brightly.

"Hi Tracey," he said, trying to return a smile half as luminous as hers. Mitch ran into her arms for a sister-hug. Clearly he was missing a woman's touch as well.

"Bathing suit? Towel? Ice cream money?" She asked in staccato military style.

"Check, check and check!" he snapped. The day could not begin without this bit of ritual. It pleased Sarnower as well to see some kind of predictability and regularity returning to their lives.

"If it's ok with you Dr. Sarnower, I'd like to take Mitch after camp. A group of us are going to play softball and then have a cookout. I thought Mitch might enjoy it."

"What do you say, champ?" he asked as his son lit up.

"Sure, Dad." Mitch was raising and lowering himself on the balls of his feet.

"I'll make sure he doesn't eat too many hotdogs," she said leading Mitch out the door to her Honda.

"Have a good one," Sarnower called after them.

Athletic too. He caught a glimpse of her lean calves, and for a brief moment coddled a visual image of a languid, sweaty Tracey removing a dusty baseball jersey, unselfconscious and comfortable in her tight, muscular body. Although tempted to savor it, he shook his head and pushed it away. Those little "lust breaks" were becoming frequent and causing distractions at important times, during therapy sessions, driving, on the phone. A patient, calling from a hastily arranged business meeting and needing to reschedule an appointment had been freaked.

"Dr. Sarnower? Are you all right?"

"Uh, sure. Why do you ask?"

"I was asking if we could change our session time. You seemed to be drifting off somewhere."

Regrouping quickly: "I'm fine, just busy. We'll see you at six tonight."

"I asked for *seven.*"

"I'm sorry. That's right. Seven."

In between patients, in the ten minute break he allowed himself to write progress notes or visit the bathroom, he would frequently drift off into a humid tableau; time would disappear until he was interrupted by the beep of his intercom that let him know his next patient was ready.

With Mitch en route to a cool swim, arts and crafts and the promise of a sticky-sweet, starchy lunch, Sarnower was ready to head to the office.

He stopped at the hall mirror to do a quick once-over. Not too bad, all things considered. Hair neatly combed, his smooth face rosy and tight with a splash of lime cologne (citrus in the summer, musk in the winter he'd once read in *GQ.*) The black polo shirt, although rumpled on the couch looked fine when tucked into his khakis. Since Cassie had left, Sarnower had lost almost twenty pounds, putting him within range of his old college weight. His closet offered things he hadn't worn in years, clothes that now draped nicely on his frame. *The Psychiatrist's Guide to Quick Weight Loss*—his next book. Chapter One: *Dealing With the Crazed*

Significant Other—that's ten pounds right off the top. Nothing like prolonged mental anguish to reverse that stubborn middle age spread. Women, he discovered, were now taking that extra moment to notice him, splashing fuel on his already hot set of fantasies.

At eight-thirty in the morning the heat was already extreme. The outside brass door handle was almost too hot to touch as Sarnower pulled it closed behind him. The air, now humid as well, bathed him in an old-world *schvitz*. On days like these, he found it hard to breath and the extra effort only made him sweat more. The car door handle, also too hot to touch, required the aid of a handkerchief. Despite a reflecting screen in the front window, the open door sent a blast of heat that almost made him swoon, like getting out of bed too quickly and seeing a checkerboard pattern before keeling over.

The task now was to turn on the air conditioner without getting third degree burns. Reaching the ignition from outside the car without touching the steering wheel would be a contortion, but he got the key in on the first try and the vents hummed to life, spewing a hot, moldy gas before the reassuring basso hum of cool air began to flood the car.

Although the trip to the office was less than a mile away, it could easily leave him depleted on a day like this. It was barely the duration of an NPR story on the radio, but it was just enough time for his thoughts to coalesce again and bring into sharp relief the full impact of his situation. Where the hell *was* Cassie? He had contacted her credit card company, and after a large cash withdrawal in San Francisco, there had been no more activity on her card. When he'd called the police and showed them the note left in her car, they had laughed at him. No way were they going to waste valuable resources on this. Couldn't he read? She'd left on her own. Sergeant O'Connor, who had talked to Sarnower a few days after the car was found had even intimated that he wasn't satisfying her sexually and that she'd had taken off in search of someone more "responsive" to her needs. He had even consulted a private investigator who claimed to have seen many cases like this.

"She'll be home, doc, don't worry. As soon as the dough runs out, she'll be back. Save your money. You'll need it to pay her bills." What was it going to take? Cassie turning up in jail, or dead?

Sarnower pulled his car into the parking lot just as he had started to contemplate going after her himself. But enough of that. It was time for work.

The Chestnut Hill Medical Center, formerly a small department store, had been purchased and remodeled by an enterprising young developer into upscale medical suites in the early nineties. Sarnower had been one of the first tenants and had a comfortable office on the ground floor. A wide, sun-lit atrium dominated the center of the building, which featured a large Japanese reflecting pool complete with naturalistic rocks and exotic fish. Offices were located on all four sides and opened up onto the spacious common area.

Frigid air blasted him as he opened the front glass door. It was an instant twenty-degree drop in temperature. Building maintenance always thought more was better. Did all those eighty-year old women who were here to see their cardiologist or orthopedic surgeon, ever contract pneumonia? At that age, and there were many at that age, the sudden climate change could be unpleasant at best.

Miroslav, the large, obsequious head of maintenance smiled at him over an industrial sized mop. "Gut mornink, doctor," he said, bowing slightly. "Morning," Sarnower returned, nodding. Miroslav was polite to the point of servility to the professionals and patients who streamed through the building at all hours, but as a Czech immigrant from the old Communist days, he was a drill sergeant who delighted in riding herd on his crew. He made sure they always had a presence in their crisp, pressed uniforms, polishing brass, cleaning glass, vacuuming, sweeping and doing whatever needed to be done to keep the Medical Center spotless. The Red Army in Chestnut Hill.

Alan Sarnower, M.D., Psychiatry, black block letters on a brass plaque announced. It had been a gift from Cassie years ago when he had christened the office. He opened the door with a fast twist of the metal knob. Inside, the air was just as cold as it was in the lobby. Sweat was beginning to evaporate and leave his hair and clothes matted and stiff.

The office looked exactly as it had the day he opened for business. A spacious waiting room with a couple of late-eighties chocolate brown leather Crate & Barrel couches were flanked by a set of oak side tables with earth-toned prairie-style lamps. *People* magazine. *Time. Money, Forbes* and *Sports Illustrated* were there for the driven, acquisitive males in his practice, although over the past few years, he noticed women were passing up *People* and were opting instead for the financials, some even going so far as to tear out articles surreptitiously.

There were expensively framed graphics by David Hockney, Alexander Calder and Robert Rauchenberg on the stark white walls. A bold, geometric Navaho rug covered the hardwood floor, and during the day, to mute the conversations from his consulting room, Public Radio's classical offerings purred gently in the background.

Off to the right side was a small glassed-off enclosure that housed a computer, a desk and a couple of filing cabinets. From there, Nina Winslow, his office manager of five years ran the practice. God, what would I do without her? Sarnower often wondered. Part secretary, part therapist for him, and over the years, guide to the unfathomable reaches of the female psyche and soul, Sarnower put her up there as one of the superb human beings he had been lucky enough to know.

She came to work for him after bouncing around a few years out of college. She exuded an energy and life force that was dazzling. Without even checking references or credentials, Sarnower had hired her on the spot, powerless to do otherwise. She was a quick study and picked up the complex mechanics of running his office in no time. Nina put his waiting patients at ease, although he noticed his male clients were often jazzed by her pulsing sexuality. She wasn't conventionally beautiful, or even very pretty, and Sarnower had spent countless hours trying to figure out what it was, but Nina Winslow gave off something that made men weak in the knees. True, she had a great figure, if a bit padded, but it was all in the right places. The shiny, long blond hair didn't hurt, nor did her skin, a natural year-round tanned, rose-gold color that reminded him of antique jewelry. The husky voice, the wide blue eyes that held you like prison-yard searchlights. Was it pheromones? Sarnower had read about those imperceptible, air-borne molecules of sexual attractants transmitted by several different species. They were supposedly important in human commerce as well. But damned if he could figure it out. Maybe it was the gestalt, the total package. The whole was so much greater than the sum of its parts.

But there she was, back turned to him, the computer printer humming. She was getting his bills out, enriching him monetarily as well as hormonally. This made her even more luscious and valuable. She was unaware he had entered the office as the air conditioner and printer combined to create a sonic wash sufficient to muffle any noise. Her ample blonde hair was up in a knot and she wore a linen peasant blouse with a flattering dark skirt and strap sandals.

Early in her career with Sarnower, they had discussed expectations of appropriate office dress, but as time passed, she had gone her own way, gradually shedding business clothes for a comfortable, upscale retro earth-mother look, her nature asserting itself. As the stock market sunk, terrorists attacked and Cassie left, Sarnower no longer gave a damn, quietly pleased at her resolute display of ease; it was part of her power. Today, he was just grateful she was still with him.

"Hi Nina," he called over the din. Startled, she jumped and placed a hand over her heart. Such a Victorian a gesture for a twenty-first century woman. She turned, flushed.

"You scared me," she gasped; relieved it was him.

"Sorry. Just me. Who can hear anything over this..."

"Mr. Zifkin is here," she said quietly, handing him the charts for the day. "I asked him to wait out here but he insisted on going into your office."

She looked at him like a guilty child expecting a reprimand.

"Don't worry about it," he said, placing a hand on her arm.

He took the folders and opened the door to his consulting room. Barry Zifkin, thirty-two, real estate prodigy, loud mouth and royal pain in the ass was standing in the middle of his office studying the diplomas on his wall. Zifkin had made his first five million by the time he was twenty-eight. He wore a dark Armani suit, crisp Turnbull & Asser French-cuff shirt and a hideous dog-vomit tie that must have cost two or three hundred dollars. He had been busted a year ago trying to score cocaine in Dorchester, and as part of his court-ordered probation, in addition to community service and regular attendance at NA meetings, he had to go for twice-weekly therapy sessions. For his admittedly handsome fee, Sarnower had to put up with Zifkin's bullshit and file monthly reports with his probation officer, who made it clear he saw his charge as a rich candy-ass, who, because of his standing had gotten a cakewalk. Sarnower could not disagree.

"I paid more for my loafers than you spent on medical school," Zifkin said still inspecting the parchment on the wall.

"You are to stay outside in the waiting area until I call you in." Sarnower answered with unexpected venom in his voice. Zifkin too was startled and became a baby-faced boy.

"Don't ever put my office manager in a compromising position again."

"Ok, ok, point made." Zifkin held up his hands in mock surrender.

"Let's begin," Sarnower said as the two of them sat. "What just happened here? That's exactly the kind of thing that gets you into trouble. How do you think people feel when you barge in on them?"

Zifkin smiled. Slowly, he took off his suit jacket, folded it neatly and put it on the table next to his chair. Christ, the guy doesn't even sweat. Even the starched white shirt showed no signs of the day's punishing heat. He knows this. He's fucking with my mind. No playing poker with this guy.

"How other people feel?" Zifkin asked, not thinking he'd heard right.

"Yes. Do you ever wonder how what you do affects other people?"

Zifkin laughed. "If I gave a rat's ass about that, I'd be super-sizing happy meals at McDonald's." He leaned forward, his upper lip curling. "Maybe you haven't picked this up yet, doc, but I'm really not all that interested in what people think of me."

"No, that comes through loud and clear." What to do with this guy? Throwing him to the penal system might bring about some dramatic attitude change. Despite his bravado and business acumen, Zifkin wouldn't stand a chance inside as someone's bitch. He'd be eaten alive for lunch. The sudden set of visuals put an unconscious smile on Sarnower's face.

"What are you laughing at?" The man-boy mogul, unnerved, caught the smile as a put-down. Not taking him seriously was his weak point. That was useful to know.

"I've got to level with you, Barry," Sarnower said, carefully sculpting his delivery. While he had the advantage, perhaps something in the avuncular lecture mode. "I really don't care what you do. You change? That's great. Fantastic. You don't? That's fine too. But I see you in a very deep vat of tapioca if you don't. You must have something on the ball to have made all that money. Where it is or what it is, I have no idea. But I'm not going to be here next time." Now rolling, Sarnower felt an unexpected jolt of rage in his chest. "I would strongly suggest you pull your act together. At least try to go through the motions, 'cause for a smart guy, you're really pretty stupid."

Jesus! What had he done? If his old supervisors in psychiatry could hear him! He'd never called a patient stupid before. What was he thinking? Zifkin was intractable, he had a character disorder as wide and deep as the ocean, but Sarnower had lost it, he'd done what he vowed he wouldn't. He'd let Zifkin get to him, taken it personally and then he'd humiliated him. A big mistake. Any first year student knew the patient's hostility was an acting-out of the transference, the therapist as stand-in for all the significant people in his life who had done him wrong. There was nothing personal in it.

Sarnower's power as a doctor was reconfirmed. What to do now? The man was wilted, deflated. Now too late, he remembered how Zifkin had described his father, a loud boor who delighted in shaming his children. Without thinking, he'd just stepped right into the old man's shoes. Zifkin needed to be rehabilitated, but at the moment Sarnower was at a complete loss, frozen by his impulsive blunder. Apologizing would be admitting to an unacceptable professional lapse in judgment, and Zifkin, with his stable of aggressive lawyers might catch a whiff of a malpractice suit: irreparable psychological harm. No, now was the time to heed the advice of one of his old teachers. If you don't know what to say, don't say anything at all.

They sat in silence, the air conditioner humming quietly. Sarnower looked straight ahead at Zifkin who returned the stare without blinking. The quartz carriage clock on the bookcase ticked softly, its second hand jerking spastically around the dial five times. Ten times.

Finally, Zifkin's glance drifted to the floor. There were tiny rippling waves under the smooth baby skin of his face. Although fifteen minutes remained in the session, Zifkin got up and reached for his jacket. Sarnower could see pools of sweat under his arms now as he put it on.

"I think I'll leave," he said in a whisper as he headed for the door. Sarnower nodded. What had he done to this guy? He'd have to come up with something before their next session.

Outside, Nina had finished his bills and had stacked them in a pile, stamped and ready to go. On her desk was a tall frosted plastic cup of iced coffee from the deli downstairs. Sarnower, already parched, depleted and wrung out at nine-thirty in the morning, eyed the container enviously.

"I got you a coffee from downstairs," she said, typing, her back still turned to him. Sarnower reached for his wallet to reimburse her.

"Don't pay me," she said turning. "Angelo gives me freebees when the boss isn't looking." She had her electric smile on. "I think he has a crush on me," she confided. Well who the fuck doesn't? Was she aware of what she did to men? He was never quite sure if she knew her own powers, but they were there all right. Today, the heat and humidity made her glow even deeper, like an orchid. Her scent filled the work area, a combination of light perfume and her own indescribable musk. The animal kingdom transacting its business, bees, elephants, monkeys, up and down the chain. He became aware of an embarrassing erection. Over the years he was sure Nina had picked up his attraction to her, but for her own reasons, and to his gratitude, she'd never mentioned it. He drifted off into one of his lust moments. Nina turned and laughed. Shit. He must have looked like a pathetic, lovesick teenager.

"Mrs. Netherworth," she said.

"What?"

"Mrs. Netherworth is ready for you," she said gently.

There on the couch was seventy-nine year old Agnes Netherworth, here for her weekly medication check and pep talk. A recent widow, Sarnower had started her on ten milligrams of Prozac and small doses of reassurance and encouragement. The old lady had seen the moony exchange through the glass partition and was not amused. But then, ever since Sarnower had taken her on she always looked as if she'd just swallowed a lemon.

"Have fun," Nina whispered.

Once one of Boston's grandees, osteoporosis and arthritis had forced an aluminum tripod cane on Mrs. Netherworth. Sarnower went over to assist in prying her out of his deep leather couch.

"Won't you get some *real* furniture in here?" she hissed, shaking and struggling to get up like an insect pinned on its back. Sarnower noted with relief that this process had immediately deflated his erection. They walked slowly into his consulting room. Mercifully, Nina had closed the door to her office and was on the phone.

"Why do you have to keep this place so cold?"

"I'm sorry. Building management sets the temperature. I can ask Nina to call down and have them adjust it."

"No, no." She gave a vague dismissive wave with a bony hand.

"How are you sleeping and eating?" Sarnower asked after she sat down.

She looked at him as though he were kidding. "I'm not."

"Your life is much different now. Adapting to change can be very difficult."

"I don't want to adapt. I want to die."

"The medication hasn't helped to lift your mood?"

"I don't want my mood lifted. Why is it all you people want to do is lift moods?"

"You're angry and that's ok, it's understandable"

"It's not ok and it's not understandable," she snapped.

Sarnower took a deep breath. "Mrs. Netherworth, how can I help you?"

"I keep telling you, you can't. You can't! You just won't listen to me!" She had a sharp metallic edge to her voice that made Sarnower shiver, like the scream of a cornered animal that knew it would be killed in seconds.

She started to cry. Tears were always just below the surface in the elderly. Does aging decay the inhibitory mechanisms of the brain? That fragile, brittle stoicism, shattered by a sneeze could bring on tears. Is that why the elderly became incontinent too? We start leaking all over, like battered rowboats. Good God. Getting old is not for the faint of heart his grandmother had told him from her hospital bed. At the time, as a boy, Sarnower had no idea what she meant; it sounded like a fortune cookie. Now here it was, right in front of him, like a highway sign warning of an imminent exit.

Again: when there's nothing to say, say nothing. Simple. He let Mrs. Netherworth weep, delicately, silently, as he passed her the box of Kleenex he always kept ready. She accepted it, and pulling several tissues, began the theatrical process of blowing her nose and wiping her eyes. When she had finished, she opened her purse and stuffed the unused tissues in with the sure, staccato movements of a squirrel hiding nuts.

"Your losses must be so hard to bear," Sarnower intoned slowly. She nodded and extracted one more tissue for a final pat down. She looked at him, sad and sagging.

"I'm sorry doctor. It wasn't polite of me to get angry with you. I know you're just trying to help."

"Mrs. Netherworth, you need to get angry, you need to scream. Do it here, do it now, you won't destroy me. Get it out."

She looked at him and smiled faintly. "Yes...yes, I'm sure that's what I need to do. You're the doctor, you went to school. You must be right."

She began to move in her seat and contemplate the mechanics of getting up. Her starched Brahmin background had years ago sealed off any hope of an expressive, emotional life with innumerable martinis, country club lunches and Sunday sermons. There must be *some* way to get through to this woman. But now she required physical assistance and Sarnower rose from his seat to help organize her departure.

The cold room had made her considerably more stiff and Sarnower could see her wince and tremble at the effort. He helped her steady herself on the cane, and when she was more or less vertical, he handed her her purse.

They walked out to the waiting room where a scruffy, T-shirted cab driver sat, waiting to drive her home. The man's gaze was firmly fixed on Nina doing her work and this made Sarnower furious.

"How did it go Mrs. N? The shrinkin' I mean," the man asked with a vulgar familiarity. Repulsed, she stiffened as he took her arm. The cabdriver turned at the door to face Sarnower. "Same time next week, eh doc?" Sarnower nodded as they left.

It was easy to understand the old woman's rage. Mounting indignities, increasing physical limitations, stupid, uncomprehending rudeness, she had to settle for less and less. Life was subtracting its gifts to her on a daily basis. One day, there'd be nothing left at all.

Sarnower was exhausted. He'd just bombed out with two patients, a pathetic start to the day. The wild shifts in environments, the heat outside and the cold air inside had thrown him badly off his game. Was that it? Something had been off, eating at him all morning, since he got up. It was too vague a feeling to pin down and now he had neither time nor energy to make the effort. Just shape up and get back on track. He had progress notes and letters to write, phone calls to return, errands to run.

There on Nina's desk was his sweating, untouched iced coffee. He grabbed the cup, tore off the lid and straw and began to chug it down in huge gulps. The coffee was watered down; the ice cubes were now the size of peas. But it was cold and wet—that was all that mattered.

Nina watched as he swallowed the drink and tossed the empty cup into the trash. "You look like you needed that," she remarked.

"I need a lot more than coffee right now."

"I'm sure," she answered cryptically.

"Who called?" he asked, gesturing to a small pile of pink message slips.

"Dr. Lane asking about Mrs. Rosten's new medication, Dr. Abravanel wondering if you can do a Grand Rounds presentation next week and Mr. Driscoll, who insisted you call him immediately."

She tapped the small pile on the desk and handed them to him. What lovely hands. Short, well trimmed nails, no polish, always the

21

same length. He noticed the cold had raised goose bumps on her arms producing a delicious golden fog of hair. God, I could eat her right now.

Mr. Driscoll, a.k.a. Tug. Former college roommate and partner in selected deviant and demented activities. Sarnower had made it a point to stay in touch with him over the years. Along with Nina, he was one of the few remarkable individuals he'd ever run into. Together at the University of Chicago in the mid-seventies, Tug came from a poor farming town in Iowa and prior to his matriculation had never even been to a city.

From their first class together, Tug had shown no interest whatsoever in school. He would sleep through lectures, write papers at the very last minute and forget to study for finals. Yet when he had to, he would invariably ace his courses. But by his senior year, Tug had had it with school. When Sarnower was preparing for the MEDCAT and applying to medical schools, Tug was off-campus learning futures and commodity trading, Cordon Bleu cooking and foreign auto repair. Although he never finished college, and knew nothing about business, he had started his own management consulting firm (on a drunken bet with a friend) long before that sort of thing was fashionable. This year the firm would be billing in excess of 200 million dollars worldwide.

As for speaking with Tug, Sarnower was definitely not in the mood. In retrospect, it was probably Tug's arrival late last night with a bottle of Absolut vodka and a bag of premium Columbian joints that was responsible for the morning's short-circuiting and professional meltdown. Sarnower was suddenly filled with a familiar disgust and self-loathing that had become common since Cassie's departure. His increasingly frequent forays into self-medication were starting to make inroads into the seamless functioning he took pride in, both in and outside the office. Yet at the time, imbibing and bantering well into the early morning hours with Tug, reliving college follies, listening to his running commentary on the sorry state of the pool of available single women, the whole enterprise seemed entirely reasonable.

Yet Tug himself (his nickname derived from an arcane masturbatory practice that he refused to divulge, even to Sarnower) never missed a beat. He was always at the office early and consistently got the job done. He could plow through his own psychic fog and bad weather like a polar icebreaker. Taking charge was second nature.

Once, as undergraduates, the two of them had been driving to Ribs 'N' Bibs, an open-all-night barbecue shack deep in Chicago's

South Side, one that Tug had been raving about for weeks. The neighborhood was clearly not one to be in at any time of day, much less at two or three in the morning. They had dropped Mescaline at some point earlier in the evening, and to take the rough edges off their return to reality were in the process of finishing off a sample bag of deluxe Panama Red that Tug was considering for quantity purchase and distribution to select clients.

While waxing philosophical on the fine distinctions between mesquite and teriyaki marinades, Tug had made an illegal right turn, and before they were half way down the block, a Chicago cop was on their tail. Frantic and sure they would be busted, Sarnower saw his future vanish. There would be a panicky call to his parents for bail money, a judge meting out a sentence, and an appearance before the University's disciplinary committee with certain expulsion. Tug's ancient Ford Falcon was too filled with incriminating smoke to attempt even a *pro forma* face saving.

"Chill out, man," Tug said, his mojo beginning to hum as a huge black cop sauntered slowly over to their car. He tapped the driver's window with a thick, Marine-ringed finger and gestured for Tug to roll it down.

"License and registration."

Pot fumes billowed forth as the cop told Tug to get out of the car. With more than mild annoyance, Tug unfolded his large frame out the door. The cop led him to the back of the vehicle, readying his handcuffs when Sarnower heard them starting to converse. Through the rear window, he saw Tug reach into his jacket, extract a large, foil-wrapped package and hand it to the officer who pealed back the top and began sniffing. Smiling, the cop stuffed the package in his own jacket pocket and began to unlock the single handcuff he had already applied to Tug's wrist. Eyes squinting and jaw jutting, Tug returned to the car and got in, slamming the door.

"Shit, shit, shit, fucking goddamn *Shit*!" he screamed, banging his hands on the steering wheel.

"Is he going to take us in?" Sarnower asked. Tug looked at him as if he were a retarded child. He shook his head. "My man, you have just been bailed out to the tune of $500."

"You bribed him?"

"Let's just say the next meeting of the Chicago Police Benevolent Association is going to have a lot of very benevolent mother fucking pigs in attendance."

"Jesus. How did you know he'd..."

"Forget it, dude."

Tug was on to his next deal.

"What did uh, Mr. Driscoll want?" Sarnower asked. A running joke, as Tug was well known to Nina, calling often and dropping by on occasion to have lunch with Sarnower. He had developed a casual, self-deprecating relationship with Nina, who thought him outrageously funny.

"Mr. Driscoll," she italicized the words, keeping the joke going "didn't say; only that you should call."

Sarnower couldn't take his eyes off her; she had never looked so desirable.

"What?" she asked.

"Nothing. Why?"

"You were looking at me funny, kind of staring."

"I'm sorry, I...I'm overloaded today. It's nothing."

"Ok." She sounded wary. Good going dick-head. Be a leering pervert.

Sarnower punched Tug's corporate number on the telephone. A cool feminine voice answered.

"The Driscoll Group. How may I direct your call?"

"Sheila? It's Alan. Alan Sarnower."

"Oh, Alan. How *are* you?" Sheila Townsand, Tug's overweight and overworked receptionist was always happy to hear from him.

"I could complain but I won't. Is he in?"

"Just a sec."

Then: "I am making it happen, captain. I am the grease on the wheels of American business and in-dus-try. I am making the world safe for capitalism." Ordinarily, Tug's trademark delivery, something between a rap-artist and a carnival barker would have gotten at least a chuckle from Sarnower. Today it was just annoying.

"Dig it, man: I just did a monster contract with these venture capitalist dudes from Hungary?" Tug had the habit, when excited, of ending his sentences in the cadence of a question. "Candy from a baby. They don't know squat. They're gonna fly me and my entourage over, put us up in some bad-ass old castle on some damn river."

"The Danube."

"The what?"

"The Danube. That's the river that runs between the ancient cities of Buda and Pest."

"Whatever, man. You're the one that finished college."

"You're the one that proved college is totally irrelevant."

"Hey, are you listening? Five years of heavy-duty consultation fees after our tutorial. I ask you, my brother, is that *phat* or what? Shit, I'm about to cream my pants."

Normally, Sarnower would pick up his end of the banter and there would be verbal jousting and parrying, but not today.

"Yeah, that's great Tug."

"Hey, you ok?"

"Just busy."

"We're all busy, man. You sound like a bus just ran you down."

"That's about how I feel."

"That crazy-ass wife of yours come back to turn the screws?"

Over the years, Tug and Cassie had honed a casual dislike of each other into a robust hatred. Tug, who thought marriage was at best indistinguishable from a life term in maximum-security prison, had been dismayed when his best friend had been lured into a web that had put serious constraints on their high-flying adventures. Tug had never forgiven her and, Sarnower suspected, was secretly glad that she'd upped and left.

"No, she's still MIA."

Tug chuckled. "I can only imagine the action she's getting."

"Knock it off. She's still the mother of my son."

"My bad. Sorry. Say, I'm thinking of growing a ponytail before we head over to Transylvania. Show 'em a little of the Wild West."

"Get your ears and nose pierced too and you'll be ready for a sales job at Dolce & Gabbana."

"Cute. I think we could find you a consulting spot on one of our teams."

"Your teams aren't ready for the likes of me." With the ball in play again, Sarnower's spirits lifted. The verbal tennis matches invariably left him mildly high and very tired. There was a buzz on Tug's line.

"I gotta go," he said. "Don't be surprised if me and Dom Perignon drop by for a little tête-à-tête and mix it up with a few of our Columbian friends."

"Shit, I'm still assessing the damage from *last* night."

"Listen, you ought to give up carbs. That's the secret. I have and it's changed my life."

"*Carbs?* What do you think's in vodka and champagne?"

"There's *good* carbs and *bad* carbs, dude, like good cholesterol and bad cholesterol. Alcohol: good carbs. Wonderbread: bad carbs."

"You missed your calling as a nutritionist. Anyway, Mitch will be home."

"All the better. We can initiate him into the glories of young manhood, introduce him to some of the ancient tribal rites and customs."

"Tug, he's *ten.*"

"Damn! What a mellow age to sally forth into life's glorious pleasures."

"You're a sick fuck, Tug."

"I do my best, buddy."

"Save it for your clients."

Sarnower hung up. Ragtiming with Tug was not a priority now. Burdened with a missing wife, mounting financial obligations and dealing with a young son who was silently retreating into a dark corner left few reserves. Tug on the other hand sat cosseted in the corner office of an air-conditioned suite, in a high-rise office building downtown, feet propped up on a huge wrap-around custom made desk, winking at attractive young female associates, high-fiving and talking sports trash with his insecure male VPs and team leaders, raking in boatloads of money, keeping the whole thing just slightly off-center and unpredictable—all with the practiced, fluent moves of an experienced surgeon.

But when you stripped away the fancy office, the expensive clothes, the nervous, toadying staff that paid daily homage to their liege, at the end of the day, Tug's riffs and charisma were pretty much all that were left, like the end of *The Wizard of Oz*: don't pay any attention to the man behind the curtain. And he knew it.

In addition to everything else, Sarnower struggled daily to cling to the hope that at least sometimes he was doing some good, helping someone. Somehow. So much for formal education. It just made you bleed out faster.

He was about to climb into a new lust moment when Nina knocked on the door and came in. She sat down in the overstuffed chair used by patients and bent forward, elbows on her thighs and looked right at him. She said nothing, sizing him up.

"Alan..." She said tentatively.

"What is it?"

"I...I hope you won't get angry with me. I took it on myself to cancel your patients for the rest of the day." She took a deep breath and continued. "Forgive me for saying so, but in the past couple of days you've looked terrible. You haven't been right. I'm sure it's all that's going on with your wife, you must be worried sick about Mitch." She stopped to tuck wayward strands of long blond hair in

back of her ears. "Some of your patients...I don't know, they've
looked kind of weird, upset, after their sessions. I've heard you raise
your voice through the wall. You've never done that before."

Her hands started to fidget, and Sarnower saw tears begin to
pool in her eyes.

"How long has this been going on? A week? Two?"

She nodded. Tears fell onto her dress. So he'd been losing it for
longer than he thought. *That* was scary.

Then came one of those moments he'd thought about and knew
was somewhere out there in space, one moment that would come
down and grace him. Somehow he couldn't put his thoughts together
and found himself moving, getting up and approaching her. He pulled
her up and into his arms, hugging her tightly, aware of the moment
and the act only after it happened. Her confessional relief and his
empathy opened a flood of tears as she tightened her arms around
him. They stood like that, in silence for what seemed like minutes as
Sarnower gently rubbed her back in small circular motions. The body
he had wondered about for so long was suddenly flush against his.
Her heat, the live, gently pulsing flesh, the dewy surface of her tear-
streaked face, the smells, the citrus shampoo scent of her hair (musk
in the winter for her too?), the sweet, slightly tangy aura of the day's
sweat that clung to her neck and breasts.

Floating, he closed his eyes and inhaled deeply. He was getting
hard again and gently began to pull away, hoping Nina hadn't
noticed the intruder between them. He held her shoulders and
looked into her swollen eyes.

"It's ok. It's fine, really. You're right. I do need some time away."

She smiled. "You're not going to fire me?"

Sarnower laughed and drew her close. "I'm going to give you a
raise." I could spend the rest of my life with this woman, he
thought. This time, Nina pulled away.

"Is there anything I can do to help you? Shopping? Watching
Mitch?"

"I think I've got that covered."

"Since Doug and I broke up, I have time. I mean it. Anything."

"I'll keep that in mind, I will," Sarnower said as she started to
pull herself back together. She grabbed some tissues from the same
box Mrs. Netherworth had used less than an hour earlier to help
salvage the remains of her fading dignity.

Sarnower looked down. His polo shirt was wet with Nina's
tears. Her fluids, her DNA were now making a talisman of this

unlikely shirt. Should he wash it? Would she ever leave her essence on anything of his again?

And Doug. He'd completely forgotten about Doug. Doug, the perpetual graduate student of Elizabethan drama had recently been given his walking papers by Nina after several hot-blooded fights. Doug the procrastinator, Doug the deadbeat, Doug the sullen and uncommunicative. But also Doug, the great lay. Nina, in her more open and assertive moments with Sarnower had, to his squeamish discomfort, gone into specific details of their rollicking sex life together. She'd never met a man who was her sexual equal before him. He could be tender; he could be rough, and lots in between, depending on her needs, which he was somehow able to divine before she herself even knew. Once an aspiring actor, years of diction practice and an ability to get his tongue around nettlesome Shakespearean couplets apparently had paid rich dividends in the sack. For the first time in her life, Nina had become multi-orgasmic. She'd never thought herself able to achieve the kind of abandon she'd found with Doug. Their first few months together were spent almost completely in bed, but gradually she had started to want more out of the relationship; enrichment, growth, new friendships. She wanted to get established publicly as a couple, and to think about marriage.

Sarnower was uncomfortable with her confidences, but felt honored that she trusted him with her closest intimacies, as she would her girlfriends. Yes, he was jealous, almost trembling at times, as if enraged. He would spend tormented hours imagining the two of them in bed, doing the things he'd heard about in so much graphic detail, hoping to keep that part of himself hidden from Nina.

He rejoiced secretly when deep cracks formed in the relationship. Maybe Nina wasn't going to be pulled away by this guy after all. He'd seen Doug's defects well before she had, and had made subtle hints and comments to her along the way, but to no apparent effect. The one time he'd actually met Doug, tall and thin with long, stringy dark hair and the pallor of a nineteenth century consumptive, he'd been virtually catatonic. No, Nina had to find her own way out and ultimately, even the incredible sex lost its magic. Doug's inability to do more than tread water and play for time, to finish his degree, to offer Nina a life together had ultimately trumped all else. Now she was single, and he...well, what was he? Not single, separated, or divorced. Abandoned, certainly. And that could lead to what? What did he want it to lead to? Nina was right. He really did need to take the rest of the day off.

Chapter 2

THE SKY THROBBED WITH black clouds as Sarnower pulled into his driveway. A brief, heavy downpour would cool things off nicely. But what was this? Cassie's recovered car that had been sitting in his driveway for three weeks was now parked in the street in front of the house. Behind it was an ancient, battered, dark blue Dodge Dart. What the fuck? Cassie was the only other person with a key.

He bolted from his car. ABBA's old disco song *Dancing Queen* was blasting from the stereo in his living room. The heavy oaken door stood open, only the screen door protected the house from the outside world. As he stepped inside, he smelled sweet, acrid marijuana smoke. He started to panic. Who was here? What was going on? He ran to the stereo and turned it off. The music had masked voices coming from a bedroom upstairs. One of them belonged to Cassie.

He took the stairs three at a time, his heart pounding, breath short, head ready to shoot from his shoulders. There in the master bedroom was Cassie and some man he had never seen before, in bed, both naked and finishing a beautiful custom-rolled joint Tug had given him the night before. Taking in the tableau took a few seconds for everyone, an unbelieving moment of stillness. They all looked at each other. Cassie was the first to break the silence. She burst into laughter, and her naked companion was quick to join in. Tug's magic carpet ride had lifted them far and away above any and all semblance of known social convention. Sarnower thought he would pass out from fury, but being clothed and vertical he figured, gave him a distinct advantage. Quickly, he ripped the sheets from the bed, exposing their nude bodies. He knew Cassie's basic geography, but the strange man was grotesque. Thin to the point of emaciation, his ribs stood out in bold relief on his chest, like a renaissance painting of the passion of Christ. That, coupled with his close-cropped hair gave him the appearance of a concentration camp survivor. His wilted, uncircumcised dick glistened with recent sex and his long bony legs and yellowed toenails made Sarnower want to retch. Cassie herself had changed. She'd become rail-thin, her eyes now in sunken cavities, her hair greasy and stringy, cheekbones protruding, her skin taking on a pale, gray color.

Awash in adrenaline, Sarnower approached the man and without thinking grabbed him by the wrists and pulled him violently from the bed.

"Who the *fuck* are you?" he hissed between clenched teeth, his white lips inches from the cadaver.

"Let go!" the man whined, squirming and struggling to free himself. Sarnower tightened his grip, digging his fingernails into the thin flesh. He pulled the man over to the wall, and threw him against it. The burst of animal rage released something so pent up and strong, so toxic, Sarnower thought for a second he'd lost his mind.

He pushed the man's head into the wall and it bounced forward like a volley ball. His mouth opened, displaying rows of crooked, yellowed teeth. His eyes were moving independently of one another and seemed unable to align themselves. Sarnower, trying to bring the situation into focus, was now the 800-pound gorilla. He gripped the man tightly by his jaw and screamed into his face.

"If you don't leave *my* house *right* now, I swear to God, I will break both your arms and throw you out the window. *You got that?*"

The man, impaled and frozen, was unable to speak. Cassie was now out of bed and getting dressed. "Leave him alone!" she screamed. Sarnower, still pinning the man to the wall by his jaw, turned and made a quick canvas of the floor. The man's dirty sneakers, worn jeans and old tie-dyed T-shirt were scattered about. He grabbed them up, opened the window overlooking the street, and hurled them out. They floated down to the lawn, into the middle of the street; one sneaker hooked itself onto a tree branch. Now freed, the man tore through the room, down the stairs and out the door. Sarnower laughed as he saw him scurry to rescue his clothes from their improbable resting places. Some of the neighbors, brought out of their houses by the high-decibel ABBA concert, remained in their yards watching in disbelief as the man struggled to get dressed, get into his car and drive off.

Sarnower turned to face his wife.

"You goddamn bitch! What the fuck do you think you're doing? You're stoned out of your mind, you stupid whore!" Cassie sat on the bed and laughed. She gathered her clothes.

"I'm not coming back," she said, suddenly sober and serious. She rose and went to the antique mirror. "I'm leaving you Alan. For good. And I'll be taking Mitch with me as soon as I get set up."

"You're taking Mitch? You honestly think I'm going to let you take Mitch? Where have you been anyway?"

She turned to face him. The physical changes in her, now close and unmistakable, were appalling.

"If you must know, I was in San Francisco. I was staying with Susan Prescott." The name rang a dim, far-away bell. She was one of Cassie's old parochial school friends, pious, obedient, and cowed as a student. But the minute school was over, she bolted for the West coast and became a radical-feminist poet, on the fringe of some Weatherman-type group forever plotting the overthrow of the government. She'd renounced men and for the past twenty years had been living with another woman. Had Cassie herself switched teams?

"Then I came back and I've been staying out in the Berkshires with Michael, who, by the way you were *horribly* rude to and could have hurt badly."

"That corpse who was just here?"

"He's not a corpse, he's a vegetarian. He takes it very seriously."

Sarnower laughed. "He's a wonderful poster boy for good eating habits. The two of you were fucking in our bed. What was I supposed to do?"

"He's tender and vulnerable, unlike you."

"He's a bony, disgusting sack of shit. Kind of like you."

Cassie was applying lipstick and mascara. With her new, caved-in features and pallid waxy skin, the makeup made her look like a punk rocker.

"When did you start using mascara?" Sarnower asked. She ignored him, throwing cosmetics into her purse. One final check in the mirror.

"I'll be in touch," she said, walking past him into the hall and down the stairs.

Sarnower started after her. He caught up and spun her around.

"Get your hands off me!" she shouted. Her bizarre appearance and the edge of fright in her voice brought up an unexpected wave of pity. He felt his rage drain; at this moment, the mother of his son was in pain.

"Cassie, stop. Please. Think about what you're doing. This is only going to end badly."

She looked at him, silently. The light had gone out of her once blue eyes, which were now pale and dull. Dead stars in a cold, dark universe. God, she's possessed, something's actually gotten hold of her soul. The ancients, the primitive cultures he'd read about were on to something, although he'd never actually seen it. Demonic possession, exorcism, shamans. At this point, she was certainly beyond the reach of any kind of therapy *he* knew about. He was powerless, out of his league.

Cassie banged the front screen door closed and headed for her car. Most of the neighbors, who minutes ago had been treated to the naked Michael show, had gone indoors. Thankfully, no one had called the police. A squad car pulling up in front of the house would be a memorable event and instantly become part of the folklore of the block. It would have a costly impact on his practice. Word would spread fast that the good doctor, an authority on interpersonal relations and emotional stability, had his own house in spectacular disarray. Heal thyself before ye bill unto others.

Now at last, there was quiet. Taking deep breaths, Sarnower struggled to center himself and bring his autonomic functions under control. During the confrontation, the surge of adrenaline and the high decibel screaming, he'd actually felt himself float above the scene observing himself as if he were someone else. He was humming like a high-voltage power wire as he wandered through the house assessing the damage.

On the dresser, he discovered that his gold watch and cuff links were missing. So were an engraved silver money clip, a vintage fountain pen and a pile of loose change. The pen, a sleek black Waterman with a fine gold nib had been a gift from his parents when he'd graduated from college, and although it hadn't worked for years, it still had sentimental value, one of the last things from them that he owned. Cassie, or that monkey she was with had taken them all, probably to sell for some quick cash. She was leaving and taking his past with her.

He stood in the middle of the room, debating whether or not to call the police and file a report. He could press charges, but what would that accomplish? The articles would be gone by the time they found her.

He went through his dresser drawers. Although they'd been rifled, nothing there appeared to be taken.

Outside, a thunderstorm had begun. He opened windows to let the cool sweet air wash through the rooms.

In the kitchen, several bottles of his favorite micro-brewed beer stood empty in the sink. Cassie and her malnourished friend had obviously been hungry as well. The heel of a loaf of French bread sat, lonely in a bed of crumbs. Crumpled sheets of deli wax paper littered the floor and counter. They'd devoured all the packages of cheese and cold cuts he'd been using to prepare snacks and lunches for himself and Mitch. Ham, smoked turkey, salami, sliced port salut, even the disgusting fatty olive loaf he secretly loved. Some vegetarians! This tacky bit of deception made him furious, rekindling the stockpiled anger at Cassie for the months of strange, hostile behavior, her abandonment of Mitch, and their disintegrated marriage. Eat the food. Drink the beer. Fine. But why lie about it?

He opened the refrigerator; its contents did not inspire confidence. While Sarnower could skip meals without noticing these days, Mitch was just at the age when he'd begun to eat voraciously, the fuel burned on growth, sports and all kinds of nervous, twitchy developmental energy. Discovering a new stage of life required fortification and good nutrition. There was a half-full container of juice, condiments in various stages of putrefaction, and a miscellany of take-out food containers. In a decisive sweep, Sarnower threw all the leftovers into the garbage. Out with the old.

The storm was breaking up. It had blown most of the pot smoke out of the house, and Sarnower walked through the rooms closing windows. Good. Action. A plan. Keep moving. A trip to Shop & Save to replenish supplies. In with the new.

The moist new air was thick with the fragrance of flowers, earth and fresh-cut grass. He inhaled deeply as he walked to his car. It was ok. Things were going to work out one way or the other, he could deal with Cassie, even her craziness, whatever direction it was going to take, he was a professional after all. But what about Mitch? He was taking all this hard and doing his best not to show it, but the signs were there. He wasn't bathing often, and left to his own devices, would wear the same clothes day after day. Sarnower was always reminding him to brush his teeth and clean up his room. Formerly an early riser, Mitch had started to sleep in, on weekends getting up in the afternoon, sometimes spending the entire day in his room with the door closed. Sarnower would have to be a more vigilant parent, more open, less critical.

At two-thirty in the afternoon, the Shop & Save was almost empty. He wrestled a stubborn cart free from the long chain in the parking lot. It was still soaked from the downpour and some soggy weekly circulars clung to the bottom of the basket. They disintegrated as he peeled them off and threw them in the trash.

Inside, the market was frigid. The disembodied voice of Karen Carpenter singing *We've Only Just Begun* further numbed the air. How ironic that the poster girl for anorexia should be featured in a supermarket. But he was seeing ironies everywhere. Irony and hypocrisy; it was getting harder to tell the difference.

Meanwhile, the metal shopping cart was channeling the ambient cold into his hands and the air conditioning had started to make him shiver. He'd get just the essentials today—real meat, not cold cuts, fruit and produce; he'd make a big salad. It was time he and Mitch started eating better. They'd cut down on the snacks and grazing. He'd get some chicken and grill it outside with some vegetables. He'd start to wean Mitch off the Ring Dings and on to peaches and nectarines.

There in aisle four was his patient, Liz Dashiell: thirty years old, grossly overweight, extremely intelligent and profoundly depressed. Sarnower had had to hospitalize her on several occasions for suicide attempts and a variety of self-destructive behavior. Seeing her for regular sessions was tricky, he never knew what to expect. Liz could be up or down, or switch back and forth in a matter of minutes. In the 1970s and eighties, when he was in training, she would have been diagnosed as a "borderline" personality disorder: supremely narcissistic, self-destructive, with highly unstable, manipulative relationships. Yet here she was in aisle four, studying the labels of heavy-duty cleaning products. He hoped she wasn't planning to drink any of them.

"Dr. Sarnower," she smiled.

"Hi Liz." He always let his patients make the first opening. Some didn't want to be recognized outside the office, and he himself was often at a loss as to how to respond. Short and sweet was usually the best course. She was putting a couple of quarts of lye-based stain remover in her cart. Reading his mind, she laughed.

"Don't worry, I'm not going to drink them."

"I don't think they'd taste very good." He smiled and moved his cart past hers. This would be just the kind of mind game Liz would play with him. He'd let her ambiguous, provocative reassurance lull him, then in a week there'd be an urgent call from his answering service at three in the morning. E.M.T.s, pink slips, early morning meetings with ward personnel, frequent calls from the attending psychiatrist, a two-week hospitalization where she'd run the staff ragged. Sarnower would have to go and present his own history with her. He knew the drill all too well. The cost to his own state of mind would be steep, especially now, overlaying his already chaotic life with another skim coat of anxiety. He should go back to her cart now, this second, remove the bottles of cleaning fluid and lay down the law in no uncertain terms. No more bullshit, no more games, no more late night calls, no more combing through the endless minutia of her hopelessly screwed up life. *I'm fed up, I've had it. Get a fucking life and leave me alone!* They don't pay me enough for this goddamn work.

He was about to turn into aisle five when he saw Liz still parked in front of the cleaning solutions, holding up yet another bottle and carefully reading the label. Sarnower shook his head. While women her age were at work, lusting after expensive, uncomfortable shoes, a promotion, the perfect man, here was Liz in the middle of the afternoon in a dirty, faded sweatshirt, shorts and sandals, becoming an eager authority on the relative toxicity of various lye compounds.

As an intern, he'd seen a couple of young women like her. One had thrown herself in front of an oncoming D train in New York City. By some miracle, the train did not hit her, but she'd landed on the third rail and had to have a badly burned right arm amputated. Another couldn't stop cutting herself with razor blades, hunting knives, anything shiny or surgically sharp. Later, as a resident still learning his craft, he was startled by the sheer drive these women had, a fascination, preoccupation, obsession, the strength of which was mind-boggling. If they'd been able to turn even a fraction of that focus onto something other than spectacular self-destruction, they could easily have been CEOs, artists, legislators, anything at all.

Of all his patients, they were the most difficult to work with, and he would frequently break down in tears after his sessions. All of them, even Liz Dashiell, had a warm and tender core, which at some point in the treatment would always rise like an air bubble to the surface. You had to put up with treachery, deception, manipulation and boatloads of anger, but if you could stay the course and slog through it all, there in the middle was a beautiful little girl—hopeful, laughing, trusting, dreaming, pristine and unsullied. But in most cases, abusive fathers, "affectionate" groping uncles, callous, idiotic boyfriends and punitive, sadistic parochial school nuns had poisoned the life force and injected lethal doses of hate and shame. They'd coat the precious core in sludge, where it would harden year after year, and become impenetrable.

Salad dressing, marinade sauce, chicken breasts, a crisp baguette, maybe some lime sorbet for dessert. He was ready to check out. Maneuvering the cart into an empty checkout line, he began to unload, two handed, on to the conveyer belt.

"Paper in plastic," he told the bagger, a small, acne-marked high school kid with coke-bottle glasses. The boy's eyes swam uncomprehending on the other side of thick lenses like exotic fish in an aquarium.

"Paper in plastic," he repeated calmly. Hold it together, he told himself.

"Doofus, put the *paper* bag in the *plastic* bag! Dig?" said the cashier turning on the hapless, challenged boy. The groceries were coming through at twice the speed they were being bagged, so Sarnower moved to the end and started helping. On getting a closer look, he saw the boy had Down syndrome and was doing the best he could. Sarnower felt sympathy for him immediately, the abuse the poor guy must get in the course of the day must be unbelievable. Yet here he was, offering no comebacks or wisecracks to his cruel co-worker. Sarnower loaded his bags into the cart. He flared suddenly.

"Hey!"

The cashier, already ringing up the next customer turned, annoyed. "Try to be more civil to your associate here, or I'll talk to your manager," Sarnower said through his teeth. The cashier snorted and returned to his work.

The sky had completely cleared to a soft, deep azure as he loaded the groceries into the trunk. Mitch would be home soon. They'd have a nice quiet evening; after dinner, maybe they'd go to a movie. His son's presence usually had a calming effect on him, sending much of the day's flotsam and jetsam out to sea. Of course the afternoon's developments put an entirely new spin on things. What if anything should he tell Mitch? That he'd seen his mother? That she wasn't coming back (or so she said)? That she looked like the living dead?

He was relieved to see the house was just as he'd left it. Tomorrow, he'd call a locksmith and get the locks changed. Surely today's performance on top of weeks of absence had deprived Cassie of the right to free access. But now it was time for a drink. He unloaded the groceries in the kitchen, poured himself a stiff gin and tonic and took it into the living room. He put a Beethoven string quartet on the CD player and lay down on the couch to let the sweet, plumy music wash over him. Another couple of good pulls from his drink and he was floating, swimming between the churning counterpoint of the master's lines.

Liz's face appeared, smiling. She lifted a large bottle of—what was it?—Coke? paint-thinner? to her mouth and winked at him as she took a long drink. When the bottle came down, the face had become Nina's. Her eyes were closed, her long blonde hair loose around her shoulders, her red lips full and slightly parted. As he moved in to kiss her, the face became Cassie's. She was laying on her side on a blanket in the middle of the quadrangles at the University of Chicago, fresh and young, long strawberry blonde hair, clear ice-blue eyes, giggling as she passed him a bottle of beer. There was sunlight everywhere, it was warm, the campus was deserted, just the two of them. In the distance, he could hear a brass band play, slightly out of tune. It came closer, the bass drum rhythmic and insistent, growing louder and louder.

Sarnower opened his eyes. Someone was knocking forcefully at the front door. What time was it? His watch said five-thirty. Shit! He'd been asleep for almost two hours. He threw himself off the couch and made his way to the door. There were Mitch and Tracey, a poorly disguised exasperation on her face, Mitch beaming, glad to be home.

"I've been knocking for almost five minutes," she said coldly, not knowing how much frustration to show an elder. "I was beginning to think you were out."

"*I* knew you were here Dad!" Mitch said, slamming into his father with a big hug.

Sarnower shook his head, guilty, mildly shamed. "I'm really sorry, I've had a terrible day. I guess I must've fallen asleep. I hope you're not late for anything."

"No, I'm fine," she answered, sunny once again. "Mitch was great. He got a single and made a terrific catch."

A terrific catch? Sarnower was confused. That's right, Tracey had taken him to her softball game after camp. The morning had seemed like a week before. The basic details of the day weren't getting registered. He'd have to start writing things down.

She turned to leave but stopped, sniffing the air, a fleeting, questioning frown on her face trying to place something.

"Bye, Tracey," he called. She nodded without turning. Great, that's all I need. Keep her waiting at the door then smother her in pot fumes.

Mitch, still wired from camp, the game, and a medley of sugar and junk food, stood expectantly waiting for his attention. Sarnower put on a big smile and turned to him.

"Looks like *you* had a great day," he boomed, mussing Mitch's sticky, dusty hair and noticing several colorful new stains on his camp T-shirt.

"It was *awesome!*" he said, rocking on the balls of his feet.

"Cool, dude." Sarnower offered a high-five, eagerly returned. "Say, how 'bout we throw some chicken and veggies on the grill?"

Mitch wrinkled his nose and shook his head. "Naw, I'm not hungry. We had hot dogs and hamburgers..."

"Ice cream and soda too, I bet"

"Yeah, how did you know?"

"Just a lucky guess," he said looking at the boy's shirt.

"Dad?"

"Yeah?"

"Did Mom call today?" His voice had come down an octave. Here was the question that signaled the fun part of the day was over. Mitch had asked it for the past couple of weeks and until today Sarnower could answer truthfully and rapidly. Now he was at a choice point. He thought of Nina; just a few hours ago pressing her body tightly against his. His scalp tingled. That was a moment he hadn't expected or been ready for. He walked to the couch and sat down.

"I saw Mom today, Mitch," he said slowly.

"When is she coming home?"

"I...I don't really know."

"Didn't she tell you?"

"No."

"Why? Didn't you ask her?" Mitch was getting agitated.

"Well, she told me she wasn't sure," Sarnower lied.

"Why wasn't she sure?" he fired back.

"Well..."

"Well what? Didn't you tell her I love her? Didn't you tell her we wanted her to come back?"

"Of course, Mitch. I told her all of that." Sarnower felt his face burn. His nose must be about eight inches long.

Looking down, Mitch stamped his foot on the floor. This was usually a prelude to tears. Sarnower reached out and brought the boy close, smelling the summer-mixture of dust, fading shampoo and soda. Mitch's head was still bent, staring at the floor, hurting too much to take in anything more than the black and white checkerboard pattern of the kitchen floor.

"Mom needs more time," he offered, stroking the boy's back. "Just a little more time." He felt Mitch start to cry, his body shaking rhythmically.

"She doesn't love us," he choked.

"No, no, that's not it at all." Sarnower said as strongly as he could. "Mom loves you very much." Mitch looked up through his tears, pouncing on the omission immediately.

"Doesn't she love you too, Dad?" The idea that Cassie could love one but not the other was incomprehensible.

"Well, I think she does. Remember how we talked about people getting confused sometimes?"

He nodded.

"She's kind of confused about me right now."

"She isn't sure she likes you?"

"Sort of, yeah."

He stopped to follow out the implication. Cautiously:

"Did you hurt her?"

Now *there* was a question. To do it full justice would take a couple of hours, to put it into terms his son would understand was beyond his ability. Did he hurt her? Yes, probably, at different points in different ways. But on balance, his offenses were small and forgivable. In the main, he had offered a good life, a wonderful son and the prospect of a future, with more comfort and enrichment to come, a smooth retirement. Sure he had foibles and peccadilloes, but who didn't? Could he be mean, vindictive, petty and self-centered? Of course, but who didn't have at least some chinks in the armor? Had he struck her, abused her or humiliated her? Emphatically, absolutely not.

"No, honey, I didn't hurt her."

Mitch nodded, satisfied for the moment. How would he understand this? Sarnower himself couldn't even begin to bend his mind around the day's events. At the moment he was at a complete dead end. Her last words to him "I'll be in touch" were all he had to work with. She would re-enter their lives at some point, but how? In person? Through an attorney? As a disembodied spirit?

The phone rang. Sarnower stood absolutely still as if paralyzed by curare, unable to move. Three, four times. "Aren't you going to answer that?" Mitch asked. Sarnower nodded, walking into the hall.

"Hello?"

"She caught the katy and left me a mule to ride," Tug sang on the other end of the line, filling in the rhythm and bass accompaniment to the old Taj Mahal song. A blast from a gentler, saner past.

"Tug," he managed.

"Dude, your symptoms require an emergency house call from Dr. Driscoll, medicine man *extraodinaire.* My acute diagnostic acumen reveals a subcutaneous malaise with chronic pernicious features. The prescription? Inhalations of a most powerful and restorative South American compound with the assist of a rare and exceedingly expensive French bubbly. The whole warranted to restore you to the pinnacle of mental health."

"Jesus, Tug, don't you ever let it go?"

"Lettin' it *go* means it don't *grow*, my man. Didn't they teach you that in medical school?

"You've been listening to too much rap. Try some Mozart or Brahms."

"Dead white males, out to dominate and repress the multicultural aesthetic." And Tug was off into another scat.

"Tug? Tug!" He stopped.

"Yo, daddy, I'm right outside your door." Sure enough, there was the shiny new black Beemer and Tug already on his way up the front walk, his bespoke English peach silk shirt untucked and flapping in the mild breeze. He'd already extracted his engraved gold cigarette case, a gift from some German industrialist whose company he'd saved, and was skillfully liberating a perfectly rolled joint with one hand. The other hand held a magnum of champagne.

"Mitch is here," Sarnower told him at the front door. He was still addled from last night's debauchery, the strain of an unreal afternoon, and now at the limit of his ability to function as a parent, he found himself not caring whether or not Mitch saw Tug light up. But no, some shred of coherence and order had to prevail; the boy needed stability now more than ever with Cassie off her rocker. Tug's freewheeling approach to fun could be more than enough to tip the boat.

"Hey, how's it hanging?" he called out past Sarnower.

"Low and mean," Mitch growled in his 1930s Mississippi delta bluesman voice, another acquisition from Tug. They banged fists in a bit of manual choreography that Sarnower had never seen before. He was glad his son could snap back so quickly and was also relieved to see Tug's joint and cigarette case were nowhere in sight. When had they disappeared? He'd been watching his friend the whole time. Sarnower rubbed his eyes. He was starting to miss everything.

"Champagne flutes all around," Tug commanded, displaying the bottle like a sommelier for Sarnower's inspection. A faded Dom Perignon label stared back at him. The year 1961 was barely visible in rubbed red numerals.

"Can I have some? Just a taste?" Mitch asked, now fully under Tug's sway.

"Whaddah ya say, pops?" Tug asked. "You know, in Europe, they start the young'uns on wine real early."

"Well, this isn't Europe." Tug didn't know of the curse that ran through Cassie's family, her constant self-medication and the possible genetic link passed on to Mitch. Today, you couldn't be too careful. In his own practice, he saw teens barely older than his son who'd already been snared into a permanent alcoholic fog. Booze more so than pot or cocaine, was now the drug of choice.

"You are such an *old fart!*" Tug bellowed. Turning to Mitch: "Isn't your Dad the oldest fart going?"

"Eeeeewwww," screamed Mitch, holding his nose.

"Eeeeewwww," screamed Tug, holding his nose.

He was outnumbered. All right. "Just a taste." Mitch lit up. He and Tug gave each other high-fives.

Tug popped the cork and poured flawlessly, turning the bottle to catch the last drop. Mitch got a full glass.

"L'chiem," he said in his Protestant Mid-Western twang. Sarnower smiled at his gawky attempt at Hebrew; Tug's only exposure had been at weddings and bar mitzvahs.

"To life," Mitch and Sarnower choroused. The three of them downed the glass in one swallow. Where had Mitch learned to drink like that? With a sudden chill, Sarnower realized he'd done this before, probably many times. Which of his friends had been stealing into their parents' liquor cabinet? He made a mental note to talk to Mitch later. He'd have to start paying closer attention.

But the champagne was incredible, smooth and dry with a delicious light fruit bouquet at the end that lingered when the gasses were inhaled. Sarnower closed his eyes, leaving everything behind, hugging the moment. It was like Nina, pressed into his arms earlier in the day. The rising vapors, floating, intoxicating and distilling all into pure sensation. By the time he opened his eyes, Tug had poured another round for all three of them. Sarnower was incapable of any protest.

The second glass went down even smoother than the first. He felt the wine invade his tissues, graceful and subtle, it began to loosen and untie his body. His breathing slowed, his pulse slackened.

Tug and Mitch were staring at him when he opened his eyes.

"I guess he likes it," Mitch said, grinning at Tug. Tug nodded and mussed the boy's hair. "You better believe it Kemosabe."

"Tug, you're going to turn him into an alcoholic," Sarnower said, suddenly annoyed. "Mitch, don't you have a room to clean up?" He wrinkled his nose. "A bath wouldn't kill you either."

"Better listen to Dad," Tug said, now serious himself, taking the boy's glass. "He and I have some man-to-man things to talk about." Mitch, puzzled and deflated by Tug's change of side, recouped.

"You guys are boring. I'm going to watch TV." He turned on his heels and pounded up the stairs.

"No need to be so quiet," Sarnower called after him. In a moment, the Sox-Toronto game was blaring.

"Order restored," Sarnower said, taking the glasses to the kitchen sink. Tug followed him, fingering the joint that had vanished in Mitch's presence. He patted down his pants for a lighter.

The cool water was soothing to his hands as he washed the rose crystal flutes, a wedding gift from Cassie's older brother. The antique set had consisted originally of four ornate glasses and a tall, graceful decanter. A couple of years before, after an angry phone call from her brother, she'd hurled the decanter against the wall, shattering it into a thousand pieces. Crystal breaks differently than glass, Sarnower discovered, the pieces were smaller, finer, in some cases almost returning to something resembling sand. To this day he was still finding tiny, glistening pink shards embedded between floorboards and under molding.

Adding dish liquid made the water comforting and velvety. Through his hypnotic, mechanical motions, the glasses became squeaky clean. I could do this forever, he thought, never look at another person, never speak another word, wash and wash until white puckered skin falls off my fingers.

"She was here today," he said, not turning from the sink. He'd decided not to go into details about their encounter.

"No shit," Tug said, perking up and lighting the joint. "Back on the cough medicine, is she?"

"No. She's off all meds now."

"And showing every inch of raw, frazzled psyche, no doubt."

Sarnower turned to see Tug take an enormous, practiced toke.

"She's not coming back."

Tug stood perfectly still, lungs and mouth ballooning with smoke. He looked like Dizzy Gillespie in the middle of a red-hot riff. Exhaling slowly, he brought the joint up to inspect its glowing tip.

"Well...maybe that's good. Maybe she needs to fly solo, be on her own."

"She's got a son here, someone still counting on her. It's not just about Cassie."

Tug looked at him, saying nothing. Family, marriage and children—he was out of his league and he knew it. Slowly he handed the joint to Sarnower who dried his hands and took the offering, something he vowed earlier he wasn't going to do. This marked the official end of the rational day. From here on out...he drew in the thick potent smoke. The two glasses of champagne and the gin and tonic before that had laid down a nice buzz, and the smoke...well...

"I think she's doing the right thing," Tug said in the authoritative voice Sarnower had heard him use with clients. "Lord knows she hasn't been much of a wife lately and she's messing with Mitch big time." All true. But kids and their mothers...the scientific literature showed that no matter how inadequate or derelict the mother, the attachment was real and strong. That horrifying classic study everyone read in Psych 101: infant monkeys would forgo nutritious food in order to hug a wire and terry-cloth stick figure, a third rate stand-in for Mom. What was all this going to do to Mitch? Cassie's threat to take him later when she was "settled" (whatever that meant) was laughable. But what if she got some goon to grab him up? Sarnower had no idea who she was hanging out with now, but judging by the character she dragged into their bed this afternoon, he wasn't encouraged. That kind of stuff happened all the time, parents kidnapping their own kids, turning up in the Middle East or deep in Central Europe.

He shook his head while struggling to think clearly. This was a classic paranoid pot fantasy wasn't it? Or was Cassie organized enough to think it through and do it? Suddenly he was scared. He couldn't figure it out.

"What's the matter?" Tug asked. The fear must have played out on his face.

"Tug, I think I need help."

"Hey, tell me something I *don't* know," he laughed, taking the joint. He thought for a moment and looked Sarnower in the eye. "Look, why don't you just have her whacked? Get the whole thing over and done with once and for all. A nice, clean break."

"Whacked? As in killed?"

"Yeah. Wasted. Blown away. Rubbed out. Dispatched. Eliminated. You know, as my old grampy back in Iowa used to say, 'some folks just need killin'.'"

Sarnower laughed. "That would solve some problems. Last I heard though, it was still illegal."

Tug shrugged. "Just a suggestion."

"No, really, I mean it. Legal help. A lawyer."

Tug looked at him, reevaluating, squinting through the smoke. He took out his cell phone and got the directory. Sarnower pushed a pad and pencil toward him.

"Nick Ballestracci," he said, writing. "Tell him I told you to call. He takes care of everything, cleans up all the mess, gotten me out of many a jam. I've got him on speed dial." He tore off the page and stuffed it in Sarnower's shirt pocket. Tug looked him in the eyes. "It's all going to work out Alan." Tug hadn't called him Alan in years; this only made him more anxious. "Call Nick. He'll make sure none of this gets out of hand."

Now that Mitch was upstairs watching the Red Sox and Sarnower had turned serious, Tug figured it was time to fold his tent and leave.

"Sorry I'm not in a more jovial frame of mind."

"Yeah, well." Tug seemed at an uncharacteristic loss. Maybe he was finally grasping the dimensions of the situation. He tucked in his shirt and headed for the front door.

"You going to be ok?"

Sarnower nodded.

"Let me know how it goes with Nick," Tug called, already out the door. "Although personally I'd opt for the first alternative."

Unlike Sarnower, he lost no sleep over problems—his or anyone else's. He offered the best fix he could and was gone, figuring that explanation, dwelling, blaming, the whole bag of confessional apparatus was a huge waste of time. Years ago, when his parents were suddenly killed together in a car accident while trying to outrun a huge tornado near their home, Sarnower was stunned to discover Tug's complete lack of any emotion. He'd handled their deaths like an annoying hitch in a business deal. He and his lawyer (likely the same Ballestracci he was supposed to contact) had flown to Iowa, all relevant papers in hand, and had wrapped up his parent's affairs and joint burial in practically no time at all. Final bills were paid, the house where he had grown up put on the market, the farming equipment auctioned, the estate such as it was, settled. End of story. Unfinished business with mother? Not a chance. Last poignant words passed from father to son? You've got to be kidding.

Years later, Sarnower had asked him if he ever regretted not being able to have any kind of closure on the relationships. "*Closure?*" he'd asked, not quite believing his ears. "You've been watching too much Oprah, man. *Everybody's* got to have closure. It's right up there with money, sex and easy credit. Fucking closure. You know when you've got closure? When they bring the lid down on your goddamn coffin, man, then you have closure."

But the vehemence with which Tug spat this out gave him away, and showed Sarnower there was a lot going on beneath the surface. But neither he, nor anyone else for that matter, was going to be privy to it. Tug's relentless serial relationships with women usually gave out at the point at which they'd begun to glimpse his private internal whirlpools and wanted to stick their toes in. He was always wary of other people's trespassing into the off-limit areas of his life. Tug would back off and be on to the next conquest. But who was to say at forty-five that the man was not entitled to live life the way he wanted?

Lately Sarnower himself had begun to think all this talking, interpreting, combing through and navel gazing might turn out to be a gigantic waste. Take the right pill, make sure the side effects weren't too intrusive and be on your way. What could be more twenty-first century? On balance, Tug was a pretty happy guy. So what if he had better things to do with his time than sit around and wring his hands? He might be one of those for whom the unexamined life was indeed worth living.

It was now eleven-thirty. Mitch had turned off the TV upstairs and had gone to sleep. At least tomorrow was Friday. A couple of patients in the morning, errands, shopping, then the weekend.

Maybe he could catch a break. He'd remember to call Ballestracci first thing in the morning and pulled out the piece of paper that Tug had jammed into his pocket. Out fell a fresh joint, and below the lawyer's number was written "happy trails to you." The guy was incorrigible.

Sarnower made a final round of the downstairs, turning off lights, straightening up. Cassie dead. He smiled at Tug's outrageous suggestion. The thought was too absurd and extravagant to contemplate, yet after today's events it had an undeniable seduction. These things did happen after all. But not to him.

Upstairs in the bedroom, he stripped the linens that Cassie and her emaciated paramour had fouled. They would go out to the garbage in the morning, and in a minute he would get a clean set from the linen closet in the hall and make up the bed. But first, just for a second, he would lie down and rest his eyes. Sleep pulled him immediately into its dark infinite pillow.

Chapter **3**

LIGHT POURED THROUGH the window as Sarnower, still fully clothed, opened his eyes. The mattress stuck to his face with sweat and early morning humidity. Sheets. He'd passed out before he could put them on. Nor had he been able to get undressed, and his stale damp clothes had soured like old milk. A muffled, repetitive thud at the back of his head tallied his tab for the previous night. It was now *two* nights he'd gone to bed wasted, and the punishment would be cumulative. He rubbed his eyes at the sting of sunlight and sat up. Stumbling into the bathroom he began removing his clothes. As he pulled the polo shirt over his head, he remembered Nina's tears, embedded in the fabric and now mixed with his own sweat. The thought was arousing.

He studied himself in the full-length bathroom mirror. Not too bad for mid-forties. There was much worse running around out there, and particularly since his dramatic and unintended weight loss, muscle and skeletal definition had returned under the thinning covering of fat. Jogging and some light weight training would detail his body like a sports car. He'd take Cassie at her word; she wasn't coming back.

In the shower, he picked up his set of fantasies of life without her. He'd definitely be dating again, probably sooner than later, as much to get on with things and quash the growing sense of loneliness as to get back at Cassie. He'd clean up his life, get disciplined, work out regularly and keep a closer eye on Mitch, who'd startled him last night by the gusto with which he drank those two glasses of champagne. Living well was the best revenge, wasn't it?

Mitch was already awake and in the kitchen. Sarnower shaved quickly, threw on some clean clothes and went downstairs. It was late and Mitch was already emptying his cereal bowl in the sink. Excellent! He'd begun to take some responsibility without being goaded. Perhaps seeing his father struggling to keep the balls in the air and the plates spinning on the sticks had started to motivate him. He should be complimented on his initiative.

Entering the kitchen, buttoning his shirt, he saw Tracey seated at the breakfast table, talking with Mitch.

"Hi, I didn't hear you come in. Care for some breakfast?" he offered. Good behavior to make up for his dereliction yesterday.

Tracey looked up at him, her eyes darting. "Uh, no thanks Dr. Sarnower." Something was up. In his twenty-plus years of practice, he had learned how to read people in fractions of a second. Here it comes.

"Dr. Sarnower...uh...I have to tell you...after today I won't be able to pick up Mitch anymore."

"Oh? Why is that?"

She looked at Mitch, the ceiling and the floor. "Well, one of your neighbors, Mrs. Gould told my Mom about some strange things going on here yesterday, and, well...I guess my folks don't think it's a good idea for me to be over here now. Also...when I dropped Mitch off yesterday...well, I thought I smelled pot." She took a deep breath.

Mitch was perturbed. "What happened, Dad?" Sarnower's heart was pounding. He knew yesterday's circus would filter through the grapevine; he had no idea it would happen this quickly. Well, gossip was information of a sort, and information now traveled at the speed of light. He should have known. He sat down to meet Mitch at eye level.

"Mitch, we had a little problem here, that's all."

"What kind of problem?" The boy would not be easily put off, he was losing Tracey—good friend and big sister. Sarnower would have to account for this in some way, but right now, he drew a complete blank. How much did Tracey know? He didn't want to become a liar as well as a total misfit, he'd just have to stall for time.

"Mitch we'll talk about it tonight, ok? I promise."

Tracey had finished organizing Mitch's backpack, and was looking to make a fast get-away. Now he'd have to find someone else.

Mitch strapped the backpack on and went out to the front hall.

"Tracey, what did your mother tell you?" he whispered.

"Enough," was her icy cut-off, looking Sarnower right in the eyes. Her new, secure moral footing had given her an added confidence boost. "I'm sorry. Mitch is such a great kid," she added sadly. He felt as if he were at a parent-teacher conference being excoriated for not motivating his son to do better in school.

"Yes, yes he is," Sarnower said quietly. "Well, thank you for all your help." He waved to Mitch who was now in her car, sitting shotgun, looking straight ahead. In days past, Tracey would climb into the driver's seat and they both would give Sarnower one last caricatured, dramatic wave. If she were feeling particularly peppy, she'd let Mitch reach over and give a couple of blasts on the horn. Today they drove off silently.

Shit, shit, goddamn fucking shit! Sarnower slammed the front door and sat down hard on the hall stairs. Now everyone knew. It wouldn't be long now before the word started spreading out from the block in ripples. If his patients started to hear, it could infect his entire practice. I have to live here. What I do for a living is based on trust, integrity, dignity and propriety. It was fragile as morning fog and could vanish just as fast.

He remembered the phone number Tug had given him. That's it. Go to the office, call this guy, get some legal muscle to staunch the bleeding. A restraining order to keep her from causing any more damage. He'd talk to the neighbors, one on one, offer an apology and be contrite. Maybe he'd have a block party, a barbecue, invite everyone over for burgers, dogs and beer. Things would be restored and back on track. Even the dour stick-in-the-mud Mrs. Gould could be brought around. He was feeling better already.

Anxious, intractable Mrs. Jessup was already deeply entrapped in his leather couch when he entered the office.

"Good morning," he offered with as much good nature as he could summon. "I'll be right with you."

Nina, already into the day's work smiled like a sphinx as she handed him his charts.

"You look like your face is going to break," she said softly.

"It is."

She was composed, in control again, without a hint of the touching insecurity and vulnerability she'd showed yesterday. Would she say anything, or go on as if nothing had happened? A new chapter in their relationship or a pit stop to change a flat tire? He'd been too far gone with Tug last night and too flustered with Tracey's mutiny this morning to give the matter any thought, and now was not the time to dwell on it. He was already seven minutes late for his appointment with phobic, compulsive Mrs. Jessup.

"Come in, please," he said and the stout, heavily made up, bejeweled woman walked slowly into his consulting room.

"How did it go on the elevators this week?" he asked.

"I didn't do it," she replied in a low monotone. "I got to the hotel lobby and just froze in fear. I had to call my husband to come and get me." Mr. Jessup, small, meek and bald, had made sea-changes in his job as an insurance adjuster to accommodate her rich assortment of fears. Sarnower had seen them as a couple several times. He'd interpreted the dynamics of the relationship, the network of control, the latent hostility, the secondary gain, the co-dependency, the factors that bound them together in chains of pathology. Things would change for a week, two at most, but as soon as the couple had tasted life without symptoms, they'd be back to square one. Sarnower had constantly to guard against powerful impulses to throttle her.

"You like it when he does that."

"Does what doctor?" Playing dumb again.

"Disrupts his entire day to help you out of a difficult situation."

"How can you say that?"

"Mrs. Jessup, we've been around this block about seven hundred times." Keep it cool and soothing. "The way you get reassurance that Bob loves you is to make him uproot himself constantly, to sacrifice his work. That shows you're the most important thing in his life."

She looked at Sarnower, mute and blank with the bovine expression he found so irritating.

"Do you remember our talking about any of this?"

She shrugged her shoulders.

"You do, don't you?"

"I guess." The submissive little girl caught in the act.

"But somehow, it's hard to remember all this when you're actually in one of those situations, like trying to get on the elevator. Isn't that right?"

She shrugged her shoulders again.

They sat in silence for a minute.

"You know, all this makes me wonder how useful I can be to you, Mrs. Jessup."

She came alive. "You're kicking me out now? You are, aren't you? You were already seven minutes late for our session." She tapped her watch crystal with a long, bright red fingernail. "So you're going to be fifteen minutes late for the next one?" She was on a roll now. "You're gas lighting me aren't you Dr. Sarnower, just like they did in that old Bette Davis movie where she keeps turning the lights down on her husband. You really want to get rid of me, don't you?"

Well, we can now add paranoia to the symptom list.

"Not at all. I was held up this morning by unexpected circumstances. I'll be happy to add the time on at the other end."

She glared at him. Some sleeping current of buried anger he'd never seen before had been aroused. Where there was anxiety, rage was never far behind.

"I think you're tired of me. I think my problems are *really* boring you."

Sometimes even the most obtuse of his patients had an uncanny knack of shooting a bull's eye. All things considered, Sarnower thought he was doing a passable job of looking interested this morning, but obviously his self-monitoring skills were deserting him along with everything else.

"Therapy is work Mrs. Jessup. Your responsibility doesn't end when you leave the office. We call this process 'working through.' You take home what we do here. You think about it, turn it over in your mind and find ways to apply it in different situations. At first, it's hard and requires a lot of effort. It can be very frustrating. After a while, things get easier; you find the new behaviors and ways of thinking are becoming more of a pattern, more automatic."

His pre-emptive bit of psychobabble had the desired effect of calming her down.

"There's no gas lighting going on here, Mrs. Jessup. No one's giving up, unless it's you."

"I don't want to do that. Bob would hate me."

"Don't do it for Bob...."

"I know, I should do it for myself."

"That's right. Lets see if you can get into that Hyatt elevator alone, ride to the top and down again. That's the goal this week. And no calling Bob away from work either."

"I'll try again," she sighed like a resigned schoolgirl asked to rewrite a paper.

The buzzer on Sarnower's phone rang. Nina was on the intercom.

"Someone here to see you."

"I'll be right out." He put down the phone. "We have to stop now Mrs. Jessup. I would really encourage you to think about what we do here during the week. If you don't fight the fear, the fear will fight you and it will win." A handy pocket-sized bromide to carry home.

Sarnower followed her out into the waiting room. A short fat woman dressed entirely in khaki, wearing men's shoes was standing there. She stood straight, at military-style attention.

"Dr. Alan Sarnower?" she asked in a cigarette-whiskey growl.

"Yes?"

She handed him a folded set of papers in a thick blue cover. "Consider yourself served."

Sarnower, numb, looked blankly at the papers. "What is this?"

"Don't read 'em, just serve 'em," she said, turning to leave.

His heart started pounding as he tried to read the document. As the page blurred and swam, he managed only to catch isolated words: Cassandra Kelly, Plaintiff, Alan Sarnower, Defendant. And there it was: Divorce—her petition for divorce. She'd actually gone and done it. In her crazy, disorganized state, somehow she was able to pull it together enough to file. He stood in the middle of the waiting room, blank, leafing through the pages, none of it making any sense. Breathe, he reminded himself. Deep. In and out. He couldn't feel his body. Was he standing upright or was he just a gigantic head resting on the floor? The next thing he knew, he was sitting on the couch.

"Alan? Alan?" Nina was standing over him frowning, concerned. He looked up helplessly. "Alan, are you all right? You're white as a sheet. What is it?"

It was all he could do to hand her the papers. She took the packet and started skimming. When she'd finished, she folded the document slowly. "Wow, that's awful." Sarnower's mouth had gone dry. He couldn't speak.

"She wants full legal and physical custody of Mitch. She wants you out of the house, she's asking for immediate spousal and child support." She handed the papers back. "There's some kind of hearing on this next Tuesday at the Middlesex Probate Court. Maybe it's time you got a lawyer. Do you want me to make some calls?"

"Huh?" He looked up at her.

"A lawyer," she repeated. "Would you like me to help you find one?"

Ballestracci. It was time to call.

"Thanks," he got out. "I have a referral."

"Would you like me to call and set up an appointment?"

"I think that's something I'd better do myself," he said. Sucker-punched again.

"Frazier, Abbott and Connors." The voice was frosty, robotic and female.

"Nick Ballestracci, please."

"May I tell him whose calling?"

"Sarnower. Dr. Alan Sarnower."

"Does he know what this is in reference to?"

Why does everyone have to know what everything is in reference to? The professional world does not like surprises, those unexpected calls for improvisation.

"I don't think so. I was referred by one of his clients, Donald Driscoll."

"Just a minute please."

Muzak. Once again, *We've Only Just Begun*, this time without the disembodied Karen Carpenter, now in an oily arrangement for string orchestra. Sarnower felt bile rising in his throat.

"Please hold for Mr. Ballestracci." Then:

"Hello? Dr. Sarnoff?" Gruff, hurried, bored.

"Uh, that's Sar-*nower*. I was referred to you by Mr. Driscoll.

"What can I do for you?"

"Well, I just found out I'm being sued for divorce."

"That's too bad. I'm sorry to hear that. You should get a lawyer."

Was this guy a comedian or an idiot? "Yeah, that's kind of why I'm calling. I was served with papers. There's going to be some kind of hearing next Tuesday."

"Uh, Mr. Sarnoff, I have to tell you, my calendar is booked solid. I'll be happy to set you up with one of our associates..." Great. Some pipsqueak with gelled, spiky hair and a bow tie.

"Tug, er, Donald told me..."

"Oh yeah, Tug. You know Tug?"

"Yes, he referred..."

"Sorry, I didn't make the connection." There were papers rustling, a brief muffled conversation with someone else in the room. A laugh.

"You say the hearing's Tuesday?"

"Yes."

"Ok. Be in my office on Monday morning, ten o'clock. Bring your petition, copies of your tax records for the last five years and a list of assets. Fifty State Street, thirty-fourth floor."

Click. The phone was dead.

Sarnower looked at the receiver. Didn't anybody say "bye" anymore? But at least it was done; he wasn't alone in this. Ballestracci and he would roll in Tuesday and squash Cassie like a ripe melon. She was nuts, clearly unfit, completely unstable, hospitalization might be necessary. How could she possibly take care of Mitch and run the house? It was out of the question, there was no way it was going to happen. The judge would take a look at her, have Ballestracci present the story, they'd be out in time for lunch. Hand this damn mess over to someone who knew what to do with it. They could wrap it up in a couple of weeks.

Sarnower slumped in his chair, eyes closed, thoroughly drenched, despite the cold of the air conditioner. His brow was gently being wiped. He opened his eyes quickly. There was Nina, kneeling in front of him, her face a few inches from his, her warm, sweet breath cutting through the cold air.

"Better?" she asked softly.

Sarnower nodded. "I have an appointment on Monday."

"This is awful. I can't help thinking about Mitch."

"I know. But he's resilient. Look, we'll all just have to hunker down and get through it."

Nina had closed her eyes and parted her lips. She moved in toward him, engaging his mouth. God, here it is, she's really doing it. He closed his eyes and tasted her mouth; it was sweet and slightly earthy. Their tongues met and chased each other, into her mouth then into his. He drew her tongue in and sucked, she moved in closer, exploring the roof of his mouth, his teeth. The hot soft breath from her nose warmed his cheek. Pulling her in closer, he was now off the chair, both of them kneeling on the floor, their kiss unbroken.

After a minute, how long was it? Five, maybe even fifteen, Sarnower broke away, opening his eyes. Nina's face was flushed, glistening. Her eyes were half closed, several strands of long blonde hair were in her face, her lips were engorged and full. This is how she must look waking up in the morning, swollen with dreams and endorphins.

"Mmmmm," she purred. "That was nice."

"Should we be doing this?" he whispered, barely able to get the words out.

"Why not?"

"Well for starters, you work for me."

"Does that bother you?"

"I...I don't know. Should it?"

She shrugged her shoulders, now covered with cascading blonde hair. Her smile was angelic, untouched by the world, by craziness, by lawyers.

"I'm technically still married."

"I'm not convinced. Anyway you're separated and," she nodded to the blue-covered papers on the floor "you're getting divorced."

It was true, but hearing it out loud, the words had an unexpected force. Until this moment, it had been a concept, a possibility, something he'd never thought of as a thing that was going to happen. *You're getting divorced* reverberated against the walls of his skull, words not yet ready to be digested and carried into the cells of his body. He thought of the hokey metaphor his humanistic colleagues used: one door opens and another closes.

They got up off the floor. Nina smoothed her dress and pulled back her hair. Sarnower brushed himself off, tucked in his shirt.

"I want to see you tonight," she said. "I don't think you should be alone."

"I'll be fine, really, I..." She put an index finger softly over his lips to silence him.

"Shhhhh. I'll bring over some dinner."

"You don't have to do this."

"I don't have to do anything," she smiled.

"Well, ok then." He was weakened, out of resistance.

"About seven?"

"About seven."

"What would Mitch like?"

"Jeeze, he'll eat anything. By the way, shouldn't Mr. Martin be out in the waiting room?"

"Oh, I forgot. He cancelled. He wanted to beat the traffic to the Cape. He'll see you next week."

"Be sure to bill him for the missed session."

"I'm all over it."

The Effect of Propinquity on Employer-Employee Relationships During Hot and Difficult Times. In seconds his life had been altered. But now to tax returns and lists of assets. Right there was an entire weekend's worth of work. Never one for orderly preservation of records, Sarnower had stashed important papers in several places, locked file cabinets in the basement, various desk drawers, cardboard boxes that might or might not be out in the garage.

Putting things in order had been a goal for years, but he'd always managed to push it to the bottom of the list.

At home, he cracked a beer and sat in the kitchen. Screw the paperwork; it could wait. Nina. What was all this about? Now *that* required some immediate attention. She'd always been attracted to desperados of one stripe or another, guys in a bind or on the fringe. She enjoyed the challenge, the rescue operations involved, giving them some kind of stability, a hot meal, a warm bed, yet sharing with them the edgy, risky side of things. Had he suddenly fallen into that camp? Did he need rescuing? Was he now officially a charity case? Where was Nina before all this shit came down? Sure, she'd sought him out as a friend, and confidant. She looked to him for the sane, analytical perspective he brought to things, a taste of the rationality that touched down only fleetingly in her other relationships.

What could she want with him, or from him? The security of someone fifteen years older? The tired father/lover cliché? Although it was possible the divorce could be wrapped up quickly, particularly when all involved saw Cassie in the midst of her meltdown, there was still the chance that it could go on for a long time. He'd treated patients for whom divorce was interminable, lasting through presidencies, stock market cycles and technological revolutions. He might be tied up, unable to commit for years. And how much did he really know about Nina? She was bright, fast, funny, with an undeniable allure. Did he want to get involved with her? Could she go the distance? How would she get along with Mitch? Would she want children of her own? Would she soon be on the prowl for another man/boy with long dark hair and exceptional lingual skills?

He looked at the clock. Two hours had passed and four empty beer bottles sat on the table. These trances, mini-fugue states were taking on a life of their own, a fog rolling in on his consciousness putting him at a sizable remove from his surroundings. The lust-moments had begun under his control, often featuring Nina herself, but recently had grown to include others; pretty women on the street, former girlfriends, models on the cover of women's magazines. They'd also branched out on their own as non-erotic daydreams to include his past, his future, even his patient's lives outside the office. He could contemplate a corn flake left on the breakfast table, or see the world in a peanut shell. This is what Zen must be about.

Sometimes his dead father would appear to him. They'd be strolling on the boardwalk at Coney Island, hand in hand, he'd be maybe five years old, entranced by the skeet-ball parlors, the steeplechase, the fascinating, grotesque carved and painted figures that adorned various rides, the gentle salty breeze coming in off the water. On the way back to the car to drive home, they'd stop at Nathan's for a hot dog and fries. If he really focused, he could conjure up the scene in startling detail: the dog, long and greasy in a soft bun, often with a bit of string still tied at the end, with a tight skin that snapped when you bit into it, the fries thick and crinkly, crunchy on the outside with a cloud-soft inside—best when dipped into a small paper cup of spicy brown mustard.

And his mother, his late mother, picking him up from kindergarten, they'd stop at a soda fountain (long since gone) for a hot chocolate in the winter or a thick malted or egg-cream in warmer weather. He could hear the hum of those old green Hamilton blenders, the tall metal cups the soda jerk would use to pour the thick malt into curvaceous glasses, then leave the cups for a refill. If his mother wasn't in one of her frequent gloomy moods, she'd offer him a Chiclet or Life Saver from a supply that never seemed to run out. Soda jerk: a term no longer in use. Mitch wouldn't even know what one was.

Ghosts were knocking around, and old pop songs, cooking smells from his grandmother's apartment on the Grand Concourse in the Bronx, fresh paint on the wall of his elementary school as the year began in September, those early television shows, Playhouse 90, Pinky Lee, Omnibus.

He got up and collected the empties. A car door slammed outside on the street. Mitch was back. Deep in his woolgathering, he'd forgotten to write a check for Tracey, who got paid at the end of each week. He dashed to the study. The small leather-covered book, usually in one of the cubbyholes in his roll-top desk, was missing. Had Cassie taken it? Not that it would have done her any good, he'd opened an account in his own name soon after her departure. In fairness to her though, the surface of his desk had become a deep, littered repository of unpaid bills, notes and receipts. Finding anything under there was going to be a long hunting expedition.

The screen door in front banged shut.

"Mitch?" he called.

"Hi, Dad."

"Is Tracey there with you?"

"I think she took off," he called from the kitchen.

Sure enough, from his study window, Sarnower saw and heard her burn rubber out of his driveway. He wondered how Tracey's mother drove when she was angry with her father.

"She said you should mail the check to her house."

Well, that was a relief, he couldn't have written a check if he wanted to. Now he'd have to find someone else for Mitch. That was going to take thought and planning. Monday would soon be here and his meeting with Ballestracci would need at least a day's worth of research and preparation. He'd worry about all that later.

Mitch opened the fridge and started to forage for a late afternoon snack.

"How's it going?" Sarnower asked.

"Good," he grunted. Mitch was sullen. Lately everyone but Sarnower had the power to cheer him up.

"Why isn't Tracey taking me to camp anymore?" he pounced. "You promised to tell me." He did. It was time to tell all, to lay the whole messy thing out. One fell swoop, let it rip like a Band-Aid.

"Mitch, why don't you get a Coke or something and let's sit out on the porch."

"I don't want a Coke."

"Then don't have one."

Mitch stamped his foot. "I'm tired of this. I want Mom to come home. I want to see her today. I want *her* to take me to camp. Why don't you let her come back with us?"

"I'm not keeping Mom away, Mitch. Mom wants a divorce." There, it was out. "Do you know what a divorce is?" Mitch nodded slowly. "She doesn't want to be married to me anymore. She still loves you, loves you a lot, and it means she's still going to be your Mom. Forever."

Sarnower was sliding into the rote talk he would give to separated parents on what to tell their own children. He was in danger of sounding glib, and his son, now hyper-vigilant to anything relating to his mother, would take it as a lack of care. He was already starting to see his father as a buffoon and royal fuck-up.

"Where is she going to live?" he pressed on like a district attorney.

"We don't know yet."

"Am I going to live with her?"

"Here, Mitch. You're going to live here. This is your house."

"But when will I see her?"

"Well, I'm not sure. We have to work out a lot of things. I'm going to see a man on Monday to help me."

"You mean a lawyer?"

"That's right. How did you know about lawyers?"

"Caleb in my class? His parents got divorced and his Mom and Dad got lawyers, only he lives with his Mom. His Dad moved to California." His voice got shaky. "Dad, you're not going to move away are you?"

Sarnower pulled him into his arms. "No. Of course not. I'm staying right here."

Mitch's lean, pre-teen body shook slightly. He's going to need time and patience, Sarnower reminded himself, and an extra-light touch.

"Why can't I live with Mom too?"

Sarnower held his shoulders and looked at his teary eyes. "Mom's having a very hard time just taking care of herself right now. She's not able to take care of you too. Besides, don't you like it living here with me, just us guys?"

A fleeting tremor in his lips gave away the full spectrum of his ambivalence, his divided loyalties. And why not, who could blame him? He loves her just as much as he did a year ago, just as much as I did. Over time, we move like points in a lopsided geometric figure, the perimeter, the internal area always moving just enough to put someone out of synch with someone else.

"Yeah, I like it ok," he said finally.

"You don't sound too sure."

Don't push it, he almost said to himself out loud. He *isn't* sure. He isn't sure about anything right now. Let him be.

"What about her clothes?" he asked.

"Her clothes?"

"Yeah, her clothes and stuff. Is she going to take them? Is she coming back for them?"

"I guess at the right time she'll figure out what to do with them."

Sarnower felt a sudden unexpected lump in his throat. Mitch was worried about her clothes. After his own father's death, his mother had lain awake at night, tormented over his father's clothes. Some boxed up their departed spouse's clothes immediately after the funeral and called Goodwill to have them removed. Others kept them indefinitely in closets, like a mausoleum, convinced in some private way that the departed would be back to wear them again. The dead remain in the fabric, their hairs, sloughed off skin cells, their oil and sweat.

"I have to be honest with you, buddy, it's going to be tough on both of us for a while. But we're going to get through it."

"When can I see Mom?" he asked again.

"We're going to have to wait." He was beginning to lose patience. "I don't know where she is Mitch."

Cassie's wake had left a gaping black hole, sucking everything in.

"I don't know what more to tell you," he said, though he knew they'd have to keep talking, like those special negotiators brought in to defuse high-wire hostage situations. Keep the floodgates open. He couldn't let his boy retreat any longer. Get angry, cry, throw things; just don't take it lying down.

"Tell me where she is. You know!"

Sarnower sat down and tried to pull Mitch toward him again, but he stood rigid and still, not moving. "Honestly, I don't. I would tell you if I knew, but I don't," he said on the fulcrum of patience between angry fatigue and unlimited father-love. "We're just going to have to wait and see. I know how hard this is."

"No, you don't!"

Going on would be futile. Mitch was spoiling for a fight and Sarnower wasn't going to grab the bait. Change the subject.

"Mitch, Nina's coming over to have dinner with us tonight."

"I'm not hungry."

"I think she's bringing something nice for you."

"Oh, is she your *girlfriend* now?" he sneered.

The boy's sadness had switched to bitterness in a flash.

"Of course not. She works for me. You know that."

"I'm going to my room!" Mitch took his backpack and banged up the stairs, slamming the door to his room. Soon, music would be blaring, some kind that Sarnower had trouble identifying. It wasn't quite rap or blues. Sometimes Mitch would listen to oldies, things that Sarnower remembered from the seventies or eighties, but he really had no idea what his tastes were. He made a mental note to get more involved, watch MTV with him, they at least could share that.

The afternoon blurred into early evening. From the kitchen, he could tell the dining room table needed attention. With his desk buried under mounds of paper and virtually unusable, he had moved administrative operations to the dining room, where the table now sprouted the same disorder that covered his desk. In addition, Mitch, following his lead, had begun to stockpile his arts and crafts projects from camp on the table as well. The sight made him anxious. Neither of them had eaten in the dining room for weeks.

They took meals in the kitchen, and when alone, Sarnower would frequently eat standing up, wolfing down his food. Surely Nina would expect to sit down at a clean table.

He walked to the living room and looked over the rows of CDs by the stereo. Music to clean dining room tables and entertain a sexy, attractive woman. Titles on the jewel box spines flew by. And there it was: Miles Davis' classic *Kind of Blue*. Just the ticket— cool, prowling, stealthy, with the sudden unpredictable baring of fangs. The CD featured a miniature photo of the original LP cover, an album Sarnower had cherished and worn out in college and then had stolen during a hell-for-leather party he'd thrown during his senior year. He opened the case and threw it on.

Miles' familiar melancholy licks filled the air, as mellow and welcoming as a strong drink. Humming along, he went into the dining room, attacking the piles of paper, the stiff, gluey collages, the lopsided ceramics, the newspaper circulars, the accumulated, unread magazines and journals. He stacked the papers and brought them into his study then arranged Mitch's artwork as the centerpiece on the dining room table, a grotesque head sitting on a tiled trivet. A fine layer of dust had settled around the clutter, leaving squares and irregular shapes like a cutout puzzle. He got a rag and a can of Pledge, and soon the mahogany surface began to shine. He hadn't set a table in months and struggled to remember what was involved. Dishes, napkins, silverware, glasses. Two places or three? He would set out three in case Mitch decided to join them.

And Nina. Well, it was pretty clear what was coming. He hadn't had sex in months, and for the most part, it really hadn't been a problem. Anxiety and fatigue had sapped his libido. The looks he was getting from women since his dramatic weight loss had rarely been reciprocated. But now, things were changing. He was going to be single again, officially. There'd be renewed interest. The summer heat, the sweet languid air, women in shorts, sleeveless tops, the sea of bare female skin. Nina without her clothes. And if Mitch was home and not out with a friend, where would they go? Wait until he was asleep? Just set the places and worry about all that later.

Carrying settings into the dining room, he saw her through the screen door, coming up the walk. In each hand was a bag from Giovanni's, the new trendy gourmet and produce store. Sarnower had tried it soon after they'd opened, but found them overpriced and not all that good. Perhaps they'd gotten their act together. He put the plates on the table and went to open the door.

"Hi," she said, smiling.

"Nina. Let me take those." He opened the door and she handed the bags off to him. They were surprisingly heavy.

"This is *dinner?*" he asked, hefting them. "You've got enough here for a battalion."

"I did some shopping for you and Mitch. I figured maybe you...hadn't...maybe you needed some food in here."

"I'd say that's a pretty safe bet."

She followed him into the kitchen as he set the bags down on the table. Her hair was done up in an expert French braid that started at the top of her head and ended at the middle of her back and she'd changed into a T-shirt, cut-off jeans and Roman-style sandals with straps that traveled up her legs like climbing vines. Her T-shirt featured a cartoon drawing of a buxom girl, like Daisy Mae of the old Lil' Abner comics, hurling a huge wrecking ball into a brick building which was exploding out from the impact. GIRL NEXT DOOR DEMOLITION the shirt read in vibrating, uneven letters, and in smaller type: *Residential and Commercial. No job too big or small.* Nina wasn't wearing a bra either. Sarnower laughed.

"What?" she smiled.

"Your shirt. I love it."

She looked down. Her profile, sweet and unaffected, was too much.

"Oh, this. My brother gave it to me years ago. He used to work summers for this crew." She laughed. "When we were kids, he would always come over and knock down the houses I built with blocks. He finally graduated to the big time."

"Did he have a boss who looked like Daisy Mae?" he asked nodding at her chest.

"I think his boss looked more like Pappy Yokum," she answered.

Sarnower couldn't move. Her clear blue eyes expanded to fill his entire visual field. There were tiny flecks of gold and green. He could see her pupils widen. Shit! This is the woman who does my billing, who schedules my appointments, whose salary I pay. What the fuck am I doing? Did I even know she had a brother? Nina's eyes began to close as she moved forward for a kiss. Her lips touched his, she began gently to nibble, prod, play, his tongue darted like a water sprite, entirely different from the passionate, plundering kiss of earlier that day. He submitted, joining in the game as the heat rose off her chest. She began to purr, almost too softly to hear, but he could feel the gentle pulsing of her body. He began to dissolve, a mass of heat and waves.

"We'd better get this put away," she said.

"Mmm," he managed.

Containers of cold Szechwan noodles, Greek olives, tahini, Italian-style marinated chicken breasts, Vietnamese spring rolls, Swedish meat balls, fruit salad, pasta salad, pepper humus, loaves of pita bread. There were bottles of water and designer iced tea. In a bakery box tied with a red and white string were jumbo chocolate chip cookies and brownies.

"I tried to find something for Mitch."

"Mitch doesn't seem to be liking much of anything these days."

"I'll bet. I'm sure he misses his Mom."

Sarnower nodded slowly. It was a hard acknowledgement. Mitch would not appreciate Nina's generosity; someone was already taking over his mother's territory and functions.

She looked at him as though reading his mind, the softness now gone from her face.

"Maybe I should go. The last thing he needs now is someone new hanging around. You need time with him alone." She started for her purse.

"No, don't. Please."

"Alan." She looked him in the eyes, resolute, taking his hands. "I'm not what you should be dealing with right now."

She was leaving. He knew it was too good to be more than a fantasy. Some nagging little voice in the back of his head had repeated that all day, he'd been too much of a pig and a dreamer to listen. More confusion he could tolerate, rejection right now would be harder to bear. Mitch was in pain, but so was he. Working day in and day out with patients, trying to maintain a normal life for both of them, it hit him. His own needs and desires had been swept aside at the first whine from his son, the first tear from a patient. He was always there with the Kleenex, the reassurance, the arm around the shoulder, the bedtime story.

His eyes must have said everything. Nina sat down in one of the kitchen chairs. She was going to talk; maybe she wouldn't go.

"Alan...Dr. Sarnower...see, I don't even know what to call you now."

"It's Alan, Nina. Has been for years. Don't back off."

She put her head in her hands. "I don't want to be a home wrecker. I can't do that."

"In case you haven't noticed, my home is already wrecked."

Why were women always doing this, offering then withdrawing? The emotional cock-tease, but obviously Nina was scared herself, unsure of her own motivations. And why not? He and his situation would hardly inspire confidence. Underneath her liberated, try-anything exterior, she was traditional. At the end of the day, she'd want a house, a husband, a kid or two. She'd be ready to hang up her spurs. But she had to be wondering just where all this was going, and he was powerless to help her.

"Any chance of salvaging a dinner?" he asked. She lifted her head and nodded. "In that case, I suggest we put something together."

They worked without talking, Miles still wailing on the stereo. Reaching for a tray on a high shelf, Nina stood on tiptoes, her back to him. Sarnower marveled at the sculpted muscles in her calves, her legs tan and sleek. Here was another choice point. He could come up and hug her from behind, but the outcome would be far from certain. It could go either way. Or, he could let the moment go. She was slipping away, that was clear.

"*Eeeeooooowww*, that music stinks!" Unheard by either of them, Mitch had come downstairs and was standing in the kitchen door holding his nose. Nina and Sarnower turned.

"Dad, can't you play real music?"

"Like what? I thought this *was* real music."

"Like maybe something with a tune?"

"Yeah, Dad, play something with a tune," Nina echoed. Dad. He was almost old enough to be her father too. They looked at each other, joining in an immediate alliance, glaring at him, both with arms akimbo, in a moment out of a cheesy sit-com.

He threw up his hands in mock surrender. "Ok, you win. I see no one here appreciates vintage jazz."

Nina and Mitch looked at each other, wrinkling their noses and shaking their heads.

"Dave Matthews," Mitch shot out.

"Limp Bizkit," Nina added.

"Nine inch nails."

"Metallica"

"Ok, ok, I get the point," Sarnower said.

"I'm thinking you don't have those in your collection," Nina said.

"And none of that Mozart crap either," Mitch added, hyped by his new empowerment.

He raced upstairs where they could hear the clack of CD cases flipping. He was down in seconds with a handful and gave them to Nina. Together, they poured over the selection on the dining room table like entomologists inspecting a rare species of butterfly. Nina pulled one out and handed it to Mitch.

"Let's give Dad a real *buzz* with this," she said. Thanks to Mitch's lucky entrance, the tension had dropped. To Sarnower, who had started bringing the food into the dining room, there was an unmistakable carnal whiff telegraphed in her words. She was back, and speaking to multiple audiences. Metallica's *Fade to Black* came to life:

> *Life it seems will fade away*
> *Drifting further every day*
> *Getting lost within myself*
> *Nothing matters, nothing else*

Nina and Mitch sang along, leaving him behind. But at least the boy was engaged, playing with an adult, something he'd been unable to do with his own father. Sarnower, out of the loop, watched as they mimed the rockers, played air guitars and sang into invisible mikes. Play. Mitch had missed it. He needed to be met on his own level, something Cassie was able to do years ago in her increasingly rare focused moments. Sarnower had completely failed him here. Mitch needed to be a boy, be treated like a boy, not a miniature man. You needed to clown with him, mix it up. Nina knew this instinctively, her rapport with him was immediate and easy, they could see eye-to-eye, speak the same pop language; she was exactly what he needed.

"I bet you can't *stand* Swedish meatballs!" She hissed at Mitch, her eyes squinting.

"No way!" he shouted, grabbing for the plastic container, emptying half of its contents on his plate.

"And I bet you just *hate* this tahini," she continued.

"In your dreams," he scowled, tucking into the meatballs.

"Dad. Dad! Aren't you going to eat?" he asked. They were already helping themselves to seconds, and Sarnower realized he had been far away, staring off into space, his plate empty. He thought of his own father, remote and awkward, never having the slightest idea how to get down on his knees and shoot marbles or teach him how to use a yo-yo. One summer evening, the old man had taken him out with his first bike and had made a feeble attempt to show him how to balance himself. That had lasted about twenty minutes, and when Sarnower had asked for another lesson the next night, his father, shrouded behind the evening *New York Post* had told him he was too busy. Busy doing what? Hiding out, of course. He saw it all now.

Nina leaned over to Mitch and whispered, just loud enough for Sarnower to hear.

"Dad's having a brain fart," she winked.

Mitch burst into laughter, small particles of food flying. "A brain fart," he repeated. "A brain fart." His laughter, spontaneous at first became forced and manic. He was finally up and wanted to make it last. Sarnower was embarrassed.

"It wasn't *that* funny," he said.

"Yes it was," Mitch answered, defiant, his mouth still full of food. Best not get baited into anything, he was already completely outclassed. Let the boy spend his laughter until it was clear even to him that there was nowhere to go with it.

"Well, that was invigorating," Nina said, beginning to organize the new chaos on the table. Genetics or early learning, women had this thing about cleaning up. His mother was always straightening, dusting, putting things away; even Cassie during her wild periods would go through the motions. Left to his own devices, Sarnower, could easily have left everything as it was on the table over night or even longer, and a day or two later sweep it all into a large black garbage bag. But here was Nina, and to his amazement Mitch helping out, getting ready to consolidate leftovers, putting away the uneaten food for future meals. She was taking care of them, making sure they were nourished, actually caring, something he'd never gotten from his mother or Cassie. He felt like crying.

He managed to down some spicy noodles and a spring roll but the new swirl of things had made him lose his appetite. Mitch and Nina were now into their own thing in the kitchen. She would sing a few bars of a rock song and Mitch would chime in, identifying the group, the album from which the song came and the year of its release. Then they would switch. Sarnower was left in the dust. She was closer in spirit and certainly in age to his son. His fantasies took off again; Nina living here with them, being the mother Cassie never could. Watching her bring the boy out of himself brought on an intense and unexpected wave of loathing for his wife.

Nina was at the sink, rinsing and loading the dishwasher as he moved in to help. Mitch had gotten into the cookies and brownies and his fingers were covered in sticky brown goo. The caffeine and sugar buzz would certainly keep him up. What would that do to the rest of the evening? Now that Nina was reassured that her presence here wasn't going to send his son to a locked ward, what would she be up for? Would she stay or want to leave well enough alone and go?

Live in the moment, forget an hour from now, the mantra he would give his patients who couldn't bear to inhabit their skins a moment longer. He could use it himself. Make some coffee, Nina's from Seattle, at least she'll have an innocent cup of coffee. Silently, he started a deep breathing exercise, in through the nose, out through the mouth. The added oxygen had the desired effect, as he felt his muscles loosen.

Dark, oily Zambian coffee beans tumbled into the Braun grinder as Nina closed the dishwasher door and turned on the machine, and the appliances began a monotone mechanical duet, drowning out the last gasps of Metallica. The sun had begun to set too as a cool dry breeze rustled the curtains.

> *Summer breeze makes me feel fine*
> *Blowin' through the jasmine in my mind*

The thought of new sex often brought to mind pop songs from the seventies and eighties, when sex was a regular occurrence, the tingle of anticipation. He turned on the coffee maker and heard it gurgle and belch to life. Soon, the room filled with the familiar rich aroma of his favorite blend. Nina wiped her hands on a dishcloth and sat down. Mitch, his face now blotched with chocolate, looked at them both, not completely sure of what was going on, but the beginning of a smile started on his face.

"What are you laughing at?" Nina asked.

"I'm not laughing."

"Yeah, but you were about to."

"Was not."

"Were too."

"Was not."

"Dad, what do you think?" That was the second time she'd called him Dad. It was starting to unnerve him.

"I think Mitch might like to wash up and go upstairs and catch the Sox-Oakland game," he said.

The boy continued to look at them silently, figuring the angles; Sarnower could see the wheels turning behind his eyes. Mitch knew what was going on now. He held the cards and he knew it. Sarnower opened his eyes wide and jerked his head almost imperceptibly in the direction of the door. Nina got up to pour the coffee while Mitch and his father stared at each other, neither giving in.

"Hot and black," she announced, bringing over two steaming mugs. Tug would surely have done a riff on that one, few things ever got by him without some kind of commentary or scat. She set the mugs down and rested her head in her hand, looking at Sarnower with slightly raised eyebrows. She was getting tired. He returned her gaze with a smile, lifting the hot mug to his mouth. Mitch was being shut out; his time commanding the stage was over.

"I'm going upstairs," he said finally, making a final plea for inclusion. Nina looked up and smiled. "Tell Pedro to pitch a no-hitter for us," she said.

"See you later," Sarnower called after him.

"The primeval struggle," she smiled. "The attempted overthrow of the feared totemic father-figure."

"Boing!" said Sarnower, his head springing back in exaggerated surprise. "Have you been reading my textbooks when I'm not around?"

"I could *write* a textbook watching the two of you."

"Are we that...dysfunctional?"

Nina didn't answer, but reached for his hands. He looked down. Midsummer had brought a deep tan to her skin, turning it from it's accustomed rose-gold to a light copper. Her nails were short and clean. A silver ring with a turquoise stone adorned the ring finger of her right hand. He wondered how much she wanted another ring on her left hand. The sun had bleached the blond hair on her arms to a pale white-yellow, which played in wonderful patterns against her darkened skin. The limbs of an honest, sensuous woman who knew who she was. She'd managed to avoid so many of the traps and pitfalls he'd fallen into by her age; there must be some internal, private compass he lacked. If he could just find it now, maybe this entire experience would be bearable, even worthwhile.

He looked up to see her wide blue eyes fixed on him. She was gently rubbing his hands; a low voltage buzz like a telephone wire connected them.

"Let's take our coffee out to the porch," he whispered. He picked up their cups and led the way through the dining room, the living room and out to the porch. Since Cassie had left, Sarnower had taken over the large screened-in porch as a private refuge. He'd moved a large couch out there, a couple of wicker chairs, some lamps and a table. On lazy weekends, he would spend hours reading the paper or a novel. He'd challenge Mitch to a game of Yatzee or Scrabble. It was nothing to spend an entire weekend day sitting, watching the arc of the sun, or following the short furious life of a summer thunderstorm from the dry safety of his new perch.

As Nina settled on the overstuffed couch he lit fat scented candles. They held the room in a soft gauzy glow, accenting the darks and lights in the new twilight air like an old Flemish painting. The light brought out unexpected planes in her face, her cheekbones, her nose. Her eyelashes, now enhanced by shadows, plumped like tiny fans, the curve of her mouth softening. Her blonde hair shone like neon. He raised his mug.

"Cheers."

"To the future."

Their mugs met in a dull ceramic clunk, the rising steam made his face flush. They sipped. The coffee, still too hot to drink caught them both at the same time. Nina puckered then licked her lips, leaving them glistening in the soft light. Sarnower put down his cup.

"God, I can't stop looking at you. I see you every day. I have no idea who you are."

She leaned over and brushed her hand against his cheek. He felt his face burst into flame. He closed his eyes and met her lips, dewy, tasting faintly of coffee. She took his head in her hands and brought him closer; she was gentle but decisive, sure of herself, leading, locking on his mouth. He gently cupped her breast, firm and larger than expected. Her nipple stood, hard at his touch, as he made small, delicate circles. She purred, deep, throaty and soft, like a vibrating bass note, and began to unbutton his shirt. Her hands went in, exploring his chest. He felt his skin leave his body, his nerves dancing in the open air. He reached for her T-shirt and began to pull it over her head, she raised her arms and Daisy Mae winked playfully as the Girl Next Door landed on the porch floor. She sat on haunches, her magnificent chest exposed, no bra needed. Gravity and children had not yet had their way with her; the ministrations of eager lovers whose tongues and mouths had engorged the lovely flowery nipples had kept them firm.

He leaned into her, taking a nipple gently between his teeth. From far away, a truck downshifted on Route Nine, boisterously stripping a gear. How long had it been since he'd been this close to a woman, especially a woman he cared about? His last perfunctory,

69

half-hearted encounters with Cassie were more than four months ago and he'd been elsewhere, just going through the motions, his tissues starved of basic nutrients, touch, skin-to-skin contact, the friction of flesh. It was all coming back now like a vaguely remembered dream.

The night he lost his virginity was gentle and fragrant, just like this one, an unexpected end to the solo, pressured fantasies of his oversexed adolescence. Kathy Mariston, the class tease in eleventh grade had sidled up to him during their junior prom, a prematurely hot May night. She'd gotten up close, the friendly touch on the arm, the look in the eye and Sarnower saw in a flash what she was after. In the end, he'd abandoned his date and had snuck off with her to her parent's empty apartment. There they picked up a blanket and a bottle of vodka and had gone up to the roof, some twenty stories above the city. They'd spread the blanket and passed the bottle. Emboldened by the hormone-liquor cocktail, he had taken charge, carefully removing her prom dress, bra and panties, while she had ripped open his rented tux shirt with such force the studs flew over the tar-covered roof like shrapnel. She sailed his cummerbund over the parapet where they watched it drift lazily down to the pavement. In moments, they had each other naked and Kathy had gone down on him. In addition to being a tease, she was also an expert. She started slowly at the top, gradually working her way down, moving faster, slowly increasing the pressure. To Sarnower, who had only known his own fantasies supplemented by a worn collection of *Playboy* and *Penthouse* magazines, another person, a live female providing the finesse his hand could only approximate, was a revelation.

When he had spent himself suddenly and uncontrollably in her mouth (and to his immense astonishment she did swallow) he took her in his arms, a naked young woman, wearing too much mascara perhaps, but luminescent against the reflected city lights. He explored her body, the curves, her smooth softness, the warm wetness between her downy thighs, her vapors delicious, adding to his high. He was hard again minutes later, and lying on his back, he pulled her on top of him and entered her, her eyes closed, her freshly done hair bigger now with spring humidity. She bobbed as she rode him, moving in a way that brought them both to trembling climaxes at the same time.

Where had she learned all this? How come her drive was every bit as strong as his? Where had he been? He was way behind the curve. After that night, Kathy must have had second thoughts; for the rest of high school she barely looked at him.

And now Nina. He was losing something all over again, his second virginity perhaps. Before she pulled him down on top of her he shed his shirt. There he was, half naked on top of his office manager. What if Mitch came down and found them? The thought added a delightful tingle of danger, and he remembered wondering years ago if Kathy's father might burst through the door to the roof and catch them. But there was the faint yet unmistakable voice of Ned Martin still calling the play-by-play from upstairs. He raised himself on his arms and looked into her gold glowing face. Jesus. In addition to being his employee, she was someone's daughter, a sister, and a lover to several disorganized and heartbroken young men. What did she see in him? Was she finally past the pyrotechnics and on to the real thing? Well, here they were, together and alone on a balmy evening. For now, that was all that mattered.

He rolled off her and pulled her to his side. They were facing each other as a gust of wind blew the candle flame so that her face moved, the sculpted tectonics undulating with the changing light. She brought him closer for a kiss and with one hand began to undo his belt. He reached for her shorts and set free the button, unzipping the fly in the next motion. She raised herself up high enough to allow him to slide her shorts off completely. Nina wasn't wearing underwear, and except for her sandals which she had propped herself up to untie, she was now completely naked. He slipped out of his own pants and kicked off an ancient pair of Topsiders, which flew and ricocheted off the other side of the porch.

Sarnower ran his hand over her body, boss and employee now equals. She stroked his back as he ran his tongue down her chest. Tiny beads of sweat had started to pool in the valley between her breasts, salt and water. We come from the sea, and to the sea we return. Do we obsess over sex because we've come so far from our origins? Perhaps there was a paper in that: *The Human Body as Analogue of the Primordial Ooze*. But not now. His tongue danced on her nipples, which hardened, tiny raspberries, willing partners. He moved south. There was a soft slope where her ribcage ended, he found himself approaching her bellybutton, delicate, an inney but not deep and free of lint. Nina had buried her hands in his full head of hair, playing and kneading his scalp. Thank God I haven't gone bald, she'd have nothing to do. The thought made him giggle involuntarily.

A fine herringbone of blond hair led from the base of her navel to a large florid bush, which overflowed its triangular boundaries down the tops of her thighs and out to her pelvis. No bikini waxing for Nina. She was at home in her skin, whatever that skin had to offer. A part of nature, not Styrofoam, she was a woman for a man who wanted a woman, not a reconstructed Barbie or an airbrushed teen.

His tongue began to explore. Her natural scent greeted him gently, a blend of musk, sweat and rising bread, she was already very wet. As if on cue she spread her legs and he found her swollen clitoris easily as she began to purr. Oral sex was an acquired taste, like herring or venison or strong English stout. Cassie had hated it, both giving and receiving. She claimed to see the faces of nuns who had taught her in parochial school floating above her during those rare times she let her husband persuade her to give him a blow job. In fact, during their entire marriage, Sarnower couldn't remember her ever having a full, earth-shattering climax; her wheels always came off at the first hints of seismic rumbling. The fear of pleasure is every bit as strong as the quest for it.

But here was Nina, eager, hungry, opening like a time-lapsed flower. He plunged his tongue down to the base of her clitoris, following it out to the tip and back again. Tiny circular motions around the base prompted her to make small adjustments of her pelvis, guiding his movements for maximum effect.

Gradually, her breathing became heavier, and Sarnower felt himself go painfully hard. Her legs came up as she began a series of involuntary shudders. She gasped sharply, ohhhh, ohhhh. The little deaths, one spasm followed the next and her breathing was shallow and quick, almost a choke. Sarnower continued. She grasped him by his hair, pulling him up.

"Fuck me, fuck me now," she gasped. She was still shaking in spasms when he entered her. He felt his entire body disappear inside, only a huge penis now, engorged and ready to explode. He kissed her, thrusting his tongue into her mouth, their sweat mixing. He flashed briefly on the polo shirt of yesterday, now lying crumpled in the hamper, remembering her tears now dried and embedded in the fabric. Yes, yes, she gave me more; she did, so much more, he thought as he fired himself into her still-convulsing body.

Chapter 4

A LOUD CRACK OF THUNDER woke him from a dark, dreamless sleep. The digital clock on the nightstand read five forty-five. Sarnower, floating between two worlds opened his eyes. Although he'd had nothing to drink, he felt hung-over. Where was he? Well, definitely upstairs in his own bed. How had he gotten there? He closed his eyes. Nina. After they'd made love, he must have fallen into a deep sleep. There was a vague memory of waking at three in the morning, naked and cold on the couch on the porch. Nina was gone; she'd left without a trace. He'd put on his clothes and gone upstairs. Mitch had fallen soundly asleep in front of the TV, the game long over. Sarnower had carried him from the chair into his bed, and still unconscious he'd mumbled a few unintelligible words and had collapsed, hugging the pillow. Sarnower had shut off the TV and gone to his room.

There, in his own bed lying on his back, he replayed the evening over and over, the impressions from all his senses, the sights, smells, textures, tastes; everything that remained in his still tingling skin, until he passed out. He'd close his eyes again for a few minutes. When he opened them again, the clock read eleven thirty.

Sunday: gray, thick and humid. Ballestracci, Ballestracci. The name rang like a coin in a tin cup as he prepared the traditional breakfast of lox and bagels. Ballestracci. It could have been the name of an early twentieth century tenor; Giuseppi Ballestracci sings *Pagliacci* at the Met. But something in his brusque conversation with him told Sarnower the guy was not an opera buff. Tax returns and lists of assets were not really the stuff of high drama and bring-the-house-down arias.

The Sunday *Times*, folded and hurled to his front steps in a wet plastic bag was going to get short-changed today. Mitch dragged himself downstairs, cowlicky and sleepy. On automatic pilot, he sat down and gulped the tall glass of freshly squeezed orange juice.

"Who won?" Sarnower asked.

The boy looked at him through half-closed eyes. "Whaa?" he whispered.

"Who won?" he repeated. "Or weren't you awake to find out?"

Before noon on Sunday, Mitch was not in a position to converse. It was just as well; he could squeeze in a section or two of the *Times* with a cup of coffee.

He went into the study. Cassie's petition lay open on his desk. Since the day he was served, he'd read it through several times. She wanted everything: Mitch, the house, the lion's share of their joint assets, outrageous support. He hadn't known whether to laugh or scream. Of course there was no way it was going to happen. It was all legal boilerplate, the opening salvo, the shot across the bow, a gesture of moxie; one that would surely be dismissed quickly by any half-witted judge. "That's fine, but let's get real" he imagined the judge saying, leaning down from the bench, removing his reading glasses and glaring at Cassie and her lawyer for wasting his time.

He dismissed the Sunday paper after scanning the first section, then sat down at his desk and cleared a small field in the middle of the clutter to work. He thought of Nina, reclining naked on a king sized bed, but pushed the image out of his mind.

Ok. Assets. Well, the house, now almost paid off. He and Cassie had purchased it years before for almost nothing. A handyman's special, they'd transformed it into a showcase, doing most of the work themselves, hauling large panels of drywall, renting floor sanders, stripping old stubborn wallpaper, painting, rewiring. Knowing nothing about renovation, he'd taken a course at a nearby community college, and with some technical assistance from a neighbor who owned a building supply company, he'd become proficient in the basic principles of construction and maintenance. They'd been approached by several hungry realtors over the years for the listing should they decide to sell. In today's inflated market, the house could probably sell for $700,000, give or take. The house across the street, smaller and with less land had recently been snapped up at $650,000. Living here all these years, Sarnower had been oblivious to the insane increases in property values, but now the time for accounting had come. Two cars, Cassie would keep her Celica, and he would hang on to his six year old reliable Toyota Camry, closing in on a hundred thousand miles and beginning to show its age. Three thousand dollars would be a charitable estimate. Their joint stock and bond portfolio, off substantially from the highs of the go-go nineties, came in at just over $70,000. His IRA and Keogh plan, perhaps another $20,000. That left a few thousand dollars from his parent's paltry estate and Mitch's college fund at an embarrassing $15,000. That was it. Furniture, pots and pans, books, their signed and numbered Erte lithograph (which had recently been pronounced a forgery by Tug)—was he supposed to itemize all this too? Well, he would, just to show good faith.

It was two in the afternoon when he finished, and by three-thirty he had located all their joint tax returns. He stacked everything neatly in a pile, placing Cassie's petition on top.

He realized, despite resolutions to change, that he'd ignored his son all day. Mitch had been upstairs. At various times Sarnower had heard the mechanical pixilated music of video games, heavy metal rock, and TV. Vaguely, he thought of doing something with him in the remaining portion of the afternoon. Mitch had been a good sport; Sarnower's tryst of the previous night had been an unknowing gift. Or had it? Did the boy know what had gone on directly below him? Sarnower would have to be alert to any clues. But now it was now too late to indulge him in ice cream or a trip to Harvard Square to look for CDs, so Sarnower spent the remainder of the day quietly sharpening his wits with the Sunday *Times* crossword puzzle.

And then Monday. Mercifully, it was cool. He would put on a dark business suit and tie, Brooks Brothers wingtips and look every bit the aggrieved, put-upon professional. After a harried chain of phone calls the night before, Mrs. Jenkins down the block had been recruited to take Mitch to camp, although Sarnower would have to pick him up in the afternoon.

He thought about Tracey Bowen—how fast things could unravel. He'd really better watch his step. Fortunately, patients had been cancelled for the day, a loss of income that was going to hurt. It wasn't clear how long the meeting was going to last, and even if it wrapped up early, he was sure he'd have nothing left to share with his patients afterwards.

At nine, showered and suited up, he grabbed his briefcase and got into the car. At this hour, Storrow Drive would be his best bet. A tuneful Haydn symphony played on public radio, and Sarnower hummed along, rerunning the night with Nina. They hadn't spoken on Sunday and he realized her silent, surreptitious exit had left him unsettled. Why hadn't she woken him to say goodbye, or at least called the next day? What was the etiquette here? Maybe *he* should have called *her*. The first post-coital contact would be awkward; they would see each other differently. Rain had started to pelt his car in pea-sized drops as he approached the BU exits. There was no point in dwelling on it now, he had to shift gears and get into warrior mode.

With wiper blades moving at top speed, he got off at Government Center. A line of cars waited on the off ramp. He drummed his fingers on the steering wheel. The Haydn symphony was over and an annoying sixteenth-century *a cappella* work had taken its place, a countertenor sounded anguished as he reached for some impossibly high note. Sarnower shut off the radio. It was only nine-thirty; he'd make the appointment in plenty of time. He'd take Cambridge to Court and on to State Street where there were plenty of expensive parking garages. Maybe Ballestracci could get his ticket validated.

By now, Nina was in the office. Should he call her or wait? Calling her now would be unpredictable and increase the chances of saying something off the cuff, unintended, something he might later regret. He was wired, but furious, he realized, at having to consult a lawyer in the first place. The last time he'd done it was during the closing on his house. Certainly this was going to be different. No, better to talk later after his meeting with Ballestracci.

The exit ramp and the sky were clearing, and for once traffic on Cambridge Street looked light. Inevitably, Nina would compare him to that deadbeat drama student, what was his name? Dan? Ned? Doug? Yes, Doug. Well, at least I did get her off; let's give a few credits here for experience. Was I too fast? Well, the circumstances were hardly conducive to long and leisurely, what with Mitch right above them. All in all, things had gone pretty well.

Without being aware of it, he'd turned into a garage, pulled a ticket from the annoying machine he was always too close to or too far from, and had found a parking space. It might be possible to go through life entirely on automatic pilot, making all the right moves and gestures externally, while living in a detached private world all your own. He collected his briefcase and emerged into the gray day.

By nine-fifty, most of the pedestrian traffic had thinned. Those still on the street were rushing, talking on cell phones and carrying covered cups of gourmet coffee and muffins. Fifty State Street loomed, brass numbers high above an intimidating, tall glass entry. Sarnower quickly inserted himself into a section of an already revolving door. It reminded him of the definition of a lawyer he'd heard years ago: someone who enters a revolving door after you and gets out ahead of you.

The brass and marble lobby with vaulted ceiling, damp, cavernous and cold still held multitudes on their way to work or appointments. The huge black directory on the wall listed hundreds of names in alphabetical order in tiny glowing white letters. Frazier, Abbott and Connors occupied several suites on the thirty-fourth floor. He walked to the bank of elevators. There were eight of them, each tall and dark as a sarcophagus. They were divided into two groups, those that went from one to twenty-five and those that went from twenty-five to fifty. One had just begun to disgorge its cargo of high-traveling passengers, and Sarnower joined the group waiting to board.

The car was tall, and although there were several recessed lights in the ceiling, it was dark; the walls were made of some sort of black corrugated metal with tiny holes, to absorb sound and light. He pushed the square indented button for thirty-four as others piled in and jockeyed to reach their numbers. The car took off silently as Sarnower and his fellow passengers assumed the standard face-forward position. An ominous red X glowed on the indicator above their heads as the car zoomed to the twenty-fifth floor. What if we get stuck on the seventeenth floor, have we entered a parallel universe? On twenty-five, a few got out, on twenty-eight, a few more. By the time he reached his destination, there were only two others left who had business at higher altitudes.

Finally, the doors opened on to an expansive carpeted hall, completely dominated by the firm. The huge office was open and visible through a plate glass window and glass doors. Frazier, Abbott and Connors was emblazoned in gold letters on the center of the doors and then again on a large hanging sign inside the office. Straight ahead was a large wrap-around wooden desk with several computer terminals and phones. Symmetrical work areas were located off to either side and the place was humming with activity. "We've got bucks, we're successful and you're in deep shit," it screamed.

Sarnower stood outside the door for a moment taking it in. He took a deep breath and pulled the door open. The handle was freezing, and even though the day had warmed, the ever-present corporate air-conditioning was blasting away. Several of the women

NOTHING TO SEE HERE

working at stations throughout the lobby had sweaters draped around their shoulders. The thought of being able to open a window here was ludicrous. He approached the main desk.

"Dr. Sarnower to see Mr. Ballestracci," he told the receptionist. She looked up from a half-eaten muffin, a young woman perhaps twenty-five, with recently cut short, streaked blonde hair, thin, with long rectangular wire rimmed glasses, edgy-corporate.

"I'll tell him you're here," she said, picking up the phone. "He's a little tied up now, why don't you take a seat over there," she turned around, pointing to a waiting area behind her. Sarnower nodded and made his way to a semi-circle of plush, comfortable chairs. In the center was a low glass table which offered a large, perfectly formed fan of current magazines. He pulled *Time* from the center and sat down. The cover was black and featured an empty crib, richly festooned with stuffed animals and a suspended colorful mobile. "Where are our missing children?" the large white letters asked. Where indeed? They're not missing, they're here somewhere on this planet, in this universe. Matter can neither be created nor destroyed— only changed into energy, and then back again into matter. Some of those missing children had undoubtedly been changed into energy, food for insects, savaging their decayed bodies, now succulent memories for craven pedophiles. Jesus, where was this going?

"Dr. Sarnower?" A deep, masculine voice. He looked up. "Nick Ballestracci," the large man said extending a huge, meaty hand.

Sarnower rose to shake it. The lawyer was big, six-five at least, but stocky as well. Nevertheless, he wore a bespoke charcoal-gray pinstripe suite that organized his bulk into a defined, proportioned man. A navy blue Hermes tie with dancing red unicorns and crisp white French-cuffed shirt shone through the dark mass like a halogen light. He was wearing gold cufflinks as big as quarters, but his larger scale made them appear normal sized. On top of the mountain of body was a large head crowned by a perfect razor-cut pompadour. He wore a light but expensive cologne (he reads *GQ* too.) Dark, sparkling eyes, and a large, clearly broken nose hung over a wide smile with brilliantly white teeth. Sarnower couldn't take his eyes off the man's teeth.

"Caps," Ballestracci said.

"What?"

"Those are caps," the lawyer laughed. "In my foolish youth I used to box, semi-pro. Most of my originals are scattered throughout various seedy gyms in New Jersey."

78

"I'm not sure I'd like to meet the guys who took them out," Sarnower said.

Ballestracci laughed. "Yeah, it didn't take long to figure there were easier ways to make a living."

"Well, I hope you can put some of your pugilistic skills to work for me."

"Let's go to my office and see what we can do."

Sarnower grabbed his briefcase and followed the lawyer down a long, wood-paneled corridor. Illuminated by soft recessed lights, the hall was lined with oil paintings in heavy gilded frames of stern, old WASPy looking men.

"Our forbearers who art in heaven," Ballestracci said without turning.

A tall, thin man approached from down the hall. As he got closer, he looked to Sarnower to be about eighteen years old. His long blond hair bounced in his eyes as he walked. He wore a pair of circular tortoise shell English schoolboy glasses, a navy blazer, striped bow tie and gray slacks, all out of a Polo ad. Ballestracci stopped in front of him.

"Stan, I was just about to call you. Stan Knowlton, meet Dr. Sarnoff."

"That's Sar-*nower*," he corrected.

"Pleased to meet you," the schoolboy said extending his hand.

"Stan's going to be working on your case," Ballestracci said. "He's one of our best family law associates."

Together the three of them walked to the end of the corridor that opened into a huge carpeted office with floor-to-ceiling windows.

"It isn't much, but it's home," Ballestracci said.

A large mahogany desk was planted ten feet from a panoramic view of Boston harbor. An antique leather swivel chair rested behind the desk. Wooden bookcases covered the walls; a large globe was suspended on a dark oak pedestal. Part of the paneled wall was taken up with diplomas and photos; Ballestracci and the governor, Ballestracci with Arthur Fiedler, Ballestracci and a local news team, Ballestracci accepting an award from a Pop Warner football team, and on.

The lawyer moved quickly behind his desk and gestured for Sarnower and the boy-associate to sit. He put on a pair of gold-rimmed reading glasses and withdrew a huge Montblanc pen from his monogrammed shirt pocket.

"So. Speak to me," he barked.

Adept at presenting case histories succinctly and dramatically, Sarnower related the story of his marriage, the beginning of Cassie's deterioration, her odd, irresponsible behavior, her current breakdown and the abandonment of her family. Ballestracci nodded and squinted during the recitation, occasionally looking down to make notes on a large yellow legal pad. Stan sat in stony silence.

"And so, that's it. Here I am," Sarnower concluded.

For a few moments no one said anything. Ballestracci chewed on a stem of his glasses.

"Let me see the papers you brought," he said.

Sarnower handed over the thick folder. The lawyer reached for the petition in the blue cover and scanned it rapidly.

"Well," he said finally, "what you've got here is a big fucking mess, not to put too fine a point on it."

The words struck Sarnower like a punch in the stomach. His mouth went dry.

"I...I thought this was going to be a slam dunk. The woman's obviously crazy."

Ballestracci smiled and leaned his huge torso over the desk. "Dr. Sarnower, I think I've got it right, yes? Dr. Sarnower, in the law, nothing's ever a slam-dunk. I know you're a professional, I'm sure you have every confidence in your diagnostic abilities. You know she's nuts, I'm sure I would too. Unfortunately, that doesn't add up to a sack of shit here. She ever burn the boy with a cigarette?"

"No."

"Chain him to a radiator in the basement?"

"No."

"Starve him? Beat him? Feed him mouse turds?"

"No."

"You see where I'm going with this? Unless there's something really outrageous, it's mothers and children. Courts just aren't going to separate them. And, they're going to make you pay to keep them together. That's the way it is. You're the breadwinner, right?"

Sarnower nodded.

"Wife currently employed?"

"No."

"That's pretty much the way it's going to stay."

Stan's head was bobbing in silent agreement, a hank of hair falling into his eyes.

"I see your wife is represented by Nora Lund." He put on his glasses and rifled through the petition again. "I've never dealt with her, but from what I hear she's all hat and no cattle. Stan, what do we know about her? What's your take?" he asked, swiveling around in the squeaky leather chair to his associate.

"Unpredictable," he said, suddenly coming to life. "She can be difficult. You've got to stay on your toes with her. Frankly, I'm bothered by the fact that they've marked up a set of motions for tomorrow. They're seeking immediate relief, they must have something aggressive planned."

Ballestracci nodded, tapping his pen on the desk.

"Stan, see if you can get this postponed. Who's sitting tomorrow?"

"Don't know, but I'll find out."

"Get it moved. A week. Five days, whatever."

"I'm on it," he said, and left.

Ballestracci sat back in his chair. "Alan," he said softly. "I'm going to call you Alan because we're going to be getting to know each other pretty well before this is all over."

Shit. This wasn't going at all as he'd thought. His stomach was heaving; he had to go to the bathroom.

"Let me spell things out, kind of give you the lay of the land here."

Ballestracci delivered his monologue. He got up from his desk, he walked, he gestured, he pirouetted, the proverbial heavy man light on his feet. Sarnower thought immediately of the old Jackie Gleason Show, the rotund comedian skipping gracefully off the stage to the "traveling music" provided by Sammy Spear and his orchestra right before the first commercial break. Ballestracci's voice faded out as he thought of the wonderful skits, now politically incorrect, with Frank Fontaine as Crazy Guggenheim, the funny, pathetic drunk, who was always persuaded by Gleason, the put-upon barkeep, to end the sketch with "a number," whereupon Fontaine would reveal his glorious tenor voice in some sappy ballad that would inevitably bring the house down. Sarnower felt himself smile at the memory, those cozy Saturday nights in front of the black and white TV with his parents, for once not bickering, everyone laughing at the foolish antics, the double takes, the over-the-top bellowing and facial contortions.

Meanwhile, Ballestracci talked on. They'd do their best to prevail at the hearing, but at a minimum, Sarnower could expect to pony up temporary support for Cassie. If he got to stay in the house (not at all a sure thing), he'd have to pay for her rent and living expenses. All efforts would be made to keep Mitch in the house and to preserve as much as possible his schedule and routine. "For the best interests of the child" the lawyer said, a phrase he would hear over and over during the proceedings.

As to who would get to stay in the house with Mitch, that would depend on the results of an independent psychological evaluation of him and Cassie by a guardian *ad litem*, a psychologist appointed by the court. Mitch himself would also be interviewed. Based on the recommendations from that evaluation, and the odds were against him, either he or Cassie would stay in the house with Mitch until a formal separation agreement was negotiated. That would take time and be inordinately frustrating. It would mean the division of all assets, a schedule of alimony, an agreement on physical and legal custody and child support, should Cassie be named the physical custodian.

Were they not able to agree on custody, the matter would almost certainly go to trial. That would be excruciating for all, especially for the boy who would have to testify. It would be extremely costly as well. Everyone's best interests would be served, Ballestracci concluded, by working together, hard as that sounded, and try to come up with a set of compromises that all could at least live with.

"Are you with me on this?" he asked.

Sarnower nodded, now completely numb.

"I bill at $500 an hour. That racks up pretty damn quick. So we're going to have Stan, who you just met, do most of the work. He bills at half my rate." He saw Sarnower start to frown and held up a large open hand. "Not to worry. I'll be consulting with him on a regular basis so everything's going to stay on track. We do this to try to save you money, doctor, because I have to tell you, this whole thing's going to run you a whole lot of dough."

Ballestracci opened a desk drawer and took out a sheaf of papers. Sarnower thought he was going to vomit.

"This is the firm's standard contract that we'll need you to sign before we can begin work for you." Ballestracci pushed the document toward him and offered his gleaming Montblanc pen, a thick black torpedo heading straight for his heart. "We'll need your signature on pages three, twelve and seventeen."

Sarnower took the packet in hand. His fingers were cold and tingling. He flipped through the pages, they might as well have been written in Urdu for all the sense they made. Lamely, he reached for the pen and signed where indicated, then pushed the document across the table. Ballestracci put on his glasses and flipped through, making sure it was appropriately signed. He collected the material Sarnower had brought and put it with the contract into a large brown accordion file folder which already bore a crisp laser-printed label bearing Sarnower's name and case number.

Ballestracci was smiling. Good that someone here was having fun.

"Finally, I'll need a check from you in the amount of $20,000. This is our retainer. Billable hours will be charged against it and you'll get monthly, itemized statements from the firm making it clear where we stand. When the retainer is spent, you'll get monthly bills against your account. My advice is not to let them go too long, because like I said, they add up. Fast. Like shit through a goose."

Sarnower nodded. The meeting was over and he was having trouble seeing. Shit through a goose was pretty much the way he was feeling, and the process of getting up and making it to the door was going to demand his full attention.

"I'll have to get that check to you in the mail," he offered weakly.

"That's fine. We're gentlemen. I'll expect it in the next day or two."

Ballestracci got up and extended his huge hand.

"Doctor? Alan? A bit of free advice? If there's any way you and your wife can work this out—I know marriage is difficult, pure hell at times, but if you can see your way, if there's any chance at all, give it a shot. This could get really...messy."

Sarnower nodded and advanced toward the door.

"By the way," Ballestracci called, already seated, dialing the phone, on to the next order of business. Time is money after all. "Stan will be in touch with you later today about the hearing. But just in case, get ready to be at Middlesex Probate Court tomorrow at ten."

He nodded vaguely. He was sure he was deathly pale. Christ. Pull yourself together. Now. People were in the corridor. A secretary might notice him, look concerned and ask if he was all right. Would he care to sit down or have a glass of water? They must see this all the time, carnage and collateral damage. This was a place where lives, futures and fortunes hung in the balance. No unwanted attention. Just get the hell out.

His breathing was rapid and shallow, and tiny black spots began to swim in front of his eyes, but Sarnower managed to stand straight and put one foot in front of the other.

People passed him in the hall. Portraits of the forefathers in heaven stared down impassively, unimpressed, unaware of the cargo of suffering that passed daily beneath their smug, frozen faces. He tried to smile. Good, hold it together just a bit longer. Out in the main reception area, the edgy blonde with the thin glasses at the desk was on the phone. She smiled and waved as he left.

Try to put things back together if you can. Why had Ballestracci said that? Sure, he'd avoid total financial ruin, be able to salvage the fruits of years of professional work, not to mention the meticulous planning, the careful investments. Mitch would certainly want his mother back; he would forgive her neglect, her sudden mood swings and the whole canvas of embarrassing, odd behavior. Having Cassie back would make things complete for him. She'd be home; the rest would fall into place. Or would it? What did he want? They could start over, fresh, but much differently. She'd need to get on the right medication, stay on it and become stable again. She might recover some feeling for him, but could he do the same? They could go for couples therapy, really try to work things through and get to the core of the problems once and for all.

He certainly had a sack full of gripes of his own. Her chronic lack of interest in sex for one thing. After his night with Nina, after a taste of what was possible, the exalted, unbound passion, was it even realistic to think of going back and never having it again? Who was he kidding? That night had confirmed what he'd suspected for years; there were women out there who could value him, who would find him desirable, that elusive combination of hunkiness and mature wisdom. At best, Cassie would put up with him, grudgingly accommodate him. Wasn't he better than that, didn't he deserve more? Sex, love, it was important. It should be. No, he wasn't going to apologize or minimize his needs any more. That wasn't negotiable.

Then, there was her refusal to grow, to learn, to get interested in new things. Since Mitch was born, she had given up her part-time career in interior design, not, as he had hoped, to nurture their son, but as he saw now, because she was incapable of handling anything that demanded her committed, undivided attention. Now that Mitch was getting older and needing less hands-on care, it seemed doubtful she would resume her career or make the effort to find something more satisfying. She'd continue to get up late, grudgingly run the house, watch soaps, read romance novels, heat up leftovers, all while he was working hard and Mitch was struggling to grow. Sarnower wanted to travel, perhaps take some courses in art or cooking, do more reading. Cassie would sit and wait for them to return at the end of the day, tense and bored.

Then, of course, he'd be married. The tomb would be sealed; he'd be out of the running, off the market. Whatever that wondrous thing with Nina was the other night, it would stop; over and done before either one of them had had a chance to explore the potential. Her wit, her sharp mind, the natural sensuality and bottomless appetite for sex; all would be gone.

He was way ahead of himself. One magnificent night of lovemaking did not a relationship make. But being single again, a teen-ager with an adult's sensibility and grasp of the world, *that* could open up a universe of interesting possibilities, if not with Nina then with someone else who was fresh, playful and alive. What a thought! The second, the *real* Mrs. Sarnower could be out there right now waiting for him to get this mess over with and move on to her.

The cost would be high, Ballestracci had warned him. He'd be severed from at least half of his assets and there was the chance, unthinkable before this morning that he might indeed lose Mitch. The thought of going on like that made him sick. He knew those weekend dads, some were even his patients, and felt a deep sadness for them. How empty they looked trying to cram days into hours, always forcing a jolly facade. They were out everywhere in suburbia on the weekends, at McDonald's and Chucky Cheese looking beaten, gray, and worried. Overly enthusiastic at little league games and soccer practice, their smoldering anger could flare up suddenly at coaches and other parents. Their hapless kids would do their best to accommodate them, flashing smiles and laughing, not wanting to hurt feelings, but in the process taking on burdens they were not ready to bear.

No. It wasn't going to happen to him. Mitch needed his father, the strong, guiding male presence. Recent psychological research had shown that fathers were every bit as important in the lives and development of their children as mothers. Mitch would have a full-time father. End of story.

Here it was, one o'clock on a Monday afternoon. He'd normally be in the office starting a session, but the rest of the day stretched out in front of him like an empty country road, the unwelcome free hours ahead would be filled with obsessive juggling of options, each of which seemed intolerable. Tug's words of the other night played in his head. Whack her and get it over with. If only.

Returning home on deserted Storrow drive, his window open, the sun beginning to peek out between the layers of cloud, Sarnower felt himself start to relax. His breathing slowed, his vision became clear. He *would* prevail, he was sure. There would be justice. Despite the vagaries of the system his cause was right. He'd make it work.

The phone was ringing as he entered the front door. He dropped his briefcase in the front hall and ran to answer it, but whoever it was had hung up by the time he picked up the receiver.

He was famished. The ordeal downtown had left him wrung out and depleted, his stomach was growling. In the refrigerator he found the cartons of uneaten food Nina had brought. There was still pasta salad, spring rolls, olives and meatballs. He emptied the boxes onto a plate and dug in. Although the food was cold, it was still tasty, and he opened a beer to wash it all down. Things began to improve with food in his stomach. Low blood sugar could lead to bad things, dark, harsh thinking.

For the first time in days, he sat in silence, without distraction or disruption. After the sweet morning rain the air had become hot and still again. A dog barked faintly on another block. From the kitchen through the dining room window, he saw a mother help her young son to steady himself on his first bike. The bells of an ice cream truck chimed in the distance, a lawnmower started after several promising pulls of the cord. The normal pulse of a quiet midsummer's day. He'd been rushing through them distracted, harried, confused, scared. These days were very precious, you would fantasize about them during a January Nor'easter. The thought of them could sustain you through the long New England winter. He was mad at Cassie again; she'd robbed him of this valuable time.

He put his head down on the kitchen table. Soon, hypnagogic images were dancing in front of his eyes, neon donuts changing color, stars against a black sky, a layer of yellow clouds above a brown earth, soothing as a Rothko painting. He dropped gently, slowly, easily into a huge pillow across the imperceptible threshold of deep...

The phone rang again, jangling loud and sharp. He let it ring once more just to make sure it was real. And again. Another ring and his voice mail would answer. No rest for the weary. He moved into the hall and picked up the portable.

"Hello?"

"Alan?" The voice was unfamiliar.

"Yes?"

"This is Bill." Bill?

"Cassie's Brother."

Bill Kelly. They hadn't spoken in years. Bill, his wife and seven children had been ensconced in Winnetka while he clawed his way up to become the Midwest king of corrugated boxes. Sarnower had last seen him when he and Cassie had gotten married. Bill had presented them with the rose crystal wine glass set, one of which Cassie had recently sent flying millimeters above his head. Since then, some twenty years ago, there had been virtually no contact from him or any of his family. Sarnower wouldn't recognize him if he saw him.

"Alan, what's going on with my sister?" His tone had an ugly, accusatory edge. Well, let's not waste time on pleasantries.

"I'm not sure I can answer that other than to say she hasn't been here in weeks and is now hell-bent on getting a divorce."

"That's what I hear. I also hear you've been smacking her around and you've thrown her out of the house."

He'd had enough. "That's a load of bullshit. Listen carefully Bill, I'm going to cut to the chase here. Cassie's very ill. She has a serious manic-depressive disorder. Up until she decided to leave Mitch and me on her own, about six or seven weeks ago, I was spending nearly every waking hour trying to get her treatment, you know? Medication and short-term hospitalization. We were just beginning to make some progress when she disappeared. Turns out she flew to San Francisco and holed up with some poet friend of hers she went to high school with. A few days ago, she turns up back here in our bed fucking her damn brains out with some idiot she met on a commune out in the Berkshires. I threw the guy out; told her we had to talk, continue to get her treatment. She laughed at me and took off again. The next day I'm served with a petition for divorce. I never, *ever* laid a hand on her, that's the absolute truth."

Bill was silent. A quick pre-emptive strike was always the best defense.

"I'm coming to Boston and I'm going to be meeting with her attorney."

"Look, Bill, why don't you come over here, let's forget the lawyers, we'll have lunch, talk like men, get this nonsense figured out."

"Under the circumstances, I'm not sure that's a good idea."

"What circumstances are those?"

"Goodbye Alan." He hung up. The phone buzzed.

Well this was spinning out of control nicely. Bill would come to Boston to throw some of his corrugated box money into Cassie's defense. Blood, even their anemic, alcohol-flushed blood, was thicker than water, thicker even than reason. He had pegged Bill as a bitter, mean-spirited lout years ago and clearly this was as much about getting shots in at him as it was helping out his sister. Years ago, when he and Cassie were dating, Bill had been around, a constant presence in their parent's house. He was always in between: girlfriends, jobs, schools, very much the one most likely to fall permanently on his face, despite being tall, jockish and rather good looking. When Sarnower dropped by Cassie's house to pick her up for a date, Bill would invariably be lurking somewhere in their long railroad house on the South Side of Chicago, always with a beer or mixed drink in hand.

It was obvious from the get-go he resented Sarnower, his smarts, his New York City background, his being Jewish. Although he didn't much care for blacks, he loved R and B and frequented the South Side blues bars. He used to enjoy embarrassing Sarnower over his lack of knowledge of important blues figures—Buddy Guy, B. B. King, Junior Wells. The walls of his room were adorned with eight-by-ten signed photographs of the famous and the not so famous, old posters, cardboard announcements of upcoming concerts in block letters and grainy photos. He had tacked and taped this prize collection to the wall so that corners had torn off and crusty yellow strips had appeared where a piece of Scotch tape had been hastily applied, dried and fallen off. Any chance the collection might have had some archival value had been destroyed by his half-assed curatorial skills.

Once he had caught Sarnower up in his room alone, flipping through a vast but poorly cared for collection of vintage seventy-eights and LPs. Completely smashed, Bill had staggered to the door, drink in hand and had shouted "Geeooutah my rooooom!" Startled, Sarnower got up and headed for the door but Bill blocked him with a thick, strong arm. He looked at Sarnower through half-closed blood-shot eyes, the rancid odor of gin leeching through his pores.

"Hey," he said, putting an arm around Sarnower's shoulder in one of his boozy, quick-change-of-affect moments that, oddly, was a trait Cassie had too.

"Hey, I din' know Jews liked the blues," he slurred, swaying, his face up close, eyes unable to find a focal point, the space between them filling with alcoholic vapor.

"Joooos like the blooos," he repeated, Sarnower still in his grip. "Joooos like the blooos," he laughed. The line was hysterically funny to him as he repeated it over and over, until finally it must have shed all meaning and existed as pure sound. His arm left Sarnower's shoulder as he doubled up in a fit of convulsive laughter, eventually falling to the floor and passing out. Relieved and revolted, Sarnower left quickly.

That was Bill—for years a complete, hopeless fuck-off, any chance at a future seemed remote at best. Then one night while drinking in a Hyde Park pub, he'd met Steffi Garrelli, out for an evening with the girls. They'd started eyeing each other, she was at a table and he was sitting at the bar. Never one for subtlety, Bill had taken her flirting as a sign she wanted to get to know him and had stumbled over with his stock of inane pick-up lines. Before the evening was over, he had managed to detach her from her pack and bring her back to the basement of his parents' house where they screwed all night on top of his father's pool table in the makeshift rec room.

Her father, a failing businessman, had inexplicably taken a liking to Bill and had offered him a job in his company. Whether to impress the man, prove everyone wrong in their assessments of him, or for some other unfathomable reason, he bit into the job like a pit bull and within a couple of years began to take over and make the company profitable. When the old man died suddenly of a heart attack, Bill had turned the corrugated box company into one of the more successful businesses in Chicago. He and Steffi married and moved to the suburbs. They'd had kids. He'd joined the Lions Club, the Rotary, and was voted Man of the Year by the Kiwanis Club. He took up golf and began ordering tailor-made clothes from London. At one point there was talk of a run for political office. Lazy boozehound degenerate to politician. It certainly wouldn't be the first time.

Sides were being chosen and causes joined. Bill had grown very comfortable in his role as big kahuna and loved nothing more than to blow into town and throw his money and weight around. He'd be pulling the lawyer's strings; that much was clear. Any doubts about Nora Lund's competence or ability to go the distance were now completely dispelled. Bill would be working behind the scenes.

Ballestracci would have to know about this and take a more hands-on role in things. Stan might be the most brilliant lawyer in Boston, but a big sneeze looked as if it could do him real damage. And the bow tie. Lose it. Bill would surely ride into Dodge City with his trademark bolo.

Sarnower got up, his brief moment of peace trashed. The phone rang again.

"Hello?"

"Dr. Sarnower?"

"Yes."

"Stan Knowlton here. We met this morning at Frazier, Abbott and..."

"Yes, I know."

"Some good news. We got the hearing on the motions postponed until Friday, so you won't need to show up tomorrow. Apparently the lawyer can't locate your wife."

"That doesn't surprise me. Well, good, I guess, isn't it? That might give us more time to prepare."

"Indeed."

Indeed? Who says "indeed?" This guy's right out of *Masterpiece Theater.*

"I'll call you on Thursday and we'll prep you for Friday morning. Oh, and Nick asked me to remind you to pop that check in the mail ASAP."

Pop that check in the mail, that's rich. Checks for $20,000 aren't popped in the mail. They're dragged like a pyramid stone, gouged right out of your gut. Stan was missing the picture.

"Uh, Stan?"

"Yes?"

"With all due respect, and I'm sure you're a fine lawyer and all, but I'm not positive you're the right one for me."

There was a silence on the other end. He'd hurt the man's feelings.

"I'm not sure I understand." Stan had turned cold and remote.

"Well, it's this Norma Lund."

"*Nora* Lund," he corrected.

"Yeah, whatever. See, I'm getting the feeling she's kind of a wild card here, plus the fact that I just found out my rich, bull-headed prick of a brother-in-law is coming to town to mix things up too. You get what I'm saying? I think we need some really heavy artillery here."

Silence again. Jesus, he'd really wasted this poor sucker. Sarnower had a vision of him on the other end of the phone trying desperately to hold back tears. Finally:

"I'm not sure what to say to you Dr. Sarnower. If you have questions about my qualifications or ability to represent you, I think you should bring them up with Mr. Ballestracci." At least the pipsqueak called him *Sarnower*. He hadn't left *his* short-term memory on the mat somewhere.

"Look, let's do the hearing on Friday and see how it goes," Sarnower said, trying to appease him and rehabilitate the conversation. "Things go our way, we'll take it one step at a time."

"Dr. Sarnower, I have to warn you, these hearings are tricky and unpredictable. We'll do our best, of course, but even Clarence Darrow would have trouble prevailing with some of these judges."

"You're not doing much to bolster my confidence."

"I'm not trying to. I'm trying to be realistic. Get used to it. For the foreseeable future, you're not in control of your life."

The lawyer hung up. Undoubtedly by now he had pegged Sarnower as a "difficult client" and would be quick to bring all this to Ballestracci's attention. Great. Now he was really fucked. But the man was right, his life was no longer under his control. This is what I get for twenty grand? No way, it didn't add up. The stakes were too high. He needed Ballestracci himself.

The phone rang again. Who was it this time? The IRS? The Medical Standards and Review Board? Torquemada himself?

"Yes?"

"I'm looking for Dr. Sarnower," An elderly woman's voice, testy and tart.

"You found him."

"We have your son Mitchell here at Sun Acres Day Camp, doctor. He should have been picked up over an hour ago."

Shit! Mitch! He'd completely forgotten. It was well after five and pick up was four o'clock on the button. The camp was strict about this policy and lines of anxious parents in their cars started forming at three forty-five. They'd miss meetings, get out of work early, drop whatever they were doing in order not to incur the wrath of the staff.

"I'll be right over. Sorry, it won't happen again," he said meekly.

Mitch was standing at the entrance to the day camp with the prim gray-haired Mrs. Watkins, program director as she titled herself. From several yards away, Sarnower could see the scowl on her face. Mitch was looking at the ground; it was obvious he'd been crying. He eased the car in front of them, rolling down the window in advance for a florid apology.

"I'm so sorry to inconvenience you Mrs. Watkins. I had an unexpected emergency to deal with."

She was not appeased. "Dr. Sarnower, we have over seventy children here. We have rules for a reason. We need close parental cooperation; we can't run this place without it." She was as stern as a disappointed one-room prairie schoolteacher.

"I understand. I assure you it won't happen again."

He looked over at Mitch, who avoided his eyes. Silently, the boy reached for the rear door handle and got in.

"How about shotgun?" Sarnower asked, turning around. Mitch said nothing and stared ahead.

"Just go," he whispered.

"Yes, sir!"

Mitch was not amused. He turned his head and looked out the window.

"How about some ice cream, buddy?"

"I'm not hungry."

"Well, would you mind telling me what's eating you, aside from the fact I was late?"

The boy continued to stare out the window as they drove down Center Street across Beacon.

"What did you do with Nina the other night?"

Sarnower shuddered involuntarily. Had Mitch been awake all that time? "What do you mean?"

"Were you having sex?"

Sarnower was silent. His mind went blank.

"You were, weren't you?"

The rocket shells and mortars were not going to stop today.

"Mitch...adults who like each other a lot... sometimes...well, sometimes they do have sex." The idea of Sarnower having this conversation with his own father was unthinkable.

"I want to live with Mom," the boy announced.

Sarnower let the words hang in the air. A statement like that deserved space around it, framed by time, a chance to sink in. Mitch sounded as though he had reached an end-point. The patchwork, catch-as-catch-can life he had been forced to accept was fraying around the edges, and Sarnower's dalliance was the final insult. He wasn't buying the edited version of his mother's condition any longer. The boy had cut him as much slack as he could.

"How would things be better living with Mom?"

"She wouldn't leave me at camp when everyone else is gone. She wouldn't be having sex with her secretary," he answered with certainty. Of course, those would be exactly the kinds of things Cassie *would* do.

He regretted instantly owning up to his reckless behavior. He should have lied. In no way was Mitch ready to deal with his infidelities on top of everything else, and by some chance if word got back to Cassie that he'd slept with Nina, it might compromise his case.

Turning on to their street, Sarnower saw Tracey Bowen in T-shirt and shorts mowing the lawn. She had cut the grass in tidy, even rows and was working on stray weeds and stalks at the edges. He honked his horn lightly and she looked up. Sarnower waved, but got no response. Soon the entire block would have him blacklisted, he could only imagine what Mrs. Gould was up to, how far from the epicenter the news of his falling-apart life had spread. *The Efficient Gossip: Some Reflections on Character Assassination in the Information Age.*

As he pulled into the driveway, Sarnower could hear the phone ring from inside the house. So this was to be his new exquisite form of torture: a circle in Dante's inferno, the perpetually ringing phone. He lunged out of the car and on to the lawn, dashing for the front door. He'd make the last ring.

"Hello."

"So you just make love to your women and leave them to fend for themselves, is that it?"

"Nina!"

"At least you remembered my name. I guess that's all a girl can hope for these days. How did it go?"

"Hard to say. Not great. They weren't all that encouraging, particularly about Mitch."

"They're not seriously thinking of letting her take him?"

"Bottom line? It's all up for grabs. There's no telling what's going to happen. Ballestracci suggested I try to put this thing back together if I can."

"After what she's done?"

"There's no way. It's too far-gone. I have no feelings for her at all."

93

Nina chewed this over, silent. Sarnower heard Mitch, already up in his room, on his phone with a friend.

"I don't know what to say."

"You don't have to say anything," he chuckled. "It's not your problem."

He regretted that instantly. No, it wasn't her problem, but that was pushing her away, letting her know that part of his life was off limits.

"I didn't mean that," he corrected. "I'm not trying to shut you out, you've got to know that. I just don't want to burden you with this crap."

"It's not a burden. Actually, I just called to give you your messages from the office."

He realized he was making a bid for her ear, her sympathy. He wanted to talk, lay it all out, get her input. But she'd called on business.

"Shoot," he said, getting out a pen and pad of paper.

"There aren't many. Dr. Abravanel. I guess you never called him back. He wants you to present at Grand Rounds on Wednesday, your paper on narcissism and depression. Mr. and Mrs. Fishburg, they needed to see you right away, I booked them for tomorrow. And..." she flipped through some papers. "I guess the rest can wait. A couple of things from building maintenance. They're going to be putting down new carpet in the lobby in a few of weeks, there will be some traffic disruption, uh...some bills, a note from management about the rent increase in September..."

That voice, familiar, gravelly. He'd heard it moan with pleasure just days ago and was filled with an immense, tender longing. It hit him hard and suddenly, like a panic attack. Cassie was gone; he might well lose Mitch, the house, even his practice after the rumors circulated, who knew? Would he get Nina? End up with her? He had to know that second. Did she really call to give him messages, or was it a veiled bid to find out what she meant to him? Her kidding around at the beginning of the call, *was* she one of his women? This was not the time to play the debonair, dangerous boyfriend.

"Sounds like a whole lot of fun. Especially the new carpet."

She laughed. "It's going to be mauve."

"I thought mauve went out in the mid-eighties." That's it. Keep it jocular and sophisticated.

"Mel Styles probably found an old abandoned warehouse full of the stuff."

Styles, their office landlord was continually looking for ways to cut corners: cheap paint, cheap carpet and cheap labor. God knew what starvation wages he paid Miroslav and his crew. Only the rent was expensive. And going up, apparently.

"No doubt a warehouse owned by his mother-in-law," Sarnower continued. The best way to keep her is to get her to want to be with you. If she gets a whiff of desperate clinginess, she's gone. Chill. She wants banter; give her banter. He heard a sharp whistle in the distance.

"I've got water boiling for tea," she said. "I'll let you go. I just wanted to get you caught up before tomorrow."

She was going to leave it at that. She wasn't going to ask to come over, nor would she invite him over to her place, where, it occurred to him, he had never been. A sudden lust moment: He was at her duplex in West Roxbury (he knew at least where she lived.) He was carrying a nice saucy bottle of Bordeaux, perhaps one of Tug's legendary joints as well. He'd hear her come to the door. She'd be barefoot, wearing a tight, worn pair of jeans, a T-shirt like the other night, no bra. Her hair would be down. Furniture would be sparse, tasteful, a sure feminine presence to the place.

There would be candles, sticks of incense, and a woven hemp rug in the living room. She'd have a bookcase with well-thumbed copies of *Zen and the Art of Motorcycle Maintenance*, *On the Road*, a couple of other titles by Kerouac, a beat poet or two, some Doris Lessing, Anais Nin, Naomi Wolfe, Sylvia Plath's *The Bell Jar*, poems by Anne Sexton, definitely a thick manual of Tantric Yoga, a Kama Sutra, *The Tao According to Pooh*. Books on organic gardening and cooking. There would be an aging but still serviceable stereo system, probably inherited in a break-up from an old boyfriend. CDs of Led Zeppelin, Metallica (of course), Eric Clapton, Aerosmith, Mozart's Greatest Hits and Vivaldi's *Four Seasons*.

He'd follow her down a small hall into the kitchen, transfixed by her curves, the way her hair fell down her back, swaying gently. There'd be a few dishes in the sink from earlier (he was sure she wasn't a neatnik.) On the counter, long glass jars with corks on top full of fresh pasta and grains, a few high-quality cooking items from Williams Sonoma, a chrome spice rack. She'd open a cabinet and take out two large glasses, more appropriate as brandy snifters, but who cared. Suavely, he'd open the bottle of wine and pour into the glasses. They'd clink, look into each other's eyes and move in together for a kiss. They'd take their wine and the bottle a little further down the hall into her bedroom.

In the center there would be a large double bed (single women always had large double beds), low to the ground. An Indian print bedspread, a braided throw rug on the floor. On the wall, an Ansel Adams-type photo of her home state, Washington: fog over the Cascade Mountains, Puget Sound at dawn. On a simple wooden dresser (ersatz Shaker), a couple of framed pictures: her parents hiking together in the woods, her brother on a motorcycle mugging like James Dean, and some half used bottles of perfume. Another candle. She'd light it and sit on the bed. He'd join her. They'd finish the wine and then smoke Tug's incredible Columbian pot. He'd...

"Alan? Alan?"

"Sorry."

"Alan, are you all right? Are you going to be able to see patients tomorrow?"

"Sure, why not?"

"You drifted away again."

"Sorry."

"Don't *be* sorry!" She was annoyed. "That's the point. If you can't pull it together now, then *don't.* You don't need to be a hero. I can take care of the office for a few days."

"I'm ok, really."

"Yeah, I can hear that."

"Getting back to the office now would be the best thing for me, take my mind off all this."

She was silent, fed up, slipping away. Sarnower felt desperation close his throat. He had to do something, say something. Now.

"Nina?" No. Don't bring up Saturday night. She doesn't even think you're in you right mind.

"Yes?"

"Nothing. I'll see you tomorrow in the office."

Chapter 5

EMANUEL ABRAVANEL, MD, Chief of Psychiatry at Beacon General stood all of five feet five inches, with a wild corona of gray hair, more white than black, and a close cropped salt and pepper beard, the mandatory Freudian look gone slightly amok. Manny, as he was known by everyone, was a valued colleague and one-time mentor who had set the tone for psychiatry in Boston for decades. He'd studied with some of the legendary greats: David Wechsler at Bellevue, Anna Freud in London, Loretta Bender and Ervin Semrad. He and Sarnower had grown close over the years. They'd shared cases, covered for each other when one was on vacation and regularly sought out the other's advice on especially difficult patients. When Manny's wife Beth was killed by a drunk teenage driver fifteen years before, it was Alan to whom he turned.

Sarnower had known Beth well, they were occasional tennis partners and discovered other interests in common too: Indian cooking, Puccini operas, crossword puzzles and British mystery novels. Although they constantly joked about running away together, there was never anything except a close friendship that Sarnower had come to treasure all the more since he and Cassie had fewer and fewer things to share.

Beth's sudden death had left Sarnower reeling too, distraught, raw and torn up for months. Manny had climbed into himself for a year or better. He'd taken a hiatus from his practice and hospital duties to stare at the walls and scream. Sarnower would drop by his large empty Chestnut Hill home frequently, bringing food, clean clothes and books. He'd arranged for a housekeeper to come twice a month to clean. At first Manny would protest, yell at him to get out, leave him alone, but Sarnower wouldn't listen, he kept charging in.

He took over some of Manny's caseload and kept him apprised of the progress his patients were making.

Gradually the man came back, at first tentative, pale and abstracted. He kept limited office hours and had started on anti-depressants, but was at least able to go through the motions with some degree of persuasiveness. Two years later he was back, supervising nervous interns, running the department, butting heads with the dead wood and playing his unyieldingly bad games of poker and tennis.

Sarnower had run interference for Manny during that terrible time, picking up slack, working as his representative and amanuensis, handling the correspondence, editing galleys of articles due by deadline at various professional journals, all in addition to his own practice. In repayment, Manny had elevated his status at the hospital to Attending Physician and had cut back on his teaching and administrative duties. Though Manny was over twenty years older, they had grown together like brothers, and if Manny wanted a Grand Rounds presentation, that's what he'd get.

But now in his car heading toward the office, he thought of Nina and that strange, ambivalent call. His distractibility, the vacant gaps now so clearly out in the open, weren't going to help his standing with her. Sure she was devoted and patient, and cared about him, but he didn't want to be cared about as an injured puppy to be nursed through one crisis after another. He needed to be assertive, taking it all in stride, proactive, smooth, making it all look easy. She shouldn't have to see the seams, the crumbs under the table, the strings being worked.

He should take a few pages from Tug's playbook. Sarnower had always suspected that Tug had gotten as far as he had because he genuinely didn't care. Whatever happened was ok, he'd buy or talk or tap dance his way around or out of anything. Why couldn't he be more like that? Devil-may-care, fuck-it-all. The only people offered sex and credit are those that don't need them, Tug had once told him. Tug didn't need anything, he really didn't. He could be just as happy living in a hut on a beach somewhere, and because his needs were truly minimal, sex, credit, money, dope all flew his way continually. But the man would never light on anything; he'd never commit himself to a woman, a house, a brand of toothpaste, or a way of life. He'd never have children, Sarnower was convinced, even though he often paid lip-service to the idea of family and stability. But at the end of the day, predictability weighed him down and made him itchy and restless. It was much easier to travel light.

Travel light. Give Cassie the house, let her have custody of Mitch, sell the practice and hit the road. Become a boxcar hobo; see the country, the beautiful USA, go wherever the wind blew. He laughed out loud. That was the stuff of dust-bowl melodramas. No one did that kind of thing anymore; it was too dangerous. He'd get his throat slit before he reached Altoona.

He pulled into the office parking lot and turned off the ignition. Ok, from here on out, new routine. No more woolgathering. Front and center. After a good night's sleep, Nina would see him rested, relaxed, ready to take it all on again.

He walked toward the building, standing tall, affecting a jaunty bounce in his step. He opened the door and received the familiar blast of cold air. Inside, the lobby was almost empty. Neither Miroslav nor his industrious crew was anywhere to be found. A couple of old women were sitting on a bench next to the fishpond, waiting for the flamboyant and perpetually late orthopedic surgeon Dr. Jaspers to make his arrival. An elderly man with a walker stood by the elevator waiting for it to transport him to whatever health care professional he was here to see. Sarnower hated the term Health Care Professional. As opposed to what? Health Care Amateur? HMOs were wrecking the language as well as the medical system. Right out of Orwell.

There in front of his door stood Dr. Mary Fontana, one of the interns he supervised regularly at Beacon General. Because she lived so close to Sarnower's office, they met there rather than at the hospital for her hour. It was always good to see Mary first thing on Tuesday morning, she was bright, learned fast and, Sarnower believed, harbored a small crush on him. Even though she was plain in a 1950s bobbed hair sort of way, and he had never had an erotic thought (well, maybe one) about her, it made him feel good to be a mentor to her. By now Mary should have been in the waiting room making small talk with Nina. What was she doing outside?

"Hi Dr. Sarnower," she said, picking up her briefcase. "The door seems to be locked."

"That's odd, Nina should be here," he said, fishing in his pocket for keys. His stomach sank. Their encounter, Nina's call last night. She's left; it was too much for her. He knew it. Shit, here he had to go and ruin a really good thing. Who could he hire now? Who could take her place, just as an office manager, never mind the bouquet of fringe benefits?

He opened the door and the rubber stripping around the jam made a soft "whoosh" like vacuum-packed coffee. The office was dark, sealed like a tomb, the air conditioner hummed softly. He turned on lights and the waiting room materialized, but somehow a bit off center as if it were tilting at a barely perceptible three or four degrees. He looked in Nina's cubicle. Nothing had changed. Folders, bills, patient charts were lying in stacks as always. The few personal items she kept, a small photo, a tiny souvenir doll were still there. She could have stepped out to go to the bathroom.

"Why don't you go into my office while I check the messages," he said. She nodded quickly, and went into his office and sat, opening her briefcase to retrieve a case file. Sarnower went to Nina's desk. Before picking up the receiver and dialing, he tried to get some sense of her presence. He sniffed the air, hoping for a lingering bit of her scent, but she would often keep a bottle of Windex and wipe the desk down at the end of the day, obliterating any trace of her. Sometimes, she left a sweater draped on her chair to use if the air conditioning got particularly oppressive. There was no sweater. He opened her desk. Inside was a half used package of sugarless gum, an old issue of *Cosmopolitan*, some barrettes, and a lottery ticket. Nothing that remotely said Nina.

He dialed his answering service. Sarnower was one of the last remaining holdouts to use a live service for his practice instead of voice mail preferred by the majority of his colleagues. For what it was worth, he was still convinced a human voice on the other end offered at least a suggestion of the contact his patients needed.

"This is Dr. Sarnower, box 327."

"Just a moment, sir." He heard rustling in the background. "You have seven messages. A mister Baluchi called twice." Baluchi?

"You mean Ballestracci," Sarnower pronounced distinctly.

"It says 'Baluchi' here." Jesus, what was he paying all this money to an answering service for? He should listen to his colleagues. He inhaled deeply.

"Ok, next."

"Nina called. Call her as soon as possible at home."

Nina! Thank God. Maybe she was hurt or sick, he'd never even considered those possibilities. A family emergency. At least she was making some kind of contact.

"What time did that message from Nina come in?" he asked.

"Uh, it doesn't say here."

No Christmas bonus for you, schmuck.

"Next."

"A Mrs. Jessup. Do you need her number?"

"No, I have it."

She rattled off more names and Sarnower scrambled to write them down. He replaced the receiver and checked his watch. It was eight-forty five; his supervisory session should have started a quarter of an hour ago. He got up and walked to his office. Mary was sitting, reviewing her case. She looked up.

"I'm sorry, something's come up and I'm going to have to make some calls. We can meet for half an hour or reschedule, whatever your preference."

"I'll wait," she smiled.

"Ok, we'll make up the balance some other time," he said.

She nodded, not at all ruffled. Sarnower sat in Nina's ergonomically correct chair and punched in her home number. One, two, three rings.

"Hello." The voice was clogged and glutinous.

"Nina?"

"Alan." Sniffles, a choked back sob.

"Are you all right?"

"No."

"What's the matter? Are you hurt? Are you sick?"

There was silence, then the sound of Nina blowing her nose.

"Nina, what is it?"

"It's Doug. He killed himself last night."

Doug, the lightweight English grad student and Shakespearean actor who had such a gratifying way with his tongue, the one Nina had broken up with weeks before.

"I'm sorry. I'm so sorry."

He heard her try to pull herself together.

"What happened?" he asked softly. She took a deep breath.

"He cut his wrists...his friend Tyler...found him in the bathtub...they were supposed to go out last night." She started to cry again.

"Good God, that's awful. What can I do to help?"

"Nothing. I don't know...I...I can't really think now. I'll need the rest of the day off."

"That's fine, take as much time as you need. Take tomorrow too."

"Thanks."

"Nina, I'm right here."

"I know, and that means so much." She let out a small gasp and continued. "I spoke to him last week. He sounded so up, like he'd gotten over us and was trying to get on with his life."

Sarnower flinched involuntarily. He didn't think they were still in touch. Once she told him when she broke up with a guy that was it, they'd never talk or see each other again. None of that phony "maybe we can be friends" crap.

"Nina, sometimes when people finally make the decision to take their lives, they become happy, serene, peaceful. I know it sounds strange, but it takes an awful burden from them."

She was silent for a moment, considering his words. "That makes sense, I guess," she said slowly. "I just feel so guilty." Her voice was hoarse and grainy.

"Nothing you could have done would have changed anything. Suicide is a solitary train ride, the pull is stronger than anything else."

"I had no idea he was hurting so much."

"No one really knows anyone at all, at least not to the extent they think they do. Listen, we've all got demons. Most of the time we can keep them under control. Sometimes they get unbearably strong, anything we do to try to put them back in their cages is useless, they tear us apart with their fury."

He hadn't meant to wax so philosophical, but the moment seemed to call for something palliative. Nina gave a sad little chuckle.

"I knew there was a reason I've been with you so long," she said softly.

Sarnower could pick up a hint of the old sensuality in her voice. She was still connected, but the roles had shifted. Now he was the strong shoulder, the support, the one she could count on. It felt good.

"Maybe I shouldn't have broken up with him."

"The maybes, the ifs, the buts, you can whip yourself endlessly with all of that. It wouldn't have made any difference. There are thousands of reasons people take their lives. Often it's for something no one ever knew about."

She wasn't convinced, but now was not the time to try to sell her on it.

"I'd better go," she said. "I told Tyler I'd pick up Doug's mother at the airport. She's flying in from Omaha. I guess she's taking his body back."

"She'll be grateful for your support."

"Yeah, well I feel like I should do something."

"Sure. Give me a call later, just check in, let me know how you're doing."

"I'll see," she said tired, and hung up.

I'll see? The shock had made her fragile and noncommittal. And who was Tyler? Sarnower had never heard her mention his name. Nina had all these layers, and all these friends he didn't know. She would often mention a name he'd never heard before. Well, what had he just said to her? No one knows anyone to the extent they think they do. Here was living proof, as if he needed more.

Was she screwing Tyler? Was he one of Doug's fringy actor friends? Sarnower pictured a tall, almost handsome man as Doug had been, but not so sickly looking. Tyler would have an earring and seductive, dark piercing eyes. Perhaps he was bi-sexual in the trendy way many young men were taking to it now, like a new style of coat or Soho cocktail. He and Nina would console each other over drinks at a new hip South End bar, their mutual friendship with Doug already giving them a bond that would weave a warm sexual cocoon; then they'd be back at his small, mattress-on-the-floor loft fucking like rabbits. As for Sarnower, he'd return to being her benevolent employer, fading back into the role of kind father, their passionate night an aberration, unlikely to be repeated.

Discouraged, he hung up the phone. At least she was still working for him; that was something. He looked down the list of calls. Ballestracci. Shit. What did he want?

"Frazier, Abbott and Connors," came the familiar female voice.

"Mr. Ballestracci, please."

"One moment." At least they didn't interrogate him this time.

"Hello."

"Alan Sarnower returning your call."

"Yes. Listen, a couple of things. Stan has been in touch with Nora Lund, your wife's attorney? They've postponed Thursday's hearing."

"Fantastic."

"Not so fast. They want to depose you."

"Depose me? Christ, I don't have time for that kind of bullshit."

Ballestracci grunted, then laughed. "Pal, you don't have a choice in the matter."

"Can't you get me out of it?"

103

"No can do. Opposing counsel has every right to take a deposition as part of the discovery process. As I told you before, you'd better get used to having your life disrupted. It's only part of what makes divorce the thrilling experience it is."

"I can do without the sarcasm, thanks."

"Yeah, speaking of which, Stan tells me you don't want him on the case."

"Nick, I've got to tell you. I need a real heavy hitter. Cassie's brother Bill is coming to town soon. He's a big businessman from Chicago and he's going to put a lot of time and money into making sure I get toasted. I need someone who can stand up to all of them."

"What makes you think Stan isn't qualified?"

"He looks like a stiff breeze could blow him over."

"Oh, so because I'm big I can mow 'em down better?" Ballestracci was getting testy. "I'm afraid it doesn't work that way, doctor. This isn't the OK Corral. I..."

"Listen, Nick. I think for twenty grand I ought to be calling some of the shots here," Sarnower interrupted, his blood boiling. When Bill puffed himself up he could be truly frightening. He was scary to Sarnower. He'd scare the pants off Stan, but that was knowledge best kept to himself. "There's just too much at stake to fob this off on one of your...assistants. I want you handling this yourself. Personally."

There was a long uncomfortable silence.

"All right then. I'll take over your case myself, if that's really what you want."

"I do."

"You recall my fee? Five hundred an hour? Is this something you really want, because in that event, given your present financial condition, I'll need to take the deed to your house as collateral." Ballestracci's voice was steely.

What? The deed to his house?

"Yes, ok." The words flew out of his mouth before he knew he'd said them.

"All right, then. I'll notify you with details. Technically they have to give us a week's notice. In the meantime, they may send over some interrogatories for you to answer."

"I can hardly wait."

"You should have them completed and ready to go ASAP. Often, opposing counsel will use your responses as a basis for questioning during the deposition. Naturally, I'll be present during the meeting to advise you. That's about it. Oh, just a reminder that we need your retainer if you haven't put it in the mail already. Enclose the deed as well."

Sarnower replaced the receiver and rubbed his eyes. What the hell had he just done? The deed to his house, his pride and joy. He could actually lose it. Was he crazy? Was he really that desperate? Without his being aware of it, this had become a game of chicken, two cars charging toward each other. Who would swerve off the road first? It sure as hell wasn't going to be him. Cassie brings in Corrugated Bill; he brings in Nick, former heavy weight from New Jersey.

He looked at his watch. It was nine-thirty. Mary Fontana! He spun the chair around and dashed into his office. It was empty. She must have left quietly while he was on the phone. There was a note resting on his chair in her large, rounded female writing:

> Dear Dr. Sarnower,
> It was getting late and I had to leave.
> I didn't want to disturb you.
> Same time next week? M.F.

He stood alone in the center of his consulting room, Mary's note in his hand, and felt something snap. It was subtle and quiet, like a barely noticed twist of the ankle which hours later swells in a nasty fracture. The floor started to slant just slightly, like being on a small boat in placid water. He saw black floaters, specks of dust start to dance and move randomly in his visual field. At that moment, he lost sensation in his body, as he had a few days before when the process server had come to his office to deliver Cassie's petition. Objects looked flat and one dimensional, as if painted on cardboard. Out in the parking lot a young mother had been pulled into a power struggle with her toddler. She was yelling, he could hear the words as sounds, but couldn't attach any meaning to them.

Slowly he sat down. So this is what losing your mind feels like. He was in brand new territory. Should he panic? He'd never felt like this before. Continuing to breathe, in and out was all he could do. You're the pro; use some of that training on yourself. Maybe it's the summer flu that's been going around. He was susceptible; he'd hardly been taking the best care of himself. He looked at Mary's note and noticed his hand was shaking. Dear Dr. Sarnower. How dear was he to her? How dear was he to anyone? Perhaps old Doug was on to something after all. Plenty of smart people thought suicide was a rational, intelligent choice. Why not? Why not take your life if it became absolutely unmanageable, if you just couldn't work the machinery of living anymore? I give up, I retire, I'm outta here. He wouldn't have to fork over the deed to his house; he'd be rid of Cassie and all her poison forever. The whole tortured thing with Nina resolved. Tug? He'd find someone else to play aging college buddy with.

But Mitch? He'd never see his son again. The boy would have to grow up without a father. That seemed like an inconceivably cruel thing to do to the only person in the world he genuinely loved, and who genuinely loved him back. Mitch hadn't asked for any of this, he hadn't asked to be born. None of this terrible mess was of his making. The thought of his son growing up alone under Cassie's haphazard, reckless guidance made him wince. The boy would drift to the wrong crowd; he'd cut school, get into drugs and scrapes with the law. A good kid who was neglected was trouble. He'd seen a lot of it in his own practice. No. That wasn't going to happen. Like it or not, he'd have to stick around and punch his way out.

He looked at the note again: "Dear Dr. Sarnower, it was getting late and I had to leave." It *is* getting late. Outside, the young mother and her rebellious toddler were nowhere to be seen. The office was perfectly still. Would it be possible to get up? Could he reconnect his brain to his legs? Getting up was generally something you did without thinking, in fact on the face of it thinking about it could make it impossible to do. *Just do it* as that silly *faux*-Zen sneaker ad commanded. Continue on this track for another five years and you'll be a *bona fide* catatonic. The thought made him laugh out loud. *Prelude to Catatonia: Some Musings from One About to Begin the Journey.* Don't think about thinking about getting up. His thoughts were folding in on themselves like an infinite Mobius strip.

One thing was clear. There was no way he was going to be able to see patients today, or tomorrow for that matter. In fact, why not take the rest of the week off? Nina's absence for what might be an indeterminate amount of time would add considerably to his workload, a strain he'd be unable to manage. In the past when she'd taken vacations, he'd held up well, he'd been nimble, had his wits about him. Now he was sitting in his consulting room wondering if he could rise from his chair.

He picked up his appointment book, opened his Rolodex and began dialing. Most of his patients were at work and he left messages on their voice mail. Surprisingly, he could still talk, although the voice felt disembodied, coming out of nowhere.

"This is Dr. Sarnower calling. I'll need to be out of the office this week and will have to cancel our appointment. Please contact my secretary to reschedule. Thank you."

Fortunately, things were lighter in the summer, people were away; there were only sixteen or seventeen patients to call.

It was almost noon. At least he was capable of some kind of purposeful activity. He closed his appointment book and stood up. There, that wasn't so hard. But now he heard voices, conspiratorial whispers. It sounded as if they were coming from his waiting room. Were they in his head or were there real humans out there? As he approached the door he saw Mr. and Mrs. Fishburg looking as tiny as small children in his overstuffed leather couch, here for their appointment. He'd completely forgotten, although Nina had told him last night. As usual, they were bickering back and forth in low, bristling tones like static on an old radio. It would be best to see them, keep the appointment and then leave. He could probably get through the session, he'd gone on automatic pilot with them before and they'd never noticed.

The Fishburgs, a small, shrinking couple in their late sixties or early seventies had been seeing him for the better part of ten years. The wife was continually distraught and anxious about one thing or another but she was firmly convinced that psychotherapy would deliver her and her husband from the constant sniping that had infected their marriage for over forty years. "Believe me, one day it's all going to kick in and we'll be out of your hair forever, doctor," she would regularly tell Sarnower as they left his office. Her husband would grunt and shrug his shoulders. Although there were chairs in the waiting area, they would always plant themselves in his low-slung leather couch. When Sarnower suggested easier seating, she would shake her head and give him a dismissive wave.

"My life with Herman, it's already a *tsimmes*. This is nothing."

Today Mrs. Fishburg was more upset than usual. "Doctor, where *are* you? We're waiting here twenty minutes."

Sarnower stood, unable to answer.

"You look pale," Herman growled.

"I haven't been feeling well. A touch of summer flu," he answered.

"We can come back some other time. You should go home and get some rest," Mrs. Fishburg said. She turned to her husband. "Come, Herman, let's let the doctor go home."

"No, no I'm fine, let's go." That seemed satisfactory. He led them into the consulting room.

It was close to two when Sarnower locked the door to his office, his hands still trembling as he put the key in the lock. He couldn't remember feeling so shaky, at such loose ends. Mitch absolutely had to be picked up by four or he'd deal with the wrath of Mrs. Watkins on top of everything else. He tried to make sense of the morning, his brush with something truly scary, a huge sinkhole that had started to open in his mind. He could sleep for a week.

He should talk to someone. Manny! He was going to call him anyway about presenting his paper at Grand Rounds. But that was before this morning and the depressing conversations with Nina and Ballestracci. He was in no shape to do it now.

Sarnower had always prided himself on his skill and showmanship as a speaker. He would choreograph his presentation, opening slowly, often with a joke or anecdote, putting his audience at ease. He'd start low, the sea of faces would be alert, all eyes on him; he'd terrace his argument, building point on top of point, then crescendo toward the end, tying the whole thing together with the grand sweep of an aria. There would be enthusiastic applause, often an ovation. Then, he'd take questions, playing with the answers, weaving disparate strands together, sometimes quoting a philosopher, Shakespeare, a Beat Poet, a Grateful Dead lyric, all off the top of his head, while casually sitting on a stool away from the lectern. Very Frank Sinatra. You could learn a lot from the Chairman of the Board.

Today he'd have to let Manny down. That in itself was bad, but now he would ask him to listen and support, to climb down into the depths with him and taste his fear. Sarnower had no doubt he'd be glad to help, but he hated to ask. The man had been through so much himself. Of course Sarnower had been there in Manny's darkest hours, and he'd come through with high honors and lots of markers. Now he was about to call some of them in. But what stupid terms to put things in! We're old friends, we go back, we trust each other. True enough, but the ecology of the friendship would shift.

Now at home in his study, Sarnower dialed Manny's private office number at the hospital.

"Hello?"

"Manny, it's Alan."

"So tell me please. What do I have to do to get your attention?"

Sarnower was warmed at once by the familiar old world schmaltz.

"I'm sorry. Look, I'm in trouble. I was hoping we could talk."

"Of course. What's the matter?"

Sarnower took a deep breath. "You know I've been having all these problems with Cassie."

"I heard. I'm very sorry. I should have called."

"That's ok. Something really frightening happened at the office today. I...I...felt as if I were starting to lose my mind."

"Where are you now?"

"At home."

"How are you feeling?"

"A little better. Still shaky. I cancelled my patients for the rest of the week."

"Good. Alan, I have to ask. Are you in danger of hurting yourself?"

Sarnower chuckled. It was odd to be on the receiving end of this question, one that he himself had asked of patients a thousand times over the years. To be completely honest, that morning he'd had suicidal thoughts, but to admit that to Manny now over the phone would not be a good idea. His candor with Mitch the other day had not been smart. He needed to be careful.

"No."

"Ok, good." He heard Manny flip the pages of his large appointment book. "Listen, I'm flat out with patients and *farshtinkiner* meetings all day. You want to come in tomorrow?"

"I'm free all day. What time?"

"First thing."

"I've got to get Mitch to camp."

"How's the boy doing?"

"As well as can be expected."

"Ach, its always so tough on them."

"How's ten?"

"I have an appointment. I'll move it, we'll meet."

"Thanks."

"Hey, we're family here, yes? No thanks required."

The line went dead. Manny never said goodbye; he considered it bad luck. For all his standing in the community, his vast knowledge, his formidable contacts, he harbored small pockets of ritual and superstition, a holdover, he would tell close friends, from his upbringing with shtetl-born Eastern European parents.

Relieved, Sarnower slumped back in his chair. We're family. Manny would take good care of him. But there'd be no pussyfooting or hand holding, he would tell it like it was, say what needed to be said. He was the same with everyone, colleagues, students and patients. "You want a soft tummy rub?" he would ask hostilely, "watch Dr. Bill on TV and save my time and your money." His seniority and stature combined with the physical appearance of an Old Testament prophet gave him a gravitas and wide leeway not granted to others, and he took full advantage of it.

At the house, an hour hung in front of him, unaccustomed time to fill before he had to pick up Mitch. He should get Ballestracci's check in the mail before he alienated the guy any further. A payment of that size would have to come from his mutual fund account. Where was the checkbook, or the deed to the house for that matter? He'd last seen the checks on his desk, but that was months ago when a large insurance premium was due. Since then, the disarray had increased dramatically. Take some time, clean it up, a place for everything and everything in its place, his grandmother used to say as she went around her small apartment in the Bronx cleaning, dusting, vacuuming on Friday mornings to prepare for *shabbos* dinner. The check he was going to write for Ballestracci would amount to two or three times his grandparents' annual income.

Piles. Separate everything into piles, weeding and throwing out as you go. He cleared a large space on the study floor. There were bills, receipts, correspondence, articles, ads, coupons, things that looked interesting at the time saved for future reading; they were all going. When it doubt, throw it out. The stacks mounted rapidly. Sarnower went to the kitchen for a large, plastic trash bag. Soon it was filled and the surface of his desk came into view like a sandbar at low tide. There was his checkbook, but now it was time to get Mitch. He'd write the check when he got back and get it out first thing the next day. He thought briefly of canceling his visit with Manny in the morning as he grabbed the bag and headed out the door.

The phone was ringing when he returned with Mitch.

"Alan?"

"Nina! Thank God. How are you?" He was almost breathless.

"Better. I'm glad it's over."

"I bet."

"Doug's mother is a real piece of work. I think she's about to blow."

"Not surprised. You should have given her my card."

"She's not going to be here long."

"Mmmm."

"Don't you have a hearing or something coming up?"

"They put it off. I have to give a deposition sometime next week instead."

"That sounds like loads of fun."

"I've cancelled all my patients for the rest of the week. You can take it off. With pay."

"You sound tired."

"I am."

"I think we need to talk."

"About the other night?"

"Yes."

Sarnower was silent. This never led to anything good. The big kiss-off.

"Can we do this later?" he asked, his stomach tightening.

"Sure."

Another silence. The house was completely quiet. The refrigerator hummed. Was Nina waiting him out as Ballestracci had? It was a technique he used sometimes with patients, to mobilize their anxiety into something useful. Now it just hurt.

"I'm worried about you Alan."

The old pity train pulling into the station. Best to back out now. What happened to the new Devil-may-care Sarnower?

"I'm fine, really." The doorbell rang. "I've got to go. There's someone at the door."

"Alan?" she asked, almost imploring.

"Yes?"

"Try to be kind to yourself." It was in the upturned cadence of a question.

"I will, Nina. Thanks."

The bell rang again and Sarnower hung up the phone and went to the door. Through the window he could see a Fed-Ex truck and the driver at his door, a thick envelope in one hand, a clipboard in the other.

"Alan Sarnower?" he asked cheerfully.

"Yes."

"Sign here, please." He offered the clipboard and a pen and indicated a blank line for the signature. Sarnower scribbled something that looked nothing like his name. The man handed him the thick envelope.

"Have a good one," he called half way down the walk. He made a fluid, gazelle-like jump into the cab of his truck and roared off.

Sarnower took the package inside. On the upper left-hand corner in bold letters: The Law Offices of Nora Lund, Esq. and the address, a street in Brighton he'd never heard of. An interesting choice of type font for a lawyer, vaguely Gothic—medieval and menacing. And how many law offices did she have? A computer-printed address label with borders in black like an "in memoriam" box in the obit section framed his name and address. Wishful thinking on her part, but he wasn't dead yet.

He ripped open the envelope and pulled out a thick stack of papers bound together by a black metal pinch clip.

"Interrogatories for Alan Sarnower, M.D." in capital letters. A few pages of boilerplate legalese. He could have an attorney present when responding. Answers must be made separately and fully in writing, under penalty of perjury, objections must be signed by an attorney, and on and on. There were questions about his training, assets, income, current positions, habits, drug and alcohol use. At the back was a return envelope for his completed responses.

He dropped the papers on the mail table in the hall. The shit just didn't stop flowing. What to do now? He'd have to be getting dinner ready for Mitch. He could call Nick. It was after five, but those lawyers worked insane hours thinking up irritating questions like these. They're the mosquitoes of the world.

"Ballestracci here," came the beefy voice after Sarnower had passed through the various phone shields.

"This is Alan Sarnower. I've just received the interrogatories from my wife's attorney."

"Ok, just fill them out. Be very brief, to the point. Don't give anything away, you'll do fine."

"One thing...it asks about drug use."

"And?" Nick was concerned.

"Well, uh, I have."

"I see. What have you used and when did you last use it?"

"Pot. Probably...a week ago. I mean my wife is a huge consumer of various substances, is this going to..."

"Look. You have to answer truthfully, you're under oath and you can be charged with perjury if you don't. We'll figure out how to handle this. I'm not saying it's going to help your case any, but it's not the end of the world, particularly if your wife uses also. But try to stay on the straight and narrow until this is all over."

"Ok."

"I'll be in touch with you before the deposition, and give you the details of the meeting. Maybe we can even get some sort of proposal out and start talking terms."

"That would be nice." He hung up the phone.

"What would be nice?" Mitch asked from the door.

"Dinner would be nice, champ. What do you feel like?"

"You weren't talking about dinner, you were talking about divorcing Mom." The boy locked on him and wouldn't let go.

"That's right, I was."

"I'm scared," he said. Sarnower drew him close. He'd grown dramatically that summer and was already inching past his shoulder. It wouldn't be long before the boy would tower over him.

"I'm scared too," he said softly as he put his arms around his son.

* * *

Beacon General Hospital sat in the long row of medical complexes that lined both sides of Longwood Avenue. The ancient building was recessed half a block in from the other structures, creating a small, protected courtyard, landscaped with lawns, benches and a miniature reproduction of a Roman fountain. On nice days, hospital personnel could be seen there eating lunch, chatting, sneaking cigarettes.

When he'd been more active in a teaching and consulting role, Sarnower would hold meetings with his interns on the lawn to discuss cases. He'd always felt the hospital environment claustrophobic and oppressive and not conducive to the lateral and creative thinking good psychotherapy demanded.

A couple of interns greeted him has he walked down the main corridor, past the information and admission desks toward the old temperamental elevators. Manny was on the third floor and had an office adjacent to the locked ward, where screams, moans and general cacophony could be heard around the clock, despite the continual refinements of psychotropic drugs. He'd once asked Manny why, with all his clout in the hospital he hadn't moved to a quieter, more remote office space. The man had looked at him with those soft blue eyes, "I have to be near my material," he said, as if asked to explain the perfectly obvious, why a pitcher and glass go together.

Sarnower got out of the elevator, rounded the first corner, and there on the door, as it had been for decades, was a varnished mahogany sign with old gold leaf lettering announcing Chief of Psychiatry. The door was literally always open. Inside, Sandra Marsh, Manny's elderly secretary who had been with him since before anyone could remember, looked up from her computer screen.

"Hi, Alan. He's waiting for you."

"Thanks, Sandra," he said and walked past her. He entered the office and there was Manny in a typical pose, feet crossed and up on his messy desk, reading glasses perched on his forehead, looking out the window. He was dictating progress notes into an old-style Dictaphone, much the same as he'd done for years. He smiled and motioned for Sarnower to close the door, finishing his sentence and turning off the machine.

"When are you going to get a real Dictaphone?" Sarnower asked.

"This *is* a real Dictaphone."

"I mean one that was made *after* World War I."

Manny ignored the remark. "So? What can I do for you Alan?"

Sarnower sat. The air was hot and close on his face.

"I had a bit of a scare yesterday. I don't really know, something snapped. One minute the world was right, everything made sense, you know, then...the floor tilted, things had a strange flatness, I got these weird floating specks in my visual field. I felt completely cut off from my body. For a while I couldn't talk."

The older man listened without speaking, squinting and stroking his beard.

"How are you feeling now?" he asked finally.

"Better, although I think it could happen again. And not go away."

"You're under a lot of stress."

Sarnower nodded. Manny leaned back in his chair.

"Your body is talking to you, Alan. Are you listening? It's asking you questions," he said finally. "What are you going to answer?"

"I'm sorry?" Sarnower was confused. Manny's oracular, elliptical style was too much now. He could only hope the old man would connect the dots.

"Well, you've got three choices. You can kill yourself, you can go insane and book a bed with us in the next room," he gestured toward the locked ward, "or you can hunker down, fight through this and continue to lead your life. You need an assist? I can write you a script. You sleeping?"

"Yes."

"Eating? Sex?"

"Yes. To both."

Manny smiled and raised his eyebrows. "Well, you're not too sick to be *shtupping*. Don't worry, I won't ask with whom."

"I'm not sure I'd tell."

"Good. You need some secrets. They keep the juices flowing."

Sarnower looked at the old man, a laugh bubbling up inside.

"Are you getting any of this?"

Sarnower was at a loss; he'd forgotten just how much of a virtuoso Manny was.

"I can see you're in awe of my clinical acumen," he chuckled. "Look, Alan, it's very simple. This depression, depersonalization you feel yourself sliding into. You're handing off responsibility, you want someone else to make your decisions, cook your breakfast and do your dirty work. That's why you're here. You want me to tell you, in the guise of some sophisticated psychobabble, what you should be doing. Yes? It's like I said a minute ago, your body, your neurons, your muscles are asking questions. 'What's next?' 'Where are we going?' You're a car, all revved up but you're in neutral. No one likes to make decisions, no one likes to grow up, you're closing doors, saying goodbye, moving on. Breaking up is hard to do."

"That's a song lyric, Manny. Cassie and I have already broken up."

"That's not what I'm saying." Manny shook his head. "For a bright man you're really *farblugent*."

"What?"

"You've forgotten all your Yiddish too? Out of it, lost. For Christ sake, you're mourning your life, Alan, the one you've known and lived in all these years. It's not one person. Your life as you've known it is gone and it's never coming back. You're starting over. From scratch. Maybe even before scratch. You're going to reinvent, rediscover the world, the whole ball of wax, from the ground up. You're scared shitless, naturally. We're all scared when we have to give up everything that's near and dear."

Sarnower shook his head. "It's not just that."

"Oh?"

"I'm..." He looked around at the closed office door and got up. "I'm having these thoughts." He took a deep breath. "About killing Cassie."

The old man smiled. "Of course you are. You're angry as hell. You've had your heart ripped out. At the risk of making a value judgment, I have to say your wife has behaved reprehensibly. We all have irrational thoughts when someone hurts us badly, throws our life into complete disarray."

Sarnower shook his head. "It's more than that. The other day I had to give my lawyer the deed to the house as collateral for his services. The fucking deed for Christ sake! Why? Because I don't have enough assets to cover his $500 an hour fee!"

"Is it money, Alan? I can float you a loan until you're back on your feet."

"It's money, it's Mitch, it's me. It's everything. The past few days, having her killed, even doing it myself is all I think about. I can't let it go. She doesn't just want a divorce Manny, she wants to destroy me."

"But surely you're not serious about this...impulse. It's totally crazy."

"I know."

Manny reached across his desk for his prescription pad and began to write. He ripped off the top sheet and pushed it across the desk.

"Xanax. You need to relax and get some rest, Alan. Continue this way and you'll destroy yourself, you won't even need her help."

Sarnower sat down and took the prescription.

Manny got up and walked in front of his desk. He leaned back and crossed his arms.

"You remember when Beth was killed?" Sarnower nodded. "I thought I was going to lose my mind too. I'm not going to revisit all that again, but the one thing I learned, it finally dawned on me. I was completely, totally alone. If I killed myself or went bonkers, or screwed up my life completely, as you seem to be contemplating, it wouldn't matter to anyone. Not a whit."

Sarnower started to say something, but Manny raised his hand quickly to silence him.

"Thanks, but no thanks for the easy sympathy you're itching to dispense. Let's be grown-ups here for a minute. Of course Beacon General would throw a lavish memorial; there'd be plenty of sobbing, wonderful, choked-up eulogies and testimonials, maybe even a scholarship funded in my name. And you know what? Inside of two years, no probably less, it's 'who's this schmuck Abravanel?' A name on a plaque, that's who. The twenty-three books and God knows how many articles I've written? They'll be no more alive than my tombstone."

A jagged scream pierced the wall from the ward. Sarnower started.

"You hear that?" Manny asked. "That guy is fighting exactly the same demons you are, but he's way ahead of you, my friend. The only difference between you and him is, I'm betting you'll find your way out. He probably won't. You're rich, so you're troubled. He's poor, so he's fucking nuts."

Sarnower felt the blood drain out of his body. He hadn't bargained for this, the full-court press, the bucket of ice-cold water, the deluxe Abravanel treatment. Talking for any length of time with Manny was like sitting through *Schindler's List* about four times. But the bone he'd hit you over the head with had plenty of meat.

"You ought to read philosophy, Alan," he said softly, coming off his peroration. "Forget all those *ferchachte* psychiatry journals. They're exercises in masturbation, pathetic pleas for tenure, worthless drek, most of it. Read Camus, Sartre, Kierkegaard, Viktor Frankel. Now those guys knew a thing or two about what a pain in the ass living could be. You know, you should also rotate through our unit once in a while too. It would keep all you fancy private practitioners honest. Come down here to earth and see what all the screaming is *really* about."

It was true. After his training, Sarnower had fled as fast as he could to the cushy embrace of a private practice in the suburbs. As an intern, he'd had it with the long hours, the terrible pay and the high-maintenance, demanding, manipulative patients. The air on the ward always crackled like a high-tension wire. It was enough. He'd make his own hours; see the mildly depressed, the vaguely anxious, the walking wounded, couples wanting to "improve their relationships." He'd work on "self-esteem issues" with upper middle-class teenagers who did Ecstasy, cracked up cars, stole money from their clueless parents and generally didn't give a rat's ass whether or not they lived or died. What a sick joke the whole thing had become.

For some reason he still couldn't grasp, Manny thrived on the hellish chaos of the ward. He drew some sort of strength from those souls in excruciating agony. Sarnower had seen him work the ward many times. When Manny passed through that heavy locked door, the decibel level would fall; an eerie calm would descend. He would speak very softly, often making some kind of physical contact, a hand on the shoulder or a touch to the elbow. He'd move slowly, training his blue eyes directly into theirs, inviting them to share his peace. Christ healing the lepers was an image that had struck many observers over the years. Nurses and attendants would relax knowing things, at least for the time being, were under control.

"Alan? Alan?" Manny was waving his hand in front of Sarnower's face. "I see I've put you in a trance, which is too bad because I no longer use hypnosis in my practice."

"At least not consciously," Sarnower retorted.

Manny laughed. "Point taken. I need to be deflated about once an hour these days." He looked at his watch, an old gold Patek Philippe Beth had given him on their twenty-fifth wedding anniversary. Sarnower had never seen him without it.

"Are we done here?" he asked. "Because if we are, I have *real* work to do as opposed to hand-holding one of my piss-and-moan colleagues. I'll expect you to contact Sandra in the next week to schedule your talk on narcissism and depression—my fee for this consultation."

Manny moved toward him to shake hands, but Sarnower pulled him into a tight embrace and held him absolutely still as his tears ran down the old man's face.

Chapter 6

"YOU FUCKING retired or what?"

"Tug?"

"I drop by your office yesterday during business hours when normal folks are earning a living, you're nowhere to be found. Shit, man, I wish I could lock up *my* doors and head for Turks and Caicos with a pound of dope and a twenty year old blonde."

"You can do that any day of the week. What are you complaining about?"

"Aren't you working anymore?"

"I'm taking some time off. The divorce is heating up. I just got a new motion from Cassie's attorney. They want me out of the house. Immediately. Yesterday."

"Damn. What are you going to do?"

"Well, I was kind of hoping our good friend Nick Ballestracci would have some answers for the money I'm throwing at him."

"You haven't even been to court yet. Now that's something to see. The guy's an animal. A Michael Jordan. You've got to have a little faith."

Sarnower snorted. "A little faith. That's rich coming from you."

"Hey, bro, I'm a Baptist boy from America's heartland. Faith is in my blood, it's what I do."

"Tug, your polyester middle-Americana is showing its grease stains."

"Everything I do shows grease stains. No one cares anymore. Look, get your sorry ass over here and hang for a couple of weeks 'till this shit clears up. It'd be like old times."

Now there was a depressing thought. Sarnower and Tug living together again. Thirty years ago it had been fun, but he'd like to think in that time things had changed. Of course Tug would love it too, for a while. There'd be a floating carnival atmosphere, the air perpetually fragrant with pot smoke. Tug would be ever the thoughtful host hell-bent on getting Sarnower laid on a regular basis, assembling a cavalcade of bimbos that would rival the Playboy mansion. Why not go down in style? An extreme turbo bachelor pad. Why not? Well, there was Mitch after all. Apparently Tug had completely forgotten he was a father.

"Thanks, I'll keep it in mind. I'd really prefer to stay here if Nick can get the motion quashed."

"From what I hear it's open season on professional husbands. Our wonderful liberal governors have packed the courts with radical lesbo-feminist judges."

"Gee, thanks for the encouraging words."

"Hey, reality is the best therapy. You of all people should know that."

"Oh, and you're qualified to talk about reality *how* exactly?"

"Touché," he laughed.

"If there's anyone living in a fantasy world it's you, pal."

"I try. It's not always easy."

"I suppose someone's got to do it."

"We're the future, man. The rate things are going? In ten years no one's going to be able to deal with any of it."

"I'm not sure I can deal with any of it now. I've actually been giving some thought to your idea. You know...the Driscoll marital cure."

"Oh that. Yeah, great. You go, boy. I knew you'd come around sooner or later. Today, it's all about downsizing, trimming the sails, getting rid of all that unwanted clutter strewn over the road to personal fulfillment. Am I right?"

"As always," Sarnower sighed.

Oh, for a quiet evening alone with Nina. Maybe some soft music and tender, easy conversation. Fun as he could be, Tug went at all his pleasures full tilt. Partying was sacred; the protocols and details were all to be scrupulously observed. Subtlety and nuance were rarely part of the program. He burned his candles at both ends and in the middle too. Mental health, peace of mind; all could be restored by extreme partying.

The call-waiting buzzer on his phone sounded.

"I've got to go. It's probably Ballestracci."

"The guest room's always free, buddy."

And Tug was gone. Sarnower depressed the flash key on the phone.

"Mr. Ballestracci calling for Dr. Sarnower. Please hold." Was there no end to the ways the big guy was going to pull rank?

"We've been served with a motion to vacate the marital home."

"Yes, I was just savoring the ornate yet caustic language in that document."

"This isn't funny, doctor."

"Granted, the humor is a bit dark."

"I can't work with you if you're going to take that tone."

"I'm sorry, but when someone is trying to boot you out of your own house, a house you love, a house you remodeled by yourself with your bare hands, a house you're actually still paying for, you tend to get a little upset, a little crazy."

"I told you this process would be frustrating."

"Frustrating doesn't begin to describe it."

"I understand."

"No Nick, with all due respect, I don't think you do."

The lawyer was silent. Could you possibly piss him off anymore?

"Would you prefer going into court alone?"

"No. I'm sorry. I apologize."

"We're going to fight this. We need to be at Middlesex Probate Court tomorrow morning at ten."

"This one's going to be a win for us isn't it? I mean, who left whom, after all? Who's been taking care of Mitch all this time?"

"I wish I could promise you something. I can't. It depends entirely on the judge."

"Wait a minute. We're the good guys here."

Ballestracci laughed. "In the law there are no good guys and no bad guys."

"Just funny and not so funny, eh?"

"No wisecracks. Wear a tie and jacket; be cool and calm. I'll do the talking unless the judge asks you a question. Got all that?"

"Sir, yes sir."

"Be on time."

This time Sarnower was first to hang up. He'd had it with the gamesmanship, the relativism, the fuzzy lines. Even those to whom he was paying exorbitant money were toying with him. Why not go in alone and argue his side for himself, *pro se*? He'd probably be no worse off. The "system" was there to take his money and buy him a small slice of justice, making sure he wasn't going to get anything resembling the whole pie. Between the lawyers and Cassie's share of the settlement, little if anything would be left.

There had been a spate of high-profile cases in the past few years featuring prominent men: doctors, a professor, a well known building contractor, who were accused of hideous crimes; murder, child molestation, in one case a ghastly torture which eventually led to death. They were all well-to-do, established, admired members of their respective families and communities. They were all clearly guilty, at least as far as the evidence went on *Court TV*. All had hired the best legal talent money could buy. They'd ponied up hundreds of thousands of dollars and as things dragged on, had signed over more assets, boats, fancy cars, art collections, whatever they had of any value, the ultimate crap shoot, freedom or bust. To a one they'd been convicted and sentenced either to death (the unfortunate soul in California) or to life without parole here in Massachusetts.

In all cases, everything was gone. Kaput. Zero. Nada. And to what end? If they had all pleaded guilty at the arraignments months before their excruciating trials, the outcome would have been identical, except for the fact that a life's worth of work and money could have been passed down to their permanently scarred, bewildered children.

It was a ritual that made little sense. The gladiator system of ancient Rome filtered through English Common Law and imported to America, where it was shot through with the hype, chicanery and hucksterism that imbued so many of its institutions. The system had created itself by itself, *sui generis*. It replenished its ranks through the prestigious hard-to-get-into law schools and had honed and refined a web of cronyism and insider wheeling-and-dealing that would make the Mafia envious. The longevity of the enterprise testified to its durability. When the big bomb finally came, all that would remain on the scarred, barren planet would be cockroaches and lawyers.

At least something was happening. Tomorrow, he'd see Cassie for the first time since the sit-com reunion in their bedroom. He'd get his first look at Nora Lund too and see how Nick handled himself on his feet. Despite the continuing heat, he'd wear a dark blue blazer, gray slacks, a shirt and tie. He'd be calm and detached, treat the situation clinically, as if he were interviewing a chronically ill patient. He could do it.

But the lashing out had to stop; he was shooting himself in the foot, fragging his own platoon. He was feeling it now in some kind of pure, distilled form, it broke over him like a wave of nausea, making him tingle, almost twitch. What had started out months ago as concern, empathy and worry had gradually morphed into fear and rage. He was reminded of Manny's comment that morning: "Your body is asking you questions. What are you going to tell it?" What could he tell his body now? What could he tell his soul? The thoughts of killing Cassie were frightening, they were sudden and disorienting, like an invisible hand on the steering wheel about to run you off the road. Most of them had not yet broken through to full consciousness; they swam beneath the surface as murky forms, like primitive fish at incredible ocean depths.

Standing alone in the kitchen, portable phone still in hand, Sarnower shook. The call with Nick had ended forty-five minutes ago, and he had fallen into the timeless region of inner space where everything around him vaporized. Each new trip to the black hole had become darker and scarier, just when he needed his faculties more than ever, to be alert, even hyper-alert, to track the entire panorama of things going on around him, anticipating surprises before they happened. He could start by picking up Mitch, who was due to be dismissed in about ten minutes.

On any other day, the thought of seeing his son, disheveled, grimy, wearing a tired but satisfied smile would remind him of their deep connection and the rewards of his fumbling efforts at fatherhood. Today with so much that was uncertain and everything in the balance, Mitch would be a burden. He hated himself instantly, he hated Cassie for dragging him to the point where he thought like that, but it was true.

Sarnower eased his car into the line of waiting parents. To his relief, the dour Mrs. Watkins was nowhere in sight. Children were pouring out of the front entrance under the watchful eyes of counselors; children who had two sane parents, who would be taken home to an intact household where they'd be indulged with expensive sneakers, their own cell phones, a fridge full of tasty snacks, state of the art computers and overpriced academic enrichment programs. At sixteen and a half, they'd get their own brand new cars, devoted parents picking up the outrageous increase in insurance premiums without batting an eye. There would be the normal, low-grade fights behind closed doors about money, vacations, bosses, promotions, care of aging parents, house remodeling, year after year until these same children had grown and left home, and the whole thing would fade slowly, imperceptibly to black. Then the cycle would start all over again.

A panel truck was parked directly in front of him obstructing the view of oncoming kids, but suddenly Mitch appeared, engaged in animated conversation with a taller boy Sarnower had never seen before. The two were laughing and the boy was gesturing wildly with his hands, as if he were explaining a magic trick at high speed. Mitch smiled and pointed when he saw his father and the boy instantly dropped his hands to his side as he searched for Sarnower, trying to manufacture a smile. The sight was somehow sad, the boy instinctively curbing his natural enthusiasm in the presence of adults. Manners, manners.

Mitch approached the open car window bubbling. "Dad, this is Jonathan Elsinger."

Sarnower was delighted to see him restored to his old high spirits. He extended his hand. "Nice to meet you John."

"Uh, it's Jonathan," he said, uncomfortable at having to correct an adult. "Nice to meet you too Mr. Sarnower."

"I'm sorry, *Jonathan*."

Mitch was bursting. "Dad, Jonathan wants me to sleep over tonight at his place. Can I?" He was bouncing on the balls of his feet, the discharge of excessive energy; a gene inherited from Cassie.

"Sure. I don't see why not," he answered with a smile. This was a gift, a break when a break was needed. God doesn't send you more than you can take he remembered one of his patients from long ago, a born-again Christian, telling him.

"Jonathan, is your mother here? I should work a few things out with her."

"Sure. She's in the blue SUV up there." The boy pointed with a long arm to a car ahead of them. Sarnower got out and started walking toward it. A woman with long, shiny dark hair was waiting in the driver's seat. As her face became visible, Sarnower gasped. She looked to be about twenty-five years old, fresh, moist, tanned skin, eyebrows expertly shaped, plump red lips. She flashed two rows of the whitest teeth he'd ever seen.

"Mrs. Elsinger?"

"Janice, please." She extended an exquisitely manicured hand.

"Alan Sarnower. A pleasure." He took her hand, soft and damp. "Jonathan tells me he'd like Mitch to sleep over tonight, I just wanted to make sure that was ok with you."

"We're delighted to have him," she smiled. "Jonathan's been talking about Mitch all summer, I'm just sorry it's taken this long to get them together." A child bride, she'll be on the prowl in a few years. Why hadn't he run into her before?

"Well, thank you Janice." Her jet black eyes glistened. She knew what she was doing.

"Uh, there is one thing," he added. "I have a very early meeting tomorrow and it would be next to impossible to pick Mitch up and take him to camp, I wonder if you..."

"No trouble at all," she said. "I'll bring him in with Jonathan." There. It was done.

"Let me give you my number in case you need to reach me," he said pulling a business card out of his wallet. He wrote his home phone number on the back and handed it to her.

"Oh, you're a shrink. I mean psychiatrist," she laughed.

"Guilty."

"I know some people who could definitely benefit from your services."

"I'm sure." How many times had he heard that very line? "Well, thanks again," he said, turning. There were Mitch and Jonathan back to their private, high-energy exchange.

"So long, champ. See you tomorrow," he said to Mitch who tightened his lips and rolled his eyes toward Jonathan.

"Nice to meet you Jonathan," he said, extending his hand. The boy now emboldened by the proximity to his mother and the prospect of more clowning with Mitch slapped Sarnower's hand and held the thumb, homeboy style.

"Later, dude," he growled.

Sarnower smiled as Mitch and Jonathan burst into riotous laughter.

"Jonathan!" Mrs. Elsinger admonished, barely able to contain her own amusement. Sarnower looked at her intently one last time before turning, hoping this vision would somehow burn itself into his retinas for permanent storage. Moms today just didn't look like the ones he knew growing up. Janice caught his gaze and held it; a glorious pink tongue darted out between her wonderful teeth. Ouch!

"Thanks again," he said smiling.

The boys had scrambled into the back seat and had already begun a noisy game of cat's cradle. Sarnower stood there drifting into a vivid lust-moment with Janice. They were somewhere in Italy, maybe Venice, on the Piazza del San Marco. It was a hot day, crowded with tourists and pigeons. Janice was sitting alone at an outdoor cafe table nursing a cup of dark espresso. He walked up behind her and placed his hands on her hot, bare shoulders and nuzzled his face deeply into her thick, dark, fragrant hair. She must have been expecting this, for instead of turning around, she let out a low, guttural moan. Although he couldn't see from that angle, he was sure her eyes were closed. He rubbed her neck gently as she continued to purr. He took a seat and faced her, her image bright and clearly defined by the noonday sun. There was a delicious bead of sweat across her upper lip as he moved in for a kiss, the blended tastes of coffee and wet, sunbathed skin.

When he returned, most of the cars and kids had gone. Only a few stragglers remained with the counselors who had started looking at their watches and checking the street for late parents. Sarnower felt oddly at peace, relaxed for the first time in days. Were Manny's pearls of wisdom sinking in or was it the unexpected pleasure of a few moments with newly discovered Janice? It didn't matter. He put his car in gear and started driving toward Nina's.

Chapter 7

ALTHOUGH HE KNEW WHERE she lived, Sarnower had never been to Nina's house despite their years of working together. At first, they'd both made an effort to keep business and personal lives separate. She always seemed to have a boyfriend in some stage of living there. On the few occasions when the question of his coming over had arisen, usually to drop off some work, she'd volunteered to pick it up at his house, preferring to wait in the front hall and conduct their transactions there, rarely even accepting an invitation to join him in the kitchen for a cup of tea or coffee.

But here he was heading for her duplex in West Roxbury, not knowing exactly why. It would be boorish to barge in on the spur of the moment. Nina was still sorting through Doug's suicide and the strange visit from his mother. She'd want to be alone, licking wounds or eating pints of Haagen Daz or on the phone with a girlfriend, away from Sarnower's simmering vat of troubles and free-floating carnal urges. She'd be polite, of course, even gracious, but distant. Why was he rushing hell bent into the arms of certain rejection?

Questions sped by like the gravel in the street. In Newton Centre, he stopped at Dan's Liquor Mart and picked up an expensive bottle of Bordeaux, heavy for a warm afternoon, but one that was sure to be fragrant, caressing and expressive. Eat, drink and be merry, for tomorrow you die, or at least begin the process of shedding everything you've come to know and love. Manny had said as much, and in different terms, his lawyer had too. The condemned man's last meal. Instead of fried chicken, mashed potatoes and chocolate ice cream, a fine wine and Nina.

He was now a man on a mission, heading south on Parker Street and making a left onto Dedham. He passed neat houses with well-tended lawns. Construction crews were out and working at several locations, putting up new carriage houses with high, open interiors, the latest fad among the young, wealthy gentry who were moving in to colonize the area. He turned on the radio where a Sibelius symphony was reaching a climax and Sarnower, windows open, sang with the lush violins of the Berlin Philharmonic, loud and raucous enough that brawny, muscled construction workers turned to look. One or two of his patients lived nearby and might be out for a late afternoon walk. Would they be shocked to see their shrink bellowing a late romantic symphony out of his car window on a summer afternoon? He didn't care.

After a mile or two the houses began to thin out, until there were no houses at all and the old Jewish cemetery came up on him. He often wondered who was resting there. In his many years in the area, he had never once seen a ceremony, a burial, even a lone visitor carrying flowers within its rusted iron fences. The gravestones were old and crumbling and the grass was poorly tended. The place looked abandoned, tired and resigned, so chock full of the restless dead that its shabby state could have been a conspiracy to keep all comers out. It always gave him a chill, filled as it was with those who'd finally, once and for all had it with the living, their feeble strutting, shouting and banging around.

He sailed up to the stoplight. Here was the VFW Parkway, once a stately high rent turn-of-the-century boulevard, now a poorer step-cousin to the more hip, ingratiating Newton. Thick oak trees planted decades ago in the median strip provided a lush green canopy, shading the early rush hour traffic. Sunlight flickered and danced on the windshield as Sarnower turned on to the Parkway. This was Nina's route after she left his office; her tires had crunched the same gravel.

Caruso Street. That was hers. It would be coming up soon on the right. Although he'd never actually seen it, the street had played a role in the countless musings and fantasies he'd had about her. She'd live in a white house, ringed by a picket fence on a tree-lined street, fragrant with the scent of some unnamed flower, but as he approached the green and white sign, the conjured up images were not what awaited him.

A small, abandoned, overgrown lot greeted him at the corner. Enclosed by a chicken wire fence, it was filled with garbage, a rusting shopping cart, parts of old bicycles, an air conditioner that no longer hummed, paper wraps from McDonalds' hamburgers, a recliner permanently reclined sprouting tufts of stuffing, now surely a condo for insects and vermin. The street was one-way and narrow. Small houses stood close together, many in need of painting and repair. Mesh fences separated property lines and there were plaster fountains and Madonnas on several of the small lawns. I should be paying her more, she deserves better.

Her house, number forty-six was in the middle of the block and was in surprisingly good shape relative to the others. It had recently been painted. There was a courageous spread of lawn, and a small colorful flowerbed abutted the porch. He parked the car, grabbed the bottle of wine and crossed the street. There was Nina's car sitting in front, her once bright red Honda Accord now dinged and dull.

He remembered when she bought it; he'd gotten her a good buy through a friend at a nearby dealership. He crunched the numbers with her, helped her get the loan and set her up with Phil Duggan, his longtime mechanic. He'd told her about upkeep, changing the oil regularly, periodic maintenance recommended by the manufacturer. Her attention to the car had started out promisingly enough, but as time passed, things had lapsed. There had been a couple of expensive repairs, which had necessitated an advance on her salary. Now, it was starting to look like a shit box. Dust to dust, chrome to rust.

He took the couple of stairs in a leap and noticed the porch boards had recently been replaced with pressure-treated lumber. The bell underneath the taped-on piece of paper that read "Winslow" was out of order, so he knocked. Sarnower felt his heart pound. This show of spontaneity was really stupid. She'd be getting dinner ready, perhaps she had a guest; he'd be barging in like a clown in the midst of a pratfall. It wasn't too late to dash for his car and burn rubber out of there, she might never know he'd shown up. But now there were footsteps approaching on a carpeted floor. Too late.

The door opened and there she was.

"Alan," she said, surprised. In that first microsecond that contained all, that grain of time he could read, she actually seemed glad to see him.

"I was going to tell you I was in the neighborhood, but that would be a complete lie," he said handing her the wine. "I know I should have called first. You're probably in the middle of something." She was wearing rubber gloves.

"No, not at all." She took the bottle. "Come in. I was just doing some cleaning." She led the way through the living room into the kitchen. He passed an old Hoover vacuum cleaner, a model similar to the one his mother had used back in the 1950s, it looked like a streamlined train charging across the floor. The odor of pine cleanser hung in the air.

"How do you keep that vacuum cleaner going? It must be older than me."

"Oh that? It came with the place. It's never really broken down, but the hard part is finding replacement bags," she answered, turning. "I have to go to some dinky out-of-the-way place in Dorchester to get them."

She led him into the kitchen, opened a drawer and took out a corkscrew. It looked like a small abstract sculpture of a ballerina in first position.

"The honors?"

"The honors," he answered, taking the object. Her clear blue eyes met his. The corkscrew fell to the floor with a clatter, its arms extended. He was back in her aura, the familiar scent, the warmth. She clasped her arms around his neck and looked up.

"I've missed you, sailor. How are the choppy seas?"

He smiled. "Gale-force winds, I'm afraid." He brushed his lips against hers as she closed her eyes and probed his mouth with her tongue. He moved in closer and put his hands in the rear pockets of her tight jeans. Eyes closed, the image of Janice sitting in the Piazza appeared, and that soft, sweat-dotted upper lip. He was hard immediately. Nina sensed his erection and pressed closer. "Shiver me timbers," she whispered.

"I think they're shivering," he said as she started to unbutton his shirt.

Something was off. Nina, here in the body that had so often pushed its way into his three-minute fantasies, just wasn't doing it for him. Instead, Janice's tan, young face appeared, that glorious mouth. Sarnower closed his eyes; he was there with her again in the Piazza. The pigeons, the tourists had all vanished, it was just the two of them now. Being with Nina had given the fantasy added force and color, it was such a short distance from her to Janice and the details were still fresh and clear in his mind.

Why couldn't he be satisfied with what was right here before him? Sure, all that crap about the hunt, the chase, once the prey was bagged, the thrill was gone and then it was on to the next. It couldn't really be that simple, so completely animalistic. Didn't this hyper-evolved cortex count for anything? Here was this beautiful woman, still decimated, run over by the suicide of her ex-boyfriend, a drip for sure but her ex nevertheless, in his arms, wanting to give herself to him, still after all of this believing in the possibility of a relationship, or of love even, happy to press herself against his aging, sagging frame. And where was he? Over in Venice with a woman he didn't even know, in love with her lips.

Was this a sign of fetishism? According to Freud it was a none too mature level of psychosexual development. Freud and his gang had a field day with fetishists, often those who went after feet and shoes, the "split-off part object" as it was now called in modern jargon. The failure to take in, deal with, love the entire person was a sign of stunted, arrested growth, selfish, narcissistic, completely given over to primitive need-gratification.

He pulled away. Nina's warm face filed his visual field like a close-up on the silver screen. "What's the matter?" she asked, darkening.

"Cassie wants me out of the house. I've got to go to court tomorrow morning." He was becoming adept at covering his tracks.

"Isn't that kind of sudden?"

"That's how they do things, this wonderful system of ours. It's an ambush. Anyone who wants a piece of you can get in line and take their best shot. You have to prove you're worthy enough to hold on to what's already yours."

"It makes me want to hate her," she said. Strong words from a healthy, even-tempered soul.

He smiled. "I know what you mean." His murderous thoughts returned. Cassie's head splattered over his white bathroom wall.

"Let me get you a drink."

"But the wine?"

Nina turned to him, smiling. "Alan, you need something stronger. This isn't a wine afternoon anyway."

"Oh?"

"I'm thinking more along the lines of a Cosmo."

"Get me drunk and have your way with me, is that it?"

"The thought did cross my mind."

She winked at him. This was her turf, her show. Best to be led along and enjoy the ride. She had plans, tricks up her sleeves.

"How's this going to turn out tomorrow?" she asked, taking two frosted martini glasses from the freezer. Sarnower, seated at her vintage 1940s Formica table heard the words but didn't attach the meaning. He'd become engrossed in a pair of bawdy plastic salt and pepper shakers. A large-busted, red lipped, scantily clad young woman (obviously pepper) was artfully dodging the impending grope of an old drunk (salt) dressed in a tattered tuxedo with a comically squashed top hat.

"I'm loving your condiments," he chuckled. Nina turned.

"Oh, those." A note of seriousness crept into her voice. "Doug got those at a flea market a couple of years ago."

"I'm sorry, I didn't..."

"That's ok," she took a deep breath. "I can talk about it." She brought the drinks over to the table and sat down opposite him.

Sarnower lifted his glass to her. "To better times. For both of us."

"Amen."

They drank. The cold pungent liquid, slightly thickened by its time in the freezer, radiated out to Sarnower's fingertips. The welcome, mellow buzz was almost instantaneous.

"To answer your question," he said, retrieving the echoic words and fixing their meaning, "I have no idea. My lawyer hasn't been very encouraging."

"So get a new lawyer."

Sarnower chuckled. "I probably should. It's not that easy. Apparently I've become a real pain in the ass. I get the feeling he'd love to drop me."

"Can they do that in the middle of a case?"

"I don't know what the protocol is when an attorney can no longer stand his client."

"How did you find this guy anyway?"

He looked at her sheepishly. "Tug," he said softly.

"Tug? Tug?" She had to contain herself from spitting her Cosmo across the table.

"I know, I know," he said, swirling the pink liquid at the bottom of the glass.

"You're getting a legal referral from Tug." She could barely stifle a laugh, almost choking.

"He's got all this high-powered muscle on retainer for his business. I figured he could help me find someone to handle a simple divorce."

"Except that it's not simple."

"No, apparently not." He chugged the last of his drink as tomorrow's events started playing on an internal screen; the huge stifling courthouse, old and poorly air-conditioned, the institutional oak furniture, once solemn and dignified, now filthy and carved up with the initials and obscenities of the trapped, the cornered, those about to get chewed up by the system. The long corridors, the high dingy ceilings, probably not painted since the 1930s, the lights—huge, dusty glass orbs.

"Hey slugger, time to pull your socks up."

"Huh?"

"You looked very far away." She got up and refilled their glasses. He followed her form as he expertly poured the drinks from a large crystal pitcher, raising and lowering, keeping an even flow until both glasses were neatly topped off a quarter of an inch below the rim.

"I can see you've done that before."

"Driving out here one summer from Washington, I bartended for a few weeks in Denver to get some extra money. *That* was an education."

"What haven't you done?"

She turned and smiled, carrying the two refreshed drinks.

"Not much. Maybe we could figure something out though."

"I'd like that."

"L'chiam," she toasted.

"Where did you pick up your Hebrew? Don't tell me," he said closing his eyes. "An old boyfriend studying at a Yeshiva to become a rabbi."

"Hardly," she laughed. "Although I've gone out with many Jewish men."

"Well, I hope I've been a satisfactory delegate."

She downed her drink in a single large gulp and Sarnower followed her lead. He was starting to get drunk and should probably stand up now while he could; sitting any longer would make him light-headed and clumsy. And his performance? Nina was clearly up for making love and she wouldn't want to be disappointed.

She followed his lead and rose, taking the empty glasses to the sink.

"I've always liked liquid dinners," she said rinsing the glasses. "There's so little to clean up."

"Booze is definitely underrated as one of the four food groups."

She laughed, turning to him "That's what's always attracted me to you Alan. Your humor. It's very sexy."

"A good laugh and an orgasm are first cousins physiologically, did you know that?"

He was on again, hoping he wasn't slurring his words. She took his hand and pulled him toward her, hungry. Sarnower could taste the cranberry juice and bitters as she planted her tongue in his mouth. "I want you to fuck me," she whispered, undoing his belt. "Fuck me silly." He was once again in her elusive fragile chemistry, so like and unlike every other woman he'd ever been with. He was hard again instantly as his hands began to trace the base of her firm breasts.

Without speaking she took his hand and led him out of the kitchen down a small hall into her bedroom. Even in his tumescent, sexed-up fog, he was startled at how closely the room resembled the one in his fantasies. The scarred oak dresser, a yard or estate sale purchase held bottles of perfume and massage oil and a delicate copper vase sprouted long sticks of incense. Instead of the Ansel Adams photo of the Cascade Mountains there was a framed print of Robert Indiana's familiar, blocky 1960s "LOVE", and a poster of the Picasso drawing of a hand offering colored flowers to another hand. A king-size platform bed dominated the room with an ornate, expensive duvet.

She pulled him down on the bed and in an instant her hand was in his pants. How wonderful to be aggressed upon. So this is what the sexual revolution had produced; women meeting their needs with the same bold directness men had for centuries before. Fair enough. What's good for the goose is good for the gander.

She tugged his pants down to his knees, and tracing her fingers gently around the top of his briefs, slowly began to lower them. Sarnower was at full attention.

"I like a man who shows interest."

He reclined on the luxurious bed, hands behind his head as Nina mounted him, her eyes closing as she finished unbuttoning his shirt. She pulled it up and over his head, collapsing on his chest in a falling curtain of blond hair and began to lick his neck, slowly working her way down to his nipples. Her tongue, deft and sure made Sarnower shiver and burn at the same time. Was this the way people spontaneously combusted? That old TV episode of *Ripley's Believe it or Not*, where a woman in some enthralled, ecstatic state had supposedly burst into flame and had wound up a pile of smoking ashes on the floor. If the same thing happens to me, that's perfectly ok.

But she had barely begun to work her brand of Tantric mysticism. She took off her T-shirt, her breasts brushing his thighs now like feathers as she made her way down to his straining purple cock. Sarnower trembled and almost seized as she took it in her mouth and began her velvet ministrations. Time and the universe stood still and shrank to a tiny black dot. Then he came like the final, blinding white-hot gasp of a dying star.

* * *

The Middlesex Probate Courthouse, huge, ugly and red, squatted like a Sumo wrestler, dominating an entire block of East Cambridge. Built at the turn of the century, it was a decaying relic of an age that no one who used it or worked there could possibly remember. Because the building also held the Registry of Deeds, Sarnower and Cassie had been there years before to close on their house. Seated at long wooden tables, they had passed papers back and forth between officious lawyers and a cantankerous old widower from whom they were buying the house. The old man, even at that late date had wavered. He nostalgically recalled his wife, their kids and the twenty-three years they'd spent in the house. At one point, it looked certain he was going to back out of the deal, his cascading memories so vivid and disorienting. The lawyers had somehow been able to coax him back and cajole and sweet-talk him through to the end. Eventually the man had signed the papers, misty and lost, and after a few moments of respectful waiting while he collected himself, his lawyer escorted him downstairs where his daughter waited to bring him home with her, holding nothing but a thin envelope with a bank check for more money than he'd ever seen in his life.

Today's outcome would be far less certain. Sarnower was running on no sleep at all; he and Nina had been up all night making love, talking, and dressing each other's wounds. He'd finally left at six in the morning and had gone home to shower and change, but with no rest, he was tremulous, headachy and vaguely nauseated. All-night escapades, easy to recover from in college, now extracted at least a day of suffering while his abused, dehydrated body regained its equilibrium.

And now, at nine-thirty, dressed in a lightweight blazer and tie, he drove down Cambridge Street, which, despite the encroaching urban renewal was still a strongly identified Portuguese neighborhood. Ethnic restaurants and bakeries dotted the blocks. Dusty, faded bilingual signs sat in the windows of tired bodegas, and used clothing and furniture stores had already exploded onto the street with their melancholy wares.

In the past ten years East Cambridge had been discovered, and young professionals, priced out of the Harvard Square and Brattle Street areas had come in to buy up the tiny crumbling fisherman's shacks that lined the quiet, shaded side streets. They would tear them down and put up small Tudors or Capes. Starbucks and expensive dry cleaners had begun to proliferate as old-time residents, now unable to pay the rising property taxes, had been forced to sell and move out.

Sarnower thought of his patient Zifkin, the real estate mogul who'd seen the trend coming years ago, and had snapped up real estate here for practically nothing, developing and building condominiums and selling them at obscene mark-ups. Arrogant and infantile though he was, at least he was a risk taker and even, Sarnower hated to admit it, a visionary of sorts. Signs for his company Zifkin Development were prominently displayed in several locations. Maybe Zifkin was on to something after all. He and Tug seemed to have lots in common; both charged ahead first, then picked up the messes and asked questions later. They were both wealthy enough by now to have others carry their water and walk behind their elephants.

And here he was, having heard a higher calling to a difficult profession, which offered harrowing work for less and less money. His balls were in a vise, having to answer to a crazy woman. He'd gotten stuffed like sausage filling into this impersonal legal meat-grinder, missing the opportunity, if there ever was one, to strike out on a different path. When Zifkin had been busted for drugs, he never even had to appear in court. His well-connected attorney had struck a deal with his good friend the DA and the whole thing was handled with a phone call. The papers were drawn up and signed within hours. Over and out. Done.

A parking space opened up miraculously as a battered Chevy, covered with decaying, peeling bumper stickers, squealed out onto the street. *My Kid's an Honors Student in the College of Hard Knocks* one of the stickers read. Well, I'm a professor emeritus in the college of hard knocks, he thought, as he gratefully pulled in. He checked himself briefly in the rear view mirror. His color wasn't good and even though the early morning humidity had subsided, he was already damp with sweat.

Inside, a line had formed to pass through a pair of tall metal detectors. A burly court officer sat at a desk checking through briefcases and purses. Another held a wand on the other side of the detectors and frisked those who had set off the alarm. Sarnower placed his briefcase on the table for inspection. The bored officer opened the case and rifled through the papers. In addition to financial statements and documents related to his legal proceedings, there were patient's charts he'd forgotten to remove, though they'd been in there for weeks now. He saw the officer stop briefly to read the names on the tabs protruding from the folders, then, satisfied there were no guns or explosives, he handed the case back with a grunt.

Passing through the detectors, Sarnower set off the alarm. Several sets of eyes focused on him as the guard with the metal wand approached. He emptied the contents of his pockets into a small plastic tray, keys, change, his wallet and spread his arms as the man patted him down. Two entirely different people for two entirely different reasons explored his body within the past few hours. The irony made him grin, which the guard, by his snarled look of disgust, took as a sign of some kind of perverse sexual gratification. When he was satisfied that Sarnower's monogrammed belt buckle was the culprit, he nodded toward the plastic tray and Sarnower walked on, returning the contents to his pockets.

It was now almost ten o'clock and the vast, vaulted marble lobby was crowded. Clients, most of them black or Hispanic, were holding impromptu conferences with their rumpled, sleep-deprived legal-aid lawyers. A group of well dressed attorneys huddled in a corner, their expensive suits and well-cut hair set them apart from the hoards of muscle-shirted men and tube-topped, big-haired women. And there was Ballestracci, his large, razor-cut head turning slowly like a beacon on a lighthouse, scoping the room for him. Sarnower looked at the man and felt a balloon of bile rise from his stomach. A light tan Brioni suit hung on his huge frame and a starched white shirt and solid maroon tie completed the look. If all else failed, perhaps Sarnower could get some reliable fashion tips from him for his new life.

Just then Nick found him and waved. Sarnower smiled weakly as the lawyer advanced.

"Things are a little backed up in courtroom three," he said nodding in the direction of one of the long corridors. "Your wife and her counsel are already here. We may have a bit of a wait. Did you bring the material?"

Sarnower nodded, opened the briefcase and took out a folder and handed it to him. He felt blood drain from his head as the lawyer flipped through the pages."

"Where are the interrogatories?" he asked.

"Interrogatories?"

"Yes, the ones you were sent a few days ago. We talked about them. I don't see them here."

Nick was right. They were sitting on his dining room table, half completed. He'd gotten distracted and totally forgot about them. Today, he'd be lucky to remember where he'd parked his car.

"I'm sorry," he said lamely. "I'm new to all this, I'm trying to hold things together as best I can."

Nick snorted and shook his head. He closed the folder and handed it back to Sarnower.

"The judge isn't going to like this one bit. We could be sanctioned."

"Oh?"

"A fine. Punishment for non-compliance."

"Great."

"Look, we'd better get going. I'll see what we can do with Judge McGraw. She's not always predictable."

"*She?*"

Nick nodded and began walking. "Nancy McGraw, a Dukakis appointment. She's been sitting for years."

"Shit! I was warned about women judges."

The lawyer looked at him and shrugged. "Luck of the draw. What can I tell you?"

"What can you tell me? You can tell me we can win this thing. You can tell me I won't be completely wiped out. You can tell me I'll get out of this with some shred of dignity and self- respect. You can tell me I'll be able to raise my son." Acid had pushed to the top of his esophagus and was ready to spew.

"Dr. Sarnower, you've got to calm down." Nick stopped and faced him. "Your demeanor in there is going to tell as much about you as everything in here," he said waving Sarnower's case-file in the air. "If you want to hold on to your life, you've got to look as though you can handle it. Cool, calm, collected. Let your wife take the nutty."

Right. The calmer he was, the more wound-up she would get. That was the old pattern.

"I'm sure her lawyer's told her the same thing," he said, the acid at the back of his throat making it difficult to speak. But Nick had already started down the corridor. He followed, staring at the back of the man's head. A bald spot he hadn't noticed before had started to appear on the large man's crown, a patch even his $150 hair cut couldn't hide, and Sarnower fixed on it to keep from throwing up. Within a few years, that area and more around it would become increasingly bare; the tall and proud finally vanquished by male hormones, down the drain and into the sewer. He was secretly pleased that Ballestracci would soon need a transplant or plugs. He'd certainly have the funds for it.

And there was Cassie, or someone that resembled her. No, it was she only she'd been completely made over. Her hair, now shiny and lustrous was freshly cut and expensively styled. Her color was back and she'd added a few pounds. Light make-up had been professionally applied and her eyes were clear, no longer cavernous and dead. She had new clothes: a white blouse and modest dark skirt tapered down to light sheer panty hose and understated but pricey black pumps. He was galled to see her wearing the antique strand of pearls his mother had given her shortly after they were married. She must have picked them up the day he'd caught her and that stooge in bed a few weeks ago, the day they'd made off with *his* jewelry too.

But even Sarnower had to admit she looked good. It was becoming obvious how this was going to go. She wouldn't be taking the nutty.

"Dr. Sarnower, this is your wife's counsel, Nora Lund." A short fat woman with a frizzy cloud of gray hair and large, outdated glasses moved in front of him. The lenses made her eyes appear huge, the size of golf balls; the effect was both scary and comical at the same time. He could easily have laughed, but in his condition, any response other than guarded caution would be dangerous. Her distorted appearance made her expression and intent difficult to read. She didn't offer her hand. "Dr. Sarnower," she nodded with a deep voice.

Sarnower smiled and tipped his head. When in doubt, say nothing, the lesson applied here too. Like his patients, best to let them fill in the blanks themselves. How were his patients doing? Were they missing their time with him or could they function just as well on their own? Perhaps they'd forgotten all about him. Tug's offer of several weeks ago to join one of his consulting teams suddenly had appeal.

"Alan?" a voice boomed. Sarnower looked up from Lund's hideous eyes. The man, tall, thin and well dressed was familiar but floated out of reach of a name. Where had he seen this guy before? TV? The papers?

"Bill Kelly, Cassie's brother," he said extending his hand, and raising his eyebrows looking for a sign of recognition. Of course. It had been what, twenty years or more? The man had morphed completely. His tall frame, now slightly stooped, was the only feature Sarnower could fit with any recollection of him. Bill had certainly grown old. His hair, what there was left of it, was now almost completely white. The prominent nose stood out more than ever, as the skin had thinned and pulled tighter to the skull. It was lined with a map of red veins, as were his cheeks; his life-long habits and addictions written in clear topography across his face. He was still an imposing man. The voice and height could project the edge of menace he remembered from college.

"Hi, Bill," Sarnower responded. He tried to raise his hand to shake, but the muscles wouldn't work. Nick stepped in to shake Bill's retracting hand. "Nick Ballestracci. I'm representing Dr. Sarnower."

Mumbles and nodding, the five of them stood there, guests at a dreadful cocktail party.

"I'll take the interrogatories," Nora Lund said, extending her hand.

"We don't have them," Ballestracci answered.

"And why not?" She glared at Sarnower and the lawyer.

"You'll get them," Balestracci grunted, looking over her head down the hall.

"I want them in my office first thing in the morning, or we can all find ourselves back here."

She picked up a large, battered lawyer's briefcase and headed for the courtroom door. Like sheep, everyone followed, holding the old frosted glass and oak door for the next.

The vast room was almost empty. Large palladium windows stretched from floor to ceiling, admitting huge shafts of dusty sunlight. A lazy Casablanca-style fan turned grudgingly over the judge's head unable to move the hot air. At the bench, the Honorable Nancy McGraw, an obese woman with a helmet of stiff, dyed, jet-black hair and a pair of half-glasses sliding down her nose, lectured a young Hispanic couple before her. The man, more of a boy really, wore a dirty T-shirt cut off at the sleeves. His head was bowed to the floor as the judge admonished him, his wife, or girlfriend clearly pregnant, looked at him shaking her head in disgust, arms akimbo. Sarnower could only make out intermittent words, "job" "support" "responsibility." A tall bailiff stood immobile in the at-ease position looking out into the courtroom.

Sitting next to him on the hard wooden bench, Nick made a last-minute run through the papers. He leaned over to Sarnower. "Don't speak until the judge speaks to you. Keep it short and polite. Say 'your honor' or 'judge.' Let me do the talking."

The bailiff showed the defeated Hispanic couple (accompanied by someone that looked to be the girl's mother) away. The two women, now animated, talked to each other in Spanish, while the young man, slumping with his hands in his pockets, walked behind them. They'd be back before the same judge in ten days for sure, when the man, unable to follow through on whatever the court had ordered, would be cited, perhaps even jailed.

Sarnower had a brief image of sharing a cell with him, basically a good kid, but in way over his head. He'd become passive and amorphous in the face of everything the world had thrown at him. Sarnower would help the young man with his English, introduce him to great books, music, art, maybe the boy would teach him Spanish. They'd confide in each other, look out for one another in the general population. The boy would help him learn street-style self-defense, some basic survival skills. Sarnower would bulk up, spend hours pumping iron in the yard, do sit-ups and one-handed push-ups. Soon, no one would want to fuck with him.

"Kelly vs. Sarnower," the bailiff called. So Cassie was going back to her maiden name. All for the best, she didn't deserve his family's name; he and Mitch would keep it. Bill probably had a hand in this too, bribing her with all those fabulous clothes.

"Showtime," Nick whispered, suddenly taut and alert. Sarnower rose. Across the isle, his adversaries stood and began to walk toward the bench. Cool, calm and collected. You're a pro; just use your training. It's all clinical. Cassie exuded a whiff of perfume he'd never smelled on her before as he followed in her wake.

Up close, Judge McGraw was huge and imposing as a circus tent, almost twice the size of a normal person. Her black robe spread out like a small mountain range, and close-up her head made him think of Mt. Rushmore, a vast fleshy expanse with features tucked into crevasses and canyons. The steel-rimmed reading glasses added a comic touch and reminded him of a cartoon character from his childhood whose name he couldn't remember. The five of them arranged themselves in front of the bench. The attorneys stood together as their clients lined up behind them. Nora Lund, poised to spring, was first out of the gate.

"Uncontested divorce your honor, petition for immediate relief." She handed the judge a folder with the motion paper-clipped to the top.

"Judge," Nick started, his voice a smooth, rolling baritone. "Some background. What we have here is a case of abandonment, infidelity, reckless behavior and substance abuse." He ticked off each count with a raised finger. "Dr. Sarnower was left by his wife two months ago when she disappeared. She also abandoned their minor child..."

"Give me a break," Lund interrupted, pumping herself up like a blowfish. "Dr. Sarnower has been an abusive tyrant for years. My client had reached the end of her rope and had to get away. It was medically necessary."

The judge took off her glasses and stared at Lund. "*Medically* necessary? That's one I haven't heard." Nick! Jump in now! Sarnower thought, here's a great opening. But Lund continued to press.

"She was on the edge of a nervous breakdown..."

"Exactly so! And should have been hospitalized, but has continued to refuse appropriate treatment," Nick shot in. He straightened his tie and planted his feet, looking straight at McGraw.

"Your honor, let's get right to the issue. This woman's behavior has been completely erratic and she's given ample evidence of her unsuitability to function as a parent, much less a sole custodian. I have affidavits here from neighbors, and friends as well as a list of psychiatrists she's seen and medications prescribed; all of it documenting her declining mental health and her failure to follow through with appropriate treatment."

He dropped a huge folder on the judge's bench with a dramatic thud. Swirling clouds of dust, like paisley patterns on a necktie, rose from the bench into beams of sunlight.

When had Ballestracci collected those? Did he have the FBI on retainer?

The judge quickly thumbed the pages and turned her massive head to Sarnower.

"So you're a psychiatrist?"

"Yes, your honor."

"Well your professional opinion counts for nothing here."

"Judge!" Lund got in. "Ms. Kelly was kicked out of the marital residence, cut off from any contact with her son and was forced to

142

live without any support for weeks at a time. In addition to that, she has suffered physical abuse at the hand of her husband." Lund glared at Sarnower through her massive glasses.

McGraw stared at Lund. "Well, what was it, did she leave or was she kicked out? You can't have it both ways."

"It really doesn't matter your honor," Lund shouted.

Nick, his thick ropy neck bulging through his tailored shirt, strained for an opening.

"She left of her own volition. Let's be clear: no one kicked her out. For the record, physical abuse never occurred in this marriage. And as for support, my client was forced to cancel her credit cards to put a stop to her erratic behavior. She abandoned a car in front of a fire hydrant, for God's sake. Do normal people do that? Dr. Sarnower was concerned only for her safety."

"If he was so interested in her safety why did he let her wander around for weeks with no money?" Lund asked.

"He had no idea where the hell she was!" Nick boomed.

"And obviously had no intention of finding out!"

"That's enough!" the judge said. "I'm not having a pissing contest with the two of you." She leaned her bulk over the bench. Sarnower wondered where her tits were inside that colossal black robe. Was she wearing a bra? *Could* she wear a bra? What would it look like? She put her glasses on and looked at Cassie.

"Mrs. Sarnower?"

"Yes?"

"Mrs. Sarnower is going by her maiden name, Kelly," Lund interjected.

Judge McGraw put up her hand to silence the lawyer.

"Mrs. Sarnower, how are you feeling?" Everyone looked at Cassie.

"I'm feeling fine, your honor." Her voice was strong and resonant, not the ghostly incantation Sarnower had heard from her over the past six months. She was poised, hands folded in front, making direct eye contact with the judge.

"Do you feel capable of looking after your..." she scanned the notes in front of her, "...your son?"

"Absolutely your honor. That's why we're petitioning for custody and to move back into my house."

My House? Sarnower started to tremble. They were being out-maneuvered. He barely heard Cassie as she described the past two months as a logical, necessary choice, a break from unbearable circumstances. There had been mistakes in judgment perhaps, things could have been done differently at times, but there was no lapse in love or concern for their son. Sarnower could not recognize the gargoyle he was being portrayed as. Nick, sensing his tension and boiling need to interject, placed a hand on his arm.

Cassie concluded. She'd been beautifully prepped. McGraw, nodding, looked as if she'd swallowed the whole thing. She turned to Sarnower.

"Your honor, we object to the characterization of Dr. Sarnower as a fascist and a termite," Nick said.

The judge glared. "She sounds fine to me, Mr. Ballestracci. Doctor, what do you have to say?"

His mind went blank instantly. A black curtain had fallen. He cleared his throat. Should he refute Cassie's charges one by one or speak in general terms? He'd tuned out somewhere in the middle of her recital, bringing to mind instead an image of what the judge could possibly look like under that robe. Cut to another image of Ballestracci in the ring with Judge McGraw. The lawyer, big and muscular in satin shorts and gloves, bobbing and weaving, the judge in her vast black robes...no, it was too messy to go further. For the money he was paying, Nick should have reviewed his testimony with him. Cool, calm and collected just didn't cut it as legal advice. He could get that from a deodorant commercial. Now he was hanging out to dry like a salted herring. Everyone was looking at him. I can handle this, just focus here. Don't put her down or refute every point. Put yourself forward as honest, caring, trying to make the best of a very difficult situation. Be likable. Dispel the characterizations through your behavior: thoughtful, kind, understanding. Keep it short. Don't think that everything you've ever wanted or worked for is this minute hanging in the balance.

He heard a familiar "click click click" in back of him and turned around. There were his parents, large as life, seated in the first row of old oak benches. His mother, wearing her ratty old housecoat was staring at him, knitting, the insistent, annoying music of her needles filling the air. His father, in dusty gray corduroy pants and his worn herringbone jacket was shaking his head in a characteristic gesture of reproach.

"Jesus, what the hell do you want?" Sarnower screamed out loud at them.

Nathan and Deborah Sarnower remained seated and silent. Sarnower rubbed his eyes. They were gone.

"Dr. Sarnower, there will be no outbursts in my courtroom," Judge McGraw thundered.

"Get a *grip*, man," Ballestracci whispered.

"I'm sorry, your honor," Sarnower said, turning toward the bench. "I thought there was someone here."

"There *is* someone here and they're waiting to hear from you. I'm losing patience rapidly, doctor."

Now, wanting nothing more than to get this over with, he began.

"Your honor, it's very simple. I have never been a bully or a tyrant. My wife left me two months ago in an impossible situation. We have a young son. I have a large practice, which has now trickled down to next to nothing. I have spared no expense to care for our son. I have done and will continue whatever is in his best interests. I have no hard feelings toward my wife, only the sincere hope that she will get help and get better."

He heard Bill snort in an attempt to check a burst of laughter. In spite of himself, Sarnower chuckled. Comedy in the face of grim tragedy, so Shakespearian. Alas poor Yorick.

"You find these proceedings amusing, doctor?" McGraw asked, astonished.

"No. Of course not," Sarnower responded weakly. Another giggle escaped. He was dying, and rather than re-group and rise to the occasion, it would take all his effort to hold back a full-blown laughing fit. He was a kid again in *shul* with his parents, and the old man sitting in back of him had let one rip. He'd exploded.

The house, the cars, the 401Ks—take them all. He might as well sign the papers now. None of it mattered. He looked over at Nick, who had turned ashen, his eyes wide and disbelieving. He looked at the filthy marble floor, biting his tongue. He should just shut up. He'd hung himself in record time and even Judge McGraw seemed unable to grasp his drive for self-destruction. Cassie, Bill and the freakish Nora Lund were caught off-guard too. *He* was the mental patient now.

"Your honor, a moment with my client out in the hall if I may," Ballestracci said.

"Counselor, I have a full docket today. I don't have time for..."

"This will take only a minute, judge. I apologize to the court for any inconvenience."

"All right," McGraw said, her voice steady and calm. "Three minutes."

Ballestracci took Sarnower forcefully by the arm and led him down the aisle, through the doors and outside the courtroom.

"Are you fucking nuts? What were you doing in there?" he hissed. A vein in his forehead had ballooned into prominence.

The whole thing had gone by so fast; the vision of his parents had been so real. There'd been lots to say, and he'd said none of it. Someone should have told him the court wanted sound bites, small, easy to digest nuggets, something that would resonate with the judge at the end of the day after she was at home unhooking that humongous bra and pouring herself a stiff drink. He could have done it. Just a little something with rhythm, a bit of rock 'n' roll to it. He was always coming up with pithy gems for his patients. One had even gone so far as to transcribe them on Post-Its and put them up on her refrigerator. He was a past master of the well-turned phrase, yet he'd been totally derailed, thrown off his game once again by that schmuck Bill. The Harvard Med School graduate tipped by an asshole who made corrugated boxes. He wanted a do-over.

"I don't know," Sarnower said finally. He was drained, completely empty. Nick stood there trying to engage him.

"Explain it to me. I don't get it. You freaked out in there. I had you pegged totally different. Articulate, educated, someone who could think on his feet. You've got to help yourself. We're going down."

Sarnower shrugged, numb, flattened. "Beats me. I dropped the ball."

His parents were walking down the hall talking to each other, their backs to him. His father slumped over in that defeated, beaten-down way he had, his mother limping slightly with osteoporosis and the arthritic hip she never had replaced.

"You laugh and make a joke out of what could be the most important moment of your life, one that could easily decide your future." Ballestracci looked down the corridor biting his lower lip. "Well, we're going to have to go back in there and do damage control. Big time. I want you to work with me here and just shut up for now. Do you think you can do that?"

Sarnower nodded.

"Ok, then."

He opened the door to the courtroom and strode up to the bench. Sarnower followed behind.

"I'm waiting, counselor," the judge barked.

146

"Sorry your honor. My client is under severe emotional duress at this time. However he is continuing to fulfill all his obligations as a parent and provider."

"Not so, Judge. In fact Mr. Sarnower is not functioning as a custodial parent. Marijuana cigarettes were found recently in his bedroom. He's away from the minor child for long stretches of time without any supervision..."

"Unlike your client, Dr. Sarnower has to work!" Nick bellowed. "And as for drug usage, a case of the pot calling the kettle black. The reports in that folder will more than document the misuse of a vast array of substances by Ms. Kelly, or whatever name she's going by."

"All right, all right!" The judge banged her gavel for order. "I'm not going to issue a ruling today." She glared at the five of them. "Real pieces of work. All of you. I'm going to review the motions and all the supporting documentation. The court will appoint a guardian *ad litem* to conduct an independent evaluation of both parties in this matter. Pursuant to the evaluation, I will rule. However, I am issuing a temporary order of spousal support in the amount of $800 per week to meet expenses, and visitation with the minor child to take place one day a week, time and place to be worked out with the principals." She took off her glasses and leaned forward. Sarnower saw up close the rough and bulbous terrain of her skin. "Do you think you can work this out among yourselves without wasting any more of this court's time?" The lawyers nodded.

"Very good. We're through for now." She stacked the paperwork from the case and handed the bulk to a clerk sitting on her right. Nick grabbed Sarnower by the elbow and led him away from the bench down the aisle and out the creaking old doors to the hall, now almost empty.

Sarnower was starting to feel drunk, that present-in-the-moment-damn-everything-else aura that would shrink his consciousness to a tunnel the size of a dime. He'd floundered, lost touch with his resources, his ability to reason, put things together. The first time that had happened, he'd been stoned out of his mind at a party in college. Tug was holding court across the room, expounding to an eager group of sycophants on some ridiculous insight he'd had about the role of entropy in the space-time continuum. Through the din, Sarnower was desperately trying to hold down a conversation with a slutty looking girl who had set her sights on him at the beginning of the evening and who, from all the evidence, was determined to rope him into going home with her later. Suddenly, he was catching every third word of hers, then he would hear Tug across the room, then back to the girl whose sentences could no longer support any meaning. The words started to swirl and fall like dead autumn leaves as his attention flitted and raced trying to scoop them up.

And what were his parents doing here in this dusty old courthouse? He knew they were long dead, but there they were, as real and solid as anything he saw. Had they returned to cheer him on or drag him down to hell? The thought that he could be hallucinating was too scary to handle.

"We just dodged a bullet in there," Ballestracci said. "For now, you get to stay in the house. But next time, we may not be so lucky. I've told you this wasn't going to be fun, but you've got to keep your cool. Judge McGraw has already formed an impression of you and I'm sure I don't have to tell *you* about first impressions."

"Can we get another judge?"

The lawyer had started to walk down the corridor. Sarnower saw that Cassie and company were now far ahead and were blending into the crowd in the lobby.

"Highly unlikely. She's on the case now. Look." Nick stopped and turned to face Sarnower. "Your best shot is a good evaluation with the G.A.L. You've got to be dazzling. Maybe we can recoup some ground there. I mean you are a psychiatrist after all, aren't you?"

"Who is this guardian *ad litem*?"

"I don't know yet. The court will select one from a roster. Usually it's a social worker or psychologist. They'll want to meet with you and your wife, maybe see you together with your son."

At least this should be straightforward. He talked to these people all the time; spoke their language fluently.

"I should know soon, later today or tomorrow." Nick shot a glance in the direction of the lobby; Sarnower followed his eyes. Cassie, her brother and lawyer had gone.

"I've got to tell you Alan, this is it. You screw up the evaluation; you can count on losing the whole ball of wax. I can only do so much; the rest is up to you. I really hope you're not one of those people who secretly wants to destroy himself. I've had plenty of clients who do."

"I lust for self-immolation, is that what you think?"

"Let's just say you're plenty horny," Nick said, and turned to walk away. Maybe the man had a point; he was cutting off his nose to spite his face. He'd developed a total contempt for the process and the entire cast of characters, the lawyers, judges, their random, capricious style of making life-altering decisions for people they didn't know, decisions that were based on the flimsiest of evidence, everything that good science wasn't. But fighting it wasn't going to win the day. It was what it was. He was going to have to work with Nick, make it easier for him; even get the guy to like him. It would be a challenge but easier in the long run. Go along to get along.

And now at eleven-thirty, he was standing in a corridor of the Middlesex Probate Court building. Mitch would have to be picked up later that afternoon at camp. Would Janice Elsinger be there? This was not the time to get lost in fantasies. The judge had ordered him to come up with $800 a week in support and now that the retainer had been paid to Ballestracci, he was pretty much tapped out of liquid resources. For sure he'd have to sell some stocks and get the practice back into high gear. It would be difficult during the summer, but at least it might get his mind working at capacity again. Keeping busy, that's what had finally pulled Manny out of his slump.

Cassie would be coming over now on a regular basis to take Mitch for visits. He'd have to find some way to deal with her that wouldn't screw things up further. He flashed on those sad divorced fathers at weekend soccer games. If he didn't pull his act together soon, that would be him too.

The beginning of a lunch crowd was starting to form around the small snack stand in the lobby. He walked toward it, aware that he hadn't eaten a thing since last night with Nina. Too wasted on her generous Cosmos to prepare anything elaborate, they'd heated up a "gourmet" pizza from the freezer. Normally particular about such things, but drunk and ravenous after his romp, he'd split the pizza with her, inhaling its stale crust and gooey, greasy toppings. Now more than twelve hours later, his stomach had started to rumble, and even the image of Judge McGraw's huge, pendulous breasts wasn't enough to shut down his growing hunger.

He recognized some of the players from earlier in the morning gathered around the stand. The proprietor, a heavy red-faced man with several days growth of beard and a filthy Red Sox cap on his head was dispensing suspect, taupe-colored hot dogs, bags of chips and sodas, while his assistant, a young black man with a shaved

NOTHING TO SEE HERE

head and two huge gold hoop earrings worked the other side of the booth. He had a headset on and was weaving to the beat of some private rap group as he worked. Even through the buzz of customers, Sarnower could hear the tinny bass guitar and drums. The man would be wearing hearing aids in ten years.

The safest bet would be a bag of pretzels and a can of Coke, the salt and sugar rush would give him the kick to get moving into the afternoon. He would have to call Nina. He should stop by the office and deal with mail, return phone calls. And Mitch. He'd have to tell him what went on this morning, the return of his mother, at least on a limited basis. He'd be delighted and reassured. Mitch was incapable of seeing his mother's flaws even though she'd frightened him with her strange and scary behavior before she left. Sarnower knew Mitch continued to blame himself for her absence; he just wasn't being a good enough son. He hated Cassie for putting this enormous burden on the boy, a burden that no amount of talking would lighten. Mitch needed her forgiveness, and seeing her again could be the sign he'd been waiting for, that he'd have the chance to make amends, reassure her that he hadn't meant to be bad. The Cassie he saw that morning, prim, proper, and perfumed could at least give him that, if only she wouldn't undercut it all with her breezy dismissals. Mitch, his heart dangerously enlarged with mother-longing would grab it and be glad.

"Yo, ma man."

Sarnower looked up. Without realizing it, he had moved to the head of the line and was now being scrutinized by the bald young black man.

"And what would be yo' plea-SURE?" he asked. Lost in his son's redemptive dilemma, Sarnower had forgotten what he wanted.

"Bag of pretzels and a can of Coke." The man continued to bop to the internal strains of 50-Cent or Eminem or whoever the rapper *de jour* was. He flipped a can of Coke in the air and caught it behind his back without looking. He handed it to Sarnower who had wrestled a mangy bag of pretzels from a paint-chipped display rack. He paid and made for the exit.

The bright sun hung directly overhead. High noon. The phrase made him think of the classic Gary Cooper film he and his father had watched together so many times; one lone man against the bad guys, fighting the good fight all by himself, those campy, ominous clocks pounding inexorably toward noon. He saw his father's face caught in the strange blue light of the old Magnavox TV, silently mouthing the dialogue, he'd seen the picture so many times, a can of Rhinegold beer in his hand. "Whoever you're going to turn out to be in life," his father would tell him, "try to be more like Gary Cooper than those other schnooks. It wouldn't hurt if you ended up with Grace Kelly either," he would add, tipping the can to his son and winking.

Well, he hadn't ended up with Grace Kelly, although Nina was turning out to be a reasonable approximation. He got into the car and popped the can. The carbonation bit into his tongue and the roof of his mouth pleasantly. The first swig always surprised him in its cold assault, then its journey into his nose and finally down his throat. The satisfying belch at the end of the can. He tore at the bag of stale pretzels. It opened without resistance and he noticed that most were broken; a hefty sandbar of pretzel crumbs lined the bottom. He would have five or six, after that the stinging salt overtook any suggestion of taste.

He thought of his patients. He'd been out of touch with his service for days. What if one of them was in crisis and needed to contact him? Liz Dashiell, the coy borderline he'd run into in the supermarket buying drain cleaner for God knows what purpose, would have to be dealt with. She'd made it clear she was not to be ignored, with a force very much like Alex Forrest, that Glenn Close character in *Fatal Attraction*. The likeness to some of his patients, past and present, was eerie. Today, they'd think nothing of bringing him up on malpractice charges if he didn't respond immediately to their demands, however infantile or unreasonable. Their lawyers would gouge hefty settlements out of his insurance company and they'd spend their ill-gotten gains on drugs, cosmetic surgery, clothes, cars or cruises. After the money was gone they'd be more desperate than ever and ready to pounce on some other sincere, unsuspecting dope. He'd seen it happen.

He thought of his sturdy grandparents before they had come to this country, peddling *shmatas* off a pushcart in some dirt-poor Austro-Hungarian village. They'd pulled themselves up and out, cried on their own shoulders. That was the extent of their "therapy." The talking cure was carried out in bedrooms, over kitchen tables and on the steps of *shul* after Saturday morning services, not on anyone's $175 an hour couch.

"God, what have we come to?" he said aloud to no one. His parents, both dead, buried and crumbling. At least they weren't here to see him being stripped and picked apart piece by piece, bit by bit.

It would have broken their hearts (you're only as happy as your most unhappy child he remembered a colleague saying once.) No, at least his parents had the good sense to die before the new millennium, the horrific terrorist attacks, the scary stock market plunge, steroid-enhanced telemarketers breeding like locusts and plaguing the dinner hour, impossible-to-use cell phones that when folded up were smaller than your erect dick.

Without realizing it, he had put the car in gear and was already en route. But to where? Rather than drive back to his office in Chestnut Hill, he found himself almost ready to cross the Charles River over the Longfellow Bridge and head for downtown Boston. Who or what was downtown that he had to see? As much as he had always resisted the Freudian doctrine of unconscious determination, a stubborn part of him still held out. Even now, with medications, self-help gurus and good old-fashioned discipline, we are still meek, cowering slaves to our instincts and primitive cellular drives. Hunger, sex, comfort, the need to get high, fly, escape. Beyond the pleasure principle as the Great One himself had described it. The obliteration of all drives and stirrings, the end even of consciousness itself. He found himself heading toward Tug's office.

Chapter 8

THE DRISCOLL GROUP. Or was it Driscoll Associates? Sarnower couldn't remember, but he thought he knew the building in which Tug maintained his lavish suite of offices. He was nearing State Street and could see the glistening tower that held Ballestracci's office, site of his first stomach-churning meeting. He could picture Nick behind his desk, leaning back in that large leather chair, twirling his reading glasses by the stem, squinting in concentration at another client, nodding in agreement.

Once a week visitation and $800 a week in temporary support. How was he going to come up with that kind of money and still have funds to live on? He felt his stomach roll, the Coke and pretzels refusing to settle. We dodged a bullet this time, Nick had said. A Pyrrhic victory at best. So he could stay in the house. For now. Big fucking deal. He was going to have to put up with Cassie again, her rages, her volatility, her unpredictable ways with Mitch. Zero to super-bitch in five seconds.

Was that why he was crashing in on Tug unannounced? The morning's court proceedings had marked the official beginning of financial and emotional ruin that was sure to continue, tearing loose bleeding chunks of everything he had made of himself, everything he had built, until finally, there would be nothing left. He'd be reduced to a spirit, *The Psychiatrist as Poltergeist*. But at the same time, the prospect gave him a strange, unexpected lightness. "Freedom's just another word for nothing left to lose." Good old Janis reaching out across the decades.

At this hour, Tug was sure to be in the midst of his wheeling and dealing, working phones, dictating memos and barking directives. He had no time for metaphysical cogitation. Tug's was a life of steady

153

enlargement and acquisition, in contrast to his own which had started to gather speed in its erosion. In the past couple of weeks, he'd lost another five pounds, and his clothes, rather than draping fashionably had started to hang on him like a stick figure. No, he was on the way out, while Tug was growing and living larger than a Thanksgiving Day parade float. At least he loved what he did. He'd been lucky to find his niche early in the game, the ringmaster and MC at stoned-out Hyde Park parties or in sedate Zurich boardrooms, unlike Sarnower for whom psychiatry had some vague, never realized promise of "career satisfaction," a phrase popular years ago but now as vacuous as the stale, nauseating air in his car.

He was starting to feel like the Flying Dutchman, condemned to float and wander the earth until the crack of doom, unable to light for more than a few minutes at a time. Formerly, his days were spent seated in his climate-controlled office, and now here he was, in the car driving endlessly to or from the office, the lawyer, or chauffeuring Mitch (what *was* Tracey Bowen doing now? He could really use her help. Could her mother forgive him for the burlesque on his front lawn?)

For the second time that day, a parking space had just opened up, a half block from Tug's office. He'd save a cool twenty dollars because someone up there was still looking out for him, however tenuously. Justice meted out in coffee spoons. At this rate, he'd be 450 years old before the scales were balanced again. He backed the car in, slicing the cut perfectly in one fluid movement. Soon he'd be teaching Mitch how to do this, helping him bone up for the written learner's permit test, taking him out early Sunday mornings to vacant parking lots to practice three-point turns; that is, if he was still Mitch's father.

Lunch hour was ending and people were drifting back to work. In the high, clear summer light, everyone looked good. Young men in lightweight suits, freshly barbered, animated, trading dirty jokes, bemoaning the Red Sox; women walking in pairs, their bare skin glowing, laughing, comparing dating horror stories, glossy, newly shampooed hair blowing gently behind them in the soft breeze. Time was moving on, everyone was so much younger than him now, he was shrinking away in his once-tight clothes, pretzel crumbs and a spent can of Coke in his lap.

He brushed the crumbs to the floor. He had to get up and out. Anything was preferable to sitting still, where he'd easily be captive to an unending stream of reflection, fantasy and unpredictable memory. He'd had patients who were frightened of going to sleep. There, they'd be attacked and ravaged by nightmares, held hostage by the dark side of their own minds. The sudden, scary episode in his office the other day, that brief step into an unreal, floating parallel world was a reminder of his own increasing vulnerability, the stress eating away at healthy defenses like an army of subterranean carpenter ants. The nervous breakdown or "psychotic decompensation," the final insult to a flayed, tender ego.

He was now on the sidewalk, blending in with other pedestrians. The sun warmed his face and he took off his jacket, suspending it by his thumb over his shoulder. An attractive young woman with severe, spiky blond hair and thin black glasses smiled at him as he passed. Did she know him? He knew that face, but from where? An old patient? One of Tug's ex-girlfriends? Placing her could become the obsession of the day and divert him from everything he still needed to do. Part of him welcomed the challenge, perhaps a fantasy or two in the bargain, he'd have her on a Caribbean island, wearing nothing but a skimpy grass skirt, her spiky hair starting to grow out, now soft and bleached white by the sun, she'd be tanned of course, all over; sea air and sweat baked into her skin.

Tug's building was smaller and more graceful than he had remembered it. How long had it been since he'd been here? Tug kept his professional and recreational lives separate and discouraged his off-hours retinue of hangers-on and merry pranksters from contacting him at work. Although Sarnower was in a different class of friend, his sudden appearance might ruffle the delicate scrim of his operation. No matter, Nina had welcomed his unannounced visit last night so why shouldn't Tug?

His first guess had been right, it was the Driscoll Group, as stated in block gold letters on a thick, burnished mahogany door. There was a discrete doorbell under a tiny brass plaque that read "please ring." Sarnower noticed a small video camera perched high above the door like an exotic bird on the branch of a tropical tree. Tug was screening his visitors now. Homeland security had come to the Driscoll Gang. Had something happened that Tug hadn't told him about? A crazed client barging in screaming and terrorizing his staff? Unthinkable ten or fifteen years ago, events like that were now commonplace. You couldn't watch CNN for more than a week without seeing someone go berserk in McDonalds or K-mart. Sarnower himself, now losing his own protective skin could almost empathize, he was getting to know the currents and undertows that would drive you to such a point.

He smiled and waved into the camera, rang and was immediately buzzed in. Apparently he could still pass for a sane person. Inside, Tug had completely renovated the suite. A dark gray carpet, so new the chemical odor was still in the air, lay like a calm, still sea on the floor. The stodgy old-boy-club heavy desks and chairs had been replaced with sleek futuristic glass and chrome furnishings. Catalogs came to his own office filled with cold, sterile stuff like this. They even featured pictures and "bios" of the designers as if they were minor celebrities, with names like Sven, Olaf and Helmut, sporting shaved heads, filigreed goatees, bilateral earrings and impossibly small glasses. They looked out with total contempt as if they were doing you a favor by selling you their wares. Sales by intimidation from the hipper-than-thou.

Although the props had changed, the swarm and buzz was the same. There was trusted Sheila at the reception desk on the phone, taking notes and carrying on a conversation with one of the associates at the same time. She gave multi-tasking a whole new meaning. Her eyes lit up when she saw Sarnower.

"Dr. Sarnower, how are you?" she asked, surprised to see him.

"Hi Sheila," he returned, advancing to take her hand.

"Donald told me about your...you know, situation," she whispered. "I just wanted to let you know I think about you, and I'm praying for you and Mitch."

"Thanks," he said, his voice breaking unexpectedly. At least someone was taking him seriously; he was touched. Prayer still had a place, even in the Temple of Paganism that was Tug's office. Suddenly, she withdrew her carefully manicured hand and turned the pages in a large appointment book at the center of her new millennium desk.

"Do you have an appointment with Donald? I don't see you in the book."

"No. Actually, I'm here on the spur of the moment."

"Oh," she said, confused. He was a monkey wrench in the well-oiled cogs, a hair in the soup. "He's pretty busy today." She looked at him, brightening. "But I'll see what I can do." She dialed the intercom. "Dr. Sarnower is here."

Tug's voice, loud and metallic as his new furniture, barked on the other end.

"Sarnower? Throw that bum out! And call security!" He hung up.

Sheila put down the phone and smiled.

"He'll see you now. But don't tie him up for too long. He's got a conference call from Japan in twenty minutes."

"Thanks," he said and headed down the familiar hall to Tug's corner office. There was recessed lighting and an occasional modern abstract graphic on the bright white walls. Although it was decorated completely differently, Sarnower was reminded of the walk to Ballestracci's office, down that corridor with portraits of long-dead partners of the firm.

And there was Tug's office, door open. He sat with his feet up on his new desk pitching a deck of playing cards into a stainless steel mesh waist-basket across the room. Sarnower knocked and walked in.

"Working hard or hardly working?" he asked. Tug smiled but remained focused on the cards.

"Ah, the rowboat moves between strokes," he said slowly in the manner of a Saturday Night Live guru on a papier-mâché mountaintop.

Sarnower smiled. "Gee, if you manage to memorize every cliché and bit of pseudo-wisdom, you too can achieve eternal knowledge and light."

Tug banged the desk. "Shit, man, you found me out." He put the remaining cards down and gestured to a chair for Sarnower.

"And to what do I owe the honor?"

"I'm not sure anyone considers it an honor to have me in their presence anymore."

Tug laughed. "We all know that."

"I had my first judicial humiliation this morning. Cassie's moving ahead full steam to grab custody of Mitch and have me thrown out of my own house. I have to give her $800 a week in support."

"Fuck. When do you have to be out?"

"No date yet. We have to be "examined" by a guardian *ad litem* to find out which of us is sane and can be a fit parent, if you can believe that."

"That should be pretty clear."

"Not really. Cassie looked good, like her old self. Someone did a great job cleaning her up and coaching her. Maybe she's on medication, I don't know. But it's becoming obvious how things are going to play out. They're claiming I'm an abusive monster; Cassie couldn't take it any more and had to leave. She was at the end of her rope, the poor, victimized woman. With me out of the picture, she'll be a terrific mom, caring, devoted, attentive. Everyone will be happy. Mitch will be better off without me. Abuse has taken on a whole new meaning since we were young. Now, just getting your kid to eat his vegetables can be spun into some kind of heinous crime in the hands of the right lawyers."

"What an abortion," Tug said softly, shaking his head.

Sarnower felt the lump return in his throat. Sheila's concern, and now even Tug was beyond his banter.

"Look, I'm not here for pity," he said barely getting out the words. This was as close as he'd ever come to pure, white-hot hatred for himself. His load, the thoughts he was carrying, it was all too much. Generations of poor, struggling ancestors, always, *always* finding some way to survive, some way to hold onto their dignity and pride in situations far more grim than his. And here he was, Alan Sarnower, M.D., the end of the line, their last spokesman, the only voice they had left. He had to do right by them, continue to represent them, bring their spirits forward for generations that were yet to happen. He got up quickly and closed the door to Tug's office.

"You record things in here, don't you? Meetings, conversations, phone calls?" he whispered.

"What?"

"Don't mess with me Tug, I wasn't born yesterday."

"I don't know what you're talking about." Tug was genuinely puzzled. "Do I look like Dick Nixon? What's this about? Are you all right? I'm sensing a little paranoia around the edges."

"I'm fine, really."

Tug stared at Sarnower, trying to add it up. He sat back in his chair, expressionless. Sarnower seemed relieved. He pushed on.

"Tug...I'm...I want to do it." He stopped, hoping not to have to spell it out.

Tug remained silent, twirling a pencil.

"I'm going to take her out. Or have it done."

Tug jerked his head back as if he'd just witnessed a car crash, then burst into laughter.

"You're joking, right?"

Sarnower sat back in his chair, silently shaking his head. That nauseating wave of self-loathing had subsided, as had Tug's laughter.

"Dude, I love a good murder as much as the next guy, but you've got to be out of your fucking mind. We shouldn't even be having this discussion." He looked around the room. "Alan. That night? We were high; remember? Stoned. Wasted. I was *kid-ding*. After thirty fucking years don't you know my twisted sense of humor by now? Buddy, take a deep breath and let's get real. Are you losing it?"

Sarnower looked at him smiling. "Maybe I am out of my mind. I'm not sure I can tell the difference anymore."

"You're freaking *me* out. I've never heard you talk like this."

Sarnower felt himself fall through space. He was vaguely aware that something important had been breeched with his friend.

"Tell you what," Tug got out finally. "I've got an important call soon. I'll take it, wrap things up here, we'll go out for a couple of beers, just like Chances R, Hyde Park. The old days. What do you say?"

The voice, the words, the all too familiar patter suddenly made him furious.

"Don't patronize me!" he shouted.

"Alan, what's with you?" Frightened, Tug backed his chair away from the desk, away from Sarnower. "You're supposed to be a shrink for Christ's sake, the voice of reason and sanity."

"Sanity is a tune that can be whistled in many keys," Sarnower pronounced slowly. He had no idea what that meant.

Tug raised his eyebrows, turned up the corners of his mouth ready to laugh, but checked himself. "You want to start this meeting over again?"

"I didn't realize this was a meeting."

Tug was struggling now, doing his best to close the sale, bring it all back to the table, but Sarnower wasn't budging. He was throwing Tug over the side too, along with everyone else. A friendship of almost thirty years, it was surely the most durable thing he had left now. But he was on a mission and it was carrying him away. Those little black floaters, the ones he'd seen before he called Manny Abravanel, were coming back too.

The phone rang. The important conference call from Japan. Still staring at Sarnower, Tug picked up the phone slowly.

"Yes?" Sheila was saying something squeaky, he couldn't make it out, but on the other side of the globe, several wealthy, well-dressed Japanese businessmen were gathered around a speakerphone on a huge, gleaming conference table. The one with the best command of English would be speaking with Tug, the others would nod their heads in unison, as he gave short, periodic translations into Japanese. They would be eager and honored to be working with the successful

American businessman Donald Driscoll. Undoubtedly, they were paying him some obscene fee too, and here was Sarnower, wasting his good friend's valuable time, perhaps for all he knew, even making him an accessory to this demented scheme.

"Can we reschedule?" he heard Tug ask. "Something's come up here...yes, I'm sure. No, I know. Thanks Sheila."

He replaced the receiver and looked Sarnower in the eyes. "I don't know what to say. I think you really mean it."

"What if I do?"

"The husband's the very first one the police look at in these cases. Especially if you're in the middle of a nasty divorce. Just how long do you think it would take before they're banging on your door?"

"I think this is turning you on," Sarnower said, smiling.

Tug looked from side to side surreptitiously, a trademark move of his when he was about to divulge something in confidence.

"I admire your initiative," he whispered. "It's dramatic, ambitious, edgy, a bold gesture. Truth to tell, on at least a couple of occasions I too have had the fantasy of your lunatic wife floating face down in a stagnant quarry in South Boston with some of Whitey Bulger's defunct associates. But you've got to know in these matters the police are much smarter than you. You're completely out of your league. Totally."

"I think I could do it," Sarnower said. He was in for a penny and in for a pound now. "It would be a challenge, kind of the ultimate chess game."

"Alan, you're not fit to play tiddlywinks, much less catch-me-if-you-can with Boston Homicide Detectives." He laughed. "I can see you now in the 'box' downtown. They won't even have to do the 'good-cop bad-cop' routine. They'd sweat a confession out of you in about seven seconds with a cup of bad coffee and a stale sandwich."

He stood up, walked to the front of the desk and sat down on a corner, retrieving the remaining cards and pitching them again.

"How about a movie tonight? I'll call a couple of lady friends, we'll catch a flick, go out for drinks afterwards."

Even Tug had had enough of his idiotic bravado and wanted to wrap it up. He must think I'm the biggest dope alive. It would be embarrassing even to attempt to socialize with Tug and his "lady friends" after making such a complete ass of himself. The best course would be to shut up and beat a retreat while he still could.

He rose. "I'll think about it. I've got to pick Mitch up at camp soon. I haven't seen him in twenty-four hours, he may need some attention."

Tug brightened. "Bring the lad along, we'll introduce him to some fine adult pleasures."

Where normally this would have irritated Sarnower, in his reduced standing it was funny. The exhaustion of an awful day was starting to blow in like a storm cloud. The fatigue from lack of sleep, his disastrous court ordeal earlier, the ghostly visitation from his parents, and now the compromised position with his old friend, four systems coming together to form the perfect headache.

"I'll think about it," he said again, moving toward the door. Tug remained seated on the corner of his desk and winked. The bum's rush, with a velvet-gloved hand.

Traffic was light as Sarnower made his way back to Newton. He was wasted, completely spent, like coming home from one of those forty-eight hour parties he faintly remembered from college. They'd start late Friday night and the last barely ambulatory stragglers would be out by early Monday morning. You could easily sleep for two or three days straight. And what was with that wink? It was something Tug might do to throw a curve at one of his clients, or to a girl he knew he had the goods on.

The full weight of the last hour was sinking in. He'd been out of control, incredibly stupid. His stock had tumbled. He'd always occupied something of a lofty position in Tug's estimation, though Tug would admit it only under duress, or the fortification of some mixture of chemicals. He had a balance, even a moral authority that Tug found lacking in his business contacts and other friendships. Tug truly valued his input, came to him on occasion for advice, particularly when going into a tricky negotiation, or to clarify a "feeling" he had about an adversary, and needed help forming a plan of attack. Now, Sarnower was no more useful than an old Ann Landers column.

Cars of parents were already lined up waiting for their charges. The scene brought him back to his fantasy of the day before with Janice, the two of them in Venice. Her wonderful face had started to soften and vanish.

Kids were beginning to stream out of the entrance where some parents had stationed themselves to wait. Several were talking to each other as if they were old friends. Neither he nor Cassie had ever been able to connect with the parents of Mitch's friends though they'd tried with cookouts and dinner parties. They'd seemed hopelessly boring and mundane with conversation centered on kids, PTA, summer camps, family vacations, or good plumbers (if you were lucky.) Sarnower would feel sad and frustrated after those limp gatherings. There must be something wrong with him that he couldn't get enjoyment from sharing these simple bonding rituals. Their impatience must have shown; they rarely got reciprocal invitations. Those loving parents who'd wrap their entire lives around their children, would be thanked later with legal scrapes, slamming doors, substance abuse, and finally severed connections. So much for Dr. Spock and Mr. Rogers.

And here were Mitch and his friend. Of course he would have to thank Janice and offer to return the invitation. Mitch spotted him in the car and was waving, pulling Jonathan with him. He was dirty and sweaty, but beaming.

"Dad, can Jonathan come over?" he asked out of breath.

"Uh, maybe some other time," Sarnower answered. "Today's not a really good day." His headache had moved to the back of his skull, pounding like a colonial blacksmith.

Mitch frowned, creating dark creases in his forehead where the field dirt had caked on his skin. "Pleeeeze, please. Why not?" he pleaded. Jonathan looked at the ground, embarrassed to be in the middle. Sarnower felt sorry for him.

"Jonathan," he said and the boy looked up, expressionless. "I promise we'll make it some other time. Tonight's just not a real good time."

Sarnower made it short and sweet, any justification would sound like an excuse and make the boy squirm even more. But Mitch wasn't going to let him off. His face turned red under the brown dirt, giving him the color of a new penny.

"Dad, you never let me have anyone over!" he stamped his foot. It was true. Sarnower considered most of Mitch's friends a pain to have in the house. They were noisy and played music so loudly he'd have to go upstairs and tell them to turn it down. They'd bring food up when he wasn't looking and Sarnower would often find candy wrappers, empty bags of chips or Fritos and spilled cans of soda, the contents creating sticky shapes on the floor. Was he really serious about killing Cassie? What would Tug make of his pathetic display? Was it possible to redeem himself?

"It's ok Mr. Sarnower," Jonathan said finally, wanting to bring this to a close. He turned to Mitch. "I'll see you later," he said and started to walk away.

"Jonathan," Sarnower called after him, getting out of the car. "Where's your Mom? I want to thank her."

The boy, now deflated by the rejection, gestured vaguely in the direction of the cars ahead. Sarnower walked behind him toward the SUV. The blurry image of Janice would become clear and corporeal. He felt his heart start to race, making the pounding in his head almost unbearable.

Janice had opened the door and was getting out, a lean tanned leg and a foot in a thin, expensive sandal with toenails polished bright red. *The Split-Off Part Object: Fetishism in the Middle-Aged Man.* Hugging her son, she caught Sarnower's eye.

"Hi Dr. Sarnower."

"Alan, please."

"Jonathan and Mitch had such a good time last night," she beamed. "We went out for ice cream, then to a movie. That new really scary one? I'm forgetting the name—you know, those shipwrecked teenagers and that psychopathic killer with the reconstructed face and those hooks for arms. I probably should have called to get your permission, but Mitch said you'd say it was ok."

"I'm sure it was fine," Sarnower said softly. The woman was energized, jacked, almost high. Her coursing adrenaline probably kept her so toned and trim; she was almost a force field. If he got too close he'd get zapped, a living Taser gun.

"I want to thank you for having Mitch over and for bringing him in today," he said. "When things settle down a bit, we'll be glad to have Jonathan over too."

She waved dismissively. "He and Jonathan get along so well, it actually makes life easier on me." She was drifting away, studying her son, brushing softball dust off his T-shirt, and straightening his hair. Jonathan rolled his eyes during the grooming ritual and strained to get into the vehicle. Seeing his discomfort, Sarnower started toward his car.

"Alan." He turned. She came up to him and gently rested her beautiful hand on his arm. "Look," she said softly. "Mitch told me about, you know...your situation. I just wanted to let you know if you want to come over some evening for some...adult company and conversation, you're more than welcome. No pressure."

"Thank you. That's a nice offer." He was surprised. He hadn't figured Janice as the sort that would reach out like that, she seemed so flighty and lightweight. Even after twenty-plus years in psychiatry, he could still come across unexpected caves and caverns of kindness and empathy. There was always more to learn; people are never, ever known.

Adult company and conversation. That phrase. It had a tantalizing, ambiguous flavor; it could be stocked with all kinds of meaning. These days everything was said in code, proposition and deniability, rolled up together in the same words. It was up to him to decipher the correct meaning. And that soft touch to the arm? It all smelled like an invitation to something.

Mitch was standing by the car watching his colleagues continuing to stream out of camp. He had the perfectly still, far away look that Sarnower was seeing more and more of, almost a trance, staring into some middle world. Mitch snapped back as his father approached.

"How did it go, buddy?" he asked, knowing as soon as the words were out of his mouth that the boy would swell with anger.

"Can it," he hissed.

"Ready to go?" He nodded faintly and walked around to the passenger side. "I want to tell you something," Sarnower said as the boy slid in. "Mom's going to be seeing you again." He turned, looking for a reaction.

"Really?" His tone was noncommittal. He continued to look straight ahead.

"You don't sound very happy about it."

"I'm happy. Is she moving back with us?"

"No. I'm not sure how that's going to work out but for the time being, she's going to be getting together with you once a week. It'll be fun. You guys can go shopping or to a movie, or have lunch together, whatever you want."

"Cool."

They were driving back to the house, each staring ahead.

"Mitch, are you angry with Mom?"

"Yeah."

"Why?"

"She left us."

"Yes, she did."

"She'd rather be someplace else."

Sarnower couldn't argue with that. The facts spoke for themselves.

"I know she cares for you. A lot."

The boy turned his head and looked out the window. Without seeing his face, Sarnower could tell from the minute changes in his breathing that he had started to cry.

"Don't feel badly, honey. Remember we talked about how confused and mixed up Mom was?" Mitch didn't respond. "I think she's starting to feel better and figure things out, and part of that is she wants to pick up on being your Mom again."

"What's the point?" he answered. There was ice in his voice. He turned to look at his father. "We're doing fine now."

"Yeah, we're doing ok, but Mitch, your Mom's always going to be your Mom. I know she wants a chance to make it up to you."

"She didn't even write or call." He certainly knew the face cards in the game of relationships.

"We're both going to have to work really hard to help Mom feel good about coming back," Sarnower said, trying to be magnanimous. He'd lead by example. "Let's try to welcome her, ok?" Immediately the words turned rancid in his mouth. Just an hour ago he'd been in Tug's office wanting to finish her off. The hypocrisy made him wince.

They pulled into the driveway. Although he'd been home earlier that morning to shower and change, it felt like weeks since he'd really been there, able to sit, stare at the wall, coddle a glass of wine, listen uninterrupted to a Mahler symphony. The day had already been stretched like warm taffy, shapeless and gooey. The lack of sleep had distorted his sense of time. He was supposed to call Nina and ask her to start rebooking patients, but now with Mitch needing him, he couldn't summon the energy.

The phone was ringing, but by the time he got in the door and picked up the receiver, the line was dead.

He stood perfectly still in the foyer. Mail had fanned out on the floor where the carrier had shot it through the brass slot in the door. There were supermarket circulars, the electric bill, credit card invitations, and a professional journal. He scooped them up and put them on the small table. In the late afternoon sun, the glossy blue cover of *The Journal of American Psychiatry* reflected a soft azure patch on the white wall. Earlier in his career, when he craved exposure and visibility, Sarnower had contributed articles, letters to the editor and had served as a peer-reviewer. He'd gotten his name out as a Young Turk, an aggressive, state-of-the-art psychiatrist, up on recent advances in medication and short-term therapy, which was becoming *de rigueur*, particularly among the new, dollar-conscious HMOs. Now it was rare if he even scanned an issue. A growing pile sat stacked in his study, unread, desolate, gathering dust, no longer even wanting to be disturbed. The new one on the hall table, announcing its arrival with the pretty blue cloud on the wall, would be joining the others in short order. He should probably throw them all out.

Sy Mischakov. That was his name, the editor of the journal. Early on he had befriended Sarnower, had called him whenever he was in Boston. They would get together for lunch or drinks at one of the hip new cafes near Sarnower's office. Sy would sit across the small cramped table and talk the entire time, barely touching his Cobb salad. That sad walleye he had made it hard to know how to look at him, although Sy himself seemed fairly oblivious to it. He would fix one eye on Sarnower and the other would roam the restaurant on its own. Sy was always bringing his trunk of *tsuris* up to Boston, his difficult wife, and his troubled children. Sarnower, who had wanted to keep his prominent standing with the journal would look at Sy intently and listen as if he were in session, smiling and nodding. Sy's parents were immigrants from Russia, and the familiar whiff of old-world sadness and resignation emanated from him like the stale odor of mothballs on a worn suit. Apparently it was impossible to escape the reach of the persecuted, the traumatized and displaced in his own lifetime. Maybe Mitch would have a shot at it.

And where was Sy now? Slowly, almost imperceptibly, he had drifted out of Sarnower's life. Curious, he opened the magazine and looked for the masthead. Sy's name was nowhere to be found. The editor now was someone named Geoffrey L. Burke Jr., M.D. Sanitized and ethnically cleansed. He'd never heard of him.

Over the years, friends, family and acquaintances had spun off into scattered orbits, growing smaller and fainter, never to be seen or heard from again. Had he ever said goodbye to the man or made plans to stay in touch? Sy could be long dead for all he knew. And he wasn't the only one. College friends, colleagues, distant relatives, all may have gotten off the big train without him knowing. He should try to keep in touch, but with whom? And ultimately why? Where was he in *their* Rolodexes?

The sun had sunk while he stood in the foyer pondering. He noticed that the blue reflected patch the journal had produced a short while ago had vanished on the darkening wall. The phone rang again. He went into the kitchen and picked it up on the third ring.

"Alan."

"Manny."

"Listen," there was an urgent edge to his voice. "I've been trying to get you all day. Why don't you get a cell phone like every other normal person?"

"I've been out. I'm just now catching up. And I don't want to be a normal person."

"That's kind of what I'm calling about."

"Oh?"

"When you were in my office the other day? I couldn't stop thinking about what you told me. I got a very strange feeling. About you. Unsettled. I've been in the business long enough to listen to my gut, you know?" Manny stopped for breath. He was wound up, riding some kind of wave. "Anyway, that night I had a dream."

"Look whose ready to be talking to Dr. Bill."

Manny ignored the dig and continued. "You and I were on a plane. Somewhere, the Southwest maybe, I don't know. It doesn't matter. For some *meshuggah* reason we were going to jump—you know, sky dive. Crazy, huh? I'm scared shitless of heights. I shake on a ladder changing bulbs in the dining room chandelier."

Sarnower looked at his watch. Manny was too much to deal with now.

"Anyway," he continued, "the time comes and we jump. We're falling, I pull my cord, my chute opens and I'm whisked away by the updraft, just like you see in those old paratrooper movies. I look down to find you. You haven't pulled your ripcord yet; you're hurtling to the ground. You're falling so fast, in a second or two you're a tiny dot and then I can't see you at all. Finally I land, but there's no sign of you. You're just...gone."

"That's it?"

"Schmuck! Haven't you been listening? You're dead. Finished."

"Dreams are symbols Manny, and not always very good ones at that."

"I'm never wrong about these things."

Sarnower laughed. "Sorry I'm not buying it." Look, Manny I have to get off the phone. Mitch wants dinner."

"So bring him over. I'll order up some Thai or Mexican."

"Mitch hates Thai and Mexican."

"Pizza then."

"No. I've got to talk with him tonight. Cassie's back in the picture. She wants me out of the house immediately so she can play at being the full-time doting mother."

"Grandiosity. It's part of the symptom picture."

"Yeah, tell that to the judge. If that wasn't bad enough I have to be seen by a guardian *ad litem* to evaluate my fitness to care for my own son."

Manny was silent. "We have to talk. Soon, Alan. Please," he said finally.

"I wish I could. I have to start up my practice again. I've been saddled with support payments too." Nina. He couldn't forget to call her. "The party's over. I've really got to get back to work."

"Next week," he said softly and hung up.

Falling to earth. What was the terminal velocity you reached in a free fall? Sarnower vaguely remembered from college physics it was something over 120 miles per hour. Friction could slow you down. Would you heat up and glow like a re-entering space module? It must be quite a way to go, all that air rushing by and your heart in your throat. Would it be hard to breathe? You'd look down and see the earth coming up at you so fast, like a huge speeding car, and it would probably be over quickly, you'd be splattered over several square yards of earth or tarmac before you could even process what was happening.

Mitch had come downstairs without him having heard a thing.

"Dad?" he shouted. How long had he been trying to get his father's attention?

His daydreaming made holes that were getting deeper and harder to climb out of. Catatonia, the endless daydream, the last refuge of the shell-shocked, the retreat of the disemboweled and torn apart, here I come.

"Mitch," he said, finally turning his attention to the boy. He was bobbing up and down on the balls of his feet again as if he had to pee badly. Sarnower noticed for the first time he was wearing different clothes from those he'd worn the day before. He must have spilled something on his shirt and pants, and Janice, undoubtedly the perfect mother, had lent him Jonathan's. She'd wash Mitch's sorry duds and return them clean, pressed and smelling like a Giverny flower garden. He was sure she used those annoying scented static guard sheets in the dryer, the ones that always ended up clinging to socks and underwear. Cassie, on the other hand, couldn't be bothered with any of that. If one of Mitch's pals got spaghetti sauce on his new T-shirt, that's how he went home. "I'm not a cleaning service," she would say. "Wash it yourself if it bothers you that much."

"What's for dinner?" Mitch asked, still bouncing. "Can we go out?"

"We've got stuff here."

"What, dorky old frozen pizza? Jonathan's family goes out all the time, and they've always got better snacks and more soda than we do."

"Mitch, I'm tired. We'll heat something up here. Plus we need to finish talking about Mom." The boy stopped bobbing and fixed his eyes on his father.

"We're trying to figure out the best situation for you and for all of us. That's what we were doing this morning. For the time being, Mom's going to be renting a place near by so she can see you regularly. We'll see how that goes and then we'll figure out if she'll move back to the house and I'll get my own place or if I'll stay here with you and Mom will get her own place. Do you follow me?" Sarnower emptied a package of pepperoni Hot Pockets on a cooking sheet and stuck them in the oven.

"Where am I going?" he asked. Tears were starting to pool on the ledges of his lower lids.

"You'll be staying right here in this house, champ, no matter what."

Mitch looked up at him, a huge drop fell onto his cheek.

"I'm sorry, I wasn't supposed to call you champ anymore," Sarnower said flustered.

Mitch smiled vaguely through the tears. "It's ok Dad, just don't do it in front of my friends."

"Promise," Sarnower said, raising his hand in a Boy Scout salute.

The mouth-watering smell of the heating food started to fill the kitchen. A breeze blew the gentle perfume of freshly cut grass in through the window.

> *Summer breeze makes me feel fine*
> *Blowin' through the jasmine in my mind*

Lately he couldn't get that old Seals and Crofts song out of his head. It pulled him back to college, or was it medical school, and a day probably very much like today, warm, bursting and generous. He could have been stretched out on the grass-carpeted quads studying for a final, that angle offering a delightful vista of bare female legs. He'd read the same sentence over and over again and reach the point of overloaded distraction where nothing penetrated and further study was useless. There had been jasmine in his mind all right, and it was taking up space where he needed to cram techniques of differential diagnosis.

He removed the Hot Pockets from the oven and heard the fine gloss of grease sizzle as it met the cool air. He poured glasses of

Coke. The boy was still and quiet, the tracks of his tears had made comical tiny roads down his face like a clown. There's certain to be a shower later. He'd also have to wash and press Jonathan's clothes and have Mitch return them tomorrow. That would be expected.

The doorbell rang. Was Mitch expecting a friend? The front door was open to catch the breeze, and he could often tell by the force and rhythm of steps on the stone walk who was approaching, he'd honed that part of his hearing to the acuity of a blind man. But he hadn't heard anyone and neither had Mitch.

He walked to the foyer. Cassie stood perfectly straight and centered in the doorframe. Since the morning, she had changed her blouse, but still wore the high priced Newbury Street look he found so troubling. Money, lots of it was behind her, propelling her forward. Her expensive haircut was blowing in the early evening breeze. He opened the screen door.

"Hello Alan," she said.

"*Mom?*" A half shout, half squeal from the kitchen. Mitch tore through the dining room and foyer and jumped into his mother's unprepared arms. The surprise and split-second recoil was lost on Mitch, but not his father. Cassie hugged her son as he buried his tear-stained face in her chest. He would surely leave a face-print of dust and dirt on her pale yellow silk chenille shirt, a shroud of Turin the dry cleaner would study tomorrow and shrug his shoulders over. "We'll do our best. Can't make any guarantees." Sarnower smiled.

"Let me look at my big boy!" Cassie held Mitch out to get a full view. "I don't believe how much you've grown!"

Any ambivalence he had shown over the past weeks was pushed aside. Sarnower felt betrayed and resentful.

"Honey, please wash your face," she said, noticing the brown smudge on her blouse. "Then we'll go out for some ice cream." Mitch darted for the first floor bathroom. Things were slipping away again.

"You should have called first," Sarnower said trying to gain some ground. "We were just sitting down to dinner."

"Oh, one of your usual frozen pizzas or chicken nuggets?" she asked, tilting her head. "I don't think so. As for calling you, the judge's ruling today is all the phone call you're going to get. And while you're up, I'll be happy to take my support check too."

"You're taking a lot for granted."

She smirked. "You still don't get it do you? I've already *been* granted. By Judge McGraw, this morning in Middlesex Probate

Court. That is, if you can remember this morning. Quite a display by the way. Are you that articulate with your patients?"

"You can't barge in here after all this time and commandeer my house and my son. And why did you tell that half-wit lawyer of yours I hit you? You know that's bullshit."

She snickered. "Abuse is abuse. This is war. What difference does it make anyway?" Her fancy makeover had given her a new balls-to-the-wall grip on her domain. She was flashing a spark he'd never seen before.

"I don't have $800 right now," he said feebly, flummoxed at his own ineptitude and inability to land a shot. He was sinking again into the same quicksand that had swallowed him earlier that day in court. Cassie's new witchcraft had pulled his defenses and verbal retorts right out from under him like a magician snapping a tablecloth, leaving the silverware and glasses in place.

"That's a crock. I know what your practice brings in."

"You're really getting off on this, aren't you? For your information, I haven't been seeing patients. All your bullshit has made it impossible to work. On top of that, I've had to pay my lawyer a huge retainer." He was shaking with rage.

"Save the sob stories and get back to your office. An order of support has been issued and you'll be held to it."

The New, Improved Cassie. He couldn't get over it; sharp, aimed, and loaded for bear. Her brother's money had airlifted her into entirely new terrain. He looked her in the eyes, now clear and steely.

"What can I say? I don't have it."

She smiled, mouth closed, squinting. "Keep it up," she whispered.

Mitch was back, pink, scrubbed and bright eyed.

"Ready?" she asked as he banged through the screen door ahead of her out to the waiting car. As soon as they'd vanished from sight, he went to the phone and called Janice. It was his time to howl. Shriek like a savage. He wanted some of that adult company and conversation. Whatever it was.

Chapter 9

TWO NIGHTS LATER, he pulled up in front of a large white Victorian mansion. A tall wrought iron fence surrounded the lush property, which spread over an entire block. A weathered mansard roof erupted with gables and dormers like eyes on a prehistoric animal; an ornate widow's walk ringed the third floor.

He parked in front. Everything about the place was oversized, as if bigger humans lived here. A wide flagstone walk ushered him from the gate to the deep porch and a large oak and beveled-glass door. The heady scent of narcissus and rare night jasmine plants rose from huge, glazed ceramic vases. He rang the brass bell and heard it's clunky antique *brrrring* echo through the cavernous hall. A moment later, through the frosted glass oval, he saw the outline of Janice, her tan legs partially hidden by a thick white terry cloth robe. There was a towel wound around her head, turban style. She opened the door smiling.

"I wasn't expecting you so soon. I just got out of the shower."

Sarnower checked his watch. In fact he was twenty minutes late. Who's counting?

"Sorry. I can come back later," he said, offering her a bouquet of tulips.

"Don't be ridiculous," she said pulling him across the threshold. She buried her head in the flowers and inhaled.

"Mmmm. Very Dutch. Let me put these in water and get us some drinks," she said, turning and walking down a long hall to what must be the kitchen.

He wandered into the living room. Dark mahogany wainscoting ran its entire length, interrupted only by a gigantic stone fireplace in which a large copper pot hung. From the shine it was clear it wasn't used for cooking. On the mantle were old carved wooden duck decoys. A tall, severe grandfather clock watched over the room. Several paintings and lithographs, landscapes and still-lifes adorned the walls, each with it's own brass light. End tables on either side of the sprawling couch displayed framed photos of Jonathan, Janice and a tall blond man Sarnower took to be her husband. He looked considerably older.

The unmistakable voice of Ella Fitzgerald was coming through on the stereo, but he couldn't locate the source of the music, there were no speakers in the room. Curious that someone of Janice's age would like vintage jazz, or maybe it was her husband's taste. Where was he, by the way? And where was Jonathan? Ella had started *How Long Has This Been Going On?* when Janice reappeared with a couple of tall frosted glasses.

"I hope these aren't too weak," she said smiling, flashing those great teeth.

"Let's put 'em to the test."

She gave him his glass and they clinked. A strong vodka and tonic charged down his throat. He thought of Nina and her expert Cosmos. Women definitely liked their booze these days; they could pound 'em down with the guys, *mano a mano*.

"Where are Jonathan and your husband?" he asked as they sat on the Chippendale sofa.

She took the towel off her head and shook her hair. "They're on some kind of father-son outward bound thing in Maine. Overnight. Jonathan's not my biological son," she added with a burst. It was important that he know this.

"Oh?"

"Roger was married before. Jonathan is his kid."

"You do look a little young to be his mother."

"I'll take that as a compliment," she beamed. "Roger is divorced from his first wife. I've never met her. She's supposed to be quite the bitch."

"How did you two meet?"

"Roger's a corporate attorney and was doing some work out in LA a couple of years ago. That's where I'm from. I was waitressing at the time to pay off some school loans. To make a long, boring story short, he came in for lunch one day, I'd just broken up with a guy I was going with, he'd just separated, we started talking and went out that night, really hit it off. A couple of weeks later, he sent me a one-way ticket to Boston. I hadn't been doing anything spectacular in LA, had never been out East, so I got on a plane. Basically I've never left. We got married about a year ago."

"The whirlwind romance."

"Sort of. Roger's a great guy, a wonderful father and a good provider. As you can see, I like nice things."

Sarnower scanned the room. "I'd say corporate law has been very good to him. And to you too."

"But...he's not very physical, if you know what I mean." She took a long pull on her drink and moved closer to him. Sarnower could feel her warm breath on his face. "I have very strong needs."

First Nina and now Janice. He'd hit the mother lode. It was hard to believe, a parallel universe of available women all around him, one as desirable and attractive as the next. Where had he been? Cooped up in a lousy marriage, that's where.

Setting down his drink, he gently opened her robe. There were two of the firmest most perfectly formed breasts he'd ever seen. Sarnower pulled her toward him and locked his mouth on hers. Oh, she was eager. He covered her perfect white teeth with his tongue and lost himself in her beautiful mouth. She unbuttoned his shirt and ran her perfect fingers over his chest.

"Roger never let's me do this," she purred. "He doesn't like to be touched. Sometimes I want to lick him all over. He'll nudge me away. I just need to feel like a woman. Is there anything wrong with that? Come."

She disengaged and took Sarnower by the hand, leading him through the living room and up a large, wide staircase. The blond oak treads were covered with a thick, muted Oriental runner held in place by gleaming, polished brass rods. The house was immaculate and smelled alternately of lemon and jasmine, the same fragrance that had greeted him on the porch.

On the second floor, Janice made a left down a long, wide hall. He passed what must have been Jonathan's room. From the open door he could see a wide-screen plasma TV and computer. There were large framed posters on the wall of sports figures and rock musicians Sarnower couldn't identify. The young were blurry, they moved at a speed too fast for him.

A bathroom on his left featured a restored claw-foot tub and Art Deco sink with shining silver plumbing. At the end of the hall they reached the master bedroom, easily as big as the living and dining rooms combined. Against the far wall was the largest bed he'd ever seen, magnificently framed at the head by a carved, pink marble arch. Sarnower stood at the entrance. He must have been gaping comically as Janice started to laugh.

"The arch, right? It gets everyone's attention. Roger and I brought it back from Tuscany on our honeymoon. Believe it or not, it was in our bedroom in the castle we were staying at, just as it is here. I told him I absolutely *had* to have it, kind of as a joke—we were both a little drunk at the time—and Roger immediately got dressed and went downstairs to the proprietor and started haggling with him. In Italian, no less. I was so impressed. At first the man refused to sell, but Roger browbeat him and must have offered an obscene amount of money; he still won't tell me how much. Finally the guy gave in. It cost a fortune to ship back here and install, but Roger says it was worth every cent. It reminds him of our honeymoon."

"Such a romantic gesture for an unromantic man."

"Yeah. Go figure."

Sarnower was figuring he'd like to be moving rose marble too, instead of paying spousal support.

She stood at the head of the bed and slipped off her robe, and Sarnower was treated to a full view of her spectacular body.

"Well, what do you think?" she asked, turning slowly.

His mouth dried instantly. Tanned all over, lean and gently curved, Janice was one of the new breed of younger women who had opted for a clean-shaven look, with a small dark "landing strip" between her perfect legs. Well, he could enjoy chocolate fudge as well as butter pecan; it was all delicious. Variety, the spice of Eros.

He was out of his clothes in seconds and on the huge bed with her, frolicking under that ponderous Italian marble arch, Roger's Italian marble arch. Like Nina, she knew exactly what she wanted and went right for it. He saw how Roger might have trouble keeping up. With twenty-plus years on her, he had to be fading.

Here he was with another man's wife in another man's bed. The thought was as seductive as it was repulsive. He was doing to poor old Roger exactly what was done to him weeks ago in his own bedroom. If Sarnower couldn't have Roger's money, his house, his marble, his easy, comfortable path through life, he'd take his wife. Fairness had to be distributed somehow. There was something very juicy about claiming your own justice.

After he was hard, Janice got on top and began to ride him. She started slowly, up and down, and gently side-to-side, in movements that made him think of a skater's figure eight. He closed his eyes and played with her incredible breasts, the nipples maroon and swollen.

Her still wet hair whipped his hands gently as she bobbed, and her breathing gradually became a soft moan that grew louder and louder.

He brought up the imagined scene of the two of them alone together on the Piazza del San Marco, leaning over, slowly licking the sweat off her upper lip. He thought of Nina, their combustion of just a few days ago, and back yet further to his first time with Cassie. They were all different and all the same, variations on a single theme.

Janice had left him far behind and was mounting the last rung on the ladder to her own satisfaction.

"Ohhhhh," she gasped as Sarnower, swimming between his fantasies came at the same time. She remained astride him with eyes closed, breathing deeply. He looked up at her, her hair dark and wild. She could have been riding a horse through the desert.

His release over too quickly, Sarnower got a sudden urge. It was nuts, he'd never done anything like it before. How would she take it? He barely knew her. It could turn her off completely. On the other hand, she might really dig it. Caution to the wind, he decided to go for it.

"I want to fuck you in the ass," he whispered.

Her eyes opened wide. "Oh, doctor," she giggled, rolling off of him. She opened the drawer to her nightstand and pulled out a handful of different colored lubricant tubes.

"What flavor?" she asked.

"Kumquat."

"No kumquat. I have Tango with Mango."

Sarnower grabbed the tube and began applying the gel to her luscious, rosy ass. He pulled her up, and, still hard and wet, entered her doggie style. Janice, for her part moved like a pro, quickly matching his rhythm. She was delightfully tight, much more so than in front, and the extra pressure on his dick brought him to a rapid, powerful orgasm. She'd done this before, a woman half his age with several obvious years of experience on him.

Now spent, he withdrew himself and flopped on his back.

"You're quite the little vixen."

Janice remained silent and stared at him.

"What?" he asked.

She shook her head and said nothing. Silence. He'd seen this odd withdrawal before with other women. Sometimes after the act something shifted, he could never understand what it was, a pang of regret, a dram of self-loathing. Even the most progressive women seemed to carry more conflicted baggage about sex than men. He'd never figure them out. Never.

"Are you ok?"

"Fine."

She dismounted and reached for her bathrobe. "I'll be back," she said padding to the bathroom. Alone, his mind a blank, Sarnower watched himself wilt. The sight was vaguely comical, like the deflating of a cartoon balloon. He should get dressed and go, he had no energy for serious post-coital talk.

Janice returned as he finished dressing. "You're going?" She sounded disappointed.

"I thought you might want to be alone."

"What made you think that?"

"You seemed..."

"Quiet? Into myself? Oh it's nothing. I just get like that. I'm very moody."

"You're entitled."

"Thank you," she snapped.

Sarnower stood up. Wading through Janice's darker emotional swells wasn't on the program this evening, though he sensed she really wanted him to stay and provide some professional solace.

"Sure you're ok?"

It was a stupid question, inviting just the thing he wanted to avoid.

"Of course. Why shouldn't I be ok? You're not the first guy I've screwed."

"That's not what I meant." What had brought up this brittle bit of dander? He wanted to leave badly, but on a good note. He kissed her on the forehead. "Thanks so much. This was really special."

She put her arms around him, looking up into his face.

"Don't think you're going to run my life now that you've fucked me in the ass."

What? Was she kidding??

"Frankly the thought hadn't crossed my mind."

Perhaps this was theater for his benefit, but she was definitely overplaying her hand. Instead of seeming alluring, mysterious and opaque, she'd come off as pouty and adolescent, probably not the effect she was reaching for. The difference in their ages was suddenly a yawning chasm. Undoubtedly, she'd broken a few hearts along the way, either before or during her marriage to Roger, but his wasn't going to be one of them.

* * *

Summer was winding down, the days were noticeably shorter, the evening air cooler, and getting back to a regular work schedule after the embarrassing morning in court and the strange but arousing evening with Janice had been difficult. Patients were straggling in slowly, languorous from vacation. Several had decided not to return to therapy. Those that did were needy; starved for his attention and validation, hungry for his voice and gestures, the cool leathery smell of his consulting room, the chance to be reassured by his diplomas and to stare at the rows of tired, leaning scholarly books with incomprehensible titles on their spines.

At times their demands had been too much and their renewed dependence on him a weight, like a young child clasping onto a leg to hang on for the ride. He wanted to throw up his hands and surrender. And through it all, he felt himself get lighter and lighter, with less and less to offer, drained and vacated. Although he hadn't seen his parents again after that day in court, there were other odd, startling apparitions in his visual field; a mouse scurrying off on the periphery, a boy in the distance he was sure was Mitch who turned out to be someone else. Once he'd heard his name called, but no one was there.

And Cassie. Her maneuverings, her court-sanctioned claims on Mitch, her pinched, acidic contacts with him had moved him closer to some kind of edge. On a short lease, she'd rented a two-bedroom condo in an upscale complex on Hammond Pond Parkway from a newly minted divorcee who had just filleted *her* ex financially and was on a three-month trip to the French wine country with a new boyfriend. To sweeten the deal for Mitch, she'd bought an expensive pedigree Airedale puppy, a large screen TV and a small dorm-style fridge that she put in his room and kept stocked with soda, candy and snack cakes. They'd spent one Saturday shopping for posters to hang in his bedroom. To Sarnower's distress, Mitch had selected large, suggestive photos of scantily clad Britney Spears, Christine Aguilera and some new teen idol he didn't know, with a drum-tight bare midriff, bellybutton rings and an ornate tattoo in the shape of an arrow leading south from her navel to the gardens of a pre-adolescent imagination. Mitch had never shown the slightest interest in girls before, but now he had taken the first steps on the road to sexualization; a small child seduced with a candy bar by a stranger, in this case his mother who was as oblivious to his needs as an abductor. She'd become expert in bribery and was buying his love on the installment plan.

One weekend, she'd taken him to Nantasket Beach. The sun had been high and strong all day and Mitch had been in and out of the water with nothing on but a bathing suit. When Cassie brought him back, he was as red as a tomato, burned all over. She'd completely forgotten to apply the sunscreen Sarnower had specifically reminded her to use. He was dehydrated and shivering. He'd vomited, and by evening small, pale yellow burn blisters had appeared on his back.

Sarnower was horrified. He'd interrogated Mitch, who was already embarrassed by the incident.

"I don't want to talk about it," he said, cringing from his burns.

He followed the boy through the house until, beaten down, he'd finally given up. Cassie had met someone on the beach and had been persuaded to go off with him for a couple of hours to get a tattoo on her ankle. She'd tried to get Mitch to come along, but frightened of the man, he'd refused. She'd returned a couple of hours later. Mitch had remained where she'd left him, unprotected, alone and baking in the sun.

When he called Ballestracci the next day wondering if her negligence constituted abuse, the lawyer was equivocal. He promised to make a note of it although it wasn't worth going back into court. Her offenses, none of which tipped the scale alone, were collectively indicting. She was killing him with a thousand tiny cuts.

Three weeks had gone by since their appearance before Judge McGraw and Sarnower was now constantly broke and forced to sell off stocks, often at a steep loss. The mandated weekly payments of $800 cut well beyond his discretionary budget into essentials. Soon Mitch would need back-to-school clothes and supplies. He had hoped to have the kitchen repainted, maybe even manage an end of summer get-away to the Cape or Vineyard, but those possibilities had faded. And Mitch, with his newly festooned room at Cassie's had become contemptuous of his own space at the house. It wasn't new or shiny. Food had to be eaten in the kitchen or dining room. The TV was old. He was moody and missed the dog, which he named Ecstasy. Appalled, Sarnower tried to ask how he'd gotten the name but Mitch had only smirked, shaking his head. The boy was being corrupted; the new freedom had lured him in like a siren.

The first meeting with the guardian *ad litem* had not been a spectacular success. As requested, he brought Mitch in with him. The office was in Arlington, and he'd gotten lost, arriving fifteen minutes late. The guardian, Eileen McCarthy, M.S.W. was in her late sixties or even early seventies. Her long white hair was drawn on top of her head in a bun and she wore an old flower-print dress. She must have seen Sarnower roll his eyes.

"You don't seem to be taking this very seriously," she'd admonished after he and Mitch sat down.

"My apologies. I don't know Arlington well at all. It won't happen again."

Turning to Mitch: "And how are you today, young man?"

She was stiff and flinty, a maiden aunt unused to talking to children.

"Ok," he answered, looking at the floor.

Silence. Eileen tapped her pen on the desk.

"Is he always like this?" she asked Sarnower.

"No. He's in a new setting; he doesn't know you. Sometimes it takes a while for him to warm up, feel comfortable."

This was pulling teeth. Eileen McCarthy could have been a clerk at the Department of Motor Vehicles for all her clinical skill.

"How has it been living with your father?"

"I don't know. Fine, I guess."

She was getting uncomfortable.

"Well, can you tell me some of the things you do together?"

Mitch looked at his father. "Not much. He doesn't even let me have friends over."

Suddenly alive, she smelled blood. "Oh? And why is that?"

"He says we're too messy and make too much noise."

Sarnower felt his face flush. "Well, that's not quite true. I do expect them to be neat and respectful of others."

Mitch turned on him. "That's crap, Dad. You wouldn't even let Jonathan come over."

She turned to Sarnower but Mitch kept going. "My Mom always lets me have friends sleep over. We can stay up late. She takes us to the mall and buys us stuff."

Sarnower jumped in. "My wife has tried to bribe Mitch in an effort to make me look like a bad parent, Ms. McCarthy. She's tried to make up for her inexcusable absence by buying his affection. She's got him going for the fake and not the ball." He felt awful for having to say that in front of his son.

"I see," she said, making notes. Mitch was looking around the room, bored.

Sarnower continued. "I've found it impossible to be Mitch's father as well as his friend. I can't do both. Sometimes you have to make rules, set limits. That's part of being a good parent. I resent having to compete with my wife to see who can have the biggest TV, the fullest refrigerator and the most freedom. I don't think that's what kids need."

Eileen looked at him. "And what is it that they do need?"

"They need love and stability before anything else."

She wrote some more. Maybe he was getting somewhere with her after all. Mitch had gotten up and was pacing around the room.

"Can we go, Dad?"

Sarnower looked at his watch. "In a minute."

Eileen finished writing, turning to the boy.

"Mitch, who would you rather live with?"

Sarnower was furious. "Hold it! That's not a fair question!" he shouted. "You can't put him in the middle like that."

"Oh? Isn't that exactly what *you're* doing? Don't you think he should have some say in this?"

"I think it's a question of who will provide the best environment and be the best parent. That simple. He's not qualified to make that decision."

Eileen glared at him in silence. He needed to shut up right now. She took off her glasses and put down her pen.

"I'll need to see Mitch and his mother together too, then schedule a meeting with you and your wife. I want to see how the two of you get along."

"Do I have to come back here, Dad?" Mitch asked, whining.

Sarnower took a deep breath. "If Ms. McCarthy thinks you need to."

At least the meeting was over. Sarnower was just relieved to be getting out of there.

She stood up. "It was nice to meet you Mitch."

"Yeah," he said going out the door.

And now back at his office, Sarnower had gotten word that Barry Zifkin, the flamboyant wunderkind real-estate developer, had been busted once again trying to score cocaine from one of his project foremen, who, it turned out was a planted undercover agent from the Boston Police Narcotics Division. This time, there'd be no cushy deal from the D.A., no probation, no therapy. He'd be arraigned and bound over for trial. It was unlikely that any of his zealously accumulated millions was going to be of help. Although not surprising, the news made Sarnower unexpectedly sad. He had enjoyed mixing it up with Barry, the battle of wills and wits, even admired his brazen narcissism.

If you looked past the flamboyant, self-destructive behavior, there was much to admire: the drive, the singleness of purpose, the ability to direct and control. Barry was not above busting balls when the need arose. Persuasion had a whole different meaning in his playbook and Sarnower had secretly hoped that by continuing their sessions, some of that gold dust might be sprinkled on him, and would come in handy in his ordeal with Cassie and the cast of characters that had inserted themselves into his divorce.

On a more crass level, Barry's two weekly office visits which had netted him $350 a week were now gone. A few more patients had dropped out after their first couple of appointments with him at summer's end. When he called to talk with them, they'd cited lack of funds, or told him, with transparent insincerity how well they were now doing "thanks to him," and how they wanted to "try things on their own." Once patients disconnected, there was no bringing them back. Sarnower wished them well in their new lives and had hung up quickly. Some would do fine, others would be in distress soon enough after the Novocain of therapy wore off.

But Mrs. Netherworth, Mrs. Jessup and her mousy husband, the slithery Liz Dashiell and the rest of his exasperating charges were back, filling his days and evenings with confession, posturing, beseeching and bellyaching. Through it all Sarnower, tired, worn and preoccupied, struggled to be present, to confront, to comfort, to assist, to heal.

Taking special care not to offend, he arrived ten minutes early for the next appointment with Eileen McCarthy. From behind the closed door of her office, he heard a man's voice, harsh and irritated, on the verge of shouting. A woman was crying hard, hiccups punctuated her sobs. Sarnower started to laugh.

He looked through the magazines. Outdated copies of *Highlights for Children* had all the games and puzzles completed, undoubtedly by the anxious offspring of divorcing parents. In some issues pages had been torn out, and a particularly angry customer had drawn large male genitalia in black crayon on all the figures, regardless of sex. A worn set of blocks and Leggos littered one corner of the room. There were copies of *Golf Digest* and *Home and Garden* from the mid-1990s. A thoroughly budget operation.

Cassie walked in a few minutes later, trailing the gentle cloud of her expensive perfume. Sarnower said hi, but she sat down and picked up a magazine without acknowledging him. From inside the office he could hear movement and muffled voices. People were getting up and advancing toward the door. Final words were said, the woman was taking a few moments to pull herself together. Then the door opened and a young couple emerged, the woman, red-eyed, was blowing her nose. The man, stiff and unaffected, stared straight ahead, oblivious to his wife's pain. Sarnower struggled not to laugh when she hiccupped again.

Eileen McCarthy appeared at the door. "You may come in now," she said in a pleasant, singsong voice completely disconnected from the trauma of the previous hour. Sarnower and Cassie rose and he followed her in. Eileen walked behind her desk and put on her glasses after assembling a pad of paper and a pen. Cassie waited until Sarnower was seated on the couch and then found a chair at the opposite end of the room.

"Well, now," Eileen said, peering over her glasses.

"You wanted to see me and my wife together," Sarnower said gently.

"Yes, so I did."

"Well, here we are," he said with a forced smile.

Cassie pounced on the woman's confusion. She must have been taking lessons from Nora Lund.

"Ms. McCarthy, I think we need to get some facts straight here before my husband massages you with his melodious, oh-so-reasonable accounts of what a head case I am."

Sarnower heard the clear buzz of her old manic self. Maybe she'd gone off the medication entirely. If old Eileen McCarthy were any kind of clinician at all, she'd be able to pick up on the pressured, anger-laced speech immediately and form her own conclusions. But it didn't seem likely. The best plan seemed to be to let her spend herself like a Roman candle and then come in to clean up the ashes.

Cassie was into her practiced monologue of grievances, this time tailored to emphasize his catalog of shortcomings as a parent. Eileen was leaning forward, nodding and taking notes. Cassie had hooked her and was reeling her in.

"...arbitrary in his punishments, never lets Mitch have any of his friends over."

"Yes, I've heard that."

"...he won't loosen up. Mitch is only a child after all. He's constantly riding him about one thing or another. Homework, bedtime, hygiene. It's endless."

Although he had tuned out, (he was back with Janice and her wonderful breasts, every bit as tan as the rest of her) he could tell by the cadence in her voice she was nearing the end of her recital.

"Yes, yes," Eileen said, taking off her glasses and looking at him.

"Mr. Sarnower, I imagine you have your own perspective on things?"

He nodded. He wouldn't be the tongue-tied fool he'd been in court.

"I understand my wife's wanting to paint me as some kind of ogre." He saw Cassie shake her head in disgust. "It's true, I have standards. We talked about this last time. I think kids today need some structure and discipline. It didn't do me any harm. If my wife had her way, Mitch would be playing video games and eating junk food all day. He'd be bounced out of school in no time. I don't think what I ask is excessive at all."

Eileen chewed on her pen. She hadn't written anything. He continued.

"I realize deciding on custody is a very difficult matter. When it comes to parenting, there's always room for improvement. But here's the point: I think we need to separate my wife's anger at me from what's best for Mitch."

Good. A three-point shot. Cassie was upset, straining at the bit. Eileen turned her attention to her.

"This bastard just sits here and makes like he's being ordained for the priesthood. He threw me out of the house at the beginning of the summer. What kind of real father would do that to his son's mother? What kind of fucking man is he?"

She was near tears. Was she acting or did she really believe what she was saying? It was hard to tell even for him. Suddenly he was back on his front steps the day Cassie had thrown her overstuffed suitcase in the trunk of her car, trying to get her to stay and talk things out. Eileen was frowning, her already wrinkled face bunched up now like a prune.

"Cassie, it was *you* who left *us*." The words came out gently, as if he were reminding Mitch to say 'thank you' after receiving a gift.

She turned to stare at him. "You *kicked* me out you son of a bitch!" Now the tears came. Eileen sat impassively, observing. Sarnower turned to her.

"Ms. McCarthy, I'm afraid it's all a matter of record. My wife left us at the beginning of the summer. She flew out to California, stayed with a friend, and on her return, shacked up in a commune out in western Massachusetts with a group of...I don't even know, hippies, derelicts, druggies. All this is documented. I'm assuming you know the history or have access to those records."

Cassie turned to him, her face a red bath of tears. "It's all a fucking matter of record for you isn't it?"

Sarnower sat looking at her, shaking his head while Cassie rummaged through her pocket book and took out a handkerchief. Eileen put her glasses back on and started making notes again.

"Are you all right Mrs. Sarnower?" she asked.

Cassie nodded. Sarnower sat quietly, his hands folded in his lap. He should leave well enough alone and not add anything. Here was plenty of evidence of Cassie's instability. But whether that would mean custody for him was another matter.

"I think we should stop for today," Eileen said, looking at both of them, taking charge for the first time. She arranged her notes and put them in a manila folder. "Frankly, You both leave me in a bit of a quandary." Sarnower felt his scalp tingle. "I don't really see any compelling evidence to recommend either one of you as the sole custodial parent. Perhaps seeing you both together with the boy will make things a bit clearer."

Well, what fucking planet was she on? There was plenty of evidence right in front of this woman to come to the correct decision. What was it going to take, how loud would he have to scream to make people see what was going on? He tried one last time.

"Ms. McCarthy, with all due respect, bringing Mitch in here and in effect asking him to choose between his mother and me is not a really good idea. It could cause a lot of damage. I thought I made that point the last time I was in here."

She turned to him sharply. "It looks as if a lot of damage has already *been* caused. Mr. Sarnower, I know how to do my job. I've been appointed by the court to perform a fair and impartial evaluation. That is what I intend to do."

Her mind was already made up. Protesting further, even armed with sound clinical evidence would do nothing but entrench her further. He threw up his hands and headed for the door.

At home and at wits end, he called Manny. They hadn't spoken since the old man's apocalyptic dream. Initially dismissing it as mumbo-jumbo, something about it had stuck, until it began to fester like an infected hangnail demanding attention. In his discombobulated state, and after the outrageous joint meeting with the G.A.L., Sarnower had to admit he was losing the ability to distinguish the meaningful from the meaningless, so better to seek the man's input than dismiss it out of hand. Despite his own craziness, he was rarely an alarmist.

At Sarnower's request, they met at Manny's palatial Chestnut Hill home. The thought of driving to the hospital and seeing him on the dim, malodorous ward complete with tortured Dante-esque screams was too much. He'd arrived for dinner and was greeted by the old man at the front door wearing comical baggy shorts, a faded Celtics T-shirt and rubber flip-flops. The man's hair was a gray-white solar flair of disarray and brought to mind pictures of Old Man Winter blowing a Nor-Easter onto a defenseless planet earth. The sight made him laugh.

"What is it, my shirt?" Dear, clueless Manny Abravanel. Totally unaware of himself as always.

"It's nothing. You're fine," Sarnower said, trying to stifle an oncoming belly laugh. The old man looked down, taking stock of his appearance.

"The flip-flops?" Yes, in truth they contributed to the overall troll look, the knurled feet attached to pale, hairless bowed legs. The shorts, sized for a man much stouter than Manny, made him look oddly shrunken and withered. Only the T-shirt with the familiar smiling green leprechaun worked well on Manny's lean torso. Sarnower was stupid to have laughed; *he* should look this good at Manny's age.

Manny looked puzzled and hurt. "Maybe I should go on one of those TV shows where they do a complete make-over." He brightened. "I could look like Sean Connery."

"You and me both," Sarnower said as they entered the wide foyer.

Nothing had changed in the huge living room and study. Obviously Manny had kept Nilda on, the Brazilian cleaning lady Sarnower had found for him years ago. The place was clean, vacuumed, in order. There on the large carved mahogany desk in the study was the familiar photo of a much younger Manny and Beth, both radiant and smiling in tennis whites, taken after a match long before her fatal accident. It had been years before Manny could even bear to look at it, and Sarnower himself hadn't seen it for the better part of a decade. The sight of it, unexpected, brought a lump to his throat. He stopped in front of the desk to get a closer look while Manny moved on, through the pantry and into the large kitchen.

The two young faces stared out at him, people he knew and loved, people who at that moment had no idea what lay ahead for them. As far as they knew, they'd go from that friendly match to a cocktail party, maybe a late dinner with friends afterwards. Manny would continue to rise as a star, teach, write influential books, travel, lecture. Beth would be the dutiful wife, entertain friends and colleagues, cook, keep a flawless home and take up painting or writing herself. Then, many years later, old and feeble, they wouldn't die so much as fade out together, their lives a rich symphony that just happened to end quietly.

"Hey, schmuck!" Manny called from the kitchen. Sarnower, who found he was clutching the picture to close the gap of years, started. He replaced it quickly on the desk. If Manny walked in on him during such an intimate moment, he might take it as an uninvited intrusion. The older colleague was about to deliver an avuncular heart-to-heart and would resent being pulled into an undertow of painful memories. In the large kitchen, on the antique French country peasant table were two place settings and a variety of aromatic take-out containers.

"We'll eat in here. Nilda gets pissed if I mess up the dining room." First Beth and now Nilda, keeping old Manny in line.

"Sure."

"I'm trying that new Thai take-out place on Langley," he said, popping open a couple of bottles of Japanese beer. "A patient recommended it."

He sat, and with brisk movements opened the containers and poured the beer. Sarnower looked around the kitchen. High ceilings, a rack of suspended copper and stainless steel gourmet pots and pans hung over a slate cooking-island with a Wolf professional chef's oven built in. Against the wall was Beth's pride and joy, a monolithic black Sub-Zero refrigerator. Here years ago, she had entertained, cooked and held court at lavish dinner parties. He was sure the pots and pans hadn't been touched since her death.

"So? Eat up already," Manny said, tucking into the steaming Pad Thai.

"I'm sorry. This place has so many memories for me."

Manny nodded silently. "I refuse to move. There's too much here. L'chayim," he offered, raising his glass. The quick-change artist. There'd be no trip down memory lane that night. He pulled a thin spring roll out of one of the containers and bit into it. Tiny crumbs settled in his beard.

"Alan, you're in trouble. This thing's eating you up. I can't let you go through with it. You're going to ruin your life." Manny looked at him, his sad, faded blue eyes offering acceptance and forgiveness. "Don't make me draw you a picture, please. We go back too far." His voice was tired and far away.

Sarnower was silent. He helped himself to some hot lemon grass shrimp.

"A sin, Alan. That's what homicide is. Someone in your position might consider suicide, though knowing you as well as I do, I'm pretty sure you'd take someone else out before you harmed yourself. You're too narcissistic."

"What makes you think I'm really going through with it?"

Manny was smiling, shaking his head. He got up and went to the Sub-Zero for two more beers. "You still don't get it, do you?" He freshened their glasses with the cold amber nectar. "You and me. We're alike. Exactly." He leaned over the table. "I'll let you in on a secret. After Beth was killed by that little piece of shit, may he roast in hell forever, I bought myself a gun. Yes, that's right. Me. Head of psychiatry at Beacon General Hospital, world-class healer and humanist. Hmmm? You're surprised?"

He took a pull from the beer and continued. "One day I was coming home from a consultation at McLean Hospital. I was driving through Watertown Square. This was maybe two, three months after the accident. Still destroyed by the whole thing. There on my left was the Ivanhoe Pawnshop. You remember it? It's not there anymore. A dump filled with bric-a-brac. Shit nobody in their right mind would want.

"Suddenly, I got this really strong feeling, like I should stop. No idea whatsoever where it came from, but there it was. I got out of the car. I remember it was pouring that day. And cold. I crossed the street and went into the store. At that moment, I...I knew I'd stepped over some sort of line, some measure of balance somewhere had shifted. It was a strange feeling. The guy behind the counter, I'll never forget the way he looked. He must have weighed 350 pounds, wearing one of those sleeveless T-shirts, shaved head, tattoos up the wazoo. Of course now everyone looks like that, but this was years ago when the look still had a little shock value.

"Anyway, he smiled, almost like he was expecting me. It was like an old *Twilight Zone* episode. On a regular day, even half an hour before, I would never have been caught dead in a place like that, but there I was and it felt right. I went up to the glass case where the guns were displayed. They had everything, rifles, Lugers, Uzis, Magnums. He came over and looked me up and down. 'I think I have just the thing for you,' he said. He unlocked the case and took out a nice sleek .22 caliber and handed it to me. 'You know how to use one of these?' 'I'll figure it out,' I tell him. He put a small cardboard box of bullets next to the gun. I nodded. 'Write it up,' I tell him. In those days, if you weren't a total criminal or an obvious whack-job all you had to do was register; name, age, address, were you ever arrested, that was it.

"I brought the piece home and just looked at it, like a thirteen-year-old with his first *Playboy* centerfold, you know? This went on for a few days. I'd put the gun in the dresser overnight and take it out first thing in the morning. I'd hold it in my hands and feel it warm up, almost come to life. It began to be like an extension of my body, a prosthetic if you will. I'd almost get phantom-limb pains if the gun were out of my hand. I'd feel incomplete. Remember that TV show, *The Bionic Man*? Well, that was me; flesh and steel annealed together in the fires of righteous hatred.

"I went to a shooting range, took a few lessons with a retired cop. I got pretty good, too. Driving out to that range, looking down the gun barrel at that anonymous silhouetted paper target, visualizing that sick, drunk fuck at the other end and putting one in his heart or between his eyes—that became the high point of my week. It was orgasmic, libidinous. Completely erotic, like visiting a very high-class hooker. But I was in training, getting ready to equalize, restore harmony. I didn't have a plan or a date set, but knew that if I were ready, truly prepared psychologically and technically, the right set of circumstances would present themselves. It was just a question of when. I have to tell you Alan, with no disrespect or lack of sincere gratitude to you, the single most curative factor in getting back on my feet was the purchase of that gun."

Sarnower sat stone still. He'd never heard any of this, nor could he even visualize Manny holding a gun. How little we really know anyone. He drained the smooth, malty glass of beer, his mouth now mildly numb and tingly.

"But that kid, what was his name? Derek..."

"Derek Carboni."

"Yeah. He's dead...isn't he?"

"Exactly so, January 27, 1993 at four twenty-eight in the afternoon. He wrapped his parent's Jaguar several times around a telephone pole going ninety miles an hour in a thirty miles-per-hour zone. Illustrating my point completely."

"What did I miss Manny? What point?" Was Manny himself losing it?

The old man sat back, satisfied. This was vintage Abravanel, elusive and opaque. Things of value were not easily apprehended with Manny; you worked hard for your enrichment. But tonight he was downright frustrating.

"Fate, my dear Alan. Karma. Kismet. Call it what you will."

"Just sit back and let fate take its course? Is that what you're saying?"

The old man shrugged his shoulders.

"I don't believe in Karma. Look, you got off easy. I can't count on chance! I don't have time. I have a son to bring up. Mitch could be forty before we get out from under this mess."

"There are always ways out," he said softly. "You just have to know where to look for them."

"Manny, I'm not one of your interns."

"Precisely."

"Will you talk to me like a friend instead of a fucking Buddha?" The beer was making Sarnower edgy.

"You're a grown man with free will and the ability to anticipate the consequences of your actions. What more do I need to say to you? You want me to sanction your infantile impulses? Tell you it's ok to kill?"

It was pointless to continue. By the time he left, the Japanese beer buzz had faded. Manny's meaning, or what he assumed it to be, remained elusive. What goes around comes around? Slog on and wait it out? Rethink everything? He couldn't even hold on to the fuzzy pseudo-understanding that came with the high. No matter, he would prepare as Manny, his old friend and mentor had prepared. He would think it all through to the smallest detail, explore every nook and cranny, bide his time, make sure all contingencies had been planned for and thought through in the most careful, meticulous fashion. But with all the preparation, would some unknown cosmic force step in and lend a hand? A real-life *deus ex machina*. That kind of thing only happened in bad movies. It was certainly nothing he could count on. The old man had been graced with justice from above. He on the other hand could live to be Manny's age and still be paying out alimony.

He wasn't even aware of driving home. His racing thoughts were jumping and spinning like break-dancers on a hot city street. The next thing he knew, he was in his study and the digital clock read two a.m. By the time he finally fell asleep at quarter to five, he had made up his mind. Enough already with the greasy, piggish lawyers, the stupid guardian *ad litem*, the bullshit, the anxiety, the intimidation and fear, even Manny's entreaty. He would deal with Cassie himself and get on with the rest of his life.

Chapter **10**

DON'T WRITE ANYTHING DOWN. No notes, jottings, doodles, nothing. Nothing on the computer. It's all got to stay in the head. Crime shows, *Court TV*, real life were full of cases that had been cracked by that kind of idiotic evidence, shopping lists, an idea scribbled on the back of a carelessly tossed napkin or Post-It. The written trail could come back to haunt. But it wouldn't happen here. And no credit cards. Everything purchased with cash, no receipts with card numbers, dates, times, places. There'd be nothing to tie him down anywhere. Freedom of movement allowing for slow, careful, deliberate purchases, keeping it all mundane, banal, and entirely forgettable.

As summer ended, Sarnower was in the grip of private machinations. It was like working a huge crossword puzzle, a matrix of intersecting parries, thrusts and retreats.

Alternatives were examined and discarded, some were resurrected and modified, and throughout, the dictum: Keep it Simple. The planning and working through, the hope of a reasonable outcome had given his spirits a lift. His appetite had returned and he'd gained back some of the weight lost over the summer. He was still slender, but no longer looking as gaunt or caved in.

The ambiguous parable of Manny and the .22 had sat in his mind like a diamond ring in a black velvet box. He'd returned to it time and again, plumbing the nuances, admiring the seductive power of the most pristine and basic impulses. It was glorious. The aggrieved man, tired and raw, helpless in his suffering had turned passivity to action. Through sheer force of will, he'd torn an opening in the destiny of his life. That wonderful cosmic symmetry could be Sarnower's too, once his ducks were all lined up.

The legal wrangling droned on. He received a certified letter from the guardian *ad litem* letting him know she had reluctantly come down on Cassie's side to be the full custodial parent. Her sealed, impounded report had been filed with the court and there'd be no chance for rebuttal or challenge. It was now a done deal. He'd have to relinquish the house. The opened letter, laser-printed on thick professional letterhead, sat on his kitchen table, where, head in his hands, he stared at it for hours, his heart choked with misery and hate.

"How did you screw this one up?" Ballestracci asked.

"The woman's a clueless moron."

"A kick in the nuts, I know." For the first time Sarnower could actually hear empathy in the man's voice. It was too late for scolding. "It's not quite as bad as it sounds. We can haggle over dates and visitation. You still own half the equity in the house and re-establishing yourself, paying rent and furnishing an apartment— that's justification for reduced support payments."

Nick had gone on and on, but Sarnower had floated above it all as if he were looking down on an ant colony. A week before, he would have become sarcastic, challenging and confrontational.

Now the words rolled off him like beaded water on a new tarp. Nick himself must have picked up something. After his monologue there was silence. "Any questions?" he asked.

"I think you summed it up." Silence.

"You sure? You seem different."

"Just going with the flow. I'm leaving things in your capable hands, Nick."

"Good."

"Mmm."

Silence.

"Is everything all right doctor?"

"Fine Nick. Everything is fine."

"Well, ok then."

Ballestracci was flustered, thrown off his game, and Sarnower took pleasure in the lawyer's confusion. His new abstracted calm had puzzled others as well, including Nina. She'd cooled since the torrid visit to her place. She'd been all business, rebooked his appointments, set up his schedule, organized his correspondence and committed him finally to Manny's Grand Rounds presentation. When he'd come up from behind to hug her, she'd stiffened.

"Alan," she'd started, not turning.

"I know. We have to talk," he finished and let go.

"As long as you're in the middle of this thing, we can't go on. It just feels like a romp." She sounded sad and degraded. "I don't want to do romps anymore." She was almost in tears.

The door to the waiting room opened and Mr. and Mrs. Fishburg walked in. Their small, wizened frames in the door made Sarnower think of a set of salt and pepper shakers.

"You're not...pregnant or anything, are you?" He asked knowing he'd made a big mistake the second the words were out of his mouth. She glared at him.

"No, as a matter of fact I'm not."

Sarnower was shrunken, chastened. "I'm sorry. That was a stupid thing to say. This whole thing has worn away my better judgment."

"When you get it back maybe we can talk."

Shaken and weak, he'd gone into his office. Of course Nina was right. She'd given him plenty of hints, practically fed him his lines any number of times. But he, the glorious reborn stud, had been too obtuse and taken with himself to get it. The message, more of a plea from the heart, had been there clear as day all along. She'd said it: no more boys, no more flings. She was ready to build a life and a future with one man and he'd blown it. Tell me we have something after this is over. He'd kept quiet.

His stupidity made him want to scream. For years he'd prided himself, sold himself in the market place, as someone who had a special sensitivity to others, who could translate the subtext, decode the subtle messages that were indecipherable to others. In truth, he was no better at it than Miroslav, the head of maintenance in his own building. Pride cometh before the fall. Worst of all, he'd hurt her, an authentic human being who still held a sense of optimism and belief in the possibilities of others and had graciously invited him into her life. She hadn't asked for much. A little talk about a future with her would have gone a long way. Perhaps he could send her a bouquet of flowers. It had been days after his last visit with her that he'd even called, and then, not wanting to get into a thicket of feelings, he'd simply asked her to reschedule patients.

The dimensions of his shoddy behavior unrolled like a huge carpet. For years he had lived unaware, of the unmade bed, the dirty socks on the floor, the unwashed dishes in the sink, his papers, books and notes scattered and piled all over the house. "Don't you ever notice these things?" Cassie had asked so many times that he rarely even heard the question anymore. And what about the things that *really* mattered? How much had he missed with his patients over the years, was he totally oblivious to their heartfelt concerns as well? Throughout it all, he'd been thinking of other things: the annual wine sale at Martignetti's, a gripping scene from *King Lear*, the state of his retirement plan, a new idea for a monograph. Had he ever really seen what was in front of him and brushed away the high-minded detritus long enough to understand the desires and needs of someone else, another soul struggling through the world the same as he was?

A bolt of self-hate cracked him like a sharp uppercut to the jaw. His teeth ached, his eyes watered, his ears rang. The handwritten notes he'd taken out to read before his session blurred as he soared away from them like a bungee jumper in recoil. He should abandon his plans for Cassie and accept whatever she and Nora Lund were going to make him eat. He deserved to live in a small studio apartment, do penance and show that he was worthy to be a father to Mitch. What if everyone else was right and *he* was wrong? Maybe he was the one going to hell.

The intercom on his phone buzzed. "The Fishburgs are waiting to see you," Nina said crisply. She tweaked "waiting" ever so slightly.

By nine that evening when his last patient had left and Nina had gone home, Sarnower was determined to make it up to her, somehow find a way to save things. Nothing was that broken it couldn't be fixed. They *could* have a future together after this mess was over. Sure, he'd been difficult, distracted, unavailable and selfish. Guilty as charged. The threat of losing his son, his house, everything he'd built had driven him nearly crazy; certainly she could understand that. But now, with plans for Cassie almost finished, he was ready to make amends, he could offer Nina the stability, comfort, nurturance they were both looking for. It could still work.

On his way home, Sarnower stopped at the supermarket for trash bags: large and strong with draw strings. At that hour there were just a few shoppers scattered throughout the store. The harsh fluorescent lighting gave the aisles a slow-motion dreamy feel, almost as if the scene were under water. There were dozens of brands and sizes to choose from. The store's own brand, probably useful for routine weekly trash disposal seemed insubstantial for the task at hand. No, he needed heavy-duty bags that could hold their cargo without disappointing. They were there at the end of the display. The boxes, large and gray, featured a border in gunmetal with ominous rivets like a tank. There was a picture of a handsome, heavily muscled man carrying a large bulging bag in each hand down the front walk to the curb. His sexy wife stood in the door, smiling. Sarnower wondered what they were going to do when the man returned from his chore. The wife looked as if she had some ideas.

He took three boxes, each containing ten bags. He could always come back for more, no need to arouse attention with a cart full. At the deserted checkout register, a bored teenage cashier was reading a copy of *The Enquirer*. She looked up at him with annoyance at the interruption. Even this pimply wallflower of a girl was joining the growing ranks of women who wanted nothing to do with him. As she rang up his purchase, he looked with amusement at the tabloid splayed open to a color photo essay on the changes in Michael Jackson's nose. What was next, when plastic surgery had reached its outer limits, when even the best Hollywood practitioners had thrown in their scalpels and there was a large gaping sinkhole in the face of the King of Pop? The dilemmas of a man who had nothing better to do with his time and money than lavish it on his physical disfigurement and self-destruction. There was a monograph in there somewhere and he made a quick mental note to give it some thought later, but now he should let this poor girl get back to Oprah's weight problems and celebrity divorces.

Outside, the night air had cooled quickly; the season had begun to turn. In days, with the languid, time-suspended summer gone, Mitch would be back in school. He returned to Nina, lying naked with him after making love. Now she might even give her notice, he'd succeeded in making her feel so uncomfortable. He knew the internal churnings of unhappy women who'd not gotten their due. You could smell it at first, like fear. The logistics of the parting would be worked out silently, privately and then one day it would be over. Gone, finished. You'd get your final itemized bill, a resolute, no-more-talking decision. Where the heart ruled, persuasion would accomplish nothing. The bell could not be unrung.

The house was dark when he approached. Mitch was out with Cassie. She now saw him for increasingly frequent periods of visitation on Ballestracci's strong recommendation. Rather than fight the inevitable, he felt a conciliatory tone would facilitate a better settlement.

He turned on the lights and went right to the kitchen with his purchase. For now the bags would fit under the sink, later, when he'd bought all he needed, they'd have to go down to the basement. He'd taken the first step; there was reason to hope.

There were no messages on his voice mail, no call from Nina. To contact her now would signal desperation, but to wait too long without talking might mean he was content to let her go. He'd bring flowers in tomorrow and invite her to talk when she was ready. His mind was swirling again. Trash bags and trips to different supermarkets. He could return in the morning to the Shop & Save, a different checkout clerk would be there. And receipts. They all had to be destroyed. He went to the shopping bag and pulled out the small strip of paper. "We're Glad to Serve You. Come Again!" it said on the bottom in purple pixilated letters. He smiled. Shop & Save was pleased to collaborate with him in his quest for justice. On the receipt was the date and time of his purchase. Big Guy Steel-Tuf Trash Bags were also itemized. He chuckled. Big Guy was certainly going to be getting some tonight by the looks of that hungry wife of his.

He went into the bathroom, tore the strip of paper into small pieces and flushed them down the toilet. Recently, a man convicted of killing his girlfriend had been done in by the discovery of a carelessly forgotten set of receipts and shopping lists. In thinking things through, Sarnower had been amazed at the stupidity, the lack of planning and preparation in some of these cases. A brilliant, well-known thoracic surgeon was spending life in prison after detectives found all his research on his computer, along with visits to some over-the-top kiddy porn sites.

A car pulled up to the house. Sarnower went to the window and saw Mitch jump out. Cassie got out too and handed him a large stiff shopping bag from the Gap. They were talking, but he couldn't hear what was being said.

There in the illumination of the front door light was a mother and her son, their bond as old as intelligent life, growing together again despite the fractures. It struck him that this might well be the last time he would see Mitch and Cassie together. He watched as they hugged. He would play this image again and again, for the rest of his life, as would Mitch. Could he really take the boy's mother from him?

He thought of his own mother, gray, depressed, brittle and withdrawn. How would he have turned out if she'd left at Mitch's age? Probably none the worse. She had been a chronic source of aggravation, she'd had enough piss and spite to hang on and pester him for years after his father had the good sense to die. There were other people, plans, goals, other things involved here besides Mitch.

There were standards to maintain and principles to keep. Too much had happened, too much damage had been done, too much trust and hope had been wrecked. The boy really didn't know what was good for him, how could he? His young pliant spirit welcomed unconditionally.

Looking out on that late summer night, the two of them silhouetted together in a pale, unearthly light, Sarnower felt his power to forgive leave him in an exhaled breath, a part of his own soul now dead. It was physical, a lightening, like putting down a heavy suitcase he'd been carrying all day. There was a void left in that space that had once been able to offer grace. Thirty feet away from where he stood nothing was suspected. The world would go on.

Mitch was coming up the walk now bag in hand, as Cassie took off. But there in the night, a small, dark, banged-up car turned on its headlights as she pulled out. Sarnower stared at it, he'd seen it before but couldn't remember where. It definitely wasn't owned by anyone on the block. Cassie had driven about fifteen yards before it fell in behind her, its muffler growling. Sarnower opened the door for Mitch, jazzed and excited, his movements spiky and sharp. Cassie must have filled him up with sugar, just the thing before bedtime. He was talking a mile a minute as his mother had during her manic phase. Sarnower listened, his heart sinking. In Cassie's custody, Mitch would become obese, TV bound and lethargic, a shoo-in candidate for juvenile onset diabetes. But he would be saved, delivered from that life. With him, Mitch would start in on sports that fall, soccer or football. Snacks and TV would be restricted. He'd develop disciplined study habits. Mitch would be fine.

"Mom says you're moving out soon."

"Well, nothing's been decided for sure."

"She said in a week or two you're going to move out and get your own place. Is that true?"

Good old Cassie, barreling right in like a hurricane. She had no understanding at all where hate for her husband stopped and care for her son needed to begin. Sarnower led him to the stairs and sat down with him.

"Mom and I really haven't made any definite plans yet," he said softly.

"That's not what she said." Mitch was defiant.

"I can't be responsible for what Mom said. What *I'm* telling you is true." There was no point in protecting Cassie any longer. Mitch got up, clutching his overflowing Gap bag. His eyes narrowed.

"I think you're lying," he said and ran up to his room. Sarnower felt his gut tighten and his face flush. God knows what horseshit she was feeding him. Whatever was tender and poignant in the scene a few minutes ago was gone.

On his way to the office the next morning, Sarnower made a quick stop at Shop & Save to pick up some flowers and three more boxes of Big Guy Steel-Tuf trash bags. A night had passed since he'd seen that reassuringly happy couple on the box. That could be him and Nina after the mess was cleaned up. At the checkout counter, the sullen, *Enquirer*-reading teenager was gone. In her place, a wiry, energetic black man wanted to engage him in a discussion of the new cool weather as he rang up the purchases. Sarnower played along, smiled and nodded and wished the man a pleasant day as he left. Outside, he retrieved the receipt and threw it in the trash. Now he had sixty bags. Another twenty would probably be enough.

He pulled into the office parking lot and sat. The thought of having to deal with Nina made him sad and the thin bouquet of supermarket carnations on the seat next to him seemed pathetically inadequate, a gesture worse than nothing at all. What was he going to say? Anything now would sound hopelessly lame, she wasn't interested in excuses, and truly she deserved more. Time was running out and he'd just have to punt.

He left the car and headed toward the office, throwing the flowers into the bronze trashcan at the door. The lobby as usual was frigid. Even in these cool, late August days, Miroslav kept a leaden finger on the thermostat. He crossed the atrium floor to his office door. It was locked. Sarnower checked his watch. It was eight fifteen. Nina should have been in a half hour before. He flashed on that day six or eight weeks before—Doug's suicide and Nina's unexpected absence. He hoped nothing was wrong.

The office was completely dark. He had eight patients, one after another and without Nina, things would be especially difficult. Why hadn't she at least called him at home? He was starting to feel like a sap for being so conciliatory. She was here to work after all, and the day was going to be a full-blown mess because of her. Well, she had it over him now, it was his own fault. He'd given her the power by blurring their professional and personal lives. She had control and apparently plenty of justification for getting back at him. He began turning on lights and entered her work area to call for messages. What he saw made him gag.

Her desk and surrounding work areas had been completely cleared out. He opened drawers. Nothing. Her sweater, often draped over the back of her chair was gone. Not a paper clip nor stick of gum remained. The few familiar *tchotchkes* that sat on her desk, a plastic Mickey Mouse doll with an oversized bobbing head from a long ago trip to Disney World, a small photo of an old high-school friend and her baby, a miniature model of the doomed World Trade Center, all gone. He grabbed the phone and pushed buttons. The laconic woman at his answering service had three messages for him: a cancellation, a call to reschedule, a request for a medication refill. That was it. Nothing from Nina. He dialed her number. The phone rang and rang. Usually by the third or fourth ring, her husky voice could be heard on voice mail: Sorry I missed your call, but please leave a message at the beep. Now there was nothing.

His legs started to buckle as the realization of what was happening spread like a wet stain on cloth. A blast of burning acid erupted from his churning stomach. He tried again. No answer. He opened the door to his consulting room. No note on his chair or end table. There was no sign at all that Nina had ever worked there.

Paralyzed and completely shut down, Sarnower stood in the middle of his consulting room, heart pounding, struggling to breathe. The carriage clock on the bookcase read eight twenty-five. His first patient, a new referral from Manny would almost certainly be on time for her eight-thirty appointment. She'd just been discharged after two weeks of in-patient hospitalization at Beacon for a suicide attempt. Donna Prestwidge, daughter of a prominent professor of ancient history, would have to be handled very carefully, correctly, by the book. She was beautiful and brilliant, and at this point had enough dealing with the psychiatric community to be able to spot in an instant anyone not on top of his game. He heard the front door open. At least it was unlocked and the lights were on. For the rest of the day he'd have to struggle to put everything else out of his mind and focus on his patients. They weren't paying hefty fees to see his life spinning out of control. He opened his appointment book to August twenty-ninth. There, over the entire page, in bright, red indelible magic marker was written:

Sorry. I really am. It was never going to work.

The note, somewhere between subway graffiti and a ransom letter in its impact, was unsigned. There it was in screaming red, bleeding and raw. There was nothing more to say.

The day dragged. "I'm a little short handed, Nina's out today," Sarnower said over and over. Patients didn't seem to mind. They'd come to see him, not her. A male patient in his forties, one that Sarnower had caught glaring at her, hoped Nina was feeling all right and would be back soon. He nodded but said nothing. It occurred to him what Nina must have had to put up with. Men checking her out, looking her up and down, their stares burning like x-rays through the glass partition. What must she have felt, looking up suddenly from her work and finding them leering at her? Maybe she'd had enough of that too; it wasn't all just him.

He managed to contain his heartbreak through the late, darkening afternoon, and mercifully, his last patient, a brief session for a medication check, arrived early.

And then it was over. Relieved, Sarnower closed up the office. He'd start looking for Nina's replacement first thing in the morning. He'd call Manny; perhaps he could recommend someone.

In the car he let the impact of the morning's blow hit him. He groaned and choked, he hadn't anticipated any of it. Likely, he'd never even see Nina again. She'd cut herself out of his life with a swift, clean surgical stroke. He'd grown to love her; he knew that. Was he too old for her, did she not want to deal with someone else's child or had she simply tired of a relationship with a burdened, distracted, middle-aged divorcing man who was treading water as best he could?

He started the car, but rather than turning right out of the parking lot to go home, he made a left and found himself without any conscious willing, heading for Nina's. This is not a good idea he said out loud when he realized what was happening, but he drove on. In minutes he was speeding east on the VFW Parkway. Don't do it, big mistake, he kept repeating, but the car hadn't heard. And soon, the familiar sign for Caruso Street appeared. He pulled over to the curb and forced himself to stop before making the right turn.

Surprisingly, the small scruffy lot on the corner, filled with trash and discarded appliances a few weeks before had been cleaned and planted. Rows of late summer flowers stood at stiff attention in the deepening twilight. Part of the lot had been fenced off and cultivated as a vegetable garden and lettuce, squash, radishes and turnips had started to push up through the gritty city soil. The sight of those unlikely flowers and vegetables, their life force inextinguishable in that hostile ground made him weep. The day's stinging chaos, the punishing summer mercifully coming to an end, pulled at his heart. He wept for Nina and for Mitch and even for Cassie and what he was about to do. He wept for his parents, so very far away now, existing only as a papery whisper and a grainy memory. He wept for himself and for the tortured soul of Liz Dashiell, who one day soon would be found dead with a bottle of Liquid Plumber by her side. He heaved uncontrollably as the poison and dreadful waste of his life squeezed itself out through his pores, his eyes, his nose and his mouth.

Then it was over. He had nothing left. Sarnower lay down across the passenger seat and fell into a deep sleep.

It was completely dark when he awoke. Cars on the Parkway were whizzing by, headlights on. It took him a moment to realize where he was. It was now almost nine. Mitch would have been back for hours wondering where he was. Or perhaps he'd called Cassie and had her come to get him, something she'd certainly add to her bill of particulars when the right time came. He looked in the rear view mirror. His eyes were red and puffy, there were pale streaks down his cheeks, his hair matted and sticky, a complete and total mess. A young couple strolled arm in arm down the block and the man bent down to glance inside the car, then turned to his companion and gestured toward Sarnower. She craned her neck and for a fraction of a second met his eyes, hers widened briefly, in disgust no doubt, and she quickly turned away.

Picture if you will a once-distinguished psychiatrist, now gathering speed down the steep slope of ruination. Surely by winter, he'd no longer even have his car to sleep in. Perhaps that was the way it should be. He watched as the couple grew small in the distance. The man made a half-hearted, furtive glance back, and then they were gone.

Sarnower pulled a package of Handi-Wipes out of the glove compartment and began restoration on his face. He ran his fingers through his hair until it regained a semblance of order. Still bleary, he put the car in gear and made the right turn onto Nina's street.

What was he doing? What did he want? To confront her? Make a scene? In his current state, feeling and looking as he did, anything was possible. He was completely in the grip of something remote and outside himself. His thoughts, his actions, nothing was his own.

He drove down the block slowly. Children rode bikes and played catch in the illumination of street lamps. Men in muscle shirts sat on porches drinking beer, reading the paper and listening to the ball game on the radio. The street buzzed with energy much as the new triumphant urban garden at the end of the block had sprung up with vibrant, defiant life. And there was number forty-six, Nina's house. He pulled over to the far side of the street and turned off his headlights.

Lights were on all through the downstairs. Everything in the living room and dining room areas could be easily seen from the street. There was Nina, her hair pinned up, wearing cut-offs and the T-shirt he had admired with the "Girl Next Door" demolition company logo. There were several large opened cardboard boxes throughout the room and she was wrapping pottery in sheets of newspaper, stacking books in piles and moving furniture. She worked with a precision and concentration that Sarnower had known from their several years together. At intervals, she would stretch and appear to talk to someone in another room. A couple of times, she looked out the large picture window, as if sensing a presence. Sarnower had parked between street lamps in a dark gulch away from the yellow cones of light, and was confident she couldn't see him.

A tall, lanky young man wearing only shorts entered the room. His long blond hair hung over his face obscuring his features, but Sarnower could tell from his lean, well tended body that the face held no unpleasant surprises. He moved in on Nina confidently and drew her close; sliding his hands down her pants and locked her in a long, penetrating kiss. Sarnower could even see their cheeks hollow and swell as the kiss grew more passionate. Nina, eyes closed, folded willingly into his form. Fuck! What a chump he'd been. Of course she'd found someone else, or more likely someone else had found her first.

Doing anything now except beating a hasty exit would mark him as a truly pathetic and desperate man. Did he want to debase himself completely and make a scene? Unhinged as he was, he realized the situation was far beyond anything he could possibly do to rescue it. Without turning on his headlights, he put the car in gear and drove off.

Chapter 11

THE HOUSE WAS DARK as he opened the front door. From the foyer he could see the ghostly blue flickering of the TV in the study and hear the excited play-by-play of a Sox game in progress. Walking back, he saw Mitch's mesmerized face in the reflected distorting light, his skin a gray lilac. There was a crumpled Coke can and an empty bag of Doritos chips on the floor.

Mitch looked up casually. "Hi Dad," he said, returning to the game.

Sarnower, still agitated by the scene at Nina's and his own lapse of parental responsibility went over to the boy and hugged him.

"Mitch, I'm sorry to be so late. An emergency I had to handle." I'm losing my mind he wanted to say. "Are you all right?"

"No biggie," he answered absently, his eyes fixed on the game.

"How did you get home?"

"Mrs. Elsinger gave me a ride. She wants you to call her."

Janice!

"What did she want?"

"How should I know? I'm not like her *psychiatrist* or anything." He spat out the word as if it were a glob of phlegm, a clever dig at Sarnower himself. The summer had changed his son there was no question about it. Mitch was no longer a little boy. He'd taken his first steps into a caustic, moody preadolescence. Sarnower had seen enough to know he was in for a long haul.

"Do you know Jonathan's number?"

Mitch rattled it off quickly, slurring the digits and making it impossible for Sarnower, already on overload, to catch. He picked up paper and pencil from the desk.

"Could you repeat that?"

This time he enunciated the numbers with exaggerated clarity, leaving an icy second of silence between each. Sarnower recorded the numbers dutifully, not falling for the bait.

"Janice? This is Alan Sarnower calling."

"Well, I know this is last minute notice, and please tell me if it won't work, but Roger and I are taking Jonathan to the Cape for the Labor Day weekend, and we wondered if Mitch would like to join us. They get along so well together."

Shit. He'd made a mental note to have Jonathan over to reciprocate weeks ago, but nothing had come of it.

"Ah, well, sure, that sounds fine. Thank you." Janice, the spirited and creative lay, the moody young spitfire.

"What should he bring?"

"Nothing really, except a bathing suit. We'll take care of everything else. We'll be by to pick him up Friday morning, eight o'clock if that's ok."

"It's fine. Perfect."

Hanging up the phone, Sarnower realized his window had opened; his opportunity had come. Cassie would be over Friday afternoon as always to get Mitch for the weekend and collect her check. He would say nothing to Mitch about it until Friday morning before camp so there'd be no chance of her finding out. This was Wednesday night. He'd have to finish his purchases tomorrow. Grabbing his scheduling book he went upstairs and began canceling the next day's appointments.

Thursday broke wet and cold. A downpour was in full fury when he awoke. This would be Mitch's last day at camp, spent indoors all day, meaning board games and crafts, if the skies didn't oblige. He'd almost certainly be coming back in a sour mood. It was now a virtual certainty he would never see his mother again. The thought hit Sarnower as something monumental, but also as too abstract and formless in all its implications to be taken on right then. There were so many small practical details to attend to, beginning with getting the boy ready. The realization of all he was going to be doing in the next forty-eight hours made his dry throat close, and a cold sweat burst out on his face.

He should reconsider the whole thing, scrap it all, get away for a week or two by himself, sort it out and put things back into perspective. It didn't have to get done this weekend. On the other hand, Cassie would be moving back into the house soon by court order. Logistical planning would become much more difficult after that. Mitch would be back in school. No, it was now or never.

Getting caught though, that was unthinkable. He remembered Tug's warning; he was no match at all for a Boston Homicide Detective. They like the husbands first in these cases. He'd prepare carefully for the close scrutiny that was sure to follow after Cassie's disappearance. The house would be searched and trace evidence, fingerprints, hair, fibers, found. What would you expect? The woman lived here for years, but there'd have to be no blood and no signs of foul play. Cassie's own flighty history, her tendency to act on impulse would lend support to the theory that she was still unstable, she could have just taken off again suddenly as she had earlier in the summer. He still had the note found in her car near Logan airport: "Split for the Coast." That lesbian poet in San Francisco, the crazy commune in the Berkshires, the ridiculous stoned-out guy she'd been screwing when he walked in on them weeks ago. It was all there, it all added up.

He'd play the concerned father. Yes, he and Cassie had their differences and were calling it quits, but it would never, ever occur to him to do anything drastic. How could he, a well-established mental health practitioner even think of depriving his son of a mother? No, this was a country of laws, not trigger-happy cowboys. They were in the process of working out an equitable settlement. Sure divorce was bruising and ugly, but they'd all heal and move on. Cassie? Who knows? She could be anywhere.

To Sarnower's surprise, Mitch was up and ready early. He took this as a good sign. In his vigilant, hyper-energized state, having a battle of wills would not be welcome.

"Way to go champ," he said as Mitch brought his cereal bowl to the sink, rinsed it and placed it in the dishwasher.

"Huh?"

"Your help. Up early. Cleaning up after yourself. I appreciate it."

"Yeah," he grunted.

Later they'd work on his attitude. Now, getting him to camp was all he could do. The offer of a raincoat was refused with a look of disgust as Mitch, wearing only a T-shirt and shorts walked slowly and deliberately out to the car in the pouring rain. When they were both inside, Sarnower handed him a towel from the back seat. Mitch sat perfectly still, water dripping from his hair into his large dark eyes. He stared at his father as if in a trance.

"Dry yourself off."

Mitch continued to stare at him without moving.

"You're going to catch cold," Sarnower said and reached for the boy's head with the towel.

"Don't!" he hissed and grabbed Sarnower's hand before it reached his head.

"You can't go around all day sopping wet."

"Ecstasy does."

"Ecstasy?"

"The *dog,* Dad. Mom's dog. Don't you remember *anything?"*

In fact Sarnower had completely forgotten about Cassie's dog. He recalled being repulsed when Mitch had first told him about the puppy bearing the name of a designer drug. This called for changes in the plan, but what? The wrench thrown into his perfectly oiled machine made his hands shake on the steering wheel. Should he call it all off now and regroup, or improvise and hope for the best? He'd come to think of the whole enterprise as an elaborately woven tapestry; dislodging one thread could potentially unravel the entire fabric. But an opportunity such as he now had would not present itself again soon.

He drove the rest of the way on automatic pilot, trying to follow out the implications of this new complication. Flighty as she was, would Cassie actually leave a dog alone and untended for an indefinite period of time? Would it be in character? He eased the car into the queue of parents discharging their kids. Mitch was out the door and walking with one of his friends before he was aware he was alone. The best idea for now would be to continue on with the original plan. In a few days he could call the police and they could break down the door and rescue the dog. He would finish his purchases and not panic. Panic would only lead to mistakes.

He headed out to the Mass Pike and on to Worcester. He wouldn't be recognized there. The rain had let up and a large expanse of western sky was clearing. It will all work out, just don't get rattled. He took the exit for downtown Worcester. Boston's poorer step-cousin, the city had always seemed especially depressing to Sarnower, although in the past ten years it had made a valiant effort to revitalize itself. It was legendary in psychiatric history. In 1909, Freud himself had come from Vienna to Clark University to deliver the Introductory Lectures on Psychoanalysis; and for that coup alone it deserved some grudging respect. The Centrum and the venerable older Mechanics Hall regularly drew A-list rock bands and symphony orchestras. Years ago, Sarnower had brought Cassie out to hear the London Philharmonic on tour. They'd played the Mahler Sixth Symphony in a shattering performance that had left him so shaken he'd been unable to speak for hours afterwards. Cassie had been bored early on. She'd looked at her watch, fidgeted, and had finally fallen asleep during the slow movement. Annoying then, it seemed funny now. Soon, he'd be listening to as much Mahler as he wanted.

He drove around the periphery of the downtown area. The promising urban renewal had not yet spread to this working class area. Small single-family homes with peeling paint and scruffy lawns filled the streets. He was reminded of Nina's struggling block. Whatever it was that had caused her to rip herself out of his life, he missed her now. She was probably completely packed and that lean beach-boy friend of hers was helping load her stuff into a rented U-Haul or Ryder truck. Perhaps she'd had enough of Boston and was heading out west with him to Washington, back to her roots, her pioneer ancestors, her family. She needed to hike in the Cascade Mountains again, sail on Puget Sound and forget about the tortured, hard-pressed, middle-aged Jewish shrink she'd bound herself up with for over five years. He couldn't blame her for wanting to be free of his unending turmoil. At the end of the day, what could he really offer her? A receding hairline, an enlarged prostate, stronger reading glasses, a sedate, comfortable blur of a life.

There in the distance was a large welcoming sign with slanted bright orange letters. Home Depot. As he pulled into the parking lot, he checked his wallet. An ATM had disgorged ten nondescript twenty-dollar bills into his sweating, waiting hand yesterday afternoon. The rain had stopped but the air was still moist and cold. Walking to the huge automatic doors, he could almost see his breath.

It was freezing inside. Did Miroslav work here too? The thought of the stocky maintenance chief out here in Worcester wearing an orange company smock and bellowing orders in a thick Slavic accent made him smile. But to business. He grabbed a frozen metal shopping cart and began wandering the aisles. Like the others he'd been to, this store was a warehouse with merchandise stocked in three high tiers, the ceiling was about four stories high. Young men drove forklifts with pallets of lumber and sheetrock through the wide aisles. The few customers at that hour searched shelves and consulted lists, wandering in awe in the gigantic caverns of the store.

He filled the cart with four rolls of duct tape, two more boxes of heavy duty trash bags (these did not feature Big Guy and his adoring wife), a box of latex gloves, a utility knife with extra blades, a nylon clothes line and a large hack saw with three packages of blades. Was anything missing? He stood in the middle of the kitchen cabinet aisle and carefully went through the well-rehearsed mental list again. That should do it.

As he made his way to the cashiers, he remembered his first trip to France, after his junior year in college. Tug had driven him to the airport for the flight and before letting him off at the terminal had given him a joint with the injunction that it must be smoked at the very highest point he could reach on the Eiffel Tower. Waiting to check in for the international flight, he'd suddenly become paranoid, convinced that his illicit cargo would be discovered and confiscated. He'd be hauled off and held for questioning and placed in custody, never making it to France. But the joint was never found and Sarnower had in fact smoked it atop the Eiffel Tower. The body remembers. And now, someone would read his thoughts, correctly deduce the purpose of his purchases, and notify store security that a crime was about to be committed.

The cashier, a man in his seventies with a white crew cut and a huge cauliflower nose, flashed a big smile. A career civil servant, bored with retirement, looking for some extra money and hours away from a nagging wife, no doubt.

"Find everything you're looking for?" he asked.

"I certainly hope so."

He scanned the items through, but stopped when he got to the hacksaw. He picked it up and examined it carefully, turning it over.

"Looks like this could do some serious damage," he said. Sarnower noticed he was missing several teeth.

"Plumbing repairs," he smiled.

The clerk continued to marvel at the saw. "Plenty of times I know my wife was fixin' to use something like this on me." He looked up, concerned. "I used to drink, you know?" He shook his head. "A mean drunk, *mean*. Gave it up twenty-two years ago, haven't been back since. Wife, God love her, she forgive me, always came back. Married forty-five years, doncha know?"

"That's very nice," Sarnower said, his cheeks starting to burn. The man gave the saw another look and scanned it through.

"You owe our fine establishment seventy-eight dollars and twenty-eight cents," he said proudly, as if he'd just earned the money himself.

Sarnower opened his wallet and took out four twenties.

"We take cash too," the man joked as he made change.

Carrying the bag to the door, the man called after him "you come back now and let us serve you again!" Sarnower turned and smiled. The man was on to his next customer: "Find everything you're looking for?"

Outside, he retrieved the receipt, tore it into small pieces and put the confetti in a waiting trashcan. No records.

Back in the car, he headed for the North Shore and on to Southern New Hampshire to look for Dumpsters. Dumpsters at construction sites, Dumpsters in back of restaurants. Nothing written, he'd remember where they all were.

Several hours later, back at home, Sarnower got to work. He brought his purchases down to the basement. There in the back was a small utility closet, unused for years, where he'd stored old cans of paint, rusted gardening equipment, a set of hub caps for a no longer owned car, a pair of ancient skis. Junk that could be thrown out, but not just yet.

He moved everything out carefully to create a workspace. He put on a pair of gloves, removed the items from the bag and placed them on the dusty bare floor. He opened a box of trash bags and began taping them to the walls, overlapping by three or four inches. There would be a solid, seamless sheet of plastic protection around the room. When the walls were completely covered he did the ceiling and then the floor.

An hour and a half later, he was finished. He'd used almost three boxes of bags and the room, save for the lone light bulb was now covered in gray metallic plastic. He checked each seam to make sure there were no fissures or gaps. For good measure, he covered the interior surface of the door and a few feet outside the door. There were over forty bags left, more than enough for the requirements of his task.

With the utility knife, he cut off a three-foot length of nylon cord. Making an effective garrote would not be as simple as he thought. It would have to slip on easily and be capable of a quick lethal choke. He tied the yard of rope into a circle and slipped it over his own head, tightening from behind. The size was about right but he'd need a lever to increase the torque and the speed at which maximum force could be applied. He flashed on Mr. Shindelman, his high school physics teacher, the lecture on torque, part of the boring unit on basic mechanics and simple machines. Looking out the window on a beautiful early spring day, the words, the writing on the blackboard had gone by in a haze. When was he ever going to come across torque again? Poor Mr. Shindelman, now long dead for sure. He knew more than I did.

Upstairs, Sarnower rummaged through kitchen drawers. There he found the solid pewter salad fork and spoon set they'd gotten years ago as an engagement present. He'd never cared for the streamlined modern Danish design, it seemed pretentious and fussy, but now the spoon, long and sturdy was an ideal lever to twist the nylon cord rapidly. He pushed it through the thick double knot and sitting down, slipped the garrote over his leg, onto his thigh and tightened. He practiced with one hand and then two. The advantage of two hands was clear but in the heat of the moment, using both might be impossible. He'd have to wait and see.

Back in the storage closet, Sarnower picked up the hack saw and inspected the blade. In the light of the single suspended bulb it shone gray and blue and the cutting edge featured thousands of tiny gleaming teeth. He picked up an old dried-out paintbrush. The saw cut through the wooden handle effortlessly, like a hot knife through butter. He was ready, there was nothing to do now but wait. A few hours remained before he'd have to pick up Mitch. He'd tell him about the weekend on the Cape, the swimming, cookouts, ice cream, staying up late with Jonathan. He'd tell him he'd talked it over with Cassie, and it was fine with her, there'd be nothing to arouse any suspicion.

Although it was only two in the afternoon, he poured himself a tall gin and tonic. Ordinarily, it would never occur to him to indulge before five at the earliest, but now he was in entirely new territory. It was all up for grabs. He thought of his last meeting with Manny. This is how it must have felt on that cold day when he was drawn into the Ivanhoe Pawnshop to buy the gun. It was like leaving a comfortable, familiar place you knew you'd never visit or see again. He was on the verge of a new life.

He thought of his grandparents leaving Central Europe in the early years of the twentieth century, crammed with hundreds of others into the dark hull of a steamer ship, bringing no money, perhaps a bag or two of possessions, torn away from a stinking, impoverished life, but at least one that was known. America stood at the end of a terrible two-week crossing as nothing more than a myth, a dream of gold and a bright space in the mind. Somehow it all had to be better. He remembered Kathy Mariston and that late spring evening on the sooty tarpaper rooftop of her apartment building when she'd gently relieved him of his virginity. Things had been different after that, a new swagger, a new life.

Mitch's birth had made him an adult. Putting another life first had been a wholesome corrective to his expensive and indulgent narcissism. Manny had been right, he was at the center of his own universe. Cassie on the other hand had felt like a grounded teenager. She'd wanted a new friend, someone with whom to shop, have lunch and go to a movie. Then his parents, their final pulling away, leaving him orphaned (the term knows no age limits he discovered), to deal with the world and his remaining years alone. Ok, not *alone* alone, but alone nevertheless. Mitch would go to college, likely out of state. He'd meet a girl and settle in a different part of the country. They'd see each other over holidays, or during the summer if he were lucky. He'd build his own family, start a career, and his presence in Sarnower's life would inevitably fade. Like Mitch, he was an only child, the sole proprietor of his own ice floe, drifting out to the open sea until land was no longer visible.

The glass was drained and Sarnower went into the kitchen to make another drink. This would be his last; he had to keep a clear head.

Mitch was animated and had lost his morning gloom when Sarnower arrived to pick him up. He was walking with Jonathan, their baseball caps backwards. Jonathan was making a funny set of noises and Mitch stopped in his tracks, doubled over with laughter. Sarnower smiled watching the two approach the car. He couldn't remember the last time *he'd* laughed that hard. What had he told Nina? A good belly laugh is a physiological cousin to an orgasm. Childhood laughter—it was their version of sex. It fulfilled the same functions, flooding the brain with endorphins, releasing pent-up tension, leaving the body limp and exhausted, sending the soul to a soft, far-away place for a few brief moments.

The boys approached the car. "What's so funny, you two?" Sarnower growled. That only sent them into another fit of laughter. Jonathan cupped his hand under his arm and let one rip. Mitch was now on the ground, doubled up, red-faced. Sarnower couldn't help laughing himself. Slowly Mitch pulled himself up, eyes tearing. He struggled to catch his breath.

"I think what Mitch is trying to ask you is if he can come to the Cape with us this weekend," Jonathan said, suddenly playing the straight man as Mitch brushed himself off.

"I spoke with your mother about it," Sarnower lied. "It's fine."

The boys looked at each other and exchanged high-fives. Jonathan leaned over and whispered something in Mitch's ear. This started another bout of laughter, but this time Sarnower was annoyed.

"Mitch, let's go. You can pick up with that tomorrow." Jonathan saw his eyes narrow and froze for a fraction of a second. He gestured to Mitch.

"See you tomorrow," he said and headed for his mother's SUV.

"You guys had a fun day," Sarnower laughed as Mitch piled in.

"Yeah."

Even in his effusive state, Mitch remained monosyllabic. Expressiveness comes with age. With Cassie no longer in his life, he'd need more contact with friends, make new ones and enlarge his repertoire. Sarnower would have to get used to having noisy, messy pre-adolescents over, like it or not. He could remodel the basement into a play den, get a pool table, wide-screen TV, stereo system. He couldn't count on Mitch's friends to entertain him forever.

"What's for dinner?" He was still bouncing from the day's residual energy.

"What would you like?"

He put his chin in his hand and leaned forward in an exaggerated pose of the Rodin *Thinker.* "Chinese," he said suddenly. "No, pizza. No. Ice cream."

"*Ice cream?*" Sarnower recoiled in mock horror. "For dinner?"

"Yeah, Dad, pleeeeeze?"

"Why not? Let's do it. Let's get some big gooey sundaes. Everything on top."

* * *

By the time Sarnower awoke on Friday morning, Mitch was already up. The sun, strong bright and hot had burned off yesterday's lingering humidity and promised to close the summer with a perfect weekend. He heard Mitch wash his cereal bowl and juice glass in the sink. The boy was learning. He'd be fine.

Turning on the shower, Sarnower ran through the plan again. This was it, D-Day. By this time tomorrow, the whole thing would be in the rear-view mirror. Done. It would just be him and Mitch, and soon their lives would be back to a regular rhythm. He felt his heart pound and heard blood rush in his ears. He could do it; he *would* do it. It was like taking his final exam in Anatomy in med school. He had to stop and puke twice before reaching the hall, but once the test was in front of him, he'd relaxed, and the months of grueling study kicked in and pulled him through to an A- in the course. He'd pass this too with flying colors.

Mitch was in the living room, his overnight bag already packed. He was absently looking through an oversized Jackson Pollack book on the coffee table.

"What do you think of abstract expressionism?" Sarnower asked.

Mitch looked up. "Huh?"

"Just kidding."

"Dad, I want to call Mom before I go."

Shit! This wasn't something he'd even thought of. Cassie had no idea Mitch was going to be away, the entire plan depended on it. Think fast!

"Uh, Mitch, Mom isn't around. When I told her you had this fantastic opportunity to go to the Cape, she went ahead and made other plans." It was improvised to be sure, but Mitch might buy it. Lying again to his own son.

"Didn't she want to say goodbye to me?" His face drooped.

"Well, you know how busy she is these days, she probably just forgot. But I know she'll be glad to see you when she gets back."

"Where did she go?" he pressed.

"I don't know. She doesn't tell me much these days."

"Did she go with that weird guy who's been following her around?"

"I don't know who you mean."

"Someone really strange. She met him this summer. He keeps bothering her. She really hates him." Mitch was anxious again, his knee was bobbing up and down.

"Has she called the police?"

Mitch shrugged and looked away. He wanted to end the discussion. Sarnower sat down on the couch and put his arm around his son.

"I'm sure Mom is fine. She's probably on a beach right now, reading a good mystery novel and working on a fantastic tan."

"Dad, will you tell me if she calls? Get her number and I'll call her right back, ok?"

"Promise. There's nothing to worry about. Mom's going to be fine." The ease with which the last sentence tumbled out of his mouth was frightening.

"You're sure?" Mitch needed the imprimatur of absolute authority on this one.

He nodded and drew the boy into a hug. His throat was closing and anything other than a guttural noise would be impossible to produce. Mitch pulled himself into his father's chest and clasped his arms tightly around his back. A horn beeped outside. He remained in the warm cave of his father's embrace.

"They're here," Sarnower whispered. Mitch raised his face, wet with tears.

"Here, champ," he said taking a handkerchief out of his pocket. Mitch got up and dried his eyes and blew his nose. He reached for his bag.

"Got everything?" Sarnower asked for the hundredth time, repeating the summer ritual for the last time.

"Bathing suit?"

"Check!"

"Toothbrush?"

"Check!"

"Clean clothes?"

Sarnower opened the front door and stepped out with Mitch.

"Dad, don't like hug me or kiss me or anything," he whispered.

Sarnower clapped him on the back as they walked to the idling SUV. There in the driver's seat was Janice, radiant, wearing a designer pair of wrap-around shades and her copious brown hair pulled back with a brilliant silk Cartier scarf. Even from several feet he could make out the signature gold and black panthers prowling the red border. Grrrrrr!

"Hi Alan," she sang as they approached. "Hi Mitch." The side door slid open and Mitch dove in. She took off her glasses and winked. He was immediately aroused. She pulled a small lavender piece of paper from the dashboard and handed it to him. In purple ink and rounded girlish script she had written their name and phone number.

"This is where we'll be just in case," she smiled. "Roger's down there already, we're hoping to be on the beach for a swim before lunch."

"That sounds great." He leaned inside the van. Unlike his car, it smelled of lime and cinnamon. "Have fun guys," he called. Already engaged in something noisy and engrossing, they gave him half-hearted waves. Janice smiled and gently squeezed his arm as the van started to roll away.

Sarnower stood and watched as it stopped at the corner, then made a left. "Off in a cloud of bat-shit," he used to say each time they'd all pile into the car for a trip. Mitch would always crack up and beg him to repeat the line several times. Now alone, he walked back into the house.

The hours until Cassie's arrival to pick up Mitch stretched out like a desert. Abruptly he grabbed his car keys from the dining room table and headed out. He got in the car and drove the now familiar route, VFW Parkway to Caruso Street. Unlike yesterday, there'd be no sleeping, no hesitation, no doubt, and no weighing alternatives. Well rested and clear, he'd have it out with her one way or the other. He'd stand up and make his case in a strong, confident voice. He didn't give a damn if that lanky stud-muffin was there. If her mind was made up and she told him where to go, so be it. But he'd have his say and make his peace.

He made the right onto her street. Unlike last night, the sidewalks were quiet and deserted. Only the buzz of a lone lawnmower was heard in the distance. He pulled the car over to the same spot he'd parked the night before. The note Nina had written in bold red letters in his appointment book ran through his mind like a TV jingle: It would never work, it would never work. He left the car and walked up the front steps. Sarnower stood at the window and looked in. He could not believe what he saw.

Nina's apartment had been cleaned out, there was nothing left except the bare floor and walls. He went to the front door and turned the handle. It opened. He was standing in her living room, where just weeks ago, warm, earthy Nina had lifted him, all of him, out of his small, grudging, jumpy corner of the universe. She'd cut the strings and helped him fly, let him breathe the cool, fresh air. Now, like his office, there was no trace of her at all.

He walked down the hall and into the empty bedroom. The antique dresser was gone, the bed gone, the Picasso and Robert Indiana prints, all gone. There were holes in the wall where they'd hung just a few hours ago. He stood in the middle of the room, inches from where they'd made love, and searched for any piece of her, anything she might have left behind, a wayward earring, a scribbled phone number on a scrap of paper, a scent lingering in the air. Other than some lone dust bunnies, there was nothing.

He jumped when he heard the front door open and close. Had Nina come back to retrieve a forgotten item? He turned quickly and saw a short stocky figure approaching. Out of the shadows of the hall a man materialized wearing greasy work pants and a sleeveless undershirt. He was holding a chewed unlit cigar in stubby fingers.

"You come about the apartment?" he asked putting the cigar in his mouth.

Sarnower felt a disappointment so strong he was afraid he'd burst into tears. He shook his head. "No. I was looking for a friend of mine who lived here."

The man smiled and withdrew his cigar. "You just missed her. Her and her boyfriend left a couple of hours ago."

"Do you know where they were going?"

"No clue. I don't poke into other people's business, know what I mean?"

The man started coughing, a deep, phlegmy smoker's cough. He's got to be inhaling those horrible cigars.

"Did you know Nina Winslow at all?" he asked when the man had regained control of his lungs.

He shrugged. "Just to say hi. Always paid her rent on time, if that's what you're asking." He squinted and looked closely at Sarnower. "You're not a cop or a fed, are you? Figured you'd show me some ID if you were."

"No, nothing like that. Just a...a friend." The word tasted like sand in his mouth. "Say, that guy she left with," how to phrase this... "he hasn't been coming around here long, has he?"

"You mean Tyler? Tall, blond, skinny?"

"Yeah, that's him."

The man scratched his bristly chin with a long yellowed thumbnail. "Dunno. Two, three years maybe. That what you mean by long?"

So it was true. He'd been betrayed from the beginning, before it ever even started. Nina had been playing both sides to the middle all along, just like everyone else. Whatever warm or protective feelings he'd had for her up until moments ago congealed into a dense, throbbing lump of disgust. He'd been played for a patsy once again. Cassie and her lawyer, her brother Bill, then even his lawyer, Ballestracci; they'd all bounced him like a handball and served him up against a hard concrete wall. He'd been had for the very last time.

"Thank you," he said to the man and started down the hall toward the living room and the front door.

"Sure you don't want to take the apartment?" the man called after him.

Sarnower didn't answer as he slammed the front door closed. Glass tinkled as the door pane shattered into tiny pieces. By the time the man was at the door screaming and shaking his fist, Sarnower was in his car peeling out of his space. So it had all been a play, an act, she was so smooth, so convincing. What had she wanted him for anyway? A raise? All she had to do was ask. Maybe she delighted in playing the men in her life like chess pieces. He, Tyler and that hapless Doug were all smitten, all balancing balls on their noses like trained seals. Female power, hear me roar, was that it? The inalienable right to flex those vaginal muscles no matter who got hurt or chewed up. Old Doug had probably walked in on Nina going at it with his good friend Tyler. That could have driven him to suicide. It would certainly make sense. Jesus, was there no honesty or fair play left at all anywhere? Everyone for themselves. The new millennium, the new glorification of the almighty self. Well, he would play too. Old, tired, crazy as he was, he could still get into the game.

Back at home he was shaking. His head throbbed and a prickling heat had developed at the back of his eyes. He took deep breaths, in and out. The room tilted under his feet the way it had done some weeks ago in his office. Slumping on the living room couch, he saw the roses on the chintz upholstery sway in a nonexistent breeze, his stomach twisted in a knot. He ought to lie down and sleep for a few hours and collect his thoughts. It didn't seem possible to execute an elaborate plan in the state he was in.

But it was far too late to reconsider. He'd already passed the point of no return. Cassie would be over soon to collect Mitch for the long weekend. What would he tell her, that he'd sent Mitch to the Cape with Jonathan for the weekend without consulting her first? That would get back to her lawyer in about seven seconds. He'd be hauled into court again for sure and humiliated in front of that monstrous judge on some bogus motion. No, he was tired. It all had to end now.

He stood up with great effort. The room spun and for a moment, he was sure he was going to pass out. Closing his eyes and continuing to breathe deeply, he regained his bearings. Deliberately, he walked into the kitchen and made himself a strong gin and tonic. He was barely aware of drinking it as he returned to the living room. On an empty stomach, the alcohol worked rapidly, bringing the room back to stability, calming his short, erratic breathing. He got up and mixed another and sat at the kitchen table.

From down the block someone had started a barbeque, mouth-watering mesquite, grilling hamburgers and sausages began to spice the air. Sarnower was suddenly ravenous; he hadn't eaten since the night before. Briefly, he considered a sandwich, but rejected the idea. The food and alcohol would slow him down when he needed to be rapid and nimble. When it was all over, he'd have a late night meal. Maybe even a glass of champagne.

He got up and went to the sink to splash cold water on his face. In moments, it would be just he and Cassie again. Long before Mitch, before Nina and Manny and everyone else he knew, it had been the two of them. They would engage in their very last, their most intimate act together, more intimate by far, than sex. Funny how things folded back in on themselves, returned to their origins to complete their cycles. The snake eating it's own tail, it was some kind of universal closure. That was part of the ambiguous message Manny had embedded into his fable a few weeks ago, wasn't it?

And there was the front doorbell. Sarnower checked his watch. Four o'clock. She was right on time. He went down to the basement to retrieve the garrote, testing its strength on the way upstairs. He ducked into his study and put it on the desk. The bell rang again and Sarnower suddenly felt everything begin to move in slow motion as if it were all happening under water. He went to the front door and opened it. There was Cassie, wearing a white polo shirt and white tennis shorts. He noticed a new, black leather Gucci clutch in her hand. He was ready.

"Last weekend for whites," he said, smiling broadly.

Cassie was not amused. "Alan are you drunk?" she demanded. Well, yes he was sort of half lit; she must have smelled the fumes.

"This isn't going to help you in the visitation and support negotiations," she said, moving into the foyer and looking around. "I see you haven't started packing up yet either."

Sarnower had trouble suppressing a laugh; she had no idea how meaningless this all was now. Visitation and support negotiations? The phrase was now a punch line to some bad joke.

"Is Mitch ready? I hope you have my check too, I'm in kind of a hurry." She continued looking in the living room and dining room as if to collect more evidence of dereliction to be used against him. Her serious demeanor was ludicrous; his drinking should be the very last thing on her mind. Come to think of it, it probably would be.

"Let's go into the study and I'll get your check," he said. With exaggerated gallantry he extended his arm to usher her in first. With her back to him now, Sarnower took a deep breath, placed his hands around her neck and squeezed. Like a huge tortured crescendo from

218

one of his beloved Mahler symphonies, a bolt of adrenalin exploded
in his blood, electrifying his muscles with a current of strength. He
pushed his fingers into her windpipe diagonally, forming a V.
Cassie, shocked and struggling to breathe; kicked him in the shin.
She snapped her elbows back into his ribs, bobbing her head in
random motions to escape his grip. Ordinarily, the blows would
have been painful, but his two anesthetizing drinks and the surge of
adrenalin had made them little more than annoyances. He felt the
force, but they were ineffective in disabling his attack.

Still gagging and struggling, Sarnower pulled her over to the
desk and with his left hand, picked up the garrote and slipped it over
her head. His left hand pinched her windpipe as his right began to
spin the long Danish salad spoon, tightening the nylon cord. He
realized he hadn't seen Cassie's face yet and was glad. The sight of
her dying might have unpredictable effects later on. He couldn't have
that horrible, wide-eyed purple balloon as his last memory of her.

Although she was still kicking and flailing, her movements had
become less forceful and articulated. She'd been quieter than he'd
expected, only an occasional gasp or animal grunt. Both hands were
now on the spoon, and he began turning it like a fireman shutting
down a large water main. By the last cinch, Cassie had almost
stopped moving; there were some random muscle spasms and
Sarnower felt her start to grow heavy. Keeping the garrote tightened
with his left hand, he was now forced to hold up her slumping body
with his right. He held her against him, counting slowly to three
hundred; that was surely over five minutes. She was in his embrace
again, a final hug goodbye.

Slowly, he let her down, her body now heavy, completely limp
and lifeless. He unwound the garrote from her neck. There was a
clear, detailed imprint of the cord, dark as red wine, an intaglio in
flesh. Her face was a horrifying bright scarlet, her tongue thick and
bloated, protruded idiotically from her mouth. Her eyes, still open,
stared up at him. He could see several of the tiny blood vessels had
burst, the classic mark of strangulation. He lay her body out on the
floor of his study and felt for a pulse. Nothing. She was definitely
gone. He leaned over and closed her eyes, then sat down on the
couch. Her bright white polo shirt and shorts brought into relief the
changing colors of her skin. Gradually, her face drained of blood.

He had no idea how long he sat and looked at her. Hours,
maybe. The day's light had faded and the room had darkened.
Sarnower pulled down the shades and turned on a lamp. In the new

light, Cassie looked like a corpse. Her skin had turned a pale bluish-gray. "We've both moved on," he said softly to her. He picked up her hand, which had started to turn cold. He let it go and it dropped with a muffled thud on the Oriental rug. It was time to continue.

From the basement, he got a pair of latex gloves and put them on. Cassie's car keys were in her new clutch, and Sarnower took them out gently. He turned off the light; she'd be right there when he got back. Leaving the house, he closed the front door gently. It was now completely dark and at the moment, there was no one on the street. Lightly he opened the door to her car and got in. Thankfully, she hadn't gotten a new one yet. Undoubtedly the police would be all over it too, if they found traces of Sarnower it would be expected, over the years he'd used it countless times. He turned on the ignition and lights and pulled out onto the road. Although he'd never been to Cassie's apartment, he knew where it was, and a couple of weeks before had innocently gotten the number of her parking spot from Mitch.

Route Nine was almost deserted as he drove east to Hammond Pond Parkway. Those who were leaving for Labor Day had already gone, those staying had packed it in for the night.

He was on the other side now in a new club of men and women, one as old as time. He'd "made his bones." Easing his car into the lighted parking area, Sarnower tried to take stock and measure the dimensions of his act, but nothing came up except the next set of moves in the plan. He pulled into spot eighteen and cut the lights and engine. It was then he remembered Ecstasy, the dog she'd bought for Mitch. He sat in the darkened car, Cassie's keys in hand. He could let himself into the apartment and at least make sure the dog had food and water for a few days, but that would be risky, someone might see him and be able to ID him later. What would Cassie do? What would be consistent with her completely inconsistent behavior? It was like a Zen koan, any answer he came up with could be proved wrong later. Best not to deviate or improvise. The dog's welfare wasn't worth getting caught.

He got out of the car and locked the door. It was a fifteen or twenty minute walk back to the house, and during the planning, he had looked forward to that interval, a chance to take a break and clear his head. The next couple of phases would require all his stamina and a strong stomach. He started a brisk walk out to the Parkway and west on Route Nine, retracing his path. So far so good, no one had seen him drop off Cassie's car. The sweet, cool night air was invigorating and lifted the alcoholic haze that had made his last encounter with Cassie darkly humorous, and now, trying to recollect it, quite vague.

What was his memory of this night going to be in a week, a year or decades from now? Would it be repressed, like the nightmares of trauma victims, or would random details stand out, like the indented, dark red weave pattern of the nylon garrote in Cassie's neck, or the indescribable, pale-gray color her skin had turned after a couple of hours? At some point, the whole thing might be little more than a dream.

On Route Nine, only the occasional car whizzed by. Some dragged close enough to the narrow sidewalk to create a vacuum that pulled him in. A couple were driven by thin teenaged boys with shaven heads and tattoos, their girls, hair dyed blue or purple or jet black, wore nose rings and pale makeup with heavy raccoon eye shadow. Mitch would be at that age soon. He'd be making those "adolescent choices" as the school guidance counselors called them, PC psychobabble for fucking up, taking the wrong turns, giving in to boneheaded peer pressure. Raising Mitch alone would be difficult. Being abandoned by his mother would always leave a cloud of uncertainty as to whether she was dead or alive. Her permanent absence was sure to cause major scarring. They'd have to do their best. Shit happens.

Turning on to his street, he prepared for the next phase of the plan. It would be ugly and dirty and he hoped he wouldn't lose his nerve. He entered the house without turning on lights. From the bright silver beams of moonlight that cut through the windows he made his way back to the study. There was Cassie, her face returned to normal proportions, lividity and gravity having drawn the blood down to the dorsal surfaces of her body. He took a moment to look at her, now bathed in icy light. If he were daring and brazen enough, he could have taken a set of photos of her in the changing lights of day and night, coupled with the hues and shades of her own beginning necrosis. It would have made a fascinating series, along the lines of Monet's famous set of paintings of Notre Dame Cathedral at different hours of the day. A Haiku sprang instantly to mind:

In the bright moonlight
A woman sleeps forever
Cure for bad karma

He picked up the body, lifting it under the arms. She was heavier than he'd anticipated and although he could feel her limbs flop, he was also aware of the beginning of *rigor mortis*. She had turned frighteningly cold. He opened the door to the basement and carried her slowly downstairs. The last time he'd carried her anywhere was across the threshold of their first apartment after the wedding, a ceremonial gesture, now bookends to their life together.

The utility closet was completely prepared. Sarnower brought her in, and still wearing his latex gloves, began stripping off her clothes. Under the light of the single bulb Cassie was now a pearlescent gray. He opened a new box of trash bags and withdrew one. He balled up her shirt and shorts, her bra and panties, took off her tennis shoes. There was a small silver toe ring on her left foot and above her ankle, a tattoo he'd never seen before, some kind of ancient Celtic symbol. This must be the one she'd gotten recently while leaving Mitch to roast alone on the beach.

Tattoos on the dead. He thought of the stories his parents used to tell of the Nazis making lampshades out of the dried skin of victims of Jewish concentration camps. Of course it was contrary to Jewish law and tradition to disfigure the body in any way; the body unadorned was art enough. Art to fade and die and be reborn again. And again.

It occurred to him it had been the better part of a year since he'd seen the naked body of his wife. In the poor light and on her failing flesh he recognized the familiar landmarks, the mole on her right inner thigh, the appendix scar, the dimples in her knees that always reminded him of the face of the man in the moon. Curiously, her pubic hair had thinned and had begun to look sparse and lifeless, no doubt the result of malnutrition, that strange diet she'd been eating at the commune. That asshole he'd caught her with, his hair had looked thin and sad too. No, he and Mitch would continue to have their occasional hamburger and broiled steak, thank you.

He reached for the hack saw and tightened the blade. After one final look at Cassie, now as lifeless as a mannequin, he made a decisive cut with the blade into the joint at her right shoulder. He was startled at the ease with which the small teeth sank into the soft flesh. There was blood, but not as much as he had expected. Below the skin was a layer of viscous yellow fat, the kind they suctioned out on those extreme makeover shows she used to watch. Then muscle that had the color and consistency of raw steak. The blade began to resist when it hit bone. He dug in and moved the saw faster, but it had lost traction. He parted the layers of skin and muscle and saw that a length of pale yellow tendon had lodged in the cut. Carefully, he removed the blade and worked the almost severed tendon out of the groove. Reinserting the blade, he began again and this time it found purchase, and, applying an opposing weight at the elbow, the bone broke with an unexpectedly loud snap. He continued to saw through the remaining skin and muscle, then pulled the arm off with no resistance.

Before placing it in a trash bag, he picked up the utility knife and carefully sliced off the pads of flesh at the tops of her fingers, taking the cut down to the first joint, severing the swirls and ridges of her fingerprints from her hands, making them forever anonymous. He lined the five flaps of skin in a row, the size of pale translucent postage stamps. The sight made him sad, like looking at premature babies on life support in incubators. In all his preparation, he had completely forgotten to plan for these tiny orphans, sightless witnesses to his obsessive madness.

Slowly he repeated the entire process with her other arm, a gory Venus de Milo. After removing her finger tips again, Sarnower placed the two arms in a waiting trash bag. The covered floor had become a wet greasy mess. Blood, fluids and yellow gobs of fatty tissue made a soup that traveled in rivulets into the valleys and crevasses of the trash bags covering the floor. The mixture had begun to soak into his pants where he'd been kneeling over his work. In places, it had started to thicken, darken and dry and become sticky. Work faster, then focus on the cleanup.

Suddenly giddy and bursting into laughter, he inserted a new blade and began to cut again, this time starting at the top of her left thigh. This was it, the real thing; he had gone totally out of his mind. Here he was in the basement of his house at the beginning of Labor Day weekend, chopping up his wife in a rising swamp of sticky red goo. Stay the course and finish the job, no turning back now, this is where mistakes get made. The plan was sound, but didn't allow for freaking out.

New blood, sluggish and dark, the color of Burgundy wine ran from the femoral artery. Jesus, he should have remembered this huge conduit. What happened to all his anatomy? How much blood did the body contain? Seven to eight percent of total body weight sprang to mind, that would mean...no, he couldn't get bogged down with inane calculations. Finish the job. Dearticulation: the complete dismemberment of the body. Exsanguination: the total bleeding out.

Terms from medical school to clothe the most primitive and savage in civilized sounds. Now they would conceal nothing, he was up to his elbows in it. The left leg was almost completely severed as he cut through the last few inches of tissue. Blood oozed like thick paint. During his brief rotation through surgery in medical school, he'd learned how to cauterize wounds. It wasn't that difficult but now he couldn't remember a thing. He should have prepared better and used the feeble remnants of his training to contain this mess. The only thing to do now was work faster and get it done.

Cassie's left leg now tied up in a bag, he began on the right. He recalled that if he cut a few inches lower on the thigh, he'd miss the large common femoral artery and hit the superficial femoral and possibly avoid so much blood. He moved the saw down and began again. What had been a foreign, weird, ghoulish procedure only minutes before was already becoming routine, a butcher cutting prime ribs for a customer.

His wife, Mitch's mother, was now a torso with a head. The original plan had called for removal of the head at the neck, but that would mean cutting through the two large carotid arteries, and another significant blood loss on top of what was already there. This in itself would be hard enough to clean up; more would create a level of mess that would jeopardize the sealed work area. What were the risks of leaving the head on? These were possibilities, contingencies, "what ifs" he couldn't even think about now. Best to keep it attached.

Sarnower surveyed the floor. It was hard to look at. Cassie was unrecognizable, a red, splattered torso with four gaping, bleeding holes the color of raw meat through which jagged pieces of bone jutted. Her face, now completely drained, had caved in and the bloodless skin clearly revealed the contours of her skull. Her hair, recently cut, fanned out from her head in a circle, drenched in drying, hardening blood. When he picked her up, it would hold its shape like the strange hair-sculptures of punk rockers in the eighties.

He checked his watch. It was two-fifteen in the morning. There wasn't time for any more weighing of alternatives, he had to begin cleaning things up. He opened a fresh box of trash bags and took out several. He picked up the torso. In contrast to the intact corpse he'd carried down the stairs, it was much lighter than he'd expected. He maneuvered it into the bag. The neck was now very stiff and he had to bend the head down with some force to get the entire mass into the bag. It was a tight fit, but he found that by pulling the drawstring forcefully he could seal the contents. There would be four bags containing body parts. One for the torso and head, one for each leg and one for both of the arms. These in turn would be wrapped in other bags and then in other bags, perhaps five or six in all, so that by the end, there would be no trace of blood left.

He changed into a clean pair of latex gloves, but noticed his hands had started to itch and become swollen and red. There were white splotchy areas where pale, sweaty welts were forming. So, he was allergic to latex; not the ideal time to find out, but he'd be done soon enough.

He began wrapping. When each part had been multiply bagged, he set it outside the door.

The floor was now covered in a sea of blood and fluids. The stuff was congealing and the clotting and hardening would make it a bit easier to gather up the layer of covering on the floor. He worked rapidly but carefully. Any trace of Cassie's blood on the floor could spell disaster. Police detectives would surely scour the entire house with Luminal looking for signs of spilled blood. He detached the bags on the floor one by one, making sure the fluids ran to the center before lifting each one by all four corners and depositing it in a fresh bag. The process was repeated until the floor was clean. He checked the corners. Nothing had spilled. He began to remove the bags from the walls and ceiling. To his relief, nothing had splattered. He gathered his tools and placed them in a bag, took off his clothes and running shoes and placed them in another. Soon, he and the room were bare. He scanned the area once more. There, near the door in a neat row were the ten drying and curled flaps of skin he had shaved off her fingertips. He bent down and picked them up. They had dried, hardened and started to curl, almost the consistency of potato chips. Sarnower smiled to himself as he thought about the possibility of a new snack food. The fingertips could be deep-fried, come in barbeque, creamy ranch or salt and vinegar flavors. Shit, he was really unraveling. He started laughing. It was almost fun.

Naked, he ran upstairs to the bathroom. There he flushed the mummifying pieces of skin down the toilet. He turned on the shower. He'd never felt so filthy in his life. As the scalding hot water beat on his back, he thought of his ninth grade English class. The sexy, just-out-of-grad-school Miss Sandow had been teaching *Macbeth*. The class had struggled through the play, their first taste of Shakespeare, and the fourteen-year old boys, awash in raging hormones wondered what her bra size was, if she had a boyfriend, and if so, were they fucking? Did she give good head? And there near the end of the play, the scary, sleepwalking Lady Macbeth went stark raving mad, her obsessive hand washing, "out damn spot, out I say...The smell of blood still, all the perfumes of Arabia will not sweeten this little hand." They'd snickered and giggled as Miss Sandow tried desperately to explain guilt and insanity. What was done could not be undone. It was yours; you bought it. That alone could push anyone over the edge.

Time was passing rapidly. Although the days were getting shorter, first light would be breaking on the horizon in just a few hours. Sarnower stepped out and dried himself. The stench was still on him, but he'd have to deal with it later. The hard part was done; the rest was simple mechanics. Now in T-shirt, shorts and old Topsiders he was back in the basement. There, in a line were the seven tied-up trash bags. He put on a fresh pair of gloves and began carrying them out through the basement door to his car. Outside the air was heavy and cool with the mossy scent of recent rain. The street was dark, deserted and quiet. He opened the trunk and placed two of the bags inside, taking care not to tear them on the protruding lip of the lock. The trunk held five bags; two would have to go in the back seat. Cassie's last ride.

He returned and checked one last time. The room was clean; there were no visible signs of his ever having been there. He locked the basement door and got in the car. It was three-twenty. Backing out of the driveway, he looked up and down the street. His neighbors still slept, their houses and cars immobile as monuments. He would head out Route Nine and take 128 North to Ninety-Five North. Following the carefully laid out plan and dry run he'd made the day before, the first drop would be in a restaurant Dumpster on the North Shore, then onto southern New Hampshire where three drops would be made and finally, if time permitted, to Maine where he would dispose of the rest of the bags.

The Labor Day crowds at coastal resort areas would be gorging themselves one last time on chowder and clams and lobster rolls at these places, their Dumpsters would fill rapidly, giving him a perfect cover. They'd be hauled away quickly after the holiday weekend and by next Tuesday, Cassie's remains would be resting securely, impenetrably in garbage dumps in three states.

Headlights on and driving north, Sarnower relaxed. The jangling screaming noises in his head began to subside. As a final gesture of farewell, he popped a CD of the Mozart *Requiem* into the player. He tried to remember Cassie before her devastating breakdown, before she got swept away by a *tsunami* of illness and hatred. What had become of her gentleness, her humor, had it ever really been there, or was it merely a veil barely covering the devastation her family had wrecked on her? She may never have had a chance at all.

Singing along with the chilling *Dies Irae,* Sarnower pulled off Ninety-Five North at Newburyport and made his way through the town. Rich, plush lawns, now black in the dark-blue of night, sprawled in front of majestic restored captain's houses. Newburyport had been an important fishing center in past centuries and had managed to retain its hold as an iconic Currier and Ives New England town. It slept in a soft, foggy quilt as Sarnower made his way out to the beach road. He'd been here before with Cassie. She'd loved the shore, and even in her acutely crazy phases, something about nature, about the swell of the waves, the smell of the ocean, had a calming effect on her like Manny stepping onto the locked ward at Beacon General. The therapeutic effects of nature on insanity were recognized years ago. The innovative nineteenth century landscape architect Frederick Law Olmsted, creator of Central Park and the "Emerald Necklace" of Boston's connected greenery had been commissioned to design the grounds of legendary psychiatric hospitals, the Menninger Clinic in Kansas and of course the grand dame of them all, McLean Hospital. Cassie would never know the benefits of Olmsted's calming touch.

Approaching the fragrant salty beach road, he found Raymond's Lobster & Clam Shack and in the back, a Dumpster. He cut his lights and drove slowly through the small parking lot, stopping a few yards from the container. He popped the trunk and dislodged two of the bags. They seemed heavier now that he was no longer in the grip of his fevered butchery. The Dumpster, slightly taller than he was, had a light plastic cover, which lifted easily as he heaved each bag in. He shut the lid. That was all there was to it. Imagining himself on his porch with a tall gin and tonic doing the Sunday *Times* crossword puzzle, he returned to the car and headed out to New Hampshire.

There were more cars on the road now and the occasional eighteen-wheel Mack truck zoomed by at terrifying speed, their drivers jacked up on black coffee and Methadrine. It was still dark but he was now racing against daylight. He crossed the state line into New Hampshire and would make a drop near Hampton Beach.

What about that idea of doing a shrink talk show? Clinical work no longer held any attraction. The repetition, the whining, the endless complaining about absolute minutia, the numbing hassles with insurance companies over reimbursements, they'd taken their toll. In truth, it would be very hard to find an adequate replacement for Nina. Learning the job was a steep curve, he'd been spoiled for years, but more than that, going into the office every day and seeing someone else at her desk? It wouldn't work.

He could duplicate the success he'd had in the eighties with a self-help book. Go to Barnes and Noble and look through the current crop of titles. In a couple of months he could easily knock one out. A well-promoted piece of pop fluff would give him name recognition, and some snappy sound bites might put him in a position to get his own show. He could start out with a five-minute call-in segment on local TV, then maybe on to syndicated radio. His old editor, what was her name? She'd moved on through a couple of publishing houses since she'd worked on his book, but had called him every so often to stay in touch. Of course Manny would never speak to him again. For him it would be a complete and total sell-out. He'd forgiven Sarnower his first book, understanding that the advance would make the down payment on his house, but had delivered a stern lecture on the integrity of the profession. The accumulated knowledge of psychiatry was to be passed on through rigorous training from generation to generation like a treasured family heirloom and not sold on the cheap to a boneheaded public that would misinterpret and abuse it. Well, Manny was comfortable and had no children to put through school. He was near retirement anyway. What the hell did he know about the responsibilities Sarnower faced?

He and Mitch could leave the East coast altogether. He'd had enough of the hard-driving competitive lifestyle here, the backbiting, the professional rivalry and jealousies. There were colleagues out in L.A. making a fortune as sports psychologists, "lifestyle" coaches, "self-actualizers," whatever that was, shrinks who were on retainer to high profile people, actors and celebrities for big money, just to be available for the occasional two a.m. pep talk. He could get a job as a consultant for one of those reality TV programs, screening contestants, spotting those who would be most likely to have a photogenic nervous breakdown on national television and those who would gladly shed any semblance of inhibition and dignity to win prize money. Shit, there was any number of ways he could reinvent himself out there. To go back to the grind here and do more of the same, tread water indefinitely until it finally closed in over his head? No thanks. Liz Dashiell would kill herself one day whether he was working with her or not.

His hands were now on fire. The itching was close to unbearable and his fingers and palms had swollen to the point where he could barely move them. Sweat had pooled in the gloves and had started to run down his wrists. In an instant, he pulled them off and threw them on the floor. The cool night air bathed them in instant relief, and he flexed his fingers, thick and red as knockwurst. Got to remember to put them back on though. He'd take some Benedril when he got home.

At the end of the exit ramp, Sarnower made a right. There down the road was the seedy Hang 'n' Bang lounge, his second drop site. The neon sign he'd seen, dark during the day was now lit and animated. A naked woman in bright pink light was swinging back and forth by her knees, upside down on a trapeze, her long hair waving in the breeze. But now the place was buzzing with activity. Hundreds of bikers, grizzled, bearded men covered with tattoos, men in leather vests and heavy women with hair below their waists, clogged the street, parking lot and entrance to the lounge. There was a long line out the door. Most of the patrons looked and sounded very drunk.

Stupid! What had he been thinking? Of course Friday night was party night, especially for this crowd. They'd be going at it well into Saturday morning. Even if he could get into the parking lot, it would be far too risky to conduct his business here, he'd have to find something quickly and nearby.

But now he was caught in traffic, wedged in among Harleys and noisy, beaten-up drag racing cars. He rolled up the windows and slumped down in the seat, an unwelcome intruder at these festivities. If Tug were here with him, he'd already be out of the car and mingling. He'd be buying rounds for these guys in no time, wanting to discuss engine mountings and recent design changes to the classic hog. Who had the best dealership? Who were the best mechanics? Would Tug ever speak to him again?

He looked at the digital clock on the dashboard. It was after four-thirty and light would be breaking soon. There was nothing to do except wait. Outside, huge, bearded, longhaired men congregated in groups, beer cans in hand. Some had their arms around women. A fight was in progress somewhere in back of the lounge, he heard shouting, breaking glass and the sound of falling metal trashcans. He wondered briefly what it would be like to pick a fight with one of these guys.

Finally, the line of bikes and cars began to move, and Sarnower drove on, leaving the last of the raucous partiers behind him. A faint gray light was rising over the top of the narrow road, and color began to return to the horizon.

Rundown single-family houses sat on either side of the road, untended, overgrown lawns held broken-down rusted cars on blocks. Old, faded furniture sat on sagging porches. It was getting later and later. He began to panic but kept on driving. He'd wasted time and hadn't thought things through nearly as well as he should have. About two miles in, he came to a clearing where heavy equipment, backhoes, long-beds and dump trucks sat waiting out the holiday weekend. The land had been cleared and dug up. A foundation was being poured. There at the end of the plot was a large trash Dumpster. He drove in and cut his lights. The car rocked and swayed as it went through potholes and over rocks. He hit his head on the roof. Phil would have to check his shock absorbers next week.

A low gray light had begun to illuminate everything; the sun was coming up. There wouldn't be time to make it to Maine and he would have to discharge the remaining bags here at this site, and quickly.

This Dumpster was huge with no cover, and its iron sides were a good seven feet high. Sarnower could see pieces of an old demolished house sticking out, two by fours, warped split pieces of siding, windows, some broken, some with frames that still had panes of what looked like old leaded glass. He opened the trunk and the door to the back seat. There were three bags remaining in the trunk and two on the seat. He grabbed them quickly and started heaving them into the container. They landed with dull thuds, falling on an already substantial lining of dusty, chalky debris. When they were all in, he was relieved to see there were none visible from his level. Tuesday, some gigantic piece of equipment would haul the entire contents into oblivion. Wiping his hands on his shorts, Sarnower returned to the car. That was it. His work was done.

He sat in the driver's seat motionless, looking over the barren construction site. There would be a new home here soon, a new family would attach itself to this piece of land, to this community, to the rough and tumble beach only a couple of miles away. Here too, at least for now, for the next several hours, was the home of the last earthly remains of his wife, the mother of his son, the daughter of the late Brandon and Deirdre Kelly of Chicago. She had been here, she had walked on this planet, gladdened some spirits, poisoned others. What of it all was her fault? Could she have made a different life, or was her path through here, this brambly, unforgiving wilderness, written in her genes, her fluids, her muscles and nerves? Sarnower, no longer seeing the gaping brown-red scar on this plot of land began to cry. Silently, he mouthed the Kaddish.

When he looked up again, sunlight was spreading quickly through the trees. He put the car in reverse and backed out of the site. Traffic was already beginning to flow to and from the beach. It was now after five. Ninety-Five South had started to hum. Trucks, SUVs, campers, cars with boats in tow, recreational vehicles were getting a late start on summer's last weekend. Mitch and Jonathan, undoubtedly having stayed up late the night before, were still sleeping. And where was Nina? She and Tyler were probably somewhere in the Midwest heading for the Rocky Mountains and then Seattle where they'd open a coffee shop or organic food store together. Could Tyler give her what she wanted? He'd never know. He'd have to let it all go. Today, there were plans to be made, futures to consider.

He realized he hadn't eaten in hours. Stop for coffee and a fast food breakfast or just continue on? He could be home in a little over an hour, scramble a couple of eggs and sack out for a nice nap. Yes, that's what he'd do.

He turned on the radio. NPR was featuring an interview with a new "cutting edge" Tribeca composer whose pieces consisted of taping and distorting a variety of household sounds: stairs creaking, doors shutting, toilets flushing, air conditioners belching and humming, and then synthesizing them all into some kind of piece, an "auditory tapestry" the man called it. "I'm raising the mundane to glorious heights so that we can listen with fresh ears to our environment," he proclaimed. God! The bullshit detectors of the entire country were now completely and irretrievably broken. Tug, to his credit had learned this decades ago and had made his fortune on exactly that realization.

And back at home, his home now, the block was beginning to wake up. There was good old Tracey Bowen strapping on a backpack, about to get an early start on a bike trip with her father. Fred Cerillo was filling his lawn spreader with fertilizer and weed-killer, his own blend, as he was fond of telling anyone who got trapped into listening to his rambling philosophy of gardening.

Once inside, Sarnower went down to the basement. There was no sign that anything had taken place there. He brought the rusted tools, the hubcaps and old skis back into the utility closet and closed the door. Upstairs, he poured himself a gin and tonic, even though it was now approaching seven in the morning. He climbed the stairs to his bedroom and turned on the radio. The majestic brass of Copland's *Fanfare for the Common Man* punched the air. Of course. It was Labor Day weekend, time to honor the working stiffs of the country. Sarnower raised his drink in silent toast to the common man and took a large swig. In less than a minute he had passed out.

He is six or seven years old again, on the deck of the Staten Island Ferry, holding hands with both his parents, cold tingling spray shooting into his face as the boat rides each wave. For the hundredth time, his father points to the approaching Ellis Island. "This was the gateway to America," he intones in a solemn voice. He has heard this phrase so many times it's truly funny now, but he keeps from laughing out of respect for his father. The island has been abandoned for decades, long before the National Park Service restored it as a museum. The large main building, run down and falling apart looks like an old castle in Central Europe. His father continues: "My parents came to that exact building in 1909. They had nothing. Can you understand that? NOTHING." He bends down and looks at his son as if he's done something terribly wrong. The shame is almost overwhelming. The shame of being. Shame at having anything at all. His bike, his baseball card collection, his small junky transistor radio, the one he turns on softly late at night to hear a game. But soon Ellis Island recedes in the distance and his father is silent, having coughed up whatever emotional hairball had welled up in his chest. And soon their destination, Staten Island is in sight, getting larger and larger. The ferry, pulling into the narrow slip always hits the wooden pilings before coming to rest. With a crash the gangplanks are lowered on to the dock and they blend into the swarm of passengers getting off the boat.

Chapter **12**

HE HAD NO IDEA WHAT TIME it was when he awoke. Where had he been? The light in the sky was dim. Was it daybreak or sunset? What day was it? How long had he been asleep? His head pounded, his eyelids scratched. Sarnower roused himself and ran his fingers through his hair.

The events of the previous night came back to him like a dream, its edges fuzzy and watery. Cassie was dead. Or was she? Looking out the window, sitting on the edge of the bed in his shorts, he tried to collect his thoughts. Had he really killed her? Was it possible? She'd come over to pick up Mitch; he'd led her into the study and choked her, then turned the garrote on her neck. The next part was murky, the trip to the basement, the dismemberment, it was all colors and sense-impressions now. He had no memory of having performed a structured, sequential series of acts. Was she really dead? He thought so but couldn't be entirely sure. Slowly he stumbled into the bathroom.

His face was red and splotchy and there were dark bags under his eyes, but the swelling in his hands had gone down. A two-day growth of beard made him look like a derelict. The face of a murderer. He turned the shower on full force and got in, not waiting to adjust the temperature. Hot blasts beat on his body, burning needles shooting into his skin. He would get purified at last and finally wash that dreadful stain away.

The story. He had to get it perfectly straight—absolutely flawless. Ok. He had spoken with Cassie before the long weekend and told her of Mitch's invitation to go the Cape with Jonathan. Ever eager to avoid her parental responsibilities, she had readily agreed to let Mitch go. Fine. It was all in character. He had no idea what her plans were for the long weekend, she hadn't told him and he hadn't asked, so he had no knowledge. Sorry, he could be of no help there. Her car would be parked in its usual space by her condo. Her documented history of taking off on impulse would be a credible background to her current absence. Maybe the pressures of renewed parenthood and the legal maneuverings of divorce had been too much for her and once again she'd split. Good. It was all of a piece. He was in the clear.

Stepping out of the shower, Sarnower dried off. His body was red from the scalding water, and the air, still hot from the day, felt cold. He went into the bedroom and pulled out a T-shirt and a pair of shorts from the dresser. He was feeling more like himself already. He went to the nightstand and downed the last of the watery gin and tonic.

Downstairs, the kitchen clock read six thirty-seven. A pink glow was pouring across the sky from the west, so it must be evening. How long had he been sleeping? Almost twelve hours. It had been daybreak when he'd returned, but he could remember nothing after getting home. Nevertheless, it was odd and discomforting having an entire day pulled out from under him. He thought of Mitch, suddenly jealous that his own son was with Janice. He resented Roger. Who were they to hog her time, which should be spent with him? Janice of the incredible lips and teeth. They'd all be back tomorrow and now that Nina was gone, perhaps the two of them could rekindle their lusty adventures.

Sarnower sat on the living room couch and thought. He'd been so consumed with the planning and execution of Cassie's murder, he'd neglected all else. Right after Labor Day, he'd have to start an intensive search for Nina's replacement. He'd call a temp agency and start there. If someone worked out halfway decently, maybe he'd hire her full time. By now Nina could be approaching Seattle, the end of the line, back to her beginnings. Had she and Tyler camped out under the stars, or had they stayed in tacky motels along the way? He could torture himself for the rest of the evening imagining the acrobatics they were up to. This was the first day of the rest of his life. He was a widower now and would have to bring up his son, a boy who would never know the facts of his mother's end.

Now with Nina and Cassie out of his life, who was left? He though of his last meeting with Tug. He'd been incredibly stupid and must have come across as completely demented. Tug hadn't called since then, a pretty sure sign their friendship was in big trouble. He was starting to feel as if there was a thick Plexiglas barrier growing between himself and everyone else. Well, in a sense there was now. He was the only one he knew who had taken a life. He had no idea where that left him with his colleagues, his patients, his friends, Mitch and society at large.

He'd talked to no one in the last twenty-four hours. He hadn't heard his own voice since his final words to Cassie. His thoughts, murky, jumbled and half-formed and that strange, poignant Ellis Island dream he'd awoken from, had been the only contents of his consciousness since the drive back from New Hampshire. Would he be able to carry on without crumbling like a stale muffin? How would he handle Mitch and the police, who within days would be in his face asking crisp, pointed questions about Cassie. Could he successfully bring off the innocent bystander? Would his voice tremble, would he be able to look the detectives in the eye and say what needed to be said? He was wearing the invisible stain of his deed, carrying the dead weight of his free will.

The late summer darkness now covered the house like a shroud. The entire day had stolen by and was gone before he'd been aware of it.

Suddenly he was ravenous. Sarnower got up and went to the refrigerator. He took out a bottle of beer and made a sandwich of smoked turkey and Swiss cheese. Who would be the first to discover Cassie missing? Well, think it through. Her lawyer is probably expecting to hear from her within the next few days. Bill would still have his greasy meat hooks in the case. They were probably talking on a regular, if not daily basis. Tomorrow when he returned, Mitch would want to see her and tell her all about his fantastic trip to the Cape. It would all play out as he'd planned. Things would fall into place all on their own.

Outside, crickets had started a diminished chorus of late summer music. He bit into the sandwich. Even the stale rye bread was delicious and he killed it in four bites. What the hell, why not finish off the six-pack too?

Thou art weighed in the balance and found wanting. A favorite admonition of his father, fresh from the Book of Daniel after he'd committed a particularly heinous misdeed. He should read the Bible and the philosophers Manny had suggested. The words rang in his head as he drank the last beer. He heard his father's voice, tight and squeaky with anger, as if he were standing right across from him, but unable to see him clearly as he had that day in court. What would his parents say if they knew what he'd done? Or perhaps they did, looking down from wherever they were. He would have been found wanting long before yesterday's events.

The expected relief of having accomplished his mission, and done it flawlessly, was still out of reach. Something nagged. He got up and went downstairs to the small tool closet. All was fine. Tools were back in place, the scene looked inviolate. He'd been scrupulous in his attention to detail. No matter what shape their friendship, Tug would never go to the cops. And Manny: he'd dismiss Sarnower's disjointed ramblings as the grousing of a stressed-out middle-aged man. Without a body, who was to know what happened?

He thought of Cassie, her scattered physical remains. When were the Dumpsters scheduled to be emptied? Tomorrow was a holiday, of course. Tuesday would be the first real opportunity. It was something he should have researched when scouting locations. He should drive up Wednesday to make sure. No, that was nuts. The criminal always returns to the scene of the crime, a great way to get caught. Chances of anything happening there were remote at best. Hold on. In just a few days, he'd be completely in the clear.

The alcohol and fatigue began an ambush of his consciousness, starting at the back of his skull and moving forward like a storm cloud. He passed out on the sofa.

The next morning, he awoke with a snap, still on the sofa and cramped. Sunlight streamed through the living room windows and he could feel the beginnings of a fall chill. Mitch would be coming back today, most likely this afternoon. He tried to remember if Janice had told him when they'd be leaving the Cape. Traffic on the last holiday weekend of summer could be brutal. Roger Elsinger, Janice's husband would likely be with them when they dropped Mitch off, he'd finally get to meet the man in person, not something he was especially looking forward to. He'd seen the photos on the fireplace and Janice had told him enough already. It was time to get off the couch and start functioning.

In the kitchen, Sarnower retrieved cleaning supplies and, putting on an old Eric Clapton CD, began scrubbing down the house, waxing the dining room table, mopping the kitchen floor, dusting and vacuuming every possible surface. Cleaning rituals were the busy work of the secretly guilty, but the activity after so much groggy and restless sleep felt good.

"Strange brew, kill what's inside of you,"

Clapton sang in that weird falsetto. He got *that* right. They'd both had more than their share of the stuff.

Outside, he could see cars parked across the street. Fred Cerillo always had his children and grandchildren over on Labor Day for a big cookout. It was something of a standing institution on the block, neighbors were welcome to drop by and share a hamburger and a beer, and in past years Sarnower, Cassie and Mitch would show up, Cassie bringing a fruit or pasta salad, he'd bring dessert. He could see Cerillo's son and daughter-in-law moving the large gas grill into position. There were small children throwing a ball in the yard, another two were engaged in a wrestling match on the grass. Soon there would be crackling, buzzing activity. A large wooden table would appear, plates, cups, liter bottles of soda and people from down the block would drop in early to share a beer and catch up on neighborhood gossip. Tracey Bowen and her family usually put in an appearance as well as the Goulds and other assorted busybodies, members of the grapevine that had so efficiently spread the news of that unreal day when Sarnower had come home to find his wife and that freak in bed together.

Now that was a scene he had no problem remembering; the absurd, random running around of that naked man, first in his bedroom and then out on the front lawn for all to see. If he was now the village pariah, it was worth playing the part in Technicolor with grand gestures. But it was a long drop from disorganized, oddball shrink to murderer. Obviously, he would not be showing up across the street for Fred's end-of-the-summer fling.

It was already September. Mitch would be starting school in a couple of days and they'd have to do some back-to-school shopping. He'd really shot up this summer and few if any clothes from last year would fit. At least now there'd be some money. Sarnower could settle his bill with Ballestracci and get the deed to his house back. He'd have the energy and the resources to pursue another venture entirely. Yes, California was looking better all the time. No more lawyers, judges, G.A.L.s. He'd left the system. Checked out. Sayonara. Case closed.

People were beginning to assemble across the street. Some brought folding chairs, others carried coolers and various pot-luck dishes. Suddenly he wanted to be part of it, that simple American ritual going on in all parts of the country, the casual, easy bonding between people who lived next door, or down the block. He didn't know any of them well, but saw their rites of passage, occasionally even participated in them; their graduations, marriages, the dazzling, quick rise in fortunes during the eighties and nineties that prompted a fortunate few to move on to more luxurious homes, or out of the Boston area entirely. Their deaths, their kids in trouble. It had all rolled by like a slow-motion soap opera. The characters would change, but the drama remained the same and would continue so without intermission long after he was gone.

And there, coming up the block was Janice's SUV. He opened the front door and stepped out onto the walk. Roger was driving and Janice was seated next to him riding shotgun. They pulled up to the curb and stopped. Roger got out first and walked around the front of the vehicle. Sarnower recognized him instantly from the pictures on the fireplace mantle, but he looked older, and in person much taller. He wore a deep tan, one that was surely cultivated year round, which contrasted nicely with his blonde and silver-flecked hair. An aging surfer, still tending a lean, sinewy body. He wore a faded Hawaiian shirt and cargo shorts, boat shoes with no socks. He bounded up the walk toward Sarnower, a high-energy animal like his wife.

"Roger Elsinger," he said extending his hand. "I don't think we've met."

Sarnower advanced. Roger's handshake was firm but brief. The man made clear penetrating eye contact and for a moment Sarnower wondered if he knew what had been going on with Janice.

"We really enjoyed having Mitch with us this weekend." His voice was unexpectedly deep and authoritative. He could certainly intimidate in the conference room. "I think the boys had a lot of fun together," he said turning to the car as Mitch scrambled out of the sliding door with his backpack.

"Dad!" he screamed as he ran toward his father. Sarnower opened his arms and caught him as he jumped in, twirling him around. He could still be a little boy in spite of himself, even in front of his friends.

The passenger door opened and Janice got out and slowly made her way up the walk, her hips swaying like leaves on a palm tree. She hooked her arm around Roger's waist. Sarnower flushed.

"Alan, we had the greatest time," she said, flashing her gorgeous, sparkling white teeth. "Swimming, movies, miniature golf, too much ice cream." There were three faces in a semi-circle beaming at him. Smile. Try to look excited.

"That's great," he got out feebly. Those were his first spoken words. Seeing Roger and Janice close together in the flesh just feet away made him want to scream. He was the chump once again. Were they trying to embarrass him? Yes, they were making a mockery of him; that was clear enough. Janice must be getting back at him for their night together, her petulant, adolescent silence. Hadn't she enjoyed their frolicking? Of course she had, but now she hated him for it, and with her delicious tan arm around Roger's waist, she was sticking it to him. How much was he supposed to take without saying anything?

He should ask her, right in front of her goofy rich husband, ask her how it felt to be fucked up the ass. Turn the tables on foolish old Roger, split their phony marriage in half with a machete. He could do it. They probably deserved it standing there smug and satisfied. They'd had a great time on the Cape while Sarnower was in the basement cutting up his wife, up to his elbows in blood. Did they know what he'd been up to? That's why they were lording their cozy relationship over him. They were better than him after all. They were still dancing on the ledge; he'd already fallen off.

He wanted them all to leave that instant and take Mitch with them. His unthinkable deed and the weekend cocoon of solitude had made social contact abrasive. He forced a smile.

"Anyone follow you here?" he heard himself ask.

"What? Follow us? No." Roger frowned. "Why do you ask?"

Sarnower shrugged. He hadn't realized the sheer lunacy of the question until it was out of his mouth.

"Can't be too careful these days."

"Are you all right?" Janice asked.

"Never better." He smiled, rocking back on his heels, thumbs in his waistband like a southern farmer on his front porch.

They looked at him expectantly. Wasn't there more he wanted to say? Questions he wanted to ask? In another second, everyone was going to be as uncomfortable as he was. Janice started to frown and Roger took the initiative, looking at his watch, a large diver's model with lots of dials.

"Well, I guess we'd better get going," he said.

"Mom! Dad!" Jonathan called from the car.

Mitch was bouncing up and down. Sarnower had to snap out of it now.

"Thank you both so much," he managed. But the moment for offering a heartfelt response had long passed. Janice and Roger nodded and turned to go. He'd blown that nicely. They'd been nothing but kind and generous to his son and that's all he could manage. He'd completely neglected to have Jonathan for a sleepover despite repeated requests. Her moodiness notwithstanding, Janice had been kind and generous with him too, soothing and giving. He was unfit for any kind of human contact.

High on sun and good times, Mitch dashed into the house, his energy annoying and grating.

"Did you hear from Mom?" he asked as Sarnower entered.

It's starting all over again. "No, I didn't."

"Let's call her," Mitch said, picking up the phone. Dialing, he turned away from his father. This terrible summer had succeeded in neatly dividing his loyalties. The phone rang and rang. He could hear Cassie's faint, disembodied voice answer on the tape.

"Hi Mom, it's me. Give me a call when you get in."

He replaced the phone and turned to Sarnower.

"When is she coming back?"

"I don't know. Mom has her own life now." In a place far, far away.

A shot rang out across the street. Sarnower started and went to the window. Fred Cerillo's grandchildren were setting off cherry bombs. Pop, pop! He'd forgotten this was part of the ritual. On July Fourth and Labor Day all hell broke loose over there. There'd be noise, loud music and boisterous conversation until late in the evening. Another pain in the ass he'd have to put up with. He felt like he was coming down with something.

The next day he went into the office. Miroslav's crew had already started redoing the atrium and workers had to move equipment and large rolls of mauve carpeting out of the way in order for him to get to his door.

He stood inside the waiting room and turned on the lights. Nothing had been disturbed in his several days of absence, but the air had turned musty, devoid of the live human scents, the perfumes, the currents of comings and goings he had found so familiar and comforting.

He went into Nina's cubicle. There was his large appointment book. He took it in his hands and opened it up to that dreaded page. There it was in blood red, the last thing he had from Nina, her note of resignation from her job, from his life. He closed the book.

He got out the Yellow Pages and began calling temp agencies. By eleven he had interviews scheduled with five candidates for the next day. Where was Nina? His anger had faded and all that was left now was a black, burned out hole. Should he try to reach her through her parents in Seattle and persuade her to come back and give it another shot? He thought he had their number somewhere; she'd given it to him years ago when she'd started to work for him, in case of emergency. No, that would be begging. He was different now, changed. He was back in charge and groveling was not on the agenda.

In the afternoon he took Mitch shopping at the mall for clothing and to Staples for school supplies. It was hard to be around him. His habits irritated, his voice was an out-of-tune violin. Looking into his face was a constant reminder of Cassie, the same eyes slanted ever so slightly, the nose turned up at the end like hers. After making their purchases, Mitch had demanded they drive by Cassie's apartment and Sarnower reluctantly agreed.

They pulled into the parking lot. There was her car just as he'd left it a couple of nights before. Mitch ran over to it and peered in the windows, he tried the handle to the driver's door but it was locked.

"She's here Dad," he said breathlessly.

Before Sarnower could respond, Mitch had gone into the vestibule and was ringing her buzzer. Sarnower could see a frown spread across the boy's face. He rang again and again, punching the buzzer forcefully. He hit it with his fist. There was no response.

"Where *is* she?" he screamed, on the verge of tears.

"Did she give you a key?" Sarnower asked stalling for time, knowing that was something Cassie would never do.

"No."

"Maybe she took an extra day of vacation."

"But why hasn't she called?"

Sarnower threw up his hands. "I just don't know." He had to be able to surf over the lies like waves, the lies to Mitch, the police and everyone else.

"Did she take Ecstasy with her?"

The dog! Good God, by now it was almost certainly out of food and water, and for sure had made several messes. Should he find the super and go in and at least save the animal or wait for the natural unfolding of events? By the time Cassie was formally reported missing, the poor animal could easily die. Maybe it's barking would alert one of the neighbors to take action.

"I don't know. Does she usually take the dog with her?"

"Why is her car here and she isn't?" Mitch continued.

"She must have gone out with a friend," Sarnower said.

"What friend?"

"I don't know who her friends are these days. Do you?"

"She could be hurt and can't get to a phone."

"I'm sure she's fine. Mom sometimes just takes off and doesn't tell anyone. You know that."

"What if she doesn't come back?"

Sarnower felt his brain burst through his eardrums.

"Let's wait and see, ok?"

"Don't you care about her?"

He'd had enough. "Mitch, you start school tomorrow and we've got a lot to do. Mom can take care of herself. She's really good at that."

"You hate her, don't you," he said, his eyes drilling into his father's face.

They ate dinner silently in the kitchen. Sarnower's thoughts turned to Janice. He had to call her and explain his bizarre behavior yesterday. That kind of performance would alienate the few remaining supports he had in no time at all. While he was at it, he should also call Tug and Manny too. He'd need to make amends and straighten things out; his friendships with both of them went back too far to let so much drift out to sea.

Without having to be asked, Mitch cleared the table and stacked the dishes in the dishwasher. He turned to look Sarnower in the eyes.

"I guess you can go ahead and marry your girlfriend now," he said softly.

"What are you talking about?"

Mitch didn't answer but went quickly to his room.

Sarnower's heart was pounding as he went into his study and picked up the phone.

"Janice? It's Alan."

"Listen, I can't talk now," she whispered.

"Look, about yesterday..."

"Yeah, what's *with* you? Are you on drugs?"

"We...I need to talk to you."

"Roger's right here. I told you I can't talk."

"How about tomorrow?" He heard Roger yelling at Jonathan in the background.

"I don't know..."

"Janice, I really need to." It came out verging on a whine.

"Call me tomorrow on my cell." She hung up.

Why the sudden desperation? He realized he was still furious, her flaunting that silly, hollow marriage to Roger. But to make more of it would be trouble. Other than a routine apology, what was there to say? The school year was starting, the flings of the summer were over, or should be, especially now. It would be moronic to carry this thing with Janice any further. He was kidding himself if he thought she was going to risk her easy life with Roger on the likes of *him*. If she were determined to throw her marriage away, surely it would be for someone younger, richer and far saner than he. Jealousy along with everything else was curling his mind.

His pounding headache returned. Life without Cassie wasn't turning out to be the joy ride he'd been looking forward to. And what was going to happen to that poor dog? It would be suicidal to go over there and insert himself into a chain of events that was going to start soon enough anyway. At this stage, why slip up with a bad mistake? Yet he couldn't shake himself of the image of that poor animal in Cassie's apartment, starving, dehydrated, dying an awful death.

After walking Mitch to the school bus stop the next morning Sarnower went to the office for his interviews.

"Have you ever worked in a medical setting before?" he asked the obese Ms. Nuttig sitting across from him in his consulting room. Sweat was pouring out of her, staining her blouse. Sarnower actually thought he saw her hair curl right in front of his eyes. Which Wal-Mart stock room had she escaped from?

"No, but I'm very fast at dictation," she answered, bouncing a soiled white pocket book on her knees.

"Well, that's fine, but it's not really one of the skills we need here. Everything's done on computers now. Any experience with billing programs?"

She looked down at her shoes. Skin from her ankles bulged over the tops like rising bread.

"No," she said softly. "I suppose I could learn."

Sarnower was annoyed; he'd been very clear about his requirements with the agency. He could throttle this poor, hapless woman for wasting his time, but of course it wasn't her fault. He had to remain courteous and professional.

"I'm sorry. I'm looking for someone who can start right in. I don't have time to train anyone."

"I guess I'm not your gal," she whispered, on the verge of tears.

Sarnower rose and extended his hand. "Thanks for coming by," he said, showing her out of the office.

The morning dragged. He called his answering service. No messages. What was happening to that dog? He wanted nothing more than to go over there and rescue it, bring it home and adopt it.

Two other candidates, each unsatisfactory in their own way came and went. In the afternoon, the agency sent over a young man. He was dressed in a three-piece, Italian cut suit with a loud purple necktie. He had several ear-piercings and a demonic goatee. Had he seen this guy before? He definitely looked familiar. Was he a spy from Nora Lund's office? Had he come to get information? Confused, Sarnower asked if he was here for the job interview.

"I hope you haven't filled the position yet," he said.

"Uh, well, no. I was sort of expecting a woman."

"Isn't that sexist?"

Sarnower flinched. "Yes, I suppose it is. I need someone who can do medical billing. Do you know MEDIFLEX?"

"Version I or II?"

"I don't really know."

"Mind if I take a look?"

Should he even let this guy near his computer?

"Ok."

Sarnower showed him to Nina's desk. The man turned the computer on and with a few lightning key strokes, called up the program.

"You have Version I. Version II is much more powerful, it would save a lot of time." He turned off the computer and looked up with alert black eyes. Sarnower was flustered.

"Who sent you over here?" he asked.

"The agency."

"Which one? CIA? FBI?"

"What are you talking about?" The man was becoming unnerved.

"Uh...I need someone with a good phone voice, who can handle patients well, pay bills, keep the office in supplies."

"Do I look like a retard?" the man asked, hostility in his voice. "I'm not a spy either."

"No, of course not. That's not what I'm saying."

"What are you saying? You were looking for a woman. You want the soft female touch to put your clients at ease? I dislike the word 'patients' by the way, it implies an outdated paternalistic power imbalance. You know, you're pretty wigged out to be treating people. What kind of therapy do you do anyway?"

Who was this guy and why had he been sent over? Sarnower still wasn't convinced he was here for the job although he'd be an asset in running the practice. But his manner. In-your-face from the get-go. And who was to say he wouldn't be snooping around.

"Mr...."

"Rock."

"Mr. Rock..."

"No, just Rock. One word. Like Sting, Cher, Madonna, you know?"

"Named after what? Rock 'n' roll? Rock of Gibraltar? Rock Hudson?"

"Who's Rock Hudson?"

Good grief. "Listen...Rock. I have a couple more people to talk to, but I'm very impressed with your computer skills. I'll get back to you in the next day or two."

The man narrowed his eyes and got up from the chair.

"Forget it," he said, heading for the door.

Compared with Nina's soothing balm this guy was coarse-grade sandpaper. He might even incite some patients to violence. Realistically, there was no way he could hire him. Where were all the young, computer-savvy college grads that weren't walking around with a chip on their shoulder and a sack full of attitude? Surely some of them must be looking for a job.

Three more women showed up that afternoon. The last one, a recent widow eager to get back to work had had experience in a dental office and was familiar with medical billing programs. Sarnower hired Adelle Havemeyer immediately and asked her to start the next day.

When she'd left, he called Janice on her cell phone.

"What's the matter with you?" she hissed.

"What do you mean?"

"You were completely out of it yesterday."

"I was? I'm sorry. Listen. I really need to see you."

"*Need?* What you need is to get a good night's sleep and straighten out your life. I'm really not taking in stray puppies this week." So things had come to this; he was getting advice from a twenty-eight year old.

"I'm sure you're right." There was silence on the other end. She sighed, then:

"Ok. Roger's in Denver for meetings until the weekend. Come over at eight. Tonight." She hung up.

What was the urgency, the big deal? He was starting to act before he thought things through, once again coming off as needy and desperate, and the mixture would lead to trouble. Now was the time to relax, take things slow, look around, pay attention and fly below the radar. People were starting to notice dramatic changes and become suspicious. Soon they'd make connections.

With the morning's goal accomplished, Sarnower headed home. He'd read, take it easy, wait for Mitch to come home from school. His first day back in a new grade might focus him on something other than his missing mother. He'd pump the boy for details on classes, teachers, friends, get him interested in the year ahead. As Cassie began to fade, they'd have their new lives open up like a new day.

The phone was ringing as he entered the house.

"Alan? Nick Ballestracci here." The familiar growl.

"Yes, Nick."

"We have a bit of a situation."

"Oh?"

"It seems your wife is missing. She was supposed to have an appointment with her lawyer yesterday morning and never showed up. Her brother's also been trying to reach her. Have you seen her? Do you know where she is?"

Sarnower felt rush of adrenaline. This was it. He was on.

"I don't have a clue. I seem to remember something about her going down to the Cape for the long weekend. Maybe she's still down there."

"She has a cell phone, doesn't she? I'm assuming she'd answer it on the Cape."

Sarnower smiled to himself. If a cell phone rings under tons of garbage in a desolate landfill and no one hears it, does it actually make a sound? That was a question he and Tug could easily ponder for a few of hours over a couple of Thai sticks.

"I have no idea. Maybe they have no reception down there. You know as much as I do."

"Hmmm. Well...it certainly does fit her M.O."

"It does. She may have just taken off again."

"Her lawyer's going to keep trying, but if she doesn't turn up in a day or two a missing persons report is going to be filed. Naturally, police detectives will be talking with you, asking questions." The lawyer was silent for a moment as if remembering something. "Is there anything you want to tell me?"

Sarnower's heart started to race. "Tell you? Like what?"

Another silence. "You don't have anything to do with this, do you?"

"Yeah Nick, I killed her, hacked her up into small bits and pieces and threw her into a Dumpster."

Ballestracci laughed. "The fantasy of every divorcing man. But seriously, when the detectives show up, just play it straight, don't offer anything. They'll know you're in the middle of a divorce action and may try to get cute with you. If so, don't, I repeat *don't* answer any more questions. Have them call me. I'll take care of the rest. Got it?"

"Got it."

"If you do hear from her, let me know. I want to start working on a settlement proposal before things get any more out of hand. By the way, I don't know if you're aware, some guy was following your wife for the past few weeks. A guy named..." he flipped through some papers. "Michael Blotz. I guess she'd been seeing him for a while and then broke it off. The jilted lover, something like that."

"How did you find that out?"

"We've been tailing her."

"You have?"

"Of course. It's standard practice. I thought you knew. We've got pictures too in case we need 'em."

That was odd. The other day Mitch had mentioned some creepy guy had been after her. In his hyper, pumped-up state, it was hard to tell if this was something of significance. He wondered if it was the jerk whose clothes he'd thrown out the window at the beginning of the summer. Knowing Cassie, it could be just about anyone. Flying high, care to the wind, she could easily have hooked up with any number of crazy, possibly dangerous characters. He could turn this to his advantage. If there were any suspicions of foul play, here was a ready-made patsy. Ballestracci and his PI had photos, so it would be nothing to ID him and bring him in. Perfect. Things were starting to break. His way.

Chapter **13**

MITCH SAT ACROSS FROM him staring silently at his plate of uneaten food.

"I want to hear all about school today," Sarnower said.

The boy didn't answer. Instead, he got up and took his untouched plate to the sink and scraped it into the disposal.

"Sit down," Sarnower commanded. Mitch hadn't said a word since he'd gotten home from school. He remained standing.

"I hate you," he said softly.

"What?"

"You heard me. You don't give a damn about Mom. You haven't called the police. You don't want to look for her. You don't care if she's dead. You just want to marry your secretary and forget about her." He stood there, red-faced and rigid, clenching and unclenching his fists.

"Mitch, there isn't a thing I can do now. It's a matter for the police if she really is missing."

"No. You hate her and I hate you!" Sarnower tried to put his hand on his shoulder, but he shrugged it off violently. In a flash it sprang back, cracking Mitch in the face. He was too shocked to utter a cry. Sarnower saw a scarlet imprint of his hand appear on his son's cheek. Vibrating like a tuning fork, the boy looked at him through narrowed eyes. He'd never struck Mitch before, and the horror of what he'd done took time to form in his mind, raising a prickly warmth and flood of tears. Instantly he was filled with remorse.

"I'm so sorry." Had he said it or merely thought the words? It was impossible to tell. His shame had eaten away all boundaries.

Mitch said nothing, backing away slowly, keeping his eyes on his father. He turned abruptly and ran upstairs. Sarnower remained in the kitchen, in shock, planted, unable to move. He'd crossed another line.

He was due at Janice's at eight, but wished now he hadn't committed to seeing her. He should be here talking with Mitch, making it up to him, working this awful moment out. He'd made a major miscalculation. Throughout the summer he'd assumed the boy would come over to his side, see Cassie's selfish, unpredictable behavior for what it was and side with him. But her bribery had worked well. He'd figured wrong and had made matters worse.

It wouldn't be right to leave now, but he had to do it. It would be best to give them both some time to cool off. They could talk tomorrow.

"Mitch, I'm going out for a while," Sarnower called upstairs. There was no response. He took the stairs two at a time and knocked on the boy's door and went in. The room was dark; Mitch was lying on the bed crying silently.

"Get out," he whispered.

"I'm really sorry about what happened."

"I don't want to live here anymore."

"Oh? Where would you like to go?"

"Away from you. Anywhere's better than here."

He closed the door and went downstairs. There'd be no chance of anything constructive tonight.

In the car driving over to Janice's, he realized he'd forgotten to shave and get cleaned up. He checked himself in the rearview mirror. Not awful, at least some of the damage from the weekend had faded with a good night's sleep. This manic dashing around had to stop. After tonight, he'd need to stay at home and be a full-time parent. Could Mitch possibly understand what he was up against? Could he possibly find some way to forgive him?

He parked in front of the gigantic house. He should have brought flowers or a bottle of wine, but the most fundamental social graces were far beyond his reach.

Janice's scented night jasmine hit his nostrils. This could be the last time its perfume would enchant him, the fragile, temperate plant couldn't take the chill of even a mild fall New England night. California Janice and her fragrant, tan, fussed-over perfection. A dear soul, but as elusive and fleeting in her own way as these delicate buds. No, she would not end up with him, she'd stay with Roger and continue to have casual trysts in her magnificent mansion, taking full advantage of his travel schedule and then resume her role as trophy wife when he was at home. Roger was rich; he'd encouraged her to do anything she wanted. The burden of having to earn a living was permanently lifted from her. That was worth giving up a lot. She only had to stay and remain on duty as wife and stepmother.

She greeted him at the door in a white blouse and tight jeans. She was barefoot and Sarnower noticed she'd painted her toenails black. Her hair was pulled back in a red scrungee that perfectly matched the color of her lips. He put his arms around her small waist and pulled her into him. She closed her eyes and opened her mouth. Sarnower tasted clove and cinnamon. Suddenly she pulled away.

"We don't have much time," she breathed. "Jonathan is at his tutor's. He'll be back at nine-thirty."

"Tutor? School's just started."

"I know." She rolled her eyes. "Roger wants him to 'hit the ground running' this year. His words. 'Start with a bang,' 'think number one to be number one,' 'first out of the gate.'"

"Careful, he's going to turn the kid into a motivational speaker," Sarnower said.

"Sometimes it makes me want to puke. Jonathan's only eleven. He's just a boy. He's got to have some fun. I'm always telling Roger to lighten up on him."

Where had he heard that before? The overachieving Dad syndrome: suiting the young up early for their futures as warriors. From the foyer, Sarnower surveyed the expanse of dining room, hall and living room. "I guess workaholism does have its benefits, though."

"It's ok for Roger, he thrives on it. But Jonathan? He's already been to a therapist for anxiety attacks. In another year he'll be drinking Pepto-Bismol out of the bottle."

"Better that than gin."

"Maybe," she said, taking his hand. She led him upstairs and down the long hall to the now familiar rose-arched master bedroom. Large candles were lit on each nightstand. Sarnower flashed briefly on Nina's bedroom; it had the same soft glow as was now illuminating this large grotto, a monument to Roger's industry. She turned off the chandelier above the bed and candlelight pushed a deep golden corona into the dark corners of the room. The flames made shadows dance. Sarnower lifted her up and placed her on the huge bed. He leaned down to kiss her hair inhaling the scent from her shampoo. She reached for his belt and began to undo his pants.

"I'm really wet," she giggled as she pushed her hand into his briefs. God, he loved it. The directness, the lack of any inhibition, the sheer, thumping good sport of it all.

In seconds they were undressed and facing each other on Janice's expensive duvet. He could see the flame of a candle reflected in both her eyes. She climbed on top and sank low on him, feeling his hardness as far as it could go. She was hot and certainly wet. She closed her eyes and removed the red scrungee from her hair, shaking it out in a billowing black sail.

"Hit me," she ordered. "Hard."

Sarnower slapped her face as he'd done to Mitch not half an hour ago.

"Again. Harder."

He obliged, this time on her other cheek. She belted him across the face, fist closed. The pain felt wonderful, purifying and cleansing. He smacked her thighs, she punched him again, continuing to ride him without breaking her rhythm, slowly building in waves to a frenzied climax, her perfect, tan breasts firm and barely moving.

She came with a shudder and a low guttural moan. Sarnower was not far behind, and after a glorious, heaving explosion lay limp beneath her, fighting to stay conscious, his face heated and pulsing.

"So doctor," she said smiling after she'd rolled off him. "What's the diagnosis? Acute pernicious nymphomania? Is there a known cure?"

"None that I'm going to do." It occurred to him that this was the first time he'd made love since killing Cassie. The thought made him instantly and desperately sad. He looked into Janice's dark burning eyes.

"I killed her," shot out of his mouth.

"What?"

"I killed her." What the fuck was he doing?

"Who?"

"Cassie. My wife."

Janice stared at him, frozen.

"You killed your wife?"

"Yes."

"You're kidding, right?"

Sarnower shook his head and sighed. "No. I killed her this past weekend. I couldn't...I couldn't stand it anymore this...divorce. It was destroying me. She was horrible. To Mitch and me. I was going to lose everything, custody, the house, all I've worked for. I had to."

Janice backed away and sat up.

"Whoa. You're scaring me."

"I'm sorry."

She was off the bed instantly, getting into her thick white terry cloth robe, frowning and moving in kinetic bursts, not sure whether to stay or make an escape.

She stood at the door.

"Have you been to the police?"

"Of course not."

"Have you told anyone?"

"Mmmm. Not really."

"Not *really*? Is that a yes or a no?"

"Well, I've hinted about it to a couple of people"

"Does that explain why you were so out of it the other day?"

Sarnower nodded. She saw tears pool in his eyes and came over to sit on the edge of the bed, unsure how close to get.

"What are you going to do now?"

He looked up at her, shrugging his shoulders.

"I don't know. Get on with my life, I guess. I hope."

Janice burst into laughter.

"Alan, you're really one of a kind. You murder your wife, come over here and fuck me, and then tell me you're getting on with you life, like...like all you've done is put the garbage out on the curb."

Sarnower smiled at the aptness of the metaphor and looked at her, speechless.

"When you put it like that it does sound a little odd."

"What other way is there to put it?"

He got up and started to get dressed. He'd made another colossal blunder. He hadn't intended to say anything; his confession had burst from his lips on its own. Now Janice was thrown into the churning wake of his lunacy and poor judgment.

"Does this change our relationship?" he asked meekly.

She shook her head trying to make sense of it.

"I don't know whether to believe *any* of this," she said ignoring his question. "If you're putting me on, I have to tell you I'm not finding any of this very funny. If it's true... Wow I've never fucked a murderer before."

"Neither have I. What does it feel like?"

She was silent, looking him over. He could see the dark cloud gathering on her face.

"Alan, I think you should leave now."

He nodded, putting on his pants.

"You're not going to say anything about this are you?" he looked up at her.

"My life's complicated enough without dealing with your crazy bullshit too. You're a sicko, Alan. Leave now. Go. Get your knob polished somewhere else."

He finished dressing while Janice, her robe cinched tight, stood over him, her anger if that's what it was, radiating in waves. His mouth had gone dry; his head throbbed. Another bridge burned, another place to which he'd never return. How could he have been such a complete idiot?

His house was completely dark as he pulled into the driveway. Usually Mitch would be up watching TV at this time and he could see the gray-blue glow emanating from his window out onto the street. Sarnower went up to his son's room. He was spread out on top of the bed, his clothes on, fast asleep, his breathing deep and heavy. Laying there, his old, tattered blue baby blanket with circus animals grasped in his right hand, a beam of moonlight playing on his relaxed child-face, Sarnower felt a lump rise in his throat. He'd never see his mother again, but worse perhaps, never know what happened to her. She'd vanished from his life forever. He'd spend the next sixty or seventy years thinking about her every day, wondering—and worse, blaming himself. It was sure to wreck him. He saw that clearly now.

Sarnower could have done the normal thing and followed through with the divorce. Millions did it every year. At some point it would have ended. He and Cassie would have picked up their lives again and healed; Mitch would have adjusted. The confessional earlier with Janice was clear and public evidence he was losing his mind.

Adelle Havemeyer showed up promptly at eight the next morning for work. She was dressed in an out-of-date pale blue Chanel suit and was teetering in high-heel shoes. Her frosted blonde hair was frozen in place with hairspray. No matter, Sarnower thought, we'll make the best of it all. He led her into Nina's office and together they went over patient record keeping, billing and scheduling. To his relief, Adelle was energetic and fast to catch on. By noon she was booking appointments.

Sarnower went into his consulting room and sunk into his chair, closing his eyes. What had made him confess to Janice? After all his meticulous planning, to open up a breach like that. The motivation was completely hidden from him. Did he secretly want to get caught or was it an impulsive act of bravado? Had he thought she'd be impressed by his derring-do? The knowledge of what he'd done was getting hard to contain, he was sure of that, like trying to keep a tiger in a flimsy wicker cage. He hadn't expected the after-shocks. It was like Raskolnikov, haunted by guilt after murdering his wretched landlady in *Crime and Punishment.* When he'd read the book in high school, it had seemed like an overwrought morality drama. Who in their right mind would want to get caught? But that was the point, wasn't it? He *wasn't* in his right mind. This was guilt, a force until now unknown, a force like an unstoppable nuclear chain reaction that had taken on a life of its own. It could make you crazy if you weren't already. It was something he'd just have to master, put down and contain with care and circumspection.

The intercom buzzed. Adelle was on the line.

"Dr. Sarnower?" her voice was shaking.

"Yes?"

"There's a...a police detective sergeant out here. He says he needs to talk with you."

He heard a muffled exchange.

"An Officer Fitzgibbons."

"Send him in please," Sarnower said.

He opened the door to his consulting room. There on the other side was a man about the same size as Sarnower. He was wearing a brown tweed sports coat and a stiff, wide polyester tie. A bad crew cut helped to frame his square, ruddy face. There was an old, faded coffee stain on his shirt.

"Dr. Sarnower?" he asked.

"Yes."

"Detective Sergeant Kevin Fitzgibbons, Boston Police Department," he said, not bothering to shake hands. Instead, he reached inside his jacket pocket with nicotine-stained fingers and withdrew a card that he handed over. "I'm investigating the disappearance of your wife." He consulted a small, spiral-bound notebook. "Cassandra Kelly. I need to ask you some questions."

"Please come in," Sarnower said, sweeping his hand toward the leather chair used by patients. The detective surveyed the room and sat.

"I understand you and your wife are in the middle of divorce proceedings," the man said, retrieving a plastic ballpoint pen from his pocket.

Sarnower remembered Ballestracci's injunction. Keep it short; don't volunteer anything.

"Yes, that's right."

"When was the last time you saw her?"

Sarnower pretended to think. "It must have been a few days before the long weekend. She brought my son back after one of his court-mandated visits."

Fitzgibbons started writing in his notebook.

"The date exactly," he said without looking up.

"I think it was the Wednesday before Labor Day weekend. I don't know the date." He picked up his appointment book and rifled through the pages. "That would have been August twenty-seventh." Thankfully, he hadn't opened to Nina's blazing farewell note.

"You sure?"

"Fairly sure, yes."

The detective squinted at him then wrote. Sarnower sat still, breathing slowly. What had Tug said? He couldn't play tiddlywinks with the police? He'd show them.

"What was the nature of your relationship with your wife, doctor?"

"What do you mean?" He could play this game too.

"Well, was it hostile, antagonistic?"

Sarnower smiled. "We were getting a divorce. Naturally we had disagreements. But we have a young son, detective, we were trying to keep things civil and workable for his sake."

"Civil and workable?"

"Yes. I guess you could say we're like any other divorcing couple. It's hard, but we're all trying to make the best of it."

"I understand your wife has taken off before and not told anyone?"

"Last spring she flew out to California without telling anyone."

"Do you think she might have done that again?"

Sarnower shrugged his shoulders and raised the palms of his hands. "At this point your guess is as good as mine."

"Do you know of anyone who might want to hurt her?"

"Apparently she hooked up with some guy this past summer who started following her around, kind of stalking her after she dumped him. My attorney had a PI on her for a while and caught them together. You might want to talk to him."

Fitzgibbons nodded and wrote some more. He put his pen away and stared at Sarnower, locking on him, saying nothing. Sarnower smiled through the laser gaze.

"Is there anything else, detective? I have a busy afternoon ahead."

The man did not respond. He got up slowly and took a final look around the room. Sarnower rose and moved toward the door.

"If you hear from your wife or learn anything about her whereabouts, please call me at the number on the card"

With an exaggerated gesture, Sarnower put the card in his shirt pocket and patted it.

"Without fail, detective," he said.

Fitzgibbons left quickly. In his wake, Sarnower caught the tangy odor of male sweat and stale cigarette smoke. The man lived in his cheap clothes and a cloud of rank tobacco fumes. Did his wife gag when they made love? Would a brisk, scalding shower get rid of that stench? He opened a file drawer and took out a can of air freshener and sprayed the room.

This was going to be his life for the foreseeable future—answering innumerable questions, playing the concerned husband and father, deodorizing the air fouled by fetid detectives. Years from now, if he made it through the jungle of this investigation, there would be those who would always suspect him of having a hand in Cassie's disappearance. Soon, everyone would know, it was only a matter of days before stories started appearing in the papers: "Psychiatrist's Wife Missing." His patients would look at him differently whether or not they were forward enough to ask him about it. It would be on all their minds; he'd be recast from the caring, concerned physician to the bereaved victim or the diabolical perpetrator; one or the other, there'd be nothing in between.

Janice had enough to deal with not to want to get involved in his headaches, or so she said. He was pretty sure he could count on her silence; part of her still thought he was being outrageous. But Manny and Tug. Did they know? Kind of. He wasn't certain. In their own different ways, they hated authority; they wouldn't give him up or betray a relationship of decades. There was no body and absolutely no evidence that a crime had even been committed. They'd need a writ of *habeas corpus*. He'd call Janice that evening and tell her he was sorry, the whole thing had been a joke, a big, sick joke.

Walking out to the waiting room, he saw Adelle on the phone.

"I have six patients scheduled for you for tomorrow," she said smiling, covering the mouthpiece.

"Wonderful."

She hung up the phone. "Dr. Sarnower, are you in any kind of trouble?"

"No, why do you ask?"

"Well, that detective. I just thought it was kind of strange; they usually don't just barge into doctor's offices. He said he'd be coming back."

"Oh?" Sarnower was suddenly anxious to get going.

"I hope I'm not speaking out of turn..."

"No. Listen, Adelle, I really have to be somewhere. Just lock up when you're finished."

She smiled and nodded. "Have a good afternoon."

In the atrium, Miroslav's crew had finished installing the new carpet; its petrochemical odor filled the air. The Czech was inspecting corners and seams and barking orders to some of the workers. Sarnower left the building and headed for the parking lot. The day had turned hot and muggy, one of summer's last gasps, a refusal to let go. He missed Nina and the image of her vacant rooms sprang to mind, the blades of yellow light illuminating the expanses of bare, blonde oak floors. Jesus, it was all so final. This had been a summer of final goodbyes, but so much hadn't been said.

Lost in his thoughts, he failed to see the large, loping figure of Tug approaching until they had almost collided with each other. He was outfitted in pressed, white khakis and a maroon polo shirt with a new pair of hip, wrap-around shades, the kind worn in Star Trek and futuristic movies. His hair had been cut very short, close to the scalp.

"Where've you been hiding your sorry, skinny ass?" Tug demanded.

"Jesus, man, what are you doing here?"

"Come to save you from yourself."

Tug removed his shades and looked at Sarnower, scowling.

"You look like dog shit. How about a stiff drink—I know I could use one. Just finished a presentation. Let's scarf a few."

"I can't."

Sarnower looked at his watch. Since that day in his office, he hadn't seen or spoken with Tug and had no idea what his standing was. His new look was not reassuring.

"Can't or won't?"

"Look, about that last time in your office."

"Forgotten, buddy." Tug laughed and put his hand on Sarnower's shoulder. "You were in the middle of a meltdown, just come from having your nuts sliced and diced and handed to you. Really, I can dig it. It was me? I'd be talking the same trash too. Might even follow through. Word to the wise though? I wouldn't be broadcasting it around, you know? Some folks might take it the wrong way."

Sarnower stared into Tug's eyes. He hadn't gotten it. In the final analysis, his good old reliable friend, psychiatrist Alan Sarnower, M.D. was incapable of such acts. Blowing off steam? Sure, but following through, doing what had been done? No. This time though, he'd keep his fat mouth shut.

"What about that drink?" Tug asked again.

Sarnower stared at him. The new haircut and shades were troubling. It was entirely possible Tug was now working in some undercover capacity. The feds could be using his international connections, or maybe he'd been recruited to watch Sarnower himself. The friendship could be a complete ruse, but he was beyond being able to put up any resistance.

At the Blue Moon, the bar/cafe a block from the office, Tug savored a double vodka martini. Sarnower ordered a beer.

"So where the hell have you been? Don't tell me." He closed his eyes. "You were pitching woo with Nina on Martha's Vineyard and were too spent to pick up the phone. I know the story. Loyalty's out the window when it comes to *cherchez la femme*, eh?"

Nina. She just kept coming back.

"Nina's gone."

Tug stared at him. "Gone? Gone as in gone shopping? Gone to powder her nose?"

"No. She quit. Left. Split. Went back to Seattle."

Tug slumped back in his seat. "Damn," he whispered. "How'd you screw that one up?"

Sarnower took a deep breath. "You're right. I did screw it up. She got tired of waiting, tired of me. I think she'd just had it. I was too much to take on. There was nothing in it for her."

Tug locked his fingers around the cold drink and looked Sarnower in the eyes.

"I'm sorry."

There was no need to delve into Nina's other suitors and boyfriends. The betrayal was deserved. He wanted to hang on to whatever golden glow remained of her presence in his life.

Sarnower nodded and drained his beer.

"I always thought when your divorce was over you two would end up together."

Sarnower smiled sadly as Tug called the waiter over and ordered another round. They sat in a rare moment of silence. He looked around the cafe. Why had Tug appeared suddenly and brought him here? There might be mikes and miniature cameras placed strategically, recording their conversation.

"Did they wire you?" Sarnower asked, examining the salt and peppershakers. Tug closed his eyes, shaking his head.

"Give it a rest. You're taking this thing out way too far."

Funny, that's exactly what they would program him to say.

"You're not fooling me."

"I certainly hope not."

"Just come clean and get it over with, ok? It's me."

"Shall I take my shirt off and show you I'm not wired? Alan, get some help for Christ's sake. First the divorce and now Nina. It's too much. You're going around the bend."

Nina. He'd never get away from her; she'd haunt him until he died. He suddenly realized Tug must have had something for her too, his charm, the constant joking. What else could it be? Of course he was flirting. But for now, he'd have to reign in his runaway suspicions.

The late afternoon heat and beer were making him woozy. It was now almost four o'clock. The bus would be bringing Mitch home from school soon.

"Much as I'd like to continue to honor the departed, I need to be getting on home," Sarnower said with a small belch. He looked across the table. Tug was staring off into the middle distance, lost in his own thoughts, his face soft and relaxed in silent contemplation, probably wondering how to dump his old friend.

"Yo, Tug."

"Huh?"

"Did you hear what I said?"

"You said something?"

"Earth to Tug: Sorry to interrupt *your* seduction of Nina, but I have to get going."

"Am I that obvious?"

"Subtlety is definitely not one of your gifts. I can read your mind like the news crawl on CNN."

Tug shook his head and downed the remainder of his drink. He pulled out a slim Italian leather wallet, withdrew a crisp new fifty and put it on the table. Sarnower got up and felt the blood drain from his head, his vision became spotty. He took a deep breath and held on to the back of the chair; sweat broke out on his forehead.

"Steady, man," Tug said, extending a hand.

"What'd they put in that beer?"

"Truth serum. The FBI's on to you."

Sarnower straightened suddenly.

"Easy! I'm yanking your chain."

As they walked out, Sarnower realized his left foot had fallen asleep. Wincing with pins and needles, he dragged himself past the patrons who were starting to come in for an after-work drink. The paranoia and his transitory disability raised a familiar wave of disgust. Like heartburn, it rose from his gut to the back of his mouth.

Outside, Tug donned his absurd shades and fished in his pocket for car keys.

"Back to the office to finish a report," he announced looking around. Attractive young women in twos and threes were entering the Blue Moon, laughing, flushed with spirited office gossip. Men in business suits with gelled spiky hair and solid-colored ties drifted in. Tug and Sarnower watched the parade in silence. In another couple of minutes, there'd be a line out the door.

"Obviously the new happy-hour spot. Some nice booty too," Tug said.

"Is that absolutely all you think of these days?"

"Of course not. There's high-grade drugs and fine wines. Not to mention Caribbean beaches."

Another throbbing headache had started. Sarnower knew he shouldn't have had anything to drink. He wanted to be home, lying down, eyes closed and fading gently into a nap. Since the killing, he had yet to get a good night's sleep.

"You sure you're going to be ok?" Tug asked. "Truth to tell, I'm worried about you Alan. How much more of this divorce shit are you supposed to take? Is Nick wrapping things up?"

"I sure hope so. He said something about settlement talks the other day."

"I hope that includes a horizontal settlement for Miss Cassandra in the family plot. But let someone else do the undertaking, if you get my meaning."

Sarnower smiled through the pounding. "Your mouth to God's ear," he said and started walking toward his car.

Chapter 14

HIS HEADACHE NOTWITHSTANDING, the tiger was back in the cage, the nasty compulsion to confess, tamed for now. Tonight he'd focus exclusively on Mitch and help him with his homework. He was determined to reconnect and become as close as they used to be. He'd struggle to take the boy's point of view on things and would need to rethink his stand as a parent; all the old automatic responses that usually involved "no" or "can't." The present would drip into the past—a black tide on its way out to sea.

An old, dark blue Dodge Dart was parked in his driveway, blocking his way when he pulled up to the house. From the vantage of his car, Sarnower couldn't see if there was anyone in it. He was sure it didn't belong to anyone he knew. No one on the block would be caught in a shit-box like that. He'd call Garabedian's towing and have it removed. Just then the figure of a man emerged from behind his house and started walking toward him. He was backlit by the sun, so Sarnower couldn't make out his features until he was about five feet away. He was thin, shockingly so, had close cut hair, and was wearing old sandals, torn jeans and a dirty blue T-shirt. He stood on Sarnower's lawn as if he owned it, his hands on his hips, a menacing glow in his eyes. Casually, he lit an unfiltered cigarette and flicked the spent match onto the grass. His teeth were crooked and discolored. Sarnower had seen him before.

"Who the fuck are you? And get off my property," Sarnower said between his teeth.

The man stood right where he was and leisurely exhaled a thick gray plume of smoke. Sarnower advanced with clenched fists. Sure. This was the guy he'd caught with Cassie months ago in their bed. Michael. The Michael Blotz Ballestracci had mentioned to him.

261

He'd roughed him up and thrown his clothes out the window, in full view of his astounded neighbors. And there on his left wrist was Sarnower's stolen watch.

"Get off my property now. And give me back my watch!" Sarnower barked, putting his fist near Michael's face. He made a lunge for the watch, but Michael was too quick for him and landed a clean upper cut to Sarnower's jaw, knocking him back, staggering. The pounding in his head was excruciating, and for a moment he couldn't focus his vision. Michael had retreated to a safe distance and brought the cigarette up to his mouth for another long drag, then dropped it on the lawn, grinding it out.

"I think you might want to hear what I have to say," he rasped, inspecting the watch. Sarnower massaged his jaw and looked around. It might be possible to take the guy down just as he had before, but this time Michael had the advantage, surprise and time of day. A couple of cars had started down the block. Neighbors were coming home from work now and he had to avoid another scene at all costs.

Michael walked to his car and leaned against the trunk. He took another cigarette out of its pack.

"Mind if I smoke?" he laughed, lighting up.

"Get to the point!" Sarnower wondered if he should rush the guy. His jaw throbbed.

"It's a long story, most of it I'm sure you won't be interested in because it concerns your wife. Your *late* wife I should say. So, I'll get right to the part about you." He removed a piece of tobacco from his tongue and continued.

"Cassie and I, we were in love. I say *were* because you and I both know what happened to her."

"I don't know what you're talking about."

He smiled and went on.

"We had a beautiful time in the Berkshires. The two of us. We made plans. She was going to dump your ass and we were going to start a life together after she got her settlement."

"You're the creep that was following her."

"No, sir. Wasn't following her. Protecting her. Making sure nothing would happen. There's a difference."

He smiled, revealing his grotesque teeth. "I was rip-shit the day you humiliated me right here on this lawn. I started to fear for what you'd do to Cassie. But ok. I got over it." He looked down at his cigarette. "I believe in justice, Mr. Sarnower, something I'm sure you have no concept of. Justice and fate. Karma. You ever study the Eastern religions?"

Jesus, there it was again. He heard Manny's voice speaking through this derelict. He thought his head would explode. Should he try to get his watch back or hear what this weasel had to say?

"I'll make the rest short and simple because I have to get going." He tapped Sarnower's prized watch with a yellow-stained finger. "I was following you the night you did that horrible thing to Cassie. Yeah. This time I *was* following. Rats need to get trapped, you know? I saw her come right here to the house. Her house. Came to collect her boy for the weekend, am I right? He's a cute one, a real live wire. I knew what you'd done to her when she never came out. She drove here and never came out. Now the part you'll like. You took her car to her place, and came back here. Saw you load those trash bags into your trunk? I knew what you'd done. Deductive reasoning, you might say. You thrown her out just like the trash."

He stopped. The recital had choked him up. His lower lip quivered, but he pressed on.

"I followed you up to Newburyport and on into New Hampshire. Know what your problem is Mr. Sarnower? You just don't know the folks you're dealin' with too well. Make all kinds of assumptions, they turn out to be dead wrong."

He laughed, shaking his head. "I'll tell you though. I do know where everything is and I've got a real heartwarming story to share with the police."

Sarnower felt himself go white. His mouth was suddenly parched. His eyes burned.

"You're bullshitting! You have nothing! You could have done it yourself. You probably did. My lawyer has pictures of you harassing my wife."

The man stood there calmly, smiling. "Well, if I did it, why are the police going to find your very own fingerprints all over those trash bags?"

"What are you talking about?" Sarnower's heart was in his mouth; his voice shook.

"Simple. You threw away those bags? Your bare hands, man. You weren't wearing nothin' over them." The man shook his head and laughed. "And you're a...doctor, right? Don't all you docs have rubber gloves?"

The gloves!

"I gotta go," he said stomping out his cigarette on Sarnower's driveway. "We'll be in touch to work something out, if you know what I mean." He rubbed his thumb and index finger together. "Or maybe we won't. Haven't really made my mind up yet."

He got into the car and started it up. The engine roared to life, belching a huge cloud of thick black smoke from the tailpipe.

When he'd disappeared around the corner, Sarnower dashed to his car and opened the door. There under the passenger seat was the pair of latex gloves he'd torn off when his hands had started to itch and swell. In the confusion with the bikers, he'd completely forgotten to put them on again when disposing of the bags. Michael was right. His prints were on the bags.

He stood on the sidewalk and threw up. He retched again and again, until there was nothing left. There were tears in his eyes as he sank to the pavement on his knees and tried to catch his breath.

There must a way out, there had to be. Surely Michael would call and make a blackmail attempt. Yes. Someone in his position, poor, living in obvious squalor, hand-to-mouth—he'd want money. That could be done, a payoff. But would it guarantee his silence? Of course not. He was a loose cannon; he could easily take the money and rat him out anyway. No, Michael himself had to be silenced, but Sarnower hadn't a clue where to find him. Wait. Ballestracci's PI would know. He had pictures, knew his whereabouts, dates, places. Yes, that was it! He'd call the lawyer and find out where Michael was hiding out. Sarnower could take care of the rest. All kinds of shit goes on in those wacky communes. Things get out of hand, just look at Manson and his gang. Helter skelter. Violence was just a tweak away from love and peace anyway. Ok, that was the plan.

He rose from his knees, covered in his own puke. Mitch would be home in minutes and he had to get cleaned up. He walked into the house and upstairs to the bathroom. The mirror gave him a bad report. There was a bright red and purple patch where Michael had hit him on the jaw. Bloodshot eyes, blotchy skin and hair that stuck out at all angles. He stripped out of his clothes and jumped into a hot shower. Moving fast, he lathered up and rinsed. He'd made the sort of fatal blunder that had hung so many before him. Large events always pivoted on the smallest fulcrum. He had to get to Michael and take care of him before he went to the police. Likely, he'd need at least some time to mull over an extortion threat. That would give him a day at the most. It was possible to do, but he'd have to act fast.

Drying off quickly, he slipped into a change of clothes and grabbed the soiled shirt and pants. He ran downstairs to the basement and dumped them in the washing machine. The large plastic gallon of detergent was almost empty, and Sarnower shook the bottle vigorously to release an anemic blue vein of the stuff before turning on the machine. Upstairs in an instant, he pounded Ballestracci's number on the portable phone.

"Frazier, Abbott and..."

"Nick Ballestracci," he wheezed. "It's an emergency."

"I'm sorry, Mr. Ballestracci has left for the day."

"No. I absolutely have to reach him right now!"

"I'm sorry sir, if you call back tomorrow..."

"Then give me his home number."

"We don't give out home phone numbers."

"Well make an exception, damn it! I told you, this is an emergency!"

"Sir..."

Sarnower slammed down the phone and pulled out the phone book from under the telephone table. The tiny print blurred before his eyes. It had been so long since he'd used his reading glasses he had no idea where they were anymore. He could do without them for most print, but the phone book was impossible. Even if Ballestracci had a listed number, he wouldn't be able to read it. Information! He'd call information.

Before he could dial, he heard Mitch's key in the front door. Why did the kid always have to show up exactly when something critical was going on? No wonder he found it difficult to give the boy his attention.

"Hi Dad," Mitch called from the door, throwing down his backpack.

Sarnower struggled to compose himself. "How's it going?" His voice was loud, shaky. Apparently though, Mitch was over his snit of yesterday. It would be important to take advantage of this fresh start, but all he could think of was getting to Ballestracci.

"I'll be right with you," he said as Mitch went into the kitchen to make a snack.

He dialed information.

"What city please?"

"Boston. I think. I'd like the number of Nick Ballestracci." He spelled out the last name for the operator.

"I'm sorry, I have no listed number for any Ballestracci in Boston."

"Try Wellesley or Weston, or Dover."

He waited.

"No, no listing for Ballestracci in any of those towns."

"Is it an unlisted number? This is an emergency."

"I'm sorry sir, I find no listing."

Sarnower hung up. He'd have to call the lawyer first thing in the morning. Precious hours wasted. No doubt Michael was calmly and deliberately putting the finishing touches to his plan. For all he knew, the police could already be combing through huge garbage dumps with bloodhounds, or however it was they located bodies. It was a search for a needle in a haystack, but it was amazing how often they found what they were looking for.

"Dad," Mitch called from the kitchen. "Don't you want to hear about school?"

No, that was the last thing he wanted to hear about.

"Sure," he answered. How to take care of Michael? A gun would be the quickest, most efficient method. But he'd need a silencer. No telling where he'd have to do it or who might be within earshot.

"Mrs. Erikson is going to teach us astronomy this year instead of yucky geography, isn't that neat?"

"Yeah." Perhaps a blunt object, a brick or cinder block to the head, a neat, clean blow. Unlike Cassie, Michael would be too difficult to restrain in an effective chokehold.

"She says we're going to have to get a telescope and keep a journal of what we see, the stars and all that stuff."

"Great." A knife. He'd know exactly where to plunge it. But what about the mess, the disposal of clothes, the clean up?

"Dad, you're not even listening."

"I am. I'm just a little distracted."

"You're always distracted."

There was never going to be any end to this, he'd never get a foothold on any peace or quiet. He wanted to jump out of his skin. Joining Liz Dashiell in a Drano cocktail was beginning to look like an attractive option.

"Mitch, I really can't talk now."

"But I need help with math."

"Start it yourself. If you have a problem, I'll come up and help you."

The boy took a long look at his father. Sarnower saw for the first time he'd lost the eyes of a child. The sparkle had faded and they'd started to recede into his skull, withdrawing as he had. How many people was he going to take down with him? He was powerless to reach out, the Plexiglas box had pushed in against him, constraining his movements, his breathing. His thoughts would choke him to death. All he could do now was get out of the way of Michael Blotz's oncoming freight train.

"Dad, what happened to your face?"

"What?"

"There's a big red mark on your jaw."

"Oh that. I bumped into one of the cupboard doors."

Mitch looked at him skeptically. "It looks like someone hit you."

Sarnower forced a laugh. "Yeah, it does, doesn't it?"

The boy continued to stare at his father's jaw as he carried his backpack upstairs.

Sarnower threw a couple of hot dogs on the stove and brought a liter bottle of Coke out of the refrigerator. He knew his time with Mitch was running out. If by some miracle Michael didn't turn him in, he'd spend the rest of his life unsure of who knew, who suspected. There'd always be phantoms in the shadows, the unexpected around corners. That was the best-case scenario. He'd be the object of constant scrutiny and speculation. The will power needed to get through each day, to place one foot in front of the other, not to mention parenting and maintaining a career, seemed staggering.

After dinner, Mitch stayed in his room doing homework and didn't ask for help with math again. Relieved, Sarnower went into the study and turned on the TV. The mindless chatter and canned laughter of inane sit-com reruns lulled him into a welcomed twilight state, somewhere between sleep and wakefulness. He didn't fight it when his eyes finally closed for the night.

The TV was still on when he awoke the next morning to the light banter of *A.M. America.* The chipper host and perky hostess were drinking coffee out of large mugs that featured prominent station logos. Wide-eyed, she was laughing and leaning in attentively as the host explained some mishap with his wife in the kitchen the night before. He turned out to the camera to deliver the perfectly timed punch line:

"So I said to Judy, my wife, 'don't call us for dinner, we'll know it's ready when the smoke alarm goes off!'"

The audience burst into laughter. The hostess spilled coffee on her dress. "We'll be right back after these messages," they said in cheery unison.

Sarnower got up and turned the TV off. He'd slept in his clothes on the reclining chair and the awkward position had made him stiff. It was seven-fifteen; Mitch had to be at the bus by seven-thirty. He wondered when Ballestracci got into the office.

Mitch was in the kitchen rinsing out his cereal bowl, his backpack bulging, ready to go.

"Why did you sleep with the TV on?" he asked.

"I guess I was too tired to make it to bed."

"Mom's not coming back, is she?"

"I don't know," he whispered.

Mitch put his arms through the straps of the backpack.

"I'm going to stop asking you about her." He looked at his father. They almost met eye-to-eye now, Sarnower no longer had to bend over to connect with him. Mitch had changed; he was pulling away, letting his mother go. A wise-beyond-his-years look had settled on his face.

"I'll walk to the bus by myself today," he said.

Sarnower nodded. "Ok." He'd decided on a gun; clean and fast. There was no time left for planning. He'd just have to get one. He'd call Manny and borrow his.

Mitch turned back to look at his father before opening the front door.

"You going to be ok, Dad?"

Sarnower smiled. "I'll be fine. You have a great day."

Mitch walked down the slate path and onto the sidewalk.

Sarnower stood on the porch and watched until he disappeared around the corner. At nine sharp he was on the phone.

"Nick Ballestracci," he told the cool voice on the other end.

"One moment please."

"Ballestracci here."

Sarnower was hyperventilating, struggling to catch his breath.

"Hello? Hello?"

"It's Alan Sarnower. Listen, that guy who was following Cassie?"

"Yeah? Speak up. I can hardly hear you."

"I need to know where he lives."

"What's this about?"

"I just need his address."

"Why? We've got this covered."

Ballestracci wasn't going to give it up.

"She's dead, Nick."

"Who...your wife?"

"Yes."

"When? How? You?"

"Yes."

"Shit. Why?"

Wasn't it obvious? "Why not?"

Ballestracci groaned. "Good Christ. Ok. I want you to call the police right now and turn yourself in. Do you think you can do that Alan? Alan?"

Without answering, Sarnower replaced the receiver. It rang immediately.

"Dr. Sarnower?"

"Yes."

"This is Adelle at the office." She was anxious. "Your first patient is here waiting for you."

"Who did you schedule?"

"Let's see." She flipped through the appointment book. "This would be a Ms. Dashiell. Liz Dashiell?"

"Tell her I said it was ok to drink that bottle of Liquid Plumber."

"Excuse me, doctor?"

"A joke. Forget it."

The day from hell had begun. He'd confessed to his own lawyer. Like that crazy admission to Janice a few nights before, it had burst out on its own. The tiger was out of the cage, now surely for the last time. Slowly, he went into the bathroom and turned on the shower. Since the murder, he'd gotten no relief from the hot pulsing water; it merely beat against his permanent, indelible stain. But now, finally, he felt himself relax, the water soothed his sore, cramped muscles and his bruised, swollen face as it carried his remaining life in small, graceful eddies down the drain.

While dressing, he heard a knock at the front door. Damn. Mitch had forgotten his lunch or his homework, the same old shit. The boy's maturity that morning had been an illusion. He tucked in his shirt and reached for a tie. The knocking continued forcefully.

"Hold on, I'm coming!" he shouted. There at the door was Detective Sergeant Kevin Fitzgibbons and two Newton city police officers. The scene on the street hit him like a punch in the gut. There were two patrol cars parked in front of his house, their blue lights flashing and spinning. Neighbors on their way to work had stopped and gathered in the street. Fred Cerillo, Mrs. Bowen, the

Goulds. One of the officers, a huge man with a completely shaved head was holding a set of handcuffs.

"Alan Sarnower?" the other asked.

"Yes?"

"I have a warrant for your arrest for the murder of Cassandra Kelly. Please turn around and place your hands behind your back." Too numb to respond, Sarnower turned and in one fluid motion the huge bald officer snapped the cuffs on him. They were surprisingly warm, and not at all as heavy as he would have guessed.

"Mr. Sarnower, you have the right to remain silent. Anything you do say can and will be used against you in a court of law. You have the right to an attorney. If you cannot afford one, one will be appointed for you. Do you understand these rights?"

He nodded. Officers on each side escorted him out the door and down the front steps. There were about fifteen people now pressing onto the sidewalk and even some who had gathered on his lawn. Kevin Fitzgibbons was trying to disperse the growing crowd. In his left hand he carried a large yellow roll of crime scene tape.

"Move it along folks, move it along," he barked. "There's nothing to see here, absolutely nothing to see here. Move it along!"

And up the street about twenty yards away, there was that car. It was clear in the bright sunlight, that beat-up blue Dodge Dart; and sitting cross-legged on the hood was Michael Blotz smoking a cigarette. He smiled and gave a little "howdy neighbor" wave. Oh, he'd been smart. The cocky son-of-a-bitch had the whole thing set up with the cops, ready to go before he even showed up yesterday. He'd dangled that inch of wiggle room, that sliver of freedom in front of Sarnower as payback, exquisite and excruciating. He never had a chance.

So that was it. Game, set and match. Sarnower felt the world begin to close in as his breathing became difficult. His legs gave way as the patrolmen supported him by his elbows. Bile rose in his throat.

"Murderer!" a man called from the crowd. Sarnower looked in his direction but only saw flat blobs of color bleeding into each other. Mitch! What would happen to Mitch? He tried to form words, to explain the situation to one of the officers who was now guiding him into the back of a patrol car, but all that came out were grunts and gasps.

He fought against the cuffs that pinned his arms in back, but they wouldn't budge. The air in the car was stagnant and hot, and filled with the strong scent of stale sweat and urine. An old skel must have relieved himself in the very spot he was now occupying. The cops on either side pressed against him, holding him firmly in the seat.

A scream erupted from the base of his diaphragm and climbed like lava through his lungs and out his mouth, charging the still air with a ringing red flood of sound. Startled, one of the cops slammed a billy club into his abdomen and Sarnower slumped over on the verge of passing out, his vision fragmenting. He struggled to stay conscious.

They'd have to let him make a phone call down at the station, wasn't that how it worked? He'd call Tug first. Maybe Tug could even take Mitch in for a few days until things got cleared up.

The car was moving slowly down the block, its lights still flashing. Yes, that's what he'd do. He'd get in touch with his old buddy Tug and together they'd put things back on track. Just like that narrow escape in Chicago years ago. He'd call Tug as soon as he got to the station, the very minute. Surely Tug would help him out now, wouldn't he?